Infidelity

Ally Bunbury

POOLBEG

Published 2018 by Poolbeg Press Ltd
123 Grange Hill, Baldoyle
Dublin 13, Ireland
www.poolbeg.com

A catalogue record for this book is available from the British Library.

ISBN 978-1-78199-824-3

www.facebook.com/poolbegpress
@PoolbegBooks

Typeset by Poolbeg in Sabon
Printed and bound by CPI Group
(UK) Ltd, Croydon, CR0 4YY

www.poolbeg.com

About the Author

Ally Bunbury is the bestselling author of *The Inheritance*. She was brought up with her three sisters and a menagerie of animals in County Monaghan. Following a serendipitous encounter at a dinner party, Ally landed a dream internship with a PR agency on New York's Fifth Avenue, which in turn led to a flourishing career in London and Dublin. Ally continues to create dynamic PR campaigns for her clients. She lives in the Irish countryside with her husband Turtle Bunbury and their two daughters.

www.allybunbury.com
Instagram & Facebook: allybunburybooks
Twitter: @allybunbury
#infidelity

Acknowledgements

I have loved every second of writing this book and I am very grateful for the extraordinary support I received from so many wonderful people. In particular, I would like to thank Sarah Beth Casey, who inspired me to write in the first place. And where would I be without my sisters? Gigantic thanks to Gilly Fogg, for unwavering goodness, guidance and crucial blurb-shaping advice; to Liz Cairns, for her eagle eye, encouragement and kindness that knows no bounds; and to Faenia Moore, for her splendid wisdom and reassurance. I would also like to give my wholehearted thanks to Rachael Comiskey, for her photographic genius and sense of humour; to Erin Van Vuren, for so kindly allowing me to include her poem in this book; huge thanks to Adam Rynne for being word-perfect; to Aisling Killoran, a beautiful rock of goodness; to Alice Forde, for gold-star advice on many things, including coffee beans and portafilters; to Nicola Coveney for helping me without even knowing you are; to Clare Durdin Robertson, for the best analogies, for brightening so many days and spurring me on! And to radio legend Mary Claire Rogers for your unrelenting effervescence. To the Charleston Avenue beauties, for keeping party themes rocking and rolling, thank you Lucy Kelly, Iona Hoare and Tiffany Black.

Huge gratitude also to Virginia Hartley for being such a wonderful aunt; to Tom and Sasha Sykes, beacons of urban pizzazz and kindness; to Ben and Jessica Rathdonnell, for being wonderful in many ways, from hen to child-sitting; to Dominique Patton Lei for those lovely walks and talks (the Bailey's is on ice), to Natasha Mann and Hugo Jellett for giving me confidence so generously, and thank you, Emily Bunbury, for coming to the rescue, in particular

vii

on that sunny Sunday when time was of the essence!

Thank you, Ahmed Salman, for symbolizing all that is good in the world; John Schwatschke, for art and merriment; Bernard Doyle for those important and often poignant lunchtime conversations; Annabel Butler, Daisy Jacquier, Coibhe Butler, Charlotte Capel Cure, Louise Knatchbull, Roly and Emma Ramsden and Joan Boyle for being such stylish, motivating reminders of London days. To Matthew Gallagher, Patrick and Heather Gallagher, huge thanks and love, and thanks also to Karmendra Jaisi, for teaching me so much about the world. Thank you, Ann Craigie, and Lily, for being so thoughtful and to Elinor and Honey Pot Skyes for making our kitchen sparkle with your fun.

Thank you to Jacquie and Herbie Brennan, for reminding me of all that is important; to Sebastian and Ali Barry, for inspiring our household to reach for the moon; to Liz Nugent, for your heartening welcome to the world of writing, to Liza Mitchell of *March* (on the Fulham Road) for *vraiment magnifique* inspirations and 'fashion edits'. Thank you, Victoria Mary Clarke, Jane Donald and Lu Thornely, for teaching me to stand like a mountain; Jane Williams, for oodles of encouragement; John McGrath, for being at the ready with advice; Jacqui Doyle and Charlie Fowler, for being so lovely.

My thanks to the Great British Bake Off Team: Theo, Matt, Charlie, Nathan and Kalyani for blurb edits; and huge thanks to the Festival of Writing & Ideas and the Hinterland Festival of Literature and Arts for making me feel ambitious. Thank you, Tara Quirke, for your empowering positivity and *merci bien* to Bernard de Croix for being so cool. Thank you, Mary McManus, for being a true light in the lives of Jemima and Bay and to Finches Fitness for keeping me sane and stretchy through the power of Pilates. Thank you 'Inspector Larry' for teaching me how to know a nice set of wheels when I see them, and to Mick Davis, our mechanic with Harry Potter qualities.

Thank you very much to Paula Campbell of Poolbeg for her continuing 'can do' attitude and sparkling humour, to Caroline

Maloney for being so super-organised, to David Prendergast for his marvellous skill and creativity, and to Gaye Shortland, thank you for lovely correspondence while editing and for keeping me on track, from wheelbarrows to bathtubs ...!

Remembering with love, Archie Moore, Joe Blackwell, Rosebud Rathdonnell, Aunty Sue, Ross O'Driscoll, Franz Fasenfeld and Cillian McDonagh.

Thank you to dearest Aunt Meike, for your immense counsel and indomitable spirit and for making me feel so special; to my godmother, Helen Price, for being such a lady of quality and kindness; to Johnny and Lucy Madden for your wisdom; to Alex and Daria Blackwell, the most stylish sailors on the planet; and to Valery Mahoney, the loveliest there is.

To my mother, Miriam Moore, thank you for being so brilliant and for all your help, in so many ways.

Thank you, Turtle, for listening and encouraging, guiding and laughter, long walks and late nights. And to my darling daughters, Jemima and Bay, who continue to twirl and smile and increasingly make suggestions as to character names and what becomes of them, and a big hurrah to Dilly and Mr Waffles.

My gratitude and admiration also goes to:

Laura Madden, Veronica Black, Kevin G. Conroy, Sue Leonard, Joanna Fennell, Roz Jellett, Amelia Raben, Gesa Cosby, Sasha Rogers, Sinéad Crowley, ER Murray, Sinéad Moriarty, Rick O'Shea, Hazel Gaynor, Maria Moynihan, The Rick O'Shea Book Club, The Abbey Hotel (Roscommon), Adam Goodwin, John McDermot, Gladys Lawless, Melissa Ellis, Kate Campbell, Kirstin McDonagh, Robert Ehrnrooth, Edmond Loder, Celeste Forde, Hugh Casey, Ned Kelly, Finlay Gallagher, Claire White, Freddie Durdin Robertson, Megan Comiskey, Jago Butler, Susy Webb, Dr. Annemie Van Der Straeten, Áine Toner, Jessie Cahalin of *Books in my handbag*, Marc Brun, Breda Brown of *Inside Books*, Jenny and Justin Green of Ballyvolane House, Christopher and Meryl Gaisford-St Lawrence, Andrew and Nicola Bunbury, William Bunbury, Andy Cairns, Larry Fogg, Simon Lewis, Lenny

Abrahamson, Melissa Ellis, Jed Kelly, James Keogh of Rathwood, Emily Musgrave, Louise Musgrave, Myles Dungan, Ross Adamson, George and Eve Fasenfeld, Robert O'Byrne, Austin and Marti Sullivan, Penny Vincenzi, Jilly Cooper, Wendy Mae Millar, Alexander Durdin Robertson and Sonia Rogers.

For soundtracks while I write, huge thanks to The Coronas, Taylor Swift, Bronagh Gallagher, Alison Krauss, The Beatles and the Greatest Showman. Also thanks to Kirsty Young of Desert Island Discs and Fearne Cotton of Happy Place podcasts, for keeping me company on long walks while working out plots.

There are four things in this
life that will change you. Love,
music, art, and loss. The first
three will keep you wild and
full of passion. May you allow
the last to make you brave.

Erin Van Vuren

For Turtle Bunbury, my husband, my love

Chapter one

Notting Hill, London

Elodie Gold, naked but for lace underwear, peered out from the fitting cubicle of the sleek London boutique, wondering what the loud thump had been. When she saw an alarmed shop assistant approaching, she hurriedly began to pull on her clothes.

"Excuse me, madam, is everything –" she heard the assistant ask, followed by a curtain being pulled back and a loud, high-pitched yelp.

Stepping out of the cubicle, Elodie saw a young woman lying on the floor, her eyes closed, her lips almost blue, her chin tilted towards her shoulder. She looked like she was in her late twenties, maybe younger. Very thin, and wearing a black jumpsuit.

A security guard was at the scene within seconds and asked Elodie not to leave the fitting area. Waiting by a rail of rejected clothes, she watched in horrified awe as a team of paramedics in luminous jackets marched through the shop, brushing their elbows against expensive clothes. The security guard stood alongside Elodie and watched as the paramedics checked the woman for signs of life, but heads nodded glumly and soon she was heaved onto a stretcher with a sheet covering her body.

"I've seen it before," said the security guard, as the woman was carried out of the shop. "Poor love."

"What happened?" asked Elodie, not knowing how to feel. She had never seen a dead body before.

"Overdose. Did ya see when they pulled up her sleeve? Arm like a pincushion. Wouldn't expect it from a posh girl like that, would you? She's been coming here for months. I nearly didn't let her in last week because her eyes were rolling around so much. I thought she looked alright this time but how wrong was I? God knows what she was on, but you can bet your life it was pricey gear."

"I can't believe it," said Elodie, her mind flashing to an image of Dominic popping a rolled-up fifty-pound note into his jacket pocket, his black suit peppered with white powder.

The security guard took her contact details and accompanied her out to the street.

"I don't think we'll need anything further, but if we do I've got your details, Miss Gold. Are you going to be alright?"

"Yes, thank you," said Elodie, as her phone rang in her pocket. "Would you mind if I take this call?"

"You go right ahead, Miss Gold."

She looked at the name flashing on her phone and decided not to answer. She knew he'd call again. Dominic always did.

The security guard looked at her curiously.

"The owner will be in touch soon," he said. "I'm sure he'll make some kind of gesture by way of an apology."

"There's really no need," said Elodie, standing on the pavement. "Goodbye."

Her phone rang again. Impatient, persistent Dominic Finchly. Her heart thumped and she felt a wave of revulsion wash through her at the very thought of speaking to him. She sent the call to voicemail.

The third time he rang, she answered.

"You're late," snapped Dominic.

"Something happened," she said.

"What do you mean *something happened*? I've been waiting here for nearly fifteen minutes."

"I've already told you that I don't want to go with you this weekend," she said, feeling heat and stress building on her face. "I told you I wasn't going."

"Well, it's not the first time you've said that," he said in his frequently condescending tone, as if she couldn't make a decision by herself. Then he changed tack, and put on the syrupy voice that he saved for getting what he wanted. "What are you going to do if you don't come? Sit at home eating too much and sketching those absurd cartoons?"

Elodie held the phone away from her ear and ran her free hand around her waist. He always had to mention her weight. It was the switch he liked to flick, knowing how it rattled her confidence. She thought of the dead woman and wondered about her state of mind. Maybe she felt as miserable as she did. Maybe someday that would be Elodie lying on a dressing-room floor, having achieved nothing in her life, just like her father.

"Elodie," Dominic said firmly. "*I'm waiting.*"

She could have told him what she had seen but somehow she felt it would cheapen the dead woman's life, to make her tragic death into some sort of an excuse to appease the man she had been dating for the past three years.

She took a deep breath and brought the phone to her lips. Surprising herself with the words which came out of her mouth.

"It's over, Dominic."

"What?"

"I'm breaking up with you."

"What are you talking about?"

"I don't want to see you anymore."

"Don't be bloody ridiculous," he said.

"I'm serious, Dominic. It's over. Don't call me, don't text me, don't email me, don't think of me. You need a show pony. I am not a show pony."

There was such a long pause that Elodie looked at her phone to see if they had been disconnected, but he was still there.

"No, you're right about that," she heard his tinny voice say as she reluctantly put the phone back to her ear. "You're no show pony. You're a silly, overindulged bitch and at twenty-seven you're a national bloody disgrace. What have you been doing all day, Elodie? Shopping again? Pathetic."

He dropped the call.

Clutching her yellow bag tight to her chest to stop herself from shaking, Elodie proceeded up Ledbury Road, the violent thud of the woman falling to the floor, like a huge sack of wet sand, so clear in her memory. Watching her breath turn into thick cloudy smoke in the late-winter freeze, Elodie put on her black hat, pulling it down over her ears, her long dark hair spilling down her back. The conversation she had planned to have with Dominic was supposed to take much longer, going into all the reasons why she wanted to break up with him. She hadn't expected that today would be the day, or that it would happen by phone.

She walked quickly through Portobello Market, head bowed, ignoring the colourful, vibrant treasures on offer at the second-hand stalls and trying not to bump into people striding along the footpath. Pausing briefly in the doorway of an estate agent's, she deleted Dominic's number from her phone. It somehow reminded her of the time she had flicked a perfect semicircle of mashed potato through the air of her old school dining room and watched it land on the forehead of her bullying house mistress.

Chapter two

The therapist, wearing Iris Apfel 'Owl' glasses, passed a box of tissues to Elodie.

"The moment you walked through the door, you wanted to cry, didn't you?" she said ten minutes later. "It's like you came here to cry."

"Maybe," said Elodie, pressing a tissue against her eyes and blowing her nose.

"Where would you like to begin?" said the therapist, crossing her legs tightly, leaning in.

Elodie stared at the five-bar heater and wondered if it actually gave out any heat – the room was freezing. Either way, she felt a kind of numbness and wondered if she should just forget the session as this woman didn't appear to be any improvement on the last therapist.

"I have broken up with my boyfriend," said Elodie. "About an hour ago, over the phone."

"And how do you feel about this?"

Elodie had secured an emergency appointment with the therapist, explaining to the secretary that she had witnessed something deeply distressing, but when it came to it she couldn't bring herself to mention the woman in the changing room. She didn't want to bring the memory into the room with her. Her therapy time was reserved for *her* family, for her own turmoil. This was her private space.

"My mother is bitching about my little brother, even though he seems to be doing brilliantly."

"He lives with you at home?"

"Usually, but he's been in LA for the past ten months and is due back this afternoon, which is why Mum has upped the bitch-o-meter in the last forty-eight hours."

"And why do you think that is?"

"Because he reminds her of our father. They look so similar. Eyebrows, nose, their smile. "

"And personality?"

"No, I don't think so. Max is happy-go-lucky, but I don't think my father was."

"Why do you think that?"

"I can remember him coming into our playroom. He'd sit on an armchair, watching us. I can remember feeling his nerves, his tension."

"He made you nervous?"

Elodie took a sip of water. "It's hard to explain."

"Is your brother a nervous person?"

"Not at all, he takes everything in his stride, whereas I analyse everything. It drives me crazy."

"It's perfectly normal for siblings to be different."

"Yes, I know that," said Elodie sharply.

The dead woman in the cubicle came into Elodie's mind again but she pushed the image aside.

"I just can't understand how my brother manages to take so much flak from Mum and has the ability to let it go over his head. It doesn't seem to bother him at all."

"And how does it affect you?"

"What?"

"The way your mother behaves."

"I think I feel guilty."

"In what way?"

"Maybe because I get everything handed to me on a plate."

"Material things?"

"Yes."

"And your mother's love? Does she hand that to you on a plate too?"

At the top of Portland Road, Elodie stood by the gate of her mother's house. It had always been her mother's house, never *their* house. As with everything she did in life, Julia Gold drew clear boundary lines around her possessions. The lights on the top floor signalled that she was home. The Queen in her castle, thought Elodie, and me in the dungeon, although the garden flat was, in fact, the sort of place most people would give their eye teeth for.

Opening the door, the pungent smell of furniture polish was a sure sign that Nosy Carol was at work. Nosy Carol swept through the entire house five mornings a week, superficially plumping and preening and polishing, replenishing fridges in both kitchens and restocking her mother's drinks cabinet. A vase of hyacinths stood on a side table at the foot of the stairs as part of the weekly order of ever-changing flowers. Her mother's interior design hadn't missed a detail. Stone blue walls, *New Yorker* cover prints, deep piled rugs and woollen curtains for winter, which would change to linen during the summer months. Sometimes it was as if they lived in a magazine for pristine interiors, mused Elodie, although perhaps a cartoon strip for a dark comedy would be more apt.

Chapter three

Portland Road, London

Julia Gold sat at her dressing table, the mirror reflecting a stuffed jaguar that lounged on the beige carpet behind her and the single-pane windows that beheld her garden. Sweeping a thick brush through her blonde hair, she thought again of how persistent Lorenzo had been after lunch.

"You're too uptight, Julia," he had cooed, in his seductive Puerto Rican accent. "You need me to familiarise you with my Latino side." And, moments later, he had eased down the zip of her designer jeans and began to send heavenly shockwaves through her body. Julia sometimes felt like he was a potential buyer inspecting a classic car, smoothing his hands across her breasts, breathing in her perfume and darting his tongue deeply, triggering loud gasps as if he were revving an engine.

Afterwards, Julia was always swift to return to her stance as the virtuous widow. "My children and my gallery are what drive me," she had told her Pilates instructor earlier that day. But there were no photographs of her children on her dressing table. No scene of the family posed together, perhaps barefoot, united and perfect. Elodie and her brother Max were more like Julia's business associates than children. Although they were both now in their twenties, they were still based at home, living off hefty allowances from her. Granted, Max had managed to fly the coop to LA for a year, but now he was back and Julia wondered how long it would be before he flew again.

Standing up from the table, Julia tapped into her Pilates straight-back posture as she prepared to once again direct commands at her only daughter. "I am forty-nine years old," she said aloud, "and in the prime of my life." But despite having the body of an athlete – well-disciplined, tanned and toned – she could not convince herself, no matter how often she repeated the mantra her therapist had tried to instil in her.

On the landing she cast an eye at the coral carpet; the deep pile wool had been dyed four times before it was laid but she still wasn't satisfied with the colour. Walking down the wide staircase, she found her two children sitting on a rug in the hallway, hunched over an iPad and giggling. Max, two weeks short of his 24th birthday, had returned home wearing a T-shirt emblazoned with *Do I Look Like I've Got a Big Wallet?*

Julia knew that her wilful daughter had just bust up with her boyfriend. And she hadn't learned that detail from either of her children.

"You've been back in the country for precisely three hours, Max," said Julia, towering over them on the last step, "and you've already cajoled your sister into watching muck on the internet."

Max looked up with a weary smile. "Oh Mum, don't be so serious. If you had come to see me in LA, like you said you were going to, then I could have taken you for the most incredible acupuncture. They've got these things called golden ear seeds that you gently press when you feel stressed and, voila, you're calm in seconds."

"I could have done with a golden ear seed today," said Elodie, her back resting against a Hirst sculpture.

"Why's that, sis?"

"I'll tell you why, Max," said Julia, glaring at Elodie. "Because your sister doesn't know when she's on to a good thing."

"Big Bad Dom causing problems again?" said Max, putting an arm around his sister. "Take it easy on her, Mum. I know there's lots of fish out there but Dominic Finchly is a particularly smelly one."

Julia wasn't in the mood for cheeky backchat.

"I'm going to make a phone call, and then I'll see you in the kitchen, Elodie," she said, summoning her daughter with a bejewelled finger and about-turning.

As soon as Julia rounded the corner, Max raised his eyebrows at Elodie.

"I broke up with Dominic this afternoon," she said.

"Well, I'm proud of you," he said. "He's an idiot."

"Thank you, Max," said Elodie. She felt so stagnant in comparison to her confident, sun-tanned younger brother. "While you've been swanning around film sets in Hollywood, I've been scratching my head over and over again wondering why I'm still living at home and what the hell I'm going to do with my life. It's like we've arrived at opposite extremes."

"Well, I can tell you what you should be doing, Elodie, but you know already. You should be drawing. That is your gift. You just need an agent. How many times have I told you that?"

"I've got nothing to show them."

"Utter balls, El. You've got heaps to show. You've got a huge folder of sketches from last summer for starters. Now you've got Dominic out of your life, what are you so afraid of?"

"Well, at this particular moment, I'm afraid of our mother. How on earth did she find out I broke up with him?"

"You know what he's like," said Max. "He probably called her straight after you dumped him. What made you do it, anyway? Not that it wasn't about time."

"I don't want to go into that now," she said. "Today has been seriously weird."

Elodie thought of the woman again, the dead woman, the dead face. She was about to say something to Max but decided it wasn't what someone who had just flown 5,000 miles needed to hear.

"So," she said instead. "Go on! Tell all – who were you hanging out with, or can you bear to speak with the public now that you're on track to be the next John Barry?"

"El, I'm longing to talk but Mum's going to start yelling if you don't jump to it," said Max, getting up on his feet and offering his hand to Elodie.

"You've become seriously muscly," she said, as he pulled her off the ground. "Did you go on one of those egg-white omelette diets?"

"Not exactly."

"Hanging out with the glitterati, I'm amazed you came back."

"Charlotte's been in contact."

"Aha, I was wondering why you look a little brighter. Honestly, you looked awful before you left."

"Well, I was at a pretty dark crossroads."

"And now?"

"Now, I'm going to make a future with Charlotte."

"Really? I figured that as soon as you got lucky out there you'd stop pining for her."

"No chance."

"But wasn't it weird the way she asked for a break like that?"

"I guess she wanted some time to herself. Anyway, she's been emailing and says she can really see a future for us."

"So, when will you see her?"

"When the time is right."

"That's a bit cryptic?"

"Maybe, but I'm sure she's ready to make a real go of it."

"And your career?"

"All in order, sis."

"I had been expecting long gossipy emails of the Hollywood scene."

"I was busy."

Elodie unwound her scarf from around her neck and tied it around the waist of the Hirst. "So how am I going to deal with Mum?" she said. "Now that you've got your life sorted out, it seems like I'm the only problematic one."

"Here's a tip I learnt in LA. Just treat Mum as if she were a really demanding actress. Take Sofia Tamper, for example. Now, there's an actress who's rising rapidly through the ranks but she's an awful bitch one second and then, whenever she needs something, she turns on the charm and you wouldn't believe how quickly her victims are dripping in buttery love. She's a genius, really, which is why I'd suggest you stay on Mum's good side, at least until you become independent. I've been gone for almost a year, and she barely even noticed when I arrived into the kitchen at lunch time.

She's so caught up in herself and her dumb gallery job."

Elodie laughed but then shook suddenly and Max put his hands on her shoulders.

"Hey, don't worry so much," he said. "Just think of today as your first step to freedom."

"Dominic is a horror, isn't he?"

"That's one word for him," said Max, raising his eyebrows. "You did the right thing. Is he still bleaching his teeth? You know he'd probably get away with that Greek God look if he didn't overdo it on the teeth front."

"So," said Elodie, resisting a smile, "I'm going to focus on my career completely now and just give up on men."

"Just like Sofia Tamper?" said Max, grinning. "You should see her girlfriend Ruby. Seriously gorgeous." Reversing with a bow, he moved towards the stairs leading down to the basement flat. "Don't sweat it, sis, this is nothing new. Just agree with everything Mum says and then do the opposite. Works for me."

Elodie smiled.

"And, sis, one more thing," he said.

"Yes?"

"How about getting an actual job? *In-da-pen-dance!*" And jumping on the banister, he slid out of view.

Chapter four

Elodie tip-toed through the tobacco-coloured dining room into the kitchen, where she found her mother leaning against the marble-topped counter, drinking a glass of white wine and smoking a cigarette.

"Don't give me that look," said Julia, trying to direct her cigarette smoke out through the sliding glass doors. The breeze blew the smoke straight back into the kitchen, irritating her. "As if Dominic wasn't going to tell me."

"Well, he had no right to," said Elodie, anger rushing into her blood.

"And what about the roses?"

"What roses?"

Elodie looked at a bunch of long-stemmed red roses, wrapped in cellophane, sitting in the kitchen sink. "Well, that was quick, I'll give him that. He must have speed-dialled the florist as soon as he hung up."

She pulled out a chair and put one elbow on the kitchen table.

"Elbow, Elodie. Off the table."

"Don't you think I'm too old for you to keep correcting my table manners?"

"You're passing up an opportunity," said Julia. "An opportunity for life-long security *and* with a man who has already professed

13

himself happy to indulge in your whimsical attempts at an artistic career."

"Oh, he's happy to indulge alright. It usually involves his nose and a tightly rolled bank note."

"What are you talking about? You couldn't find a more suitable man. Always so beautifully mannered, handsome and a family line that goes straight back to the Conqueror. Plus he's just been made a partner in Peregrines."

"Hardly surprising, Mum – his uncle owns the company."

"Do you know what he said to me, Elodie?" said Julia, ignoring her daughter's comeback. "He said: 'I simply want to take care of your beautiful daughter, if only she'd let me.'"

Elodie looked at her mother incredulously, and decided she resembled a waxwork at Madame Tussauds – short blonde hair pushed back with sunglasses, jeans adorned by a Hermes belt, navy polo neck and Tiffany necklace.

"But then, of course, nobody is perfect enough for Elodie," said Julia, finishing her wine.

"He's not for me," said Elodie, trying not to lose patience with her mother's sarcasm. She picked up a pencil, tore a page from a message pad and began sketching a woman slumped against a mirror. "I've decided I want to be alone. An independent woman. *Libertatem*."

"Well, at least you have an ounce of Latin to show for your education," said Julia, throwing her cigarette in the direction of an ashtray on the terrace table. As it fell to the floor, Elodie tried not to smirk.

"I think you'll change your mind when I stop your allowance," said Julia.

"I will not change my mind," said Elodie evenly, keeping her focus on her drawing, feeling her mother's eyes burning into her. "Besides, I've decided I'm going to call a temping agency and get an office job."

"Oh, come on, Elodie, you and I both know you are about as suited to office life as a fish out of water."

"And I can draw in the evenings," she said, trying to stand up to her mother's pessimism.

"You really think you can make money out of those silly little doodles?"

"Yes, I do," said Elodie defiantly. "I have a degree in architecture, remember? I can draw."

"Oh, yes," said Julia, lighting another cigarette. "I remember the day you flunked out of your degree. I remember that alright. Which has led to what exactly?"

"Architecture isn't for me. As well you know, it was *your mother* who made me go to Edinburgh. If it hadn't been for Odette, I'd have gone to Central Saint Martins and, who knows, I might be a household name by now."

"Instead of a household bin," snapped Julia. "Your kitchen downstairs is filled with luxury food, and what thanks do I get? You don't as much as have to make your bed, Elodie."

"So you frequently remind me," said Elodie, pressing the pencil lead so hard against the page that the point broke.

"Ah, yes, blame anyone but yourself. You are the classic Millennial, aren't you? Or is it Generation Y? Let me think of the buzz words around you lot … lazy, entitled, self-obsessed. Ring any bells?"

"I just want space, Mother."

"And I give you that," protested Julia. "An entire basement of space on one of London's most prestigious streets."

"Yes, but with three floors of you weighted on top of me?"

"Watch your mouth, Elodie, or you can leave this instant."

Elodie said nothing. She could leave, but then there was the thought of having to fend for herself.

"As for Max," pressed Julia. "He's still obsessed with that blasted vicar's daughter, isn't he?"

"Charlotte is good for him, Mum, you know that. She's so gentle, she suits him."

"Then why on earth did he abandon her to go to LA?"

"For experience, Mum. If he's going to get into the film-score business, he needs experience."

"I'd arranged a perfectly good job for him in the city with a perfectly solid chartered accountancy firm, but would he take it?"

"Can you really see Max putting on a pink shirt and tie every day?"

"Well, I've just about had enough of you both, quite frankly," said Julia, opening the fridge and reaching for the wine bottle.

Elodie emitted a fake cough.

"What?" said Julia defensively.

"Did I say anything?" asked Elodie, her eyes drifting to another empty bottle of Chablis by the sink. "Actually, while I'm here, can I have a cigarette?"

"Apart from the fact that you can't even say please – no, buy your own."

"If Odette were alive, I'd have my own place by now," said Elodie. "She'd have insisted. A room of one's own, as Virginia Woolf put it."

"Your grandmother was very keen on independence."

"Then why don't you encourage me to get out and work?"

"Call me old-fashioned, but I see you as a wife, Elodie, and what's more Dominic Finchly was quite prepared to take you off my hands, but now you've gone and blown it."

Chapter five

Soho, London

"I know the precise nature of the role isn't very clear," said the temping agent's voice, "but we think you'll be a good fit. Honestly, I doubt you'll have to type as much as an email. It's more about you being on hand to support his PA."

"So I'll be a personal assistant to a personal assistant?" said Elodie, ear pressed to her iPhone as she strolled down Regent's Street with kohl-rimmed eyes, in a fitted trouser suit.

"Basically, yes," replied the agent, sounding disconcertingly vague, "but try not to look bored, Elodie. It took me ages to get you back on the books after the last time."

"That was months ago," said Elodie carefully. "I was only sketching."

"Sketching a wolfhound when you were supposed to be scanning documents, I believe," said the agent. "You need to stay focused this time, alright?"

"Alright." Elodie already felt lethargic at the thought of sitting at yet another office desk all day.

Arriving at the revolving doors of a tall grey building, she slipped her iPhone into her shoulder bag and exchanged her runners for a pair of smart slingbacks. A security guard shot a disapproving look at her through the doors. Pushing on through,

Elodie caught the eye of a receptionist with purple hair pulled back into a tight bun.

"We are the choices we make," boomed a silver-haired man from a giant plasma screen, promoting coffee beans. Above the screen, she saw the name *Giles Hampton Advertising* emblazoned in huge letters.

"Ah, the very girl I'm waiting for, I'll bet," said the receptionist, stretching her hand across a dark-grey desk and shaking Elodie's hand. "From the agency, are you?"

"Yes," said Elodie, taking in a series of more large screens, suspended on wire and displaying ads, all presumably created by Giles Hampton. "I was told to go to the penthouse?"

"The Playpen more like," said the receptionist, pointing to a row of silver-faced lifts. "Choose any magic door and press P for Penthouse."

"Any chance I can take the stairs instead?" asked Elodie. "Lifts make me a little claustrophobic."

"Just over there, love. Stairs are better for your figure anyway, aren't they? My Charlie says I should do the same, but he's not exactly one to talk. You should have seen the size of the korma he wolfed down last night in front of the telly."

Elodie raised a little smile at the receptionist before dashing through the door leading to the stairwell.

By the time she had panted her way up to the third flight, she realised the tiny buckle on her heel-strap was about to give way.

"*Bugger!*" she swore, as a man in a dark-brown corduroy suit descended the stairs.

Standing up straight and holding her handbag to her chest, Elodie mustered a smile but he completely blanked her.

"I am a professional," Elodie said to herself, checking her face in a square mirror on the landing. Her father's dark hair, her mother's eyebrows and sapphire-blue eyes. A combination for better or for worse.

"Only six flights to go," she muttered and, taking off her shoes, she stomped all the way to the top floor. Red-faced and out of breath, she pulled open a heavy steel door with tinted glass and found herself standing in a circular hallway with a carpet so deep it felt like a lawn of moss beneath her stockinged feet. Yellow walls lined with prints ran into red-velvet curtains which pooled to the floor. Side-tables were graced with framed photographs of important-looking people, air-kissing and holding up trophies. It looked more like a member's club than an office.

As Elodie slipped her shoes back on again, a curvy young woman in a peach-coloured blouse approached her with an extended hand.

"Tina Blake," she said.

"Elodie Gold, from the agency."

"Yes, that's the one," said Tina, whose handshake was unexpectedly puny. "I knew it rhymed with melody. Foreign, is it?"

"French. My grandmother was from Paris."

"Well, wasn't she the lucky one?"

"I guess."

"My family are all East End. Apples and pears, know what I mean?"

"Sort of," said Elodie, looking around for a clock to see how long she had to go until she could break out.

"Cockney through and through. Not a smidgen of a foreigner between the lot of us, more's the pity. Well, except for my sister's husband."

"Oh?" said Elodie, sensing that Tina expected her to enquire further.

"He's Welsh. Does that count as foreign? He's not sexy though. Not like Tom Jones or that rugby player with the fancy boots. The one who married Charlotte Church. Oh, what's his blinkin' name?"

"No idea," said Elodie.

"Not to worry. Now then, your desk is just over there, nicely tucked away in the corner. Won't take you long to settle. I've only been here two months and already I'm indispensable to Mr Hampton."

"Good for you," said Elodie.

"Now, I've left a pile of important letters for you to deal with. You'll see that each one has been typed on headed paper, and I need you to take the rubber stamp, press it into the ink pad and neatly print Mr Hampton's signature at the end."

"Sounds easy."

"Easy once done precisely," said Tina. "Mr Hampton insists on perfection and that is what must be delivered. Then simply fold each letter and place in a tissue-lined envelope. Got it?"

"Think so," said Elodie.

"They're thank-you letters from Mr Hampton following his exclusive sixtieth birthday celebrations. You know he has extensive property on Paradise Island?"

"Nice," said Elodie.

"And he even –"

Tina jumped as a tall man stepped out of the lift, while Elodie made a beeline for her desk, pulling out a black-leather chair and sitting down as the newcomer approached Tina's desk.

"Is Giles in?" he said. He wore dark jeans and a grey shirt.

"Mr Hampton is at a very important meeting right now," said Tina, speaking very slowly and exaggerating every syllable so that she sounded like a student from an elocution academy. Her accent was quite different to the one she had spoken with earlier. She swayed as she spoke, running the tips of her long fingernails through her tight perm. "I'm afraid I can't possibly say when he will be back."

The man glanced in Elodie's direction. She leant into her computer screen and pretended not to notice him, but she couldn't resist looking twice to take in his easy smile.

"Don't worry," he said. "I'll catch him on his cell."

"American, are we?" said Tina, pushing her bosom out a little further. "You do have a name, I take it? Who shall I say called?"

"No need to say anything."

He about-turned back to the lift, pressed the button, and the silver doors opened immediately as if they had been awaiting his return.

"*Phwoah!* He was a bit of alright, wasn't he?" said Tina, reverting to her East End twang as soon as the doors closed. "D'ya think he was single, Elodie? Did he look single? Can you look like that and still be single? He kept one hand in his pocket, so I couldn't see if there was a ring."

"I don't know," said Elodie, pulling a green-suede pencil case and small pad of paper out of her shoulder bag.

"Well, he was a dazzler, that's for certain. Those brown eyes, like melting Maltesers. Bit of a cheeky bugger, mind you. Wouldn't you say? Breezing in and out like that."

When Elodie didn't reply, Tina walked over to her desk and stood in front of her.

"What you drawing?" she asked, genuinely curious as Elodie curved the pencil down the centre of the page.

"Nothing," said Elodie. It was a sketch of a miniature dachshund she'd noticed being walked through Notting Hill earlier.

"It's pretty good if that's what you call nothing," said Tina. "You don't say much, do you?"

"Sometimes," said Elodie.

"You got a fellah?"

"No."

"Well, let me give you a little advice when it comes to fellahs," said Tina, putting her hands on her hips. "See the way I stood when I was chatting with that American bloke? That was my *Wonder Woman* position. Hands on your hips like this, see?" And she began swaying again, from left to right. "This position gives me confidence, so that I can – " and then she let out a tiny squeak as the lift opened again. "Good morning, Mr Hampton, sir," she said, returning to her clipped English tones, hands still on her hips, as she strutted purposefully towards her desk.

"Looking lovely this morning, Tina," said Giles Hampton, dark-rimmed glasses rising above a crinkled nose. "Fine weather for a run down a mountain on a pair of skis."

"Like your new light beer ad, Mr Hampton," said Tina, with all the confidence of a student who had been paying attention in class.

"Exactly," said Giles, rubbing his hands before taking off his glasses and looking in Elodie's direction. "And who do we have here?"

His voice reminded Elodie of Jack Nicholson: a slow drawl, a dash of humour.

"Miss Elodie Gold," said Tina, grandly. "She's my new assistant."

Elodie gawped; it hadn't occurred to her that Tina was to be her immediate boss. She tried to say good morning to Giles but he had already turned his back and disappeared into a room which Elodie assumed to be his office.

Chapter six

"Don't worry about Mr H," whispered Tina. "Better leave the small talk out with him."

Elodie sat back in her chair while Tina began tapping her shoe against the desk leg as if she had absolutely nothing better to do.

"See this?" said Tina, holding up a book. "It's called *Get Thrifty.* My partner and I are saving for a deposit and this is the Holy Bible for how you do it. It's going to be egg sandwiches all the way for us."

"Good idea," said Elodie, feeling inadequate still living at home.

Opening a desk drawer, Tina pulled out a green Tupperware container, tore off the lid and dipped in a fork before taking five consecutive mouthfuls.

"Lentils," she explained, her mouth full. "Very filling, and keeps me regular too, know what I mean?"

She opened the drawer again and this time she held up an egg.

"Hardboiled," she winked. "Only two years to go, and then we'll have a deposit. And it's good for waist-conditioning too." She stood up, hands on her hips once more. "See this waist? Twenty-two inches. Used to be thirty-four. All thanks to this book. I'm sure it's the reason I look so good."

Frankly, Elodie thought Tina looked a little washed out. A night of cocktails and a big fillet steak certainly wouldn't go amiss.

"How about you, Elodie, me melody? On the property-ladder yet?"

"Not yet," said Elodie, glum-faced.

"Not to worry. I can lend you my book if you like? We've got our hearts set on a semi-d in Cockfosters."

"I've been to Cockfosters," said Elodie, adding a park bench to her drawing of the dog. "I once fell asleep on the Tube and ended up there."

"Yeah, it's the end of the line," said Tina, her eyes shining with enthusiasm. "And here's another good tip on being thrifty. Double up your shampoo with washing-up liquid. You wouldn't believe how much you'll save each year, especially with your long hair. You just add an egg yolk once a month to bring back the shine. Simple as."

Elodie nodded and couldn't think of anything more disgusting.

"When you're ready, ladies," said Giles, popping his head out of his office door. He had one of those smiles that Elodie imagined would continue smiling even if he was furious. "Get Jane Blake on the line for me, Tina, will you?"

"Of course, Mr Hampton," said Tina. "Won't be a moment."

"And you?' he said, looking at Elodie and tightening his tie. "Edith, is it?"

"Um, no, it's Elodie."

"A glass of freshly squeezed orange juice and a lightly toasted bagel – no butter," he said, nodding curtly and then smoothing his tie down his front before closing the door.

"She'll do that right away, sir," said Tina, covering the mouth of the telephone. "You'll find Chef in the kitchen," she said, gesturing Elodie towards an alcove on the right. "Off you go and arrange the juice. And remember, no small talk to Mr H."

Elodie shook her head and wondered what sort of job she had taken on. Walking through the double doors of the alcove, she espied a short man with a friendly, freckled face chopping what looked like a large wedge of ginger.

"Alright?" he said. Putting down his shiny chopping knife, he swooped his hand into Elodie's. "Jimmy. You're new?"

"Yes, Elodie," she said, returning his smile. "I'm working as an assistant to Tina."

"Oh," chuckled Jimmy, as he returned to ginger-chopping duties. "Well, you'll need to watch out for that one."

"Why?" said Elodie, mildly alarmed.

"All sorts of weird things happen on this floor. You wouldn't know who's having it off with who."

"Really?"

"Really," said Jimmy. "Now, looking for a bit of juice for the big man?"

"And a toasted bagel," said Elodie, wondering if Jimmy was employed purely to cook for *the big man*.

"Lightly toasted, no butter, right?" Gathering three bright oranges from a fruit bowl, Jimmy pulled a fresh knife from a wooden block, then chopped and squeezed them one by one into a tall glass. "Mr H is constantly on a diet. It's all fish and fruit this month. The two f's, or three if you count his swearing."

"He seems pretty slim to me."

"That's why. The f's keeps him that way. It's his Californian roots, you see. They're very health-conscious over there."

"Mr Hampton is a Californian?"

"Well, sort of. He's one of those geezers who made good over there and then came back here. You should Google him. There's more juice in his past than a crate of these bleedin' oranges."

Balancing the glass of juice carefully on a tray, Elodie pushed back out through the double doors, walked towards Giles Hampton's office and hesitated at his door.

"Go on then," said Tina, standing by her desk as she polished her nails with a glittering turquoise file. "He won't bite."

"Can you knock on the door for me, please?" said Elodie.

"Sorry, no can do. I'm at a crucial point with me nails."

"It's just that if I take my hand off the glass, I'm afraid it will unbalance," said Elodie, putting on her puppy-dog eyes, which usually worked.

Not with Tina.

"Oh, I think you can manage, don't you? Not terribly complicated, is it?"

Balancing the tray on one hand, Elodie knocked on the door until she heard a voice yell "*Enter.*"

Turning the handle, Elodie opened the door and breathed in the scent of expensive aftershave.

As she neared his desk, she noticed broken veins across Giles' nose. He didn't look up as she placed the juice down and she decided he was pretty rude.

"I like the violin," she said, admiring a fine Stentor mounted on the wall.

"Excuse me?" he said, tapping his pen onto the desk.

"The violin, it's very nice. My brother used to play when he was younger. He's very musical. In fact, he's just got back from LA. Work experience in Hollywood, you know, creating film scores."

Giles responded by flashing her a huge smile, and running his fingers inside his shirt collar.

"Didn't Tina brief you?" he said.

"Brief me?"

"When my mind is in flow, I am not to be spoken to."

His knuckles pressed into his desk as he stood up from his chair, like a gorilla about to pounce.

"Right," said Elodie. "No speaking then."

He nodded and returned to his writing and she retreated backwards through the open door as if she were exiting Her Majesty's drawing room.

Chapter seven

"How come you didn't take your full forty-five-minute lunch break?" asked Tina, patting the tight curls at the back of her head before taking off her leather coat. "Keen to impress on your first day? Fair enough, I can understand that. It isn't every day a position comes up in Hampton's Penthouse, as we like to call it."

"I just thought I'd come back early," said Elodie, having read an intimidating article on Giles Hampton on her iPhone in a café nearby. Apparently he liked to leave his opponents *breathless and broken*. "I'm hoping this place will inspire me to get my own business up and running."

"And what sort of business would that be?" said Tina.

"I'd like to sell my drawings."

"Your drawings, eh?" said Tina, squirting hand cream onto the palm of her hand. "Like the dog you drew earlier? Well, we can all dream, can't we? Any messages on the answering machine? Oh, don't worry, I haven't run through the phone system with you – we'll do that later, shall we?"

"Actually I did take a call from Mr van der Pol," said Elodie, feeling smug that she had been there to answer the phone.

"Johan van der Pol?" Tina's eyes darted from left to right as she quickly rubbed in the hand cream.

"Yes, you mentioned him this morning and how he and Mr Hampton are on the cusp of striking a massive deal about the airline ad campaign."

"What did he say?" said Tina, speaking very slowly through tight lips.

"Well, it wasn't Mr van der Pol as such. It was his driver."

"And?" Tina pulled up a chair and sat down across from Elodie, her face profoundly serious.

"He asked me for the address."

"For?"

"For the Sugar Club."

"The where?"

"The driver said that Johan was meeting Mr Hampton for lunch at the Sugar Club, and he wanted me to verify where it was."

"Okay, to verify where it was," repeated Tina. "And you told him?"

"I did."

"How did you know where it was?"

"It was a cinch. The address came up on Google maps immediately. I solved his query in about fifteen seconds flat, I'd say."

"And what was the address, Elodie?"

"Spitalfields," said Elodie.

The word had hardly left her lips when Tina leapt out of the chair and began swiping through her phone by the window.

"Do you have the driver's name?" she demanded.

"Um. Carlos, I think?" said Elodie, puzzled.

Within seconds, Tina had the phone to her ear.

"Carlos? Tina here. What? Fuck a bloody duck. Mr H will go mental. Get him back to the Nobu Hotel in Shoreditch, okay? They've just scored another Michelin star, so that should soothe his nerves. He is a serious foody, that one. "

Tina stormed towards Giles Hampton's office.

"*You can thank your lucky stars I've caught this before Mr Hampton finds out!*" she yelled at Elodie before slamming the door behind her.

Feeling increasingly nervous, Elodie gingerly arose from her desk and then realised she had forgotten to pass on a second message to Tina. Tiptoeing over to Giles' door, she knocked meekly three times.

"Tina?" she said, turning the handle and peeping around the door.

"What is it, Elodie?" said Tina who was sitting behind Mr Hampton's desk, typing at speed on the desktop.

"Sorry to disturb. I just realised ... well, I meant to tell you that a courier arrived earlier."

"My, it's been busy here, hasn't it, Elodie?" she sighed. "So tell me," she pushed her fingers together, her long nails making her look rather spikey, "when did this courier arrive?"

"About fifteen, maybe twenty minutes ago?"

"And?"

"And he wanted an address for Mrs Hampton."

"To send what exactly?" Tina's nostrils were beginning to flare in a rather unbecoming way.

"A small sort of package," said Elodie, sensing that she might have possibly made the wrong call on saying anything. "It was from Boodles. Gorgeous packaging. But don't worry, I checked the card to make sure it was definitely for Mrs Hampton."

"And where did you send it?"

"Well, I gave the Hampton's address in Gloucestershire, as in the same address that was on the headed paper."

"Hell's bells," said Tina, "and did you see what it said on the card?"

Elodie hesitated. She wasn't sure she should admit to having read the card but Tina's eyes had narrowed so much that she couldn't stop herself.

"Well, it was in French actually," said Elodie. *"Jusqu'à la prochaine fois, mon étoile."*

"And what the clucking bell does that mean?"

"Until next time, my star ... does that make sense?"

Tina's face paled as Giles Hampton arrived into the room.

"Oh bugger," said Elodie, looking from Tina to Giles. "Did I send it to the wrong address? I presumed the package was for your address in the country?"

28

"'Oh bugger' is precisely correct," said Giles.

"I just presumed that –"

"*Enough!*" said Giles, holding up his hand. He maintained the stance dramatically for several long seconds and then slowly walked towards Elodie until his face was only inches away.

"Why must we never presume?"

"I really don't know, Mr Hampton," said Elodie, longing to leave the room.

"Because presumption is – *the – mother – of – all fuck-ups*!"

"Ah," said Elodie, stepping backwards towards the door, "I think I'll get my coat, as they say."

"*They* would be right," said Giles Hampton.

Chapter eight

Notting Hill, London

"It was a bit of a sitcom," said Elodie, sipping a coffee at the bar of Sam's Kitchen, her best friend's Notting Hill café, two days later. "Was it really the end of the world that I sent a package for his wife to their country house, and how was I supposed to know that there are two bloody Sugar Clubs?"

"Maybe there are two Mrs Hamptons as well," said Sam. "Like a mistress going by that name?"

"Honestly, I'm exhausted by the whole ordeal, I don't ever want to hear the name Hampton again – unless I'm invited to go on holiday to the actual *Hamptons,* as in Long Island."

"So what you're telling me is that you sent the high-powered Dutch exec straight to a brothel in the East End rather than to a gentleman's club in Chelsea?" said Sam, cracking up. "That is absolutely priceless."

But Elodie couldn't laugh, yet. The chances of the temp agency getting her another job was almost zero.

"Look, El," said Sam. "We're only open for another hour. Why not help out here for a bit and then we'll lock up and go out and get sozzled?"

"Honestly, Sam, I'm just not in the mood. I think I need to go home and take to the sofa."

"Okay," said Sam, mildly exasperated. "I hope you won't mind me saying this, but if you want to get out from under your mum's skirt, you need *your own* money, Elodie."

Sam, dressed in sleek black trousers and a fitted black shirt, glossy fair hair pulled back into a ponytail, was always solid as a rock. Her can-do attitude did much to re-centre Elodie when she was wavering.

"Alright," said Elodie, slipping off the bar stool. "Pass me an apron, you slave driver!"

"That's more like it. Good times are coming, Elodie. So just hold steady, get the hours in and you'll be exhibiting in the Tate before you know it."

"Hah, I'm more likely to be exhibiting fish and chips at a takeaway in Grimsby at the rate I'm going. Isn't that how ninety-nine per cent of wannabe artists end up?"

"Not you though, Elodie. You're different. Now, I'm going to start winding things down in the kitchen so can you be my front of house for a while? See if you can convince somebody to buy the rest of the quiche, will you? Bat those lovely eyelids of yours."

Sam went into the kitchen, leaving Elodie amid the various waifs and strays of pastries and pies in the empty café. Feeling a little peckish, she cut off a sliver of red onion tart, which made her feel mildly better. Then, picking up the notepad meant for taking table orders, she began drawing a chauffeur delivering a package to a herd of cows standing in front of a huge country house.

"Hi there," said an American voice.

Elodie looked up to find a tall man with brown hair smiling at her.

Dark eyes, so familiar. She smiled and squinted for a moment. They had definitely met before. Then, with a jolt, she realised it was the guy who had waltzed into Hampton's office, the man Tina had an immediate crush on.

"We're about to close," she said, wiping her mouth and taking an instant dislike to anything to do with Giles Hampton.

"Really? But it's only six and you look pretty open to me. I've been told the Shepherd's Pie here is incredibly good."

"Well, I'm afraid it's off the menu," she said, straightening fliers on the counter for a yoga sanctuary. The thought of even having to heat up Shepherd's Pie was too much, let alone having to make small talk while the oven whirled away.

"But it's chalked on the board, right there," he said, pointing to *Today's Special*.

He was styled like a Hilfiger model and Elodie decided he was far too good-looking and full of himself. Grabbing a cloth from the sink, she ran it under the tap, huffed over to the blackboard and wiped it clean.

"Alright then," he said, amused. "I'd like a wheatgrass smoothie, with avocado and lemon."

"Sounds far too healthy," she said.

"Well, it's your menu."

"It is not *my* menu, actually."

"Wow, why are you being so rude?"

He was still smiling, which annoyed Elodie even more.

"Rude? I might ask you the same question. Anyway, the smoothies are off the menu. We have a shortage."

"A shortage of what?"

"Smoothie material. In any case, I'm busy. I don't have time."

"Wow, well, that is a shame," he said, not taking his eyes off her. "So, how about dinner?"

"What?" said Elodie. "You're joking?"

"Would you like to have dinner with me?"

"That's very impulsive?" said Elodie, fiddling with the coffee grinder to busy herself and nearly burning herself on the steamer. "*Ow!*"

"Are you alright?" he said, sounding genuinely concerned.

"I'm fine," snapped Elodie.

"I've seen you before, haven't I?"

"Have you?" asked Elodie. She felt an absurd compulsion to cry. How had she become such a failure that she couldn't even serve a customer properly?

"In Hampton's, right? You work there as well as here?"

"No. As it happens, that was my first and last day." Her eyes started to brim with tears and she turned away.

"Woah, you didn't last too long then?" he said, raising his eyebrows.

Pulling out a bar stool, he sat down, folding his long legs in front of him.

Elodie took a deep breath and tried to channel some of her mother's matter-of-fact attitude. "Mr Hampton is a piece of work," she said. "A complete horror, and his PA is a totally two-faced ..." She trailed off, wondering if Mrs Hampton ever received her package from Boodles.

The American, still smiling, was about to reply when the coffee machine began making a strange noise. Elodie didn't seem to notice.

"Um, the coffee," he said, looking over her shoulder. "I think it's ready."

Turning around, Elodie squealed and ran over to the machine which was now burbling black coffee down its sides onto the floor.

"*Oh bugger, bugger, bugger!* Okay, that's it," she said, beginning to lose her cool. "I'm closing up now. Sorry, you'll have to leave."

"Bagels," he said.

"What?"

"Bagels. I hear Sam's Kitchen is famous for its bagels."

"We don't have any of those either."

"Really?" said the American, pointing towards a tray laden with bagels.

"Alright, so go for it. Happy?" said Elodie.

"Yes, it's a sale! I'll take them."

"What? All of them?"

"Yes. Why not? They freeze really well. I'm not a big breakfast eater. Brunch is more my thing. I need at least two cups of coffee before I can eat."

Beneath the counter, Elodie found a paper bag with handles and proceeded to tip the bagels into the bag.

"Fortunately, I'm not fussy if my bagels are out of shape and broken," he said.

Elodie refused to smile back.

Taking a brown leather wallet from his jacket, he produced an AMEX card and handed it to her.

"Shall I tap?" she said and, looking at the card, she closed her eyes. "Luke ... Hampton."

"That's me," he said, grinning.

"Oh God, as in … are you related to … Giles Hampton?"

"Yes, I'm the son of the aforementioned *horror*."

"Oh Christ, I'm sorry," said Elodie. Shaking out her hair, she turned her head around, opened the fridge and thrust her head inside, pretending to look for something. The cold air cooled her a little as she took a deep breath. She turned back again, slammed the fridge behind her and briefly made eye contact with Luke as she tapped his card against the machine.

"So how about dinner, then. Is it still a no?" he said.

"What?"

"Dinner? It's a meal you have in the evening? Usually involves a knife and fork?"

"Yes," she said, "I mean, yes, it is definitely a no."

"Okay, as long as you're sure," he said, dismounting from the stool and heading towards the door.

As he reached the door, she called his name, "Luke?"

"Changed your mind already?"

"No," she said. "You forgot your bagels."

"Of course, thank you. So now that you know my name, it seems only fair that I know yours?"

"Elodie," she said, stepping around the counter and handing the bag to him. "Elodie Gold."

"Elodie Gold. A pleasure to meet you."

"Likewise," she said, trying not to smile.

As he exited the door, he looked back at her, raised his eyebrows and smiled one more time. It really was a most delicious smile.

Chapter nine

"So, you've finally taken your finger off the self-destruct button?" said Sam, studying the cocktail menu. They were seated in The Cow, their favourite Notting Hill bar and Elodie was trying to make eye contact with a waiter.

"Yes, I have," said Elodie. "No more Dominic."

"What about Max? He must be thrilled that you've got rid of Big Bad Dom. Isn't that what he calls him? How is Max?"

"Max is still mad about Charlotte and seems utterly certain that she will come back to him."

"It's entirely possible, what with her being a vicar's daughter," said Sam. "Vicars' daughters are generally considered a safe bet."

"Charlotte certainly used to tick all the reliability boxes before she went AWOL. Max thinks she's found herself again but until she actually finds him again, it's the single life for both us Gold siblings."

"According to Sheryl Sandberg," said Sam, "you can date all the bad guys you want but just make sure you marry the nerds, the good guys."

"I've no interest in good, bad or nerdy," said Elodie, catching a waiter's eye. "I'm flying solo from now on."

The waiter arrived and Elodie ordered a pair of Rhode Island Reds.

"Nice choice," said Sam. "How's your mother taking the news about Dominic?"

"You mean now that her prospects of having a rich and incredibly vain son-in-law have been blown out the window?"

"Precisely."

"I actually don't care what she thinks. When I saw that woman in the changing room, just lying there, it was so weird. It was like some sort of an epiphany. I just realised how much I need to get my act together. And I thought of all the times that Dominic called me stupid or fat."

"Oh yeah, all eight and a half stone of you," said Sam. "That guy has some nerve."

"I know dumping my boyfriend and a failed attempt at an office job isn't exactly ground-breaking, but it's a start. More of a start than that poor woman will ever get to make."

Elodie and Sam swiftly picked up the cocktails as they arrived with the waiter.

"You must have got such a fright seeing her there," said Sam.

Elodie nodded but then regretted bringing it up again and decided to steer clear of the topic.

"When I spoke with Dominic on the phone afterwards, I had a weird realisation about the way he always talks down to me. I thought of all things he's said to me over the past months, like how I'd never survive without Mum's money and that I'll never make it as an artist."

"He's such a creep, El. Honestly, getting rid of him is the best thing you could possibly have done," said Sam, clinking her glass against Elodie's. "The only thing is, and again please don't take this the wrong way, but you *have* been living at home since you left Edinburgh."

"Don't you think I bloody know that?" snapped Elodie.

"Alright, steady up. No need to fly off the handle. I'm just saying."

"Sorry. I'm really sorry, Sam. I just sometimes feel like my head is going to burst, between Mum breathing down my neck and just not having a clue about what it is I'm meant to be getting on with."

"Okay, let's focus on having a fun night, deal?"

"Deal," said Elodie. "Now, I'm just going to pop out for a ciggy."

"Okay, but before you do, tell me … who was that dishy guy you were chatting to at the café?"

"Oh, him? Well, it turned out he was Giles Hampton's son. Can you believe it? Seriously awkward."

"What? The advertising guy you were working for? What did he want?"

"Shepherd's Pie, as it happens. I couldn't really handle him though. I mean, it was so weird to see him standing in your café."

"I'm not surprised that threw you. Small world or what? It's like something out of *Casablanca*. Of all the café joints in all the world …"

"He doesn't eat breakfast apparently," said Elodie. "Prefers brunch."

"I see. So, you've already discussed breakfast habits with … what's his name?"

"Luke."

"Luke. Let's call him Handsome Luke."

"No, don't give me that look, Sam," said Elodie, grabbing her yellow clutch bag. "I'm off men, remember? And I'm also really trying to stop smoking. Damn, I'll have to start again tomorrow."

Chapter ten

Portland Road, London

"Morning, sis," said Max, walking into the kitchen in a crumpled shirt and scratching his chest. "Fun night?"

Elodie slumped her head into her arms at the kitchen table. "Yes, I'm terrific. I've got a stonking hangover, no career, no boyfriend and no one understands why I could possibly be miserable because our mother is dripping in glorious bloody money."

"Oh, come on, Elodie. You've just got to take hold of your own destiny. That's what I'm doing."

"And you think that's enough?"

"No idea," said Max, reaching for the muesli, "but if all else fails I could always do what Gramps did and marry an heiress. He hasn't done a hard day's work in his life, has he?"

"Max, I think you and I know that living with Odette would have been non-stop hard days, work or no work. She ran Bellamore like it was the Guggenheim. How the staff managed to keep up with all the polishing and dusting was a miracle. We could barely tiptoe into half the rooms in case our breath touched anything, remember? It must have been like living in a china doll's house for Gramps, except his wife was the only one who got to decide which room the dolls could sit in."

"And wasn't it weird how she wouldn't let us call her Grand-mère or Granny or anything even vaguely hinting that we were related?" said Max, lashing on milk and sugar.

"I guess she just wanted to be thought of as a stylish Parisian rather than an old granny, don't you think?"

"And yet she fetched up living in a monster of a house, in the middle of the Irish countryside, a million miles from what she was used to in Paris?" said Max. "Strange move, don't you think? To marry a dreamer like Gramps and then become a recluse. I miss those breakfasts though. Croissants straight out of the Aga, I can still taste them."

"And what about Dad, do you still miss him?" said Elodie, tearing the edge off a piece of toast and marmite.

Max put the palms of his hands on the table and there was silence for a moment.

"You know what, El? When I was in LA, I'd hear all these stories about fathers and sons and how it's every man's ambition to create a big family dynasty, but it wasn't like that for us, was it? We never had much of a relationship with him. How could we? You were seven and I was four. It was a tiny age to lose a parent."

"But don't you even miss his presence?"

"His presence? No, I was far too young. Sometimes, though, I look at these hands," said Max, "and I wonder if they're like his. But you know what? I don't want to be like him and so, to be honest, no, I choose not to miss him."

"He must have loved us though?" said Elodie.

"Really?" said Max. "I don't think there was any *must* as far as Dad was concerned. Mum and Odette always said he put himself first, every time, even ducking out when the bank caught up with him."

Elodie pushed her plate of toast to one side.

"What's bringing all this on, El? Is there a reason why you're thinking of him now? I mean, I'd understand if you wanted to talk about Dominic, or even Odette, but Dad? It's so long ago."

"It's nothing," she said, thinking of the woman's face in the fitting room. "I'm just trying to work out why I can't seem to get my life on track."

"Okay, first up, you're not massively off track, are you? You love to draw and so you know your passion – and that counts for a lot. Secondly, and I think this is relevant, Mum's hardly made it easy for you."

"That's another thing I've been thinking about," said Elodie. "Mum's relationship with Ireland. What did her family do to her?"

"From the moment Odette took to her bed, things changed, and when she died Mum made Bellamare completely off limits. That's seven years ago. Can you believe it? It was like a travel ban to the place. Why was that? They all obviously had a massive falling-out."

"Now, there is a veritable mystery," said Max. "And do you remember Odette thumping her walking stick on the floorboards whenever she wanted a G&T? That'll be Mum in twenty years, just you wait."

"I guess it will," said Elodie.

Chapter eleven

Odette, the Golds' grandmother, had died seven years earlier. Max and Elodie didn't fly back to Bellamore for her funeral because there wasn't one. Instead, she donated her body to the anatomy department at Trinity College Dublin. They had been told there would be a service two years later, when her body had fulfilled its purpose for experiments, but the service never happened. Like Elodie's father, Odette's death somehow melted away.

Douglas Gold's existence had been eliminated from the entirety of Julia Gold's house with the remarkable exception of his office, which Julia kept as a virtual shrine to him, replete with his desk, a tall brass lamp and his golf bag wedged between the log basket and skirting board.

As Elodie sat on the floor of his office, she could still hear his voice. "*Are you two being good little people for your mother?*"

She remembered glaring up at his puce face, trying not to notice the throbbing vein down the centre of his forehead. He had rarely engaged with them, not even when Max pointed at James Bond's car on the television and squealed "*Double O Seven!*". She could see her father now, in her mind's eye, walking out the door, brown shoes, yellow-and-navy striped socks.

The first clue that something had happened was when Elodie

heard the screams emanating from this very room.

"*What about the children? You have to help me, I cannot do this alone!*"

Elodie could recall the moment so vividly, when she stood in the doorway, watching her mother scream into the telephone. Then little Max pulled on Elodie's cardigan, and they retreated to the playroom. It had always been like that, Max instinctively pulling Elodie away from difficult situations.

"What are you doing in here?" said Julia, her voice booming into the silence and making Elodie jump. "Eleven o'clock," she said, dramatically tapping her watch. "Really, Elodie, what sort of time is this to be in your pyjamas?"

Walking over to the curtains, Julia slapped at the heavy material. It was the only room in the house that she hadn't yet torn apart and redecorated to the nth degree.

"I'm working at Sam's Kitchen this afternoon," said Elodie. "I've got plenty of time."

"Really?" said Julia, pulling her full-length mustard cardigan around her waist as she settled in to interrogate her daughter. "That still doesn't explain why you are in here?"

Elodie moved to the mantelpiece and sat down on the club fender.

"Max and I were talking about Dad earlier, that's all. I thought I'd come in here and sit. I didn't know it was illegal."

"That's all very well," said Julia, "but it's still high time you got dressed. What if Dominic were to call by?"

"What? Mum, how many times do I have to say it? Dominic is not going to call by. Because we have broken up. He is past tense. *Finito.*"

Julia opened her mouth to retort but Elodie beat her to it.

"Before you say anything, Mother, yes, I am sure it is over. And yes, I am trying to find a proper job but, until then, I'm helping out Sam in her café."

"Right," said Julia, momentarily lost in her daughter's big blue eyes. She didn't feel like challenging Elodie anymore.

"Have you ever thought of giving Dad's golf clubs away?" said Elodie.

"Who could possibly want them?" said Julia, turning to the window. "They're far too old-fashioned."

"I just don't understand why this room has to be kept like something out of *Great Expectations*. Miss Havisham's wedding cake wouldn't look out of place, though I have to hand it to Nosy Carol, she hasn't let a single cobweb get past her."

Julia looked at the diary on the desk. 1996. His fountain pen next to it, an executive's game of mini-billiards next to that, and a calculator. The calculator that got it all so wrong.

"Mum?"

Julia looked at Elodie. Behind those defiant eyes, she could see the spirit of Douglas. She had so much of her father in her, although Julia could never bring herself to say it. No therapy in existence could bring her to say those words. Julia reached out and ran her hand tenderly down the back of her daughter's head, feeling the softness of her hair, remembering what it had been like to brush it before school in those long-distant days. With little maternal example to follow, Julia hadn't been the most affectionate of mothers but, today, at this moment, she felt a wave of immense and unexpected sympathy for this burgeoning young woman next to her.

"What made you fall for Dad?" said Elodie, recoiling from her mother's touch.

"Your father?" Julia thought for a moment. "It wasn't difficult. He was good-looking, of course, but I think it was his sense of Englishness. Eton-educated and a promising career as a banker ahead of him. I just wanted to get away from anything Irish – or French for that matter."

"Were Thomas and Odette that bad?"

Julia ignored the question. "This house was going to be full of children," she said. "Maybe four or five. We wanted a large family, a big English family."

Her mind drifted back to the Brompton Oratory where she and Douglas married, and to the after-party at the Dorchester. All so splendidly British.

"I also loved Portland Road," she continued. "Of course, Notting Hill was quite different then. It wasn't *trendy* but I loved the challenge of redecorating the house and converting it into what it is now."

"And you loved Dad?"

"Yes," she said, "I suppose I did."

"You suppose?"

Julia looked at her hand, the engagement ring with its row of large diamonds, and her mother's signet ring on her little finger. Why did she torture herself by wearing reminders of Douglas and Odette every day?

"Mum, you look so sad," said Elodie.

Like a rubber band, Julia pulled back to her default setting.

"Oh blast, is that the time?" She checked her Rolex. "I'm due to have my eyebrows done at the salon in fifteen minutes. Sorry, Elodie, the traffic on Beauchamp Place is dreadful at this time of day."

"Why do you clam up anytime I ask you about Odette and Thomas," said Elodie, following her mother to the door.

Julia flashed her eyes angrily but she said nothing.

"Bellamore was where Max and I spent our summers," said Elodie. "You can't just expect us to erase it all.'

"As I have said before, Elodie, families are complicated, and I don't see why you choose to bring this up now. And," she continued before Elodie could speak, "if you're still here when Carol arrives, try to be polite. She's complained more than once about your rudeness to her lately."

"Nosy Carol."

"Call her what you like but don't let her hear you, and remember to close that door tightly behind you."

Chapter twelve

Beauchamp Place was the pearl in London's oyster when it came to make-up. Over the past decade, the salon's expertise had turned Julia's life around with her deftly tattooed eyebrows and Middleton-style eyeliner. Then there was the Botox clinic in Switzerland, to which she would fly every three months in order to iron out any disagreeable cellulite and attend to her upper-lip pout. She gave her face a quick, last-minute check-over in the mirror by the front door. Julia had always found her reflection difficult to look at for long, which partly explained her fixation on continually amending her image. Wide eyes, high cheekbones and pointed chin, all so reminiscent of her late mother, Odette. According to her therapist, her face was a perennial spotlight on the tangled relationship they had endured.

Lorenzo Arbore, officially Julia's personal shopper, though Max, Elodie and Nosy Carol knew better, was key to her regime. By continuously refreshing her wardrobe, he made her feel good about herself, in every way. A former lawyer, Lorenzo had tapped into the obsessions of the time-poor long before time-poor had even been identified as a trend. Combining this target market with his love of fashion, he was inspired to establish a personal shopping service, *Simply Lorenzo*. Now fifty years old, he had developed a first-rate reputation for delivering ready-made outfits in which his clients could simply walk out the door, looking fabulous. He got it right every time. Lorenzo's particular set of skills appealed enormously to Julia and made her feel sexy and desirable in a way her late husband had never done. Even on her honeymoon, Douglas had never made her feel particularly special. But with Lorenzo, it was all about the personal attention, right down to his choosing her underwear.

"There must be no strings to our relationship, Lorenzo," she had said, following a shattering orgasm.

"You are so right, my darling Julia," murmured Lorenzo. "No strings, unless they involve the letter G – only lingerie."

Julia had inherited her mother's slender waist and full bosom, but it was her exercise routine and regular trysts with Lorenzo that kept it all in shape. If it wasn't for him, she would have let herself go by now.

Pulling the heavy grey front door shut behind her, Julia was trying to tap into positive thoughts after her disconcerting encounter with Elodie in Douglas's office, but then she spotted her annoying Italian neighbour standing next to a white Range Rover. Julia couldn't bear the way the woman insisted on wearing a sleeveless puffa coat, or a Chelsea lifejacket as Lorenzo called it. The colours she wore were an insult to the gilet.

"*Ciao*, Julia!" shouted the woman, lifting up her sunglasses. "Where have you been? You must come over for coffee. I've just bought a machine that makes the strongest espresso I have ever tasted."

"I'm off coffee at the moment," said Julia curtly.

"Ah, you are having another health kick, yes?"

"Something like that. Now, as much as I'd love to chat, I'm running late for a meeting. Must dash."

But the woman was in no hurry. "Yes, I see. But I must tell you very quickly about this coming weekend. I will go to my daughter's house in Berkshire, but how will I cope? I have only Nanny to help me with the twins. I said to my daughter, you *must* go. She has taken, for one week, a very massive villa in Ibiza. It is massive, I tell you. *Enorme*. 'Sweetheart,' I said to her, 'you need to get out. It is not good to be home with Nanny and the twins all the time.' You know, she barely has a moment to herself by the time she goes to the gymnasium, and all the dinners she must go to with Gregory. You know he's been made a partner. Did I tell you?"

"Quite so," said Julia, who was about to explode with a combination of boredom, and more than a hint of jealousy at the woman's intuitive kindness as a mother. "Good luck with the twins."

"No, darling, it's more like, good luck with the nanny. Managing the staff, that's my greatest challenge," she said grandly.

The moment she managed to escape from her neighbours one-way dialogue, Julia speed-dialled Lorenzo on her mobile.

"Lorenzo, it's me," she said. "Once I've been to Beauchamp Place, can you meet me, please? I feel a tremendous need to unwind with my credit card, and then can you unwind inside me?"

Chapter thirteen

Notting Hill, London

Luke awoke with one thing on his mind: Elodie Gold. In fact, he was so distracted thinking about her that he burned two bagels before he managed to toast a third one properly. Maybe he was trying to divert himself from the frustrating phone calls he'd had with *both* his parents since his return to the flat the night before. One needy, the other plain old bossy. Actually, his mother was in relatively good form, having received a 'darling' pair of earrings from Boodles, as a surprise gift from Giles.

"Clearly, your father wants to bring back the romance," she said. "Must be getting soft in his old age."

Meanwhile his father rang in a foul humour, demanding to know when Luke was going to set a date to take up his role as VP of the company's New York office. But Luke was feeling very much at home in the anonymity of London and wanted to make the most out of every second of his 'personal sabbatical'. He loved the relaxed efficiency of Notting Hill, its diverse fashion, its spontaneous mayhem. He had even found a record store that he had fallen for. Exclusively vinyl, stuffed with 45s and 78s, acid jazz, soul, art punk, delta blues, roots reggae, ragtime, funk, the whole works. For weeks now he had been daydreaming about what the logo of his record label might look like, or what sort of artists he would sign up.

He had tried to explain to his father that he was still trying to decide whether he would continue with his cushioned seat at Giles Hampton Advertising, but Giles was unimpressed. He regarded his son's indecision as blatant disrespect and took it as a personal insult. The conversation had ended unsatisfactorily, with Giles very tersely conceding to Luke's request for more thinking time.

As he walked towards Sam's Kitchen, Luke tried to think of which dish he could order and what would take the longest to prepare, hoping Elodie would be working there. He had time to kill and he was interested; a romantic adventure was all part of the London sabbatical he had so long awaited.

At the entrance to the café a lady emerged carrying a quiche and two sticks of French bread in a basket on her arm. Luke held the door open for her and spotted Elodie, with her long hair tied up into a ponytail, fidgeting with the coffee machine. Grasping the coffee filter-basket handle, she yanked it out of the machine and banged it noisily against the edge of the sink.

"Another bad day?" he said, walking up to the counter.

"What?" said Elodie, turning around. When she saw him, he could have sworn she blushed, if only for a second. "You."

"Me," he said.

They looked at one another awkwardly before Elodie turned around and began rummaging in a cupboard.

"I can't find the coffee beans."

"Up there?"

"What?" she said.

"Above you. Top shelf, Italian roasted coffee beans?"

"Oh, I see," she said, reaching for a chair.

"Want me to get it down for you?"

"No, I can manage," she said firmly and then, looking less than happy, she muttered, "Thank you."

Having done a balancing act on the chair, Elodie brought down the coffee beans and quickly filled up the grinder.

"If you'd like to take a seat, ladies, I won't be a sec," she said, blasting the coffee grinder as three middle-aged women ambled in. She then shook the ground coffee into the filter and levelled the grains before pushing it back into place in the coffee machine.

"Sounds like you need to adjust the portafilter?" he said.

"The what?"

"There's a little flat-bottomed weighted thing called a tamper, which levels out the coffee."

Elodie closed her eyes as if she was inwardly swearing.

"If it's done too heavily the coffee won't extract through it properly."

There was that stubborn expression again. Not a great fan of manual labour, he deduced.

They looked at the machine for a while. Nothing happened.

"It still isn't working," she said.

Then suddenly the portafilter came crashing to the floor, knocking over a milk carton on the way down.

"You have got to be kidding me!" said Elodie, stamping her foot.

"Let me take a look?" said Luke.

"Sam isn't answering her damned phone," she said. "If I can't fix it, I'll have to close up."

"Come on, I won't bite."

"Okay," said Elodie, as if she was doing *him* a favour.

Luke came behind the counter but, sensing Elodie's patience was running low, he refrained from making any wisecracks.

"I think the portafilter just wasn't connected properly," he said, turning to Elodie. "Elodie?"

She had disappeared. Instead, he found himself looking at a sort of young version of Robert Redford in a pink shirt, who had just walked in.

The man, whose blond hair was smoothly brushed back from his forehead, looked irritated.

"Elodie, did you say?" said the newcomer. "Funny you should say that name, she's the very person I'm looking for."

"Sorry?" said Luke, wiping his hands on a paper towel.

"Get her, will you?" said the man abruptly.

"Get who?" replied Luke, taken aback by the man's rudeness.

"Elodie, of course," snapped the man, rubbing his forehead with his fingertips, his eyes darting from left to right.

Luke felt a tug at his ankle and looked down to see Elodie

crouching beneath the sink, finger to her lips, urgently shaking her head at him.

"I'm afraid you just missed her," said Luke, in his politest American manner. "She's stepped out, but how can I help you?"

"Stepped out?" scoffed the man. "Really? So how come you were calling her name when I arrived in?"

"I wasn't calling her. I was cursing her. She was supposed to heat up a pie before she left."

"Oh," said the man, whose flushed cheeks clashed against very white teeth.

Out of the corner of his eye, Luke could see Elodie frantically texting on her phone.

"Looks like you could do with a coffee though?" said Luke, moments before Elodie thumped his shin.

"If I wanted a coffee, I'd have asked for a coffee," said the man. "I actually wanted a word with my girlfriend. When's she back?"

"Your girlfriend?"

"Yes, girlfriend. I think you have them in America too? Elodie is my girlfriend. I gather from her mother she's working here."

"I don't think she's coming back," said Luke. "She said she was leaving the country."

"She said what?"

"You know, what with all the stuff about the duke."

"The duke? What are you talking about?"

Luke reached down to open a cupboard and glanced at Elodie, who drew a line across her neck, suggesting he immediately cut the conversation.

"Look, sorry, pal," he said to the man. "Elodie's split. If she comes back I'll tell her you called, but I wouldn't bank on her coming back."

"Now, you listen to me, *chum*. I don't believe a word you're saying but you tell Elodie, when she manages to crawl into work, that I'll be at Claridge's this evening and I would very much like to talk to her. 8pm sharp."

"Well, should I happen to ever meet Elodie again, I'll be sure to tell her that. Can I get you something to go? A glass of ass-milk perhaps?"

"Sorry?"

"A glass of milk?"

The man eyed him sternly and marched back out through the café. He paused in the doorway, looked around the room and muttered, "Damned shambles, this place," before exiting onto the street.

Luke remained where he was until he saw the man cross to the far side of the street. He then crouched down behind the counter. "He's gone," he whispered, and was about to laugh until he saw Elodie's face. She looked upset, even a little scared and refused his hand when he tried to help her up.

"Are you okay?"

Suddenly the door burst open again and they both froze.

"Elodie?" hollered a familiar voice.

"My God, Sam, at last," said Elodie. "Dominic's just been here."

"What did that creep want?"

"He desired to meet with Miss Elodie at Claridge's this evening, ma'am," announced Luke in his most courtly tone, stepping back around the counter.

Sam looked up at him, eyelids fluttering.

"I'm Sam,' she said, stretching out her hand. "You must be the knight who rode in to the rescue?"

"Luke," he said. "Great to meet you."

"And Luke is just leaving, aren't you?" said Elodie, putting one hand on his back and directing him towards the door. "Thank you for your help and –"

Sam interrupted her midway. "Hold on, El. Judging by that text you sent, Luke did you a favour by throwing your louse of an *ex-boyfriend* off the scent. So why don't you take a seat, Luke, and I'll rustle you up a proper English breakfast by way of a proper thank-you. Never too late in the day for breakfast."

"I could think of nothing nicer," he said, but looking at Elodie he could see that she was shook by the whole episode and he suddenly felt out of place. "But I've got to push on. Maybe another time? Thanks for the offer though."

Turning just before he left the café, he looked straight at Elodie and smiled that smile of his. "Don't worry," he said. "It'll all work out."

Elodie kept her arms folded, eyes to the floor, but the moment the café door closed she burst into tears. "God, I'm so embarrassed. Dominic is just so pushy – I can't believe he came in here."

"Well, if it's any consolation, he is now officially barred from here," said Sam. "Can't believe he had the nerve. Does he not understand that you've broken up with him?"

"You know what he's like. He's so bossy and always gets his own way, and guess who told him I was here? My bloody mother. He said so."

Checking out the coffee machine, Sam poured a cup and took a sip. "This coffee is perfect, El? What was the problem?"

Elodie rubbed her eyes. "Luke must have fixed it, I don't know what he did." She thought of how helpful Luke was being before Dominic arrived, and she hated the thought that he had been speaking to Dominic. She must have looked like such an idiot. "God, I need to get out of London."

Chapter fourteen

Portland Road, London

Still reeling from Dominic's unexpected cameo at Sam's Kitchen, Elodie had only just returned home when she heard a loud crash coming from the hall above her. Dropping her handbag, she ran up the stairs to find her mother crouched next to the legs of the hall table.

"I'm absolutely fine," said Julia, trying to pull herself up from her knees.

Elodie tried to help her.

"Oh, stop fussing, Elodie," said Julia, slurring her words. "You always fuss."

"Mum, what's going on?" said Elodie, slipping her hand under her mother's arm and hoisting her onto a chair.

"Bloody glasses," said Julia, steadying herself on the chair and sweeping her hands down the front of her blouse. A trail of red appeared upon her blouse.

"Mum, your thumb's bleeding. Please let me take a look."

Ignoring Elodie's hand, Julia strode into the kitchen with exaggerated concentration.

"I'm going to tell Carol to throw the highballs out in the morning," she said. "Dreadful quality, breaking at the slightest tap."

54

She must have been drinking all afternoon. Elodie followed behind and watched as her mother grabbed a roll of paper towel and broke off a long sheet to wrap around her wounded thumb. The blood seeped in like ink into blotting paper.

"Did something happen at the gallery?" said Elodie. "You had a meeting this morning, didn't you?"

"They no longer want me," said Julia, pressing her finger on the kettle switch.

Elodie suspected her mother had little intention of having a cup of anything other than booze.

"Why, Mum?"

"Oh, they'll happily take my donations, of course, but they'd rather do so without my opinions."

She paused for moment, as if on the verge of saying more, and then abruptly about-turned, opened the fridge and pulled out a bottle of Chablis. "Want some?"

"No thanks, not now," said Elodie, trying to work out what to do. She had seen her mother like this before. Challenging her was no use, it just made her even more determined to drink herself into oblivion.

"I told them that if they don't want my opinions then they won't get my donations, and so I shall take my money elsewhere."

"Are you sure you didn't, you know, misread them?" said Elodie.

"No, Elodie, I did not *misread* them and please don't talk to me like I'm a child."

"I'm just trying to –"

"I've had it with charity," said Julia. "I'm going to dig a second basement instead, that can be my new project. I'll have an underground heated swimming pool and gymnasium installed. In fact the fates have presented me with the perfect opportunity to make it happen."

"Mum, why don't you sit down?" Elodie could see her mother ramping herself up to become hysterical.

"Why don't *you* bloody well sit down?" Julia fired back.

Elodie watched as her mother took a tumbler from the cupboard and filled it with wine, adding a splash of water from the tap. As if dilution was going to make any difference.

"Fresh blood," said Julia, taking a slug of wine and looking at her bloodied thumb. "They said they wanted fresh blood and isn't it ironic that I am now standing here in my own kitchen with my thumb cut, bleeding like a pig."

Elodie sat at the table, silent, hoping her mother would follow.

"I'm sure the gallery would be happy for you to stay on part-time?" said Elodie, trying to suggest something positive. "Behind the scenes?"

"Behind the scenes?" said Julia, taking an enormous gulp of wine. "I've spent my entire life behind the scenes. No, they can forget their funding. Not a penny shall they have."

At last she sat down and looked at her daughter for a moment, her eyes narrowing as she sought a focus.

"I've been thinking about hosting a dinner party."

"In aid of?" said Elodie, trying to be patient and knowing the chance of a sensible conversation with her mother at this stage was increasingly remote.

"You," said Julia. "I'll invite catches from across London. You know there's a feature on Orlando de Croix in this month's *Tatler*? Rumour has it that he's ready to settle down. He's got a place in Hampshire to die for."

"Mum –" Elodie desperately wanted to talk about how lost she has been feeling and how she couldn't seem to find direction. "Last week, when I was shopping –"

Her mother began to cackle. "Elodie, you are always shopping!"

"When I was in the shop, there was this woman who was trying on some clothes in the cubicle next to me and, well, she dropped dead."

Julia looked at Elodie and shook her head.

"Oh," she said. "Go on."

"It really spurred me on to try to decide what I want to do with my life."

Julia reached out for Elodie's hands and pulled them towards her.

"Elodie, Elodie, my dear Elodie. It's perfectly simple what you should do. You're twenty-seven years old. You should be married by now, with children. The conversations between us should be about where you have registered the children for school or whether you want to holiday in Tuscany or the Seychelles. And yet instead you're still stumbling between these fatuous temping jobs and that chip shop or whatever it is your friend runs."

Elodie pulled away. "Can't you see that I'm not interested in getting married?"

"But there are plenty of others like Dominic –"

"And certainly not to someone like Dominic. I can't even believe I spent nearly three years of my life with the guy." Elodie held her hands out in front of her. "I want a career, Mum. Something I can be proud of."

"Such as?"

"Such as drawing."

"Oh no, and back to the doodles again! Always back to the doodles," said Julia, looking around for her glass of wine. "You know your problem, Elodie? You aren't capable of making a decision."

Julia had pushed a cigarette into the side of her mouth as she spoke and now she was trying to get her lighter to work. It emitted a series of weak sparks but she persisted. Elodie tried to take over the operation but Julia dismissed her offer with a swipe of her hand.

"If you had your way," continued Julia, "you'd be sitting in a studio, covered in paint and hidden away like a hermit for the rest of your days."

"And would that be so bad?"

"Elodie, look at yourself. You have a perfect figure and the face of an angel. You have no idea how good you have it. I'm telling you, time flies quicker and quicker for all of us. Before you know it, you'll be booking yourself in for Botox and facelifts. Mark my words, young lady, now is the time to find your chap and get settled."

As Julia finally got the lighter to ignite, Elodie thought back to Dominic and how he would scold her if she so much as looked at a pizza. He and her mother were from the same narcissistic school of thought, utterly obsessed with beauty and perfection.

"You know what, Mum, I'll be perfectly happy if I end up alone. I don't give a damn if I fetch up as an old spinster or a hermit. At least I wouldn't have you breathing wine fumes down my neck and cutting me down every time I try to stand up for myself."

Julia drew a sharp intake of breath and was about to respond except that the smoke she'd inhaled sent her into a small coughing fit. She had only just regained her breathing when a very handsome and immaculately attired Lorenzo appeared in the kitchen doorway.

"Lorenzo," said Elodie.

"What is going on, ladies?" he said, in jeans and sports jacket, with a scarf carefully draped around his neck, making him look like a perfect date.

Kissing Elodie on both cheeks, he walked over to Julia and took the cigarette from her hand, extinguishing it in the sink.

"What has happened, my love?" he said, resting his hand gently on her back.

Julia slumped against him and, as he held her tightly, he reached for the kitchen towel and examined her thumb, which had by now stopped bleeding.

"How about a little lie-down, my sweet?" he said. "Then we can go out to dinner and talk about it all. You'll let me help you upstairs?"

Elodie wondered what possessed him to be so very good to her mother. He was gentle and so loyal, despite finding her mother in this state many times. If it hadn't been for Lorenzo, she doubted her mother would even be alive. For all her expenditure on her exterior image, Julia seemed determined to turn her inner self into complete wreckage.

Julia resisted Lorenzo's efforts and, having escaped his embrace, she reached for her wineglass once more.

"Mum, please listen to Lorenzo," said Elodie. "How can I live here when you keep doing this to yourself?"

Julia pointed towards the door. "You don't have to stay," she said. "You want to be an independent woman? So, why wait? Go on, leave. Pack your bags and get out. I'm fed up of you slouching here, wasting your potential and taking endless handouts."

Elodie froze to the spot. This time her mother sounded like she meant it.

"Why the hesitation, Elodie? Thinking about your bank card?"

"Oh come now, Julia," said Lorenzo, removing the glass from her hand. "You don't really mean that."

"Fine," said Elodie, her lips trembling and eyes brimming with tears. "If that's what you want, I'll move out."

"No, no," said Lorenzo. "Elodie, don't go. We can talk this over with your mother, no?"

Julia said nothing.

"I've got to go," said Elodie, composing herself, "Sam's asked me to cover the evening shift in the café."

"Bully for you," slurred Julia. "Go and serve coffee, that's about all you're good for."

"Elodie, be safe and take your time," said Lorenzo, looking at her with eyes reassuring her that this would all blow over. "I will take care of your mother, don't worry."

Chapter fifteen

Notting Hill, London

Settling into the evening shift at Sam's Kitchen, which was mercifully empty, Elodie stretched her arms up to release the tension she felt after the encounter with her mother. Thankfully, the evening was quiet and so far she'd had only a handful of customers.

"Max," she said, answering her phone, "you got my message?"

"Elodie, you're banging your head against a brick wall if you think you can do anything to change Mum at this stage," he said. "She's a loose cannon. Always has been, always will be. She'll sleep it off and then in the morning she will go to her Pilates. Lorenzo will bring her round. He always does, and it's no surprise the gallery has booted her out. The only time she went there was to criticise, you know that."

"I actually feel a little sorry for her, you know?"

"Don't, there's no point," he said.

"But I'm not like you, Max, I can't shake her off like that. It's really been quite a ..." Her voice trailed off as she saw Luke Hampton walk through the door. "Sorry, Max, I've got a customer. Got to go."

"Hi," said Luke.

She didn't know whether to smile or frown. She still felt so mortified about the episode of hiding behind the counter while he dealt with Dominic.

"Hello," she said, picking up a tea towel, avoiding eye contact. "Back again?"

He nodded, hair falling over his forehead, his smile so wide that she found herself compelled to smile back, just a little bit. "I'm afraid we're all out of bagels today."

"There's something on your lips," he said.

"What?"

"Your lips," he said, touching his own. "Marshmallow, perhaps?"

Elodie licked her lips and wiped her hand across her mouth.

"A teacake," she said. She could feel herself blushing again. Why was she blushing? She never blushed. "I just ate one, a few minutes ago. I missed lunch."

"And you're working late?" asked Luke, sitting down on the high-back chair.

"Just until eight thirty. It's a favour for Sam. She's been such a good friend to me, especially lately."

"I could tell, when we last met."

In the short silence that followed, Elodie battled with herself but she had to say it.

"I'm sorry for being rude to you the other day."

"Not at all," he said quickly. "No need."

"And ... thank you for your help."

"Like I said, no need," he said, and then, standing up suddenly, he asked, "What time did you say you get off work?"

"Eight thirty."

The words had hardly left her mouth when a petite woman wearing a smart fitted coat arrived through the door, carrying a blue clipboard.

"Here we go," said Elodie, under her breath.

"Good evening," said the woman,

"Good evening," said Elodie.

"I have a slight problem," said the woman, slapping her clipboard on the counter.

"Go on," said Elodie.

"Ruth is my name."

"Hello, Ruth," said Elodie.

Luke was sitting out of the way, idly flicking through a copy of *The Week*.

"We had a booking at the Frog's Inn on Ladbroke Grove."

"Okay," said Elodie.

"And they've let us down, badly. Double-booked. But, being a Thursday, there's no hope of getting a booking anywhere else around here."

"Right," said Elodie.

Looking around the café, Ruth started counting the chairs. "How many can you sit?"

"Sorry?" said Elodie, glancing fleetingly at Luke.

"What is your capacity?" said Ruth.

"In terms of?"

Elodie was slow to catch on but Ruth was not to be deflected.

"I know it's short notice but could we come here, please? It's just that I'm rather desperate."

"Well, I'm here by myself, you see, so I'm not sure we're really equipped for big numbers this evening."

Luke was longing to step in and steer the conversation along but he had inherited his mother's patience. He could see why Elodie hadn't lasted very long in his father's office.

"So, here's how it is," said Ruth, looking as if she could do with a shot of tequila. "I've a minibus parked just around the corner from here, inside which there are fifteen very sweet, very old and very hungry old dears from Hillview Home. We take the 'Over Seventies Club' on an outing to the city every February, you see?"

"February's a good month for outings," said Luke, seizing the opportunity to join in. "An antidote to the short days and cold winds, hey?"

"Exactly," said Ruth, pleased by this handsome young man's participation. "Some of our pensioners really don't have it easy, so we do like to lift their spirits whenever we can. So, like I say, they're all pretty ravenous at this point, and the driver and I thought this place looked just the ticket."

Elodie had stepped back towards the coffee machine, pulling at her ponytail and rubbing the back of her neck. Luke suspected she must be grappling with her conscience.

And then she stepped forward again, saying, "I'd love to help but I'm afraid most of our food has been sold."

"I see," said Ruth, her smile waning.

"Also, I'm here alone and I couldn't possibly manage a group of sixteen people."

"Seventeen actually, "said Ruth sadly, "including Barry the driver."

"Okay then," said Luke, standing up and rubbing his hands together. "Throw me an apron."

Elodie looked at him and shook her head. "Oh no," she said. "We don't ... I can't ... I don't even know what we could give them."

"We have hot water?" he asked.

"Yes," said Elodie.

"Great, so that's a yes to a cup of tea for everyone while they're waiting. And what about cheese and bread?"

"We have cheddar and mozzarella," she said, "and a few loaves of sourdough."

"Amazing," said Luke. "Pickle?"

"Yes, we have pickle."

"Couldn't be better. So, Ruth, how would seventeen toasted cheese sandwiches suit you?"

"That sounds just heavenly," said Ruth.

"And we have quite a few pastries left over," said Elodie, warming to the prospect.

"Oh heavens!" said the woman, pressing her hands together. "My prayers to Saint Jude have been answered!"

"And we have some quiche left over," said Elodie.

"Oh, they will be so happy," said Ruth.

Taking up her clipboard, she hurried to the door, where she paused and turned back to look at them.

"Bless you both."

"You sure about this?" said Elodie to Luke, after she had gone.

"Yes, but I have just one condition."

"Go on?"

"I'd like to take you out for dinner afterwards?"

Elodie had just placed her hand on a pile of laundered tea towels and aprons, and now she hesitated. Feeling her cheeks heat up again, she hastily threw one of the aprons at Luke to stop him from noticing.

"Is that a yes?" he said, slipping the apron over his head.

"Yes, as long as *I* take *you* out to dinner," she said, "and as long as you make the toasties."

One by one, Ruth's group arrived through the door, some chattering, others silent, glancing hungrily towards Elodie as she filled teapots from the water boiler.

"Oh, I love a bit of salmon quiche, I do," said a man in a heavy green overcoat, peering through the glass at the counter. "Haven't had it in donkeys."

As Luke stitched the ham and cheese sandwiches together, he watched Elodie directing the newcomers to their seats. She struck him as the kind of girl who hadn't had much experience of being in control.

Within fifteen minutes, all the old timers, together with Ruth and Barry the driver, were feasting on a banquet of cheese toasties, pastries, quiche and tea. Luke had cut the toasties into triangles and laid them out on a large wooden chopping board. As he did the rounds, handing them out, a very elderly lady, with blue-rinse hair and eye shadow to match, placed her hand on his leg.

"You're a little bit saucy, aren't you?" she said. "You remind me of my Norman. Will you sit with me a moment, son?"

"Well, thank you," said Luke, checking Elodie was okay before pulling up a lone chair to sit beside the lady.

"He passed away eighteen months ago," said the lady.

"I'm very sorry," said Luke.

"Never a cross word between us in fifty-six years," she said. "Hard to believe, isn't it?"

"Incredible," said Luke, as she moved her head closer to him.

"You know what the secret is?" she said softly. "Come here, I'll tell you."

"I'm listening," said Luke, inching forward a little.

"Respect," she said, nodding her head. "If you haven't got respect for each other, you haven't got anything."

"Respect," said Luke.

"Yes, as long as they don't die on you, that is," she said, with a hearty cackle and, taking his hand, she held it for a moment.

"I'd better let you get on, son. You'll remember what I said, won't you?"

"I'll do my best to," said Luke, slowly rising from his chair. "Thank you."

Elodie started to clear empty plates away and heard the old woman say, "Made my week, that has. Chatting with that nice American, never seen eyes so kind."

Luke looked around the café and felt terrific. The place was humming with the happy sound of Ruth and her venerable friends munching and sipping. Harry Connick Junior's voice oozed out from the overhead speakers. He had never been in a situation quite like this before: serving food to a proper community, who appreciated every mouthful. He thought of all the corporate Sunday lunches his parents hosted in New York and of the big Christmas parties where they always hired the same band: a string quartet, talented, no doubt, but so formal and predictable. As a child in his bedroom, he would listen to the muffled sound of the music rising up to his bedroom window, take out the drumsticks Santa Claus had given him and start belting them against the brass fixtures on his bed and windows, losing himself in his own rhythm.

He was shaken from his momentary reverie by a polite "excuse me" behind him. He turned to see Elodie standing with a stack of plates, trying to get past.

"Sorry," he said, moving in to relieve her of the plates.

"I've got it," she said, smiling and holding her own.

He backed away, against the wall, to let her pass. Her body brushed against his and he caught his breath.

"Happy crowd in tonight," he said quickly.

"Very happy," said Elodie, placing the plates on the countertop. "I don't quite know how you've done it but I think you've actually managed to feed seventeen people with bread and cheese."

"You mean, how *we've* done it, Elodie."

"I'm just going to give Sam a quick call," she said. "I'm not sure what to charge for this."

"No need," said Luke.

"What do you mean?"

"I'll cover the bill."

"What? For all of them?"

"Yes."

"Are you sure?"

"Very sure."

"Well," said Elodie, "that very kind of you."

When Ruth found out, she was over the moon. Luke's generosity meant her February budget might now stretch to the acquisition of a new keyboard she'd had her eye on ever since one of her younger charges told her how he used to have piano lessons as a child.

While Barry led the group out of the café and back to the bus, Ruth stayed for a moment to thank Elodie and Luke again.

"I had a quick look at the Hillview website," said Luke.

"It's pretty basic," said Ruth, "but it gives the gist of what we do."

"Oldies and teenagers in the same house, right?"

"That's it," she said, "and it works surprisingly well. Where wisdom meets youthful exuberance. Or at least that's how I like to think of it."

"How many are living in the house?"

"We've exactly thirty. The fifteen who were here this evening, and then another fifteen younger ones, teenagers, who are back at the house. We take them on separate outings generally but, when they're at the Hillview, they all mingle together."

"How did the teenagers end up there?" asked Elodie.

"They've all had a tough time. Some are orphans, or may as well be because their parent or their parents just couldn't cope. We brought in most of them. Found them sleeping rough, offered them a bed. Simple as that really."

"The website says you're one hundred per cent voluntary," said Luke.

Ruth nodded and smiled rather shyly but said no more.

"And you live there too?" said Elodie.

"Yes, and Barry comes in most weekends, bless him."

"That's a lot of people to live in one house," said Elodie.

"We manage quite well. Hillview was left to me by my godmother, who had no children. I'd known Barry for years, through helping out at a nursing home, and when it was closing down, I knew I had to open my own door. The government helps a little, otherwise we rely on donations. But people are so good, just as you have both been this evening."

Ruth reached out to hug Elodie, and then Luke.

"God bless you both, truly, thank you," she said, before letting them go, adjusting her hat and disappearing out the door.

"Thirty people?" said Elodie after she had gone. "She invited thirty people to live with her in her house?"

"Makes you think, doesn't it?" said Luke.

Elodie nodded and felt immediately guilty for feeling upset about her own circumstances.

"You okay?" said Luke.

"Are you sure you still want to have dinner after feeding all that lot?"

"I've never been more sure."

Chapter sixteen

"So, where did you have in mind?" asked Elodie, locking the door of Sam's Kitchen behind them.

"How well do you know the place?"

"I think you could probably blindfold me and I could still lead you around Notting Hill."

"Blind-folded? Now there's a thought. So, you've lived here all your life?"

"Mostly, except for a boarding school I went to in Gloucestershire and summers in Ireland."

"Ireland? I hear it's a beautiful country."

"It's gorgeous. I had family there or sort of still do. It's a long story, or maybe it's a short story, but anyway, it's not for now," said Elodie. She was trying not to think about the blowout with her mother earlier on. "How about we head for an off-the-beaten-track place, about a ten-minute walk?"

"Sounds perfect," said Luke, "and Elodie, I don't want to put you off your stride but ..." he leaned in to whisper, his breath giving her goose bumps, "I think you almost smiled."

"Hah," said Elodie, who then really did smile. "The place we're going doesn't take cards," she said, walking towards a bank machine, "so hold on a sec and I'll get some cash."

Luke checked his phone and began reading out the history of the street they were on.

"Did you know," he said, putting on an English accent, "that Lord Walthamstow established a salubrious brothel on this very street in 1778?"

"He did?" giggled Elodie, pressing her pin-code into the machine.

"He also founded a charitable hospital for pregnant women," he said, reading on. "What a well-balanced guy he was, eh?"

He looked over at Elodie. She was no longer smiling.

"You okay?"

Elodie stood back from the machine. "I don't believe it."

"What is it?"

"Nothing," she said, scrunching up her face.

"Nothing? Well, you look pretty worried about nothing."

"I didn't think she'd actually do it."

"Who did what?" said Luke. "Tell me."

"It's nothing."

"Come on, tell me," said Luke, standing closer to her.

Then Elodie shook her head. "No, it's ... I can't remember my pin-code, can you believe it? Stupid, stupid."

"Really? I thought I heard you say 'I didn't think she'd actually do it'. Who are we talking about here? Sam? She doesn't seem like the sort of girl who'd screw you."

"No, it's not Sam," said Elodie, agitated. "It's nothing. I just ... I forgot my number, okay?"

"Hey, steady," said Luke. "Forget about it. Your intentions were first rate. Come on, supper, as the English like to call it, is on me."

Elodie felt like she was rolling through a tidal wave. She hadn't thought that her mother would actually follow through with her threat. Her bank account had been emptied, completely cleared out. It was her own fault. Julia had insisted upon a joint bank account – it was all about control.

"Oh god, I feel like I've just joined Ruth's oldies," she said.

"Hey, it's no sweat, really," he said. "Don't worry about it. Let me get some cash out and then we can continue with this outrageous behind-the-scenes tour of Notting Hill."

Turning to Elodie, he lowered his head and looked her eye to eye.

"We can go Dutch on our next hot date," he winked.

She sensed that he was on the cusp of leaning in to kiss her when a boy whirled down the pavement towards them on a skateboard; Luke nimbly stepped in towards the bank machine to let him pass.

"Besides, a tour guide of your calibre would cost me a fortune in the daytime," he said, withdrawing a wad of notes.

"In that case, you can definitely foot the bill," she said, trying to rally herself.

The jazz speakeasy was hidden between a newsagent's and a butcher's on Mirabelle Alley. Stepping off the pavement, they walked into a dimly lit bar and found a vacant booth. A pianist was playing a Duke Ellington tune just across the room.

"What can I get you?" said Luke.

"Anything," she said. "I really don't mind."

"Well, how about the crab cakes, with chilli jam, on the specials board up there?"

"Sounds good," said Elodie. "I'm really not that hungry."

"And white wine?"

"Sure," said Elodie, pretending to focus her attention on the pianist.

Luke stepped towards the bar and the moment his back was turned, she began to panic. With not even a credit card to fall back on, she realised she was now in a bar with an almost complete stranger. A nice, handsome stranger, granted, but she didn't feel particularly desirable, plus she *had* spent a disastrous day working for his awful father. But, most of all, if her mother had followed through on cutting off her allowance, then what if she meant it when she told Elodie to pack her bags?

In the short space of time that Luke took to order from the bar, Elodie's mind had spiralled into a state of quiet, unbridled anxiety.

"I ordered a bottle of Californian," he said, cheerfully. "Couldn't resist."

Elodie stood up. "I'm sorry, Luke, I have to go."

"What? Oh shit, have I upset you?"

"No," she said, shaking her head. "I'm sorry, I've got to go." Picking up her clutch bag, she slid out of the booth, pushed past him and ran out the door.

Chapter seventeen

She heard him call after her, but she ran on. She didn't even have enough money to hail a taxi. Stopping by a lamp-post she fumbled for a pack of cigarettes in her bag and popped one in her mouth. She was about to call Max when Luke caught up with her.

"Elodie," he said calmly, "whatever it is, please can we at least talk about it?"

"I'm a mess, believe me. If I were you, I'd just walk away."

"Come on," he said. "It can't be that bad, whatever it is."

"I'm not sure who you think I am," she said, holding her bag tightly against her chest, the unlit cigarette in her hand, "but I'm not sure that I'm the sort of person you'd want to get to know."

"Let me decide for myself, will you?" he said gently. "I put you under too much pressure, I'm sorry. I've got an impulsive streak, you see. I get an idea and I just want to run with it."

"Whereas I do the opposite, I overthink things."

"If it's easier for you, I've got a couple of pizzas in the fridge at my apartment, and some beers too. How about that? No pressure, no jazz, no Californian wine. Was it the Californian that put you off? My father keeps telling me I should order French. Maybe I need to loosen up a little and step away from my roots?"

He had managed to make her laugh, if only a little.

"Freshly made pizza?" she said, lighting her cigarette.

"Bought from the market this morning. A couple of irresistible-looking margheritas."

As they walked along the pavement, a stream of black taxis zoomed by.

"Lighting a cigarette always brings on the taxis. I've always found that. If you step out of a club and you need a taxi, just light a ciggie and one will magically appear."

"Is that so? And are you trying to catch a taxi?"

She thought about what her mother had said, about her being incapable of making decisions.

"Or pizza with me?" he said, pausing in a pillared doorway. "Tough call."

"Pizza with you," she said firmly.

"You know, when you brought me to that jazz bar I thought you must have been psychic?"

"Really?" she said. "How come?"

"Look up," he said. "My apartment is on the second floor."

She realised now it was a large townhouse, with lights shining from the windows above like fireflies in a jar.

"You live here?"

"I moved in a couple of months ago," he said, taking a key fob out of his pocket and buzzing the door open. "Step this way, ma'am."

"I feel like I'm in a *Harry Potter* novel," said Elodie, taking in the thick trails of ivy that clung to the brick interior. Large iron candlesticks were mounted on the walls alongside a staircase of grey flagstone steps.

Luke led the way up to a room that was more like a vast loft, complete with exposed metal beams and high ceilings.

"Lichtenstein," she said, looking at a huge canvas hanging between windows. "He's amazing – this is a print, right?"

"Actually, no. It belongs to my father. He bought it last summer, figures my place is a better bet than a vault and who am I to argue? Mind you, I suspect the main reason it's here is so that he has a decent excuse to drop in whenever he wants."

"You sound like you're not so happy about that."

"Family can be tricky," he said, taking a couple of beers out of the fridge.

"You said it," she whispered. "Is that your bike?"

He hesitated, wondering whether to ask about her own family, and thought better of it.

"Yes," he said, passing her a beer. "The cleanest mountain bike on the planet because I haven't actually taken it for a ride yet. So now it sits there like a gym membership, giving me nothing but guilt."

"And that?" she said, pointing towards a drumkit that sprawled upon a tapestry rug.

"Now that I do use. I can play, but badly."

A tish of cymbals came from the surround-sound speakers, followed by string and bass as Luke pressed a remote control.

"This is Nina Simone," he said. "*Little Girl Blue*. Her first album."

"Cool," said Elodie, as Nina's voice, upbeat and vibrant sang 'Mood Indigo'.

"This album is perfection," said Luke.

"Do you play in a band?"

"No, but I'd like to find one. A band or a solo performer."

"What, to drum with?"

"No," he said. "Part of the reason I came to London was to work out what direction I want to go in. My father wants me to join the firm."

"As an ad guy?"

"Something like that. It would be pretty convenient, joining the family business, but a huge part of me wants to go out on my own and start up a record label. That's what I've always wanted to do."

Elodie picked up a pair of drumsticks and sat on a small tanned-leather bench.

"If I come across a musician with the right potential," continued Luke, "I might just take the leap."

"I don't think I've ever held drumsticks before" said Elodie. "They're heavier than I'd imagined."

Setting his beer down, Luke slipped his hands over Elodie's, positioning the drumsticks between her fingers.

"If you hold them like this," he said softly, directing her hands to the drum kit, "then it's just a matter of feeling the rhythm."

Elodie began to slowly tap the brass cymbal with one stick and the bass drum with the other.

"I feel silly," she said.

"Enjoy it. The walls here are very thick. I haven't had a single complaint from any of my neighbours."

She turned her face towards him, and Luke almost kissed her but she turned away.

"Can we be friends, Luke? Just friends, for now?"

He swept a strand of hair from her eyes, and they held each other's stare.

"Friends like this?" he said, kissing her top lip as she closed her eyes.

"Maybe?" she whispered.

"And this?" he said, kissing her neck.

The drumsticks fell from her hands as they pressed the palms of their hands together.

"Luke, I'm sorry," she said, pulling away. "I'm really not in the right headspace …"

"No trouble at all," he said, "my mistake. I misread the situation."

"No," she said, "you didn't. I'm just, I don't know how to explain it, I'm all over the place."

"Look, how about I put the pizza in the oven and we rewind for a moment or two," he said. "Maybe we could watch a movie?"

"That would be nice," she said.

When Luke went into the kitchen, Elodie sat on a sofa and took her phone out of her pocket. She felt emotionally drained. She thought about texting her mother with an apology, and sending another to Max to let him know what had happened. Would they be worried about where she was? Did her mother really mean it? Christ, she thought, I'm supposed to be a grown woman. Can't I just forget about it all for an evening? She took a sip from the bottle of beer and sank back into the cushions. Anyway, her phone was out of battery.

Nina was singing about raindrops and there were many raindrops in Elodie's life.

She wondered if her mother had access to her email account. One reason she had never kept a diary was because she knew her mother could never resist going through it, and as Nina started to sing about the fish in the sea, she closed her melancholy eyes for a brief moment.

Coming out of the kitchen a few minutes later, Luke found her fast asleep on the sofa. The angst in her face had softened away, and she looked almost peaceful. He fetched a duvet from his bedroom, placed it over her and blew her a kiss goodnight.

Chapter eighteen

Ed Sheeran's voice drifted out from the kitchen singing 'Thinking Out Loud' as Elodie awoke, disorientated but cosy in a duvet that smelled simultaneously strange and familiar. She squinted in the morning light that glared through the huge iron-framed windows. She was still wearing her leather cowboy boots from the night before, not exactly how she had planned things. Knowing that her eyeliner must have smudged overnight, she felt like a failed rock chick. She couldn't even remember going to sleep. God, had she been snoring? Dominic had always berated her for "snoring your head off all night".

She shuffled out of bed and wandered through to the kitchen where she found Luke, dressed in shorts and a long-sleeved shirt, reading a magazine with a mug of coffee.

"Good morning," said Luke. "How are you? I hope you slept okay?"

"I feel a little embarrassed," said Elodie, searching for a hair-tie in her pocket. "I managed to pass out on your sofa without even a drop of alcohol."

"Not entirely true," he said. "You drank at least three millilitres of beer. How about I make you a coffee? This is the famous machine that taught me how to work the machine at Sam's."

"God, I'm a disaster," said Elodie, taking off her jumper – she had a long-sleeved top underneath.

"Not at all. I'm sorry for hitting on you inappropriately," he said.

"It … you didn't … it's okay …. and we kept our friendship agreement, didn't we?"

"Yes, I'm happy about that," he said distractedly. "Now, would you like to try one of my celebrated defrosted bagels? All the way from Sam's Kitchen. You'll be the first person in London to do so."

Wearing her long camel coat, Elodie walked alongside Luke towards Portland Road. She had to stop herself from wondering what Luke meant by 'I'm happy about that' when she mentioned their friendship agreement. She had sworn herself off men, and yet this was typical of her. Put something off and then wish it was on. It was such a twisted aspect to her personality and she knew it.

"What happens when you don't want to inherit your parents?" said Elodie, stepping over a puddle.

"That's a bit of an out-of-the-blue question. What do you mean?"

"If you don't like, or even understand, the things you find out about your parents."

"You mean their flaws?" he said.

"Yes, I suppose I mean their flaws."

"Well, I guess it's all part of human nature, isn't it?" said Luke, putting his arm around her briefly. "My father is no exception, he has more chips on his shoulder than a newly laid highway."

"Yes, but he's alive, isn't he? You can talk things through with him," said Elodie.

"And your father?"

"He shot himself," she said. "In his office, in the city, he sat at his desk and shot himself."

That was the first time Elodie had ever said it out loud, though people had always known, at school girls had whispered about it, house mistresses had tilted their heads when speaking with Elodie, making exceptions for her having grown up without a father. It had always been the big excuse as to why Elodie was making slow progress through life, though her mother had not once discussed it with her. Even speaking with Max, they had never discussed the suicide element of their father's death. But strangely she could speak to Luke about it, even though she barely know him. She felt at ease and more open than after any therapy session.

"I've very sorry to hear that, Elodie," he said. "How old were you?"

"Seven."

"So your mother brought you up?"

"Yes, and my brother too. He's three years younger than me."

"Tough on your mom," he said.

"Yes."

"Was it depression?"

"Desperation, I think. He had embezzled money, would have gone to prison apparently and he couldn't bear the thought of it."

"So you all paid the price," said Luke. "And you were so young."

"I don't think it's great for any child, is it? Usually I push it back, you know?"

"I can imagine," said Luke.

"I remember sitting on the stairs and Max put his little arm around me. It was horrible, not a great start," she said.

They stopped by a letterbox.

"It makes me think of a guy called Sonny," said Luke. "A great guy, he worked at my parents' place in Connecticut. Chewed tobacco, a regular Clint Eastwood. I spent most of my summers hanging out with him – fixing fences, herding cattle, catching horses, catching rattlesnakes. And, boy, could he play guitar. He was the man who got me into music. I'd bang on paint pots in the barn while he strummed but even then, when I was ten or eleven, what I really wanted to do was to get him to record an album."

"And did he?"

"No, a bull got him. It charged out of the paddock and straight into Sonny. Killed him stone dead."

"Oh god, were you there?"

"No, I was New York. I didn't even know what happened until years later. My mom took it badly. She felt so responsible – I guess because she and my father employed him and it was their bull. But he was such a character. I can remember his voice so clearly. He told me I'd have my own record label one day, I've never forgotten it."

"Do you think you will?" said Elodie, lighting her first cigarette since the previous evening. Her mother's house was rapidly approaching.

"Thirty-two years on the clock and I'm still tied up in my father's web, so it's anyone's guess."

"Well," she said, waving her hand to stop the smoke from going in his face, "apart from smoking, I'm afraid you have yet to learn about my other vices."

"Such as?"

"I'm a hopeless cook?"

"Well, luckily I love eating out."

"I'm very untidy."

"I believe large spaces are meant for spreading things out. What else?"

"I'm a colossal disappointment to my mother."

This time Elodie didn't smile. She turned her face away, blowing smoke towards the view of her house.

Two women were jogging side by side down the pavement towards them.

"I should take up jogging," she added vaguely.

"Elodie, I don't know what's going on between you and your mom right now but, trust me, you're a whole lot more perfect than you think you are."

Elodie shook her head and stubbed her cigarette out on a wall before throwing the butt into a rubbish bin. Luke took her other hand and kissed each of her fingers slowly.

"It's good to see you smiling," he said, brushing his hand against her cheek. "You have the most beautiful smile, you know that?"

Elodie could actually see her reflection smiling in his sunglasses. She couldn't quite grasp how at ease she was with him.

"You got me," he said.

"I got you? What do you mean I got you?"

"You got me hook, line and sinker, Elodie Gold. What about this evening? Are you up to anything?"

'Well, my most immediate plan is to have lovely long soak in the bath."

"Can we make a plan? Maybe you can call me?" he said, taking a slim white card from his wallet and passing it to her. "Or you could give me your number?"

"What's your name on Instagram?"

"You won't find me on any social media, I'm afraid."

"Why?"

"I guess I don't have anything I particularly want to share with the world."

"When you start your record label you'll want to share everything," she said.

"If, and that's a big *if*, I start my label," he said. "I do use email though."

"How very twenty-first century of you," she said.

"How about your email address?" he said.

"Elodiegold@yahoo.com, and that's Elodie with an i and an e at the end."

"Wouldn't expect anything less," he said. "Call me later?"

"If you like."

"I like," he said, lowering his sunglasses.

Chapter nineteen

Portland Road, London

The hydrangeas bordering the front of her mother's house still held last year's blooms, and were beginning to bud small green shoots of pure optimism. The daffodils and crocuses were also shooting up. As Elodie walked along the path towards the door of her garden flat, she felt good about herself for the first time in months, possibly years. Her mind began to race with the possibility of a relationship with Luke, one in which they could take time to get to know one another and then, step by step, maybe progress to romance.

Opening the door, painted in her mother's favourite colour, stone blue, Elodie heard an unfamiliar sound, muffled and kitten-like, emanating from her kitchen.

There was a large navy leather case at the foot of the stairs, and a long brown cape hanging on the coat rail.

"*Max?*" she yelled, throwing her bag onto an armchair. "*Max, it's me, I'm home!*"

Closing the door behind her, Elodie heard the sound again. Maybe a bird had got in through an open window, or the neighbour's annoying cat.

"*Max?*" she called again.

Walking into the sitting room, she found her brother on the sofa, staring zombie-like at his phone.

"Hey, Max, what's going on?" she said, sitting next to him and putting her hand on his back. "You look awful. You're sweating. My god, are you alright? What's going on? Who's here?"

He didn't react, just squeezed his phone between his fingers. Then, rubbing his eyes, he put it down on the coffee table and splayed out his fingers on his knees.

"There it is again," said Elodie. "Did you hear that, Max? It sounds like a bird or cat, or –"

Elodie leapt off the sofa as a woman in a brown uniform appeared at the door holding a baby. She gave Elodie a cursory glance. "I'm looking for a wee towel," she said.

Scottish accent. Stout, with brown hair cut into a tidy bob, early thirties.

Elodie looked at Max, then at the woman – and then at the baby.

"The baby," said Elodie. "It was the baby making the sound."

"Oh, aye," said the woman, coming forward. "Baby Fleur's a little bit colicky today, aren't you, petal?"

"Baby Fleur," repeated Elodie, looking at Max, whose head was now bowed.

"You must be Miss Gold?" said the woman, putting out her hand. "Morag Brown. I'm the nanny."

"The nanny?" said Elodie, dazedly shaking the proffered hand and looking at the baby clasped in Morag's left arm. She was a gorgeous child, with white-blonde hair, and wearing a pink Babygro.

"Hard to believe she's going to be six months old on Tuesday, isn't it?" said Morag.

"I'm sorry?" said Elodie. "Whose baby is this? Max, for god's sake, would you say something?"

Morag brought the baby over to Max. "Now, Mr Gold, this wee lady has had her bath and she is clean as a whistle now. I'll be taking her upstairs, getting her settled for the evening. Say goodnight to your daddy, Baby Fleur," and she tilted the baby's head towards Max.

Max looked up blankly.

"Would you like to say goodnight to your daughter?" asked Morag.

"*Daughter?*" said Elodie. "Good god, Max, what the hell?"

"Not the sort of language a young lady should hear. I can see you two have some talking to do and I'll not be part of it," said Morag, frowning.

"Wait, please," said Elodie. She reached out to touch Fleur's little feet, almost to check that she was actually real. "Is this Charlotte's baby?"

"*Ms* Wentworth has gone to visit her parents in the country," said Morag. Her emphasis on the word '*Ms*' suggested she was unimpressed by Max and Charlotte's ambiguous state of marital affairs. "I'm to look after Baby Fleur for the next month."

"The next month?"

"Yes, as instructed."

"As instructed by Charlotte?" said Elodie.

"No, Ms Wentworth is not my employer, if that's what you mean?" sniffed Morag. "My employers are Lord and Lady Broadbent." She said their names with reverential grandness. Baby Fleur began to squirm in her arms but Morag held her firmly. "Though I don't see the relevance of that to you?"

"Broadbent … you mean Charlotte's friend Petra … her parents?"

"Aye," said Morag, towering over Max. "And let's be quite clear. I'll clean up after the baby but I'll not be responsible for any area beyond the baby."

"Absolutely," said Elodie, finding it impossible to disagree with this woman.

Max was clearly in complete shock.

"Now," continued Morag, "as I was saying to Mr Gold earlier, Baby has had her bath and it's beddy-byes now. Tomorrow we'll be up at six to begin a new day … and I will continue with her routine, which must not be tampered with at *any* time."

"Where are you sleeping?" said Elodie.

"Upstairs, of course, as directed by Mr Gold," said Morag, looking at Max. "It's all nicely organised," and then she looked Elodie up and down. "I take it you don't live upstairs?"

"Our mother lives upstairs."

"The guest room is entirely adequate and Baby Fleur's Moses basket will suffice for now."

"My niece," Elodie muttered. "I'm sorry, but this is a little bit of a shock for me."

"I don't see why?" said Morag, eyeballing Elodie. "Now say goodnight to Daddy, Baby Fleur," and she once more tilted the baby's head towards Max, who was still sitting bleary-eyed. He seemed clueless about how to react.

"Kiss her forehead, Max," said Elodie. "Max?"

"Goodnight," said Max, reaching out to briefly touch the baby's hand.

The baby began screeching.

"*Tsk tsk!*" said Morag sharply, walking towards the door. "There'll be none of that carry-on, wee lady." She looked over at Elodie. "Oh yes, and there's a delivery on its way over now with my supper, which I'll take in my room, and don't worry, I'll listen out for the door. Tomorrow I'll begin ordering groceries for Baby Fleur's weekly menu. Goodnight to you both."

"Goodnight," said Elodie, and she stood rooted to the spot for many long seconds after Morag and the baby exited.

Chapter twenty

Max dive-bombed his head into a large cushion as Elodie stood feeling like she was taking part in some kind of twisted school play where she was playing an aunt, and Max a father – a father on the verge of a breakdown. Up until now, Max had always been the sorted one, strong and positive, gliding along without a worry. Now, he was in a crisis, frightened and childlike, hunched over his knees, shaking. Her happy-go-lucky brother seemed to have vanished overnight.

"Max?"

"How can I be a father, El?" he said. The dark shadows beneath his eyes made him look like one of the lost boys from *Peter Pan*. "And Charlotte ... a mother?"

Elodie sat next to him, trying to work out what would be the best move.

"So are you saying that Charlotte broke up with you because she was having a baby? Your baby? That doesn't make sense, does it?"

Max sat up and wiped his eyes. "No. I don't know what she was thinking. And I just don't know how the hell this is going to play out."

"You're in shock," said Elodie.

"Entirely," he said. "And I won't be alone. This evening, the perfect world of the Reverend and Mrs Wentworth is going to be shattered when their only daughter confesses that for the past twelve months she has not been studying horticulture in France, but instead has been hiding away on a hippy commune with their granddaughter."

"Charlotte came here with Morag and the baby?"

"They appeared at lunchtime and I was still in bed. Charlotte knocked on my bedroom window and you can picture the scowl I got from that terrifying nanny when I opened the curtains in my pyjamas."

"What about Mum? I take you haven't seen her?"

"She shot off to Switzerland with Lorenzo this morning, thank god. She left a note for me in the hall – and one for you too, by the way. She's only going for two nights."

Elodie was going to have to make peace with her mother to get her allowance reinstated, but for now she had to work out what the hell to do with Max and the baby.

"So when is Charlotte coming back? Tonight? Tomorrow?"

"No, El, longer than that," said Max. "She said she needed time out … I don't know? She literally landed the baby on me, threw me Fleur's passport and a bunch of notes. She was so upset leaving Fleur but insisted she didn't want to take the baby to her parents. Not until they've had time to process the news. Next thing, it's just me, the baby and that nanny who starts telling me she's going to be staying here for the next four weeks."

"So Charlotte is leaving for four weeks? Are you serious?"

"I don't know, El."

"Right," said Elodie. "So let's assume Charlotte isn't thinking straight at the moment and that she *does* need time out. I take it she's been staying with Petra if Petra's parents are footing the bill for the nanny?"

"Charlotte says they've paid for everything. I'll have to pay them back."

"Hold on, Max, let's just take this one step at a time."

"She didn't want to tell me she was pregnant because she didn't want me to miss my chance in LA."

"Maybe she was right?"

As Max dropped his head back into the cushion, Elodie found

herself looking at a photograph on the mantelpiece of the two of them as children. Max was hanging upside down inside a tunnel while she looked up at him. The picture had been taken in Ireland the summer before their had father died. Nothing in their lives had ever been straightforward – why would it stop now?

On the stairs up to the hall, Elodie spotted an envelope with a large 'ELODIE' written in blue ink. Inside was a letter, penned in her mother's extravagant handwriting, in which Julia explained that she would be gone for two nights, she would be available via text message unless there was an absolute urgency, and she expected a complete turn-around of Elodie's behaviour upon her return if 'perks' were to resume. It was no surprise that Julia had left London; she often whistled up Lorenzo for a quick getaway after she'd had a big row. But how exactly did she expect Elodie to survive without any bloody cash?

Crumpling up the letter in her hands, Elodie ran down to the basement kitchen, opened the fridge and found a fish pie, which had arrived with the weekly delivery from Selfridges food hall. She put the pie in the microwave, gave the central heating a boost and put the kettle on. They were going to need as much comfort as possible. As she made a pot of tea, she knew one thing for certain: she had to get Max and the baby out of the house before their mother returned. There was no way Julia would go for this.

Back in the sitting room, she found Max was now stretched out along the sofa. She put a mug of tea within his reach and sank into an armchair across from him.

"I've stuck a pie in the microwave," she said, "and please drink your tea, would you, Max?"

"I will when I'm ready," he said.

She felt mildly like Dr Frasier Crane assessing a patient.

"Max, I'm sorry to ask … you know how fond I am of Charlotte?"

"But?"

"Are you totally sure the baby is yours?"

"Elodie, for fuck's sake," he said, "of course I'm sure. You only have to look at Fleur."

"Okay, I'm sorry," she said hastily.

"It's just so surreal," said Max. "I honestly thought we were taking a break so that Charlotte could work out what she wanted to do with her career. Landscaping or whatever. It never occurred to me that she was bloody well pregnant."

Elodie's tea was cold already and the smell of fish pie coming from the kitchen was making her feel nauseous. She felt sick about the entire situation.

"Nosy Carol will totally snitch to Mum if we don't make a move," said Elodie. "Thank god she's off until Saturday."

"What kind of move?"

"You can't stay here with the baby, Max. There's just no way. Mum's in what Thomas used to call one of her 'unpredictable Ayatollah moods'. I mean, can you really see her coping with a baby in the house? Let alone that nanny. She's a piece of work."

"Who are you telling? I can't be a *dad*."

"Max, get a grip," said Elodie, standing up and tossing options around in her mind. She needed to come up with a solution fast. A place where Max could land with a baby, and a nanny, somewhere completely away from the beady eyes of their mother's social circle, with no risk of word getting out while Max worked out the next step with Charlotte.

Elodie looked at the tiny goldfinch charm on the bracelet on her wrist, which Gramps had given to her on her twenty-first birthday, and there she found the answer.

"Max, I know this is going to seem a little out there, but what if –"

"Yes?"

"What if you went to Bellamore?"

"Bellamore?" said Max. "You are joking?"

"I'm deadly serious."

"Go to Ireland? Land on our grandfather completely out of the blue, and with a baby?"

"You'll have Morag with you, she'll look after the baby and then you can work out what to do from there. You'll simply be a father, travelling with your nanny."

"Elodie, you are suggesting I take refuge in a place we haven't been for … how many years? Ten? No way, El, I won't do it."

"Do you know what Fleur's full name is? Where's her passport?" Elodie began googling flights from Heathrow to Dublin on her phone. "If we can book flights this evening, then it's just a matter of making a call to Bellamore and, of course, letting Charlotte know."

"Oh Christ, you are actually serious, aren't you?" said Max, reluctantly getting up from the sofa.

"Yes, I am."

"Follow me," he said, walking to the kitchen. "Let me find the envelope of notes Charlotte gave me. It's about the only thing she handed to me instead of to the bleeding nanny." He grabbed a large brown envelope from the dresser and passed it to Elodie. "Here you go," he said.

Pulling out a passport, Elodie opened it up. She held the passport up to the light, looking at Fleur's photograph. "There really is a big likeness between you and Fleur."

"But your idea is off the wall, Elodie. I can't just rock up to our grandfather with a baby, and a nanny."

While he hesitated, Elodie thought of the options. The last time she saw her mother she had been asked to vacate the building. Maybe Julia would cool down but there could be no guarantees.

"So what if I were to come with you? Just for a week or so, help settle you in and we could both go on the charm offensive with Gramps?"

"Maybe, and it isn't as if we ever fell out with him, is it?" said Max.

"Exactly. Mum stopped us from going there. I don't think it had anything to do with Gramps, did it?"

"Remember how Odette objected to us calling him that?" he said.

"Only she could have insisted on us addressing our grandparents by their names."

"It was Odette's way, that's all. But Gramps it was and Gramps it continued to be."

"Okay," said Elodie. "We needn't land on him out of the blue. Let's contact him and find out if this idea is actually a runner."

"We don't even know if he's still alive," said Max.

"We'll find out soon enough, won't we? One thing we can be sure of is that he won't be straight on the phone to Mum."

"True," said Max.

"One more thing, Max. I'm completely out of cash. Mum has cleared me out."

"She finally did it? After all the threats?"

"My penalty for breaking up with bloody Dominic, and most probably because I tried to get her to stop drinking the other night."

"Well, if it's any consolation I'll most likely be in a similar boat when Mum discovers that I've not only bolted, but with my progeny," said Max. "We'd better book those flights fast while my card is still working, assuming Gramps says yes, that is."

Chapter twenty-one

Yorkshire

Charlotte arrived in her VW Golf and parked in front of her parents' house, which was surrounded by immaculate tarmac, small potted plants and pottery woodland creatures. Wearing a long cardigan with red trousers and a striped scarf, Charlotte tightened her French plait of blonde curls and tried to rub a muddy mark from the toe of her leather boot.

The shine of the brass doorknob made Charlotte remember her mother's lemon-juice trick to get a true shine and, as she rang the doorbell, she could imagine the conversation taking place on the other side of the door.

"What sort of time is this for one of your parishioners to call round, Gerald," her mother would be saying. "Don't they all know we watch the *Bake Off* at this time?"

Through the frosted glass, Charlotte could see the blur of a figure approaching.

The door opened and her father stood there, looking stunned.

"*Mary?*" he called out, over his shoulder.

"*Not now, Gerald, Paul Hollywood is about to taste the Pavlova!*"

"*Mary, I think you should turn off the television and come to the door!*"

"Surprise?" said Charlotte, kissing her father on the cheek. She could see her mother peeping her head around the sitting-room door, as she so often did when one of Gerald's flock bared their souls on the doorstep, creating draughts.

"Charlotte, it's never you?" said Mary, coming to meet her.

"Hello, Mum," said Charlotte, trying to feel relief in seeing her parents.

"Come in then, don't just stand there," said Mary, "and look at those boots, take them off, there's a good girl."

As Charlotte unlaced her boots, she looked up at her parents who were exchanging glances.

"Leave the boots on the mat," said Mary. "That's it."

It had been twelve months since they'd seen their daughter and taking off her boots was the first instruction. Charlotte's expectations had never been particularly high when it came to her parents.

"Have you had your tea, Charlotte?" said Mary, leaning in to awkwardly kiss her daughter's cheek.

"Not really," she said.

"That's your car you arrived in, is it?" said Gerald.

"Yes," said Charlotte. "Isn't it lovely?"

"How did you pay for it, Charlotte dear?" said Mary.

"I wrote essays."

"Essays? You wrote essays? What, in exchange for a car?"

"I did," said Charlotte. "Students who were too busy asked me to write essays for them. It proved to be lucrative. Enough for a second-hand car anyway."

"I'd like if I could get a car like that for writing sermons," said Gerald, but nobody laughed.

"Now," said Mary, walking into the kitchen and putting on her apron, "the problem is, I don't have any more lamb chops. If you'd just called beforehand ..."

"No, Mum, it's okay. I'm a vegetarian now."

"You're a *what*?" said Gerald.

"You've never turned into one of those!" said Mary.

"Yes, Mum, I have," and, seeing the horror on her mother's face, she wondered how on earth she was going to break the news to them that they had a grandchild.

The next morning, Mary fussed over spider plants in the kitchen with a small watering can and simultaneously sobbed into a tea towel.

"A baby, Gerald, not a baby!" she kept repeating, over and over. "How could you not have told us, our Charlotte? All this time, I've been going to church, standing by your father as he says the Lord's Prayer, and there's our own daughter with a baby out of wedlock."

"Easy now, Mary, take it easy on the girl," said Gerald, pushing his cornflakes, untouched, to one side.

"I'll make you some toast, Charlotte," said Mary, putting down the watering can and blowing her nose on a piece of floral paper towel.

"No thanks, Mum, I've already had cereal."

"I've got that berry jam that Mrs Darndale makes. You remember Mrs Darndale, don't you?"

"I think so," said Charlotte, "though it's been a while since I've been to any of your gatherings, Mum."

"What about a slice of flan? I've put flaked almonds over the cream, just like on the telly. Though the *Bake Off* hasn't been the same since Mary Berry left, has it, Gerald?"

Charlotte looked at her father, wondering how on earth they were going to cope.

"Though I do like Prue's colours," said Mary. "Bright and bold, and I'm sure all her clothes come from high-end shops."

"Aye, love," said Gerald, "no doubt they do."

"But, Mum, about Fleur, I'd really like you to meet her," said Charlotte, leaning against the sink. "You are her grandparents and I'd really like you to be part of her life."

"Actually," said Mary, ignoring Charlotte's suggestion, "I've got a cranberry loaf in the freezer. Let me find it and I'll make you a toasted cheese sandwich, like I used to when you came home from the Brownies."

"Mum, really –"

"You were such a sweet little Brownie," said Mary, beginning to cry again.

"Mary, she doesn't want any ruddy toast," said Gerald, slightly raising his voice, at a loss as to what else to say. "I'm sorry but, woman, can't you see that Charlotte doesn't want any more breakfast? Sometimes people just don't want any more, of anything. Do you see?"

Mary took off her apron which had small white lilies detailed around the pockets, and pulled out a chair to join her husband and daughter at the table.

Charlotte kept one eye on the door in case she had to bolt.

"Make a fresh pot of tea, Gerald, would you?" said Mary.

Then Mary pulled Charlotte's hands into hers, resting them on the table as if they were going to play one potato, two potato ...

"Tell me where you've been, Charlotte dear? France, you said, studying gardening, that's what we've been telling people."

Charlotte closed her eyes and felt so bad about having lied to her parents. "At the Broadbents', Mum. Petra's parents have been so kind and I'm so sorry, Mum and Dad – I desperately wanted to tell you but I didn't think you'd understand."

"You mean to tell me Lady Broadbent took in my own daughter without so much as a word to me?" said Mary and, getting up from the table, she took a bag of flour from a cupboard and poured a large amount into a bowl.

"Aren't you going to use the scales, Mary? How can you get an accurate bake without the scales?"

"To hell with the measurements, Gerald. Now, pass me six eggs, please."

"I'm sure the proportions can't be right, Mary," said Gerald, passing the eggs, which Mary proceeded to crack one after another on the edge of the bowl.

Charlotte felt dreadful for driving her parents into such a state.

"I thought you'd broken up with Max?" said Mary, stirring the mixture in tight circles. "No, Gerald, this wooden spoon just isn't working – pass me a whisk, please."

"We did take a break," said Charlotte, responding to her mother's question. "It was my idea, when I discovered I was ..."

"Pregnant," said Gerald.

"Yes, pregnant," said Charlotte.

"What about your qualifications?" said Gerald, trying to steady the situation.

"I'm still passionate about gardening, Dad, and I'm sure I'll get a job with a couple of years of course-work under my belt."

"How can you have a baby and be a gardener at the same time?" said Mary. "It's like serving jam sponge next to Shepherd's Pie – as Prue and Paul would say on the *Bake Off*, the flavours just don't work."

"Fleur is so beautiful, Mum," said Charlotte, her eyes brimming with tears as she smiled. "Just the other day she started to make the sweetest sounds – like vowels, you know? Her mouth '*as clean as a cat's*' as Sylvia Plath would say – remember when you used to read that poem to me, Dad?"

"I do, love, that I do."

"I think you're going to love her," said Charlotte, her voice beginning to break as she turned to her father. "If you'll just give us a chance, I know Max and I will make good parents."

"But you still haven't told us where the baby is, Charlotte," said Gerald.

Charlotte sat back on the chair, and held her hands together. "Ireland," she said.

"*What?*" said Mary.

"Fleur has gone to Ireland with Max, and his sister Elodie."

Mary and Gerald looked at each other, eyeballs popping.

"Why on earth would your child be in Ireland with Max?" said Mary.

"And the nanny."

"The nanny?" said Gerald. "What nanny?"

"They are staying with Max's grandfather in Ireland," said Charlotte, "and don't worry, Dad – Petra's parents are paying for her."

"*They are what?*" said Mary, lifting the whisk out of the bowl and spilling cake batter onto the floor. "Now look what I've done! Oh Gerald!"

"Steady now, Mary," said Gerald, going into the utility room and returning with a mop, as Mary laid out a couple of cake tins on the kitchen unit.

"Charlotte," said Mary, "have you thought through all the options?"

"Options?" said Charlotte.

"There's an agency in Birmingham, isn't there, Gerald? That girl from Burnsley, she went there, didn't she, Gerald?"

"She did," said Gerald, bowing his head and avoiding eye contact with Charlotte.

"What exactly is it that you're suggesting?" said Charlotte, desperately hoping she was misreading her parents.

"Adoption," said Mary.

Charlotte stood up and stared at her parents for several moments in silence. "You are actually suggesting that I give my daughter away?"

"We'd make sure she went to a good home, wouldn't we, Gerald? A home with stability."

"This is your granddaughter we're talking about!" said Charlotte. "How can you ..." She fought for words but she couldn't find any.

"Where are you going, Charlotte dear," said Mary, as her daughter descended the stairs with her overnight bag.

"I'm going to begin my life with Max and Charlotte."

"But you can't just stay one night and then leave?" said Gerald.

"I love you both," said Charlotte, resting her case on the floor and pulling on her boots by the front door, "and I am truly sorry for embarrassing you – especially you, Dad, with your job and everything."

"Charlotte," said Gerald, "you know, sometimes there isn't a solution, sometimes you just have to pray."

"I don't need a solution, Dad, I know where my future lies," and she walked out the front door.

"Your laces, Charlotte," called Mary. "You can't go off with your laces untied."

"Let her go, Mary," Gerald said, "let the lass go."

"We can't just let her go, Gerald," said Mary, "and I was going to make a trifle for tea tonight."

Chapter twenty-two

Dublin Airport

Elodie had never held a baby before and surprised herself by feeling such comfort as Fleur pressed her warm little face against her cheek.

"I told you I wasn't a keen flyer," said Morag, emerging from the bathroom by the luggage carousel, dabbing a handkerchief on the edges of her mouth before taking Fleur into her arms.

"We thought the chocolates might distract you from the noise of the engine," said Elodie, checking her cigarette supply in her hand luggage.

"Well, that proved to be correct, but not in the way you intended I presume?" said Morag, pulling Fleur's hat over her ears. "I've never been a fan of airports either, they make me anxious."

"I thought nannies weren't supposed to be anxious," said Elodie, who was feeling increasingly nervous about returning to Bellamore.

"Correct, just as nannies are not supposed to be forced into uncomfortable situations," said Morag, shooting Elodie a dark look.

Elodie wished Max would hurry up and retrieve their luggage. She hated being left alone with Morag. Her prayers were unexpectedly answered when her mobile sprang to life. A call was coming through from an Irish mobile number.

"Hello?" she said, answering it.

"Is that Elodie?" came a loud voice in what sounded like a Dutch accent.

"Yes."

"Oh, so you have landed. This is Anika. I've come to collect you."

"Okay," said Elodie. "That's so kind of you. We'll be –"

"You'll find me in the set-down area," said Anika. "I'm driving a burgundy jeep," and she hung up.

Elodie felt too exhausted to react to the abruptness of the call. She had got rid of Dominic, fallen out with her mother, had been stripped of her money, had fallen for Luke and now she had instigated the return to a place of haunting memories. Self-doubt had never felt so heavy on her shoulders.

Seeing Max pushing a trolley laden with bags towards them, she pulled out a ciggie to smoke as soon as they got out of the building. She raced ahead of the others to light up, but she had barely ignited the cigarette when she heard a series of beeps from the set-down area. She looked up and saw a jeep with the front door open. A tall blonde woman was standing there, leaning into the driver's seat, presumably pressing the horn. As Max, Morag and the baby joined Elodie, all four of them found themselves staring at this woman who stood glaring at them. She was dressed in long black riding boots and jodhpurs, with a tight black polo neck accentuating her large bosom beneath an open Puffa jacket.

"*Come on, you lot!*" she yelled.

Max and Elodie looked at each other.

"Remind me, who is she again?" said Max, steadying the luggage as his trolley rattled towards the woman.

"She said her name was Anika," said Elodie. "A friend of Gramps', I guess?"

Anika had pouting lips and shoulder-length hair with a fringe sweeping across her forehead. Her eyes lit up when she saw Max.

"Hello," she said, kissing him on both cheeks, with a waft of freshly applied perfume. "You must be Max?"

"Yes," he said. "This is Elodie and –"

"Later, later," said Anika, waving him to silence and opening the boot of the jeep.

A pair of terriers began yapping from the back seat.

Anika was clearly about to say something else when she saw Fleur. "And what is this?" she said.

"This, madam, is a baby," said Morag, nose pointing high.

"And you are?" said Anika.

"I am Baby Fleur's nanny."

"Baby Fleur? Thomas didn't mention anything about a baby."

"We did tell him," said Elodie, "when we phoned."

"He must not have heard," said Anika. "He sometimes doesn't over the phone."

The terriers continued to yap.

"*Bonnie and Clyde, will you shut up,*" roared Anika into the window.

"The baby is mine," said Max as he began to load luggage, including Fleur's foldable pram, into the back.

"Really?" said Anika, sizing him up with smoky eyes. "If I had known you had so much stuff I would have brought the horsebox. How much luggage does a baby need?"

"I like to have clothing for every eventuality," said Morag. "Now, there is a problem. I will not travel with dogs."

"And why is that?" said Anika, her blue eyes narrowing.

"I'm allergic to their smell," said Morag brashly. "I also personally think it's very unhygienic to have dogs and a baby in close proximity."

"What utter poppycock," said Anika, turning her back on Morag, "and, I can assure you, my jeep is the only mode of transport that will get you to Bellamore this afternoon, so you'd better make your mind up pretty sneppity."

"Sneppity?" said Elodie. "I don't think that's a word, is it?"

"Are you commenting on my use of English?" said Anika. "I had my own slot on MTV, you know? You think they'd put me in that position for my looks alone?"

"I'm sure Elodie didn't mean to be critical," said Max, stepping in diplomatically as Elodie rolled her eyes.

"Okay, Maxy," said Anika, putting a hand on his shoulder, "you travel in the front with me."

"Actually," said Elodie, "if you don't mind, I'd like sit up front. I tend to get very car sick."

"Allergic to dogs? Car sick? Am I an ambulance? No, I am not. Elodie, you will sit in the back, as I asked you – Bonnie and Clyde can sit on your lap – you have strong thighs, no? Maxy, you and your long legs must sit in the front."

"Can't I – "–" began Elodie.

"Enough," said Anika, "and put out that cigarette. I can't bear the stench of smoke. Now, you, Nanny, what is your name?"

"Morag, and I will not be –"

"Morag, have you made your mind up? Are you going to jump in or will you be joining us later by helicopter?"

Morag huffily clambered into the back seat beside the baby-seat Max had strapped in position.

"Good, and now you, Elodie, come on – *chop-chop*!" said Anika.

Elodie and Max looked at each other as Anika jumped into the driver's seat, started the engine and began revving like she was on a Formula 1 racetrack. They reluctantly took their seats in the car, Elodie squeezing in beside the terriers who promptly jumped on her lap.

Max hadn't even closed his door before Anika shot off, instantly double-beeping her horn at a white BMW sports car which swerved in front of her.

"No doubt it's a woman behind the wheel," she said.

"Women are better drivers than men," said Morag, "no question about it."

Bonnie and Clyde began yapping again and Fleur howled in response.

"*Godverdomme,*" shouted Anika.

Fleur and the terriers were all startled into silence.

"I'll thank you not to raise your voice in the presence of my charge," said Morag.

"Sorry about the wheels," continued Anika in her bellowing voice, completely ignoring Morag. "I had meant to have the jeep valeted but somehow the days pass by so quickly in the country. First it's Monday, then you count to five and it's Friday and then it's Monday all over again."

"And you might take it handy with your driving," said Morag,

"I don't trust these jeeps. I think they're out of proportion and lacking style."

"I used to drive a Bentley in Amsterdam," said Anika, "but when I came to Ireland I decided a jeep was more fitting for the countryside."

"You'd be better off in a tractor with the state of these roads," said Morag.

Easing onto the motorway, heading north, Anika slowly ran her left hand across Max's knees to the glovebox, from which she extracted a box of Ferrero Rocher. Without offering them to anyone, she single-handedly unwrapped three in a row and wolfed each one down.

"So what are you up to in London, Max?" said Anika, rummaging in a side pocket of the door and pulling out a lipstick.

"I've just got back from LA," said Max, nervously watching Anika apply red lipstick in the rear-view mirror as she sped up the motorway.

"Such a fabulous city, I used to fly in for Fashion Week."

"Organising parties or something?" said Elodie, from the back seat.

"No," said Anika, with an irritated flick of her hair, "I was modelling, obviously."

"Obviously," said Max, wondering what on earth his grandfather could have in common with this woman.

"So what about the baby's mother?" said Anika.

Morag leaned forward, "The baby's mother is –"

"She's on holiday," said Max, glancing back at Morag. He didn't want Gramps to think that Fleur had been abandoned by her mother.

"What's that?" said Anika. "This engine is so noisy."

"Charlotte is visiting her parents," said Elodie.

"I have a son, you know," said Anika, gliding her hand back across Max's crotch and lunging across him to find a pack of Tic Tacs in the side-pocket of the passenger door. "He's in the Swiss Alps. Twenty-three years old, girls draped around his shoulders, on the slopes all day long. Just like his father."

"Your husband?" said Elodie, wondering if Anika's perfume was Chanel or Givenchy.

"Ex-husband, and a snake. I sent him packing years ago. They say you have to kiss a lot of frogs, don't they? Still, I gained a townhouse in Amsterdam, compliments of my ex, so all was not lost."

"And now you live in Ireland permanently?" said Max.

"I don't think there's any such thing as 'permanently'," said Anika, shaking half the contents of the Tic Tac container into her mouth. "Right now I live just outside Drummare, about ten minutes from Bellamore. I have a marvellous house with a couple of stables. Riding helps me to keep my weight in check."

Everyone closed their eyes as Anika overtook a lorry with an oncoming car in view.

"You see, I have a weakness for cheese and chocolate," she said, seemingly oblivious of the near-miss. "No matter how I try, I can't seem to avoid them. Particularly as your grandfather loves blue cheese."

"Do you see a lot of him?" said Elodie.

Anika rolled her eyes. "Of course."

"And have you known each other for long?" asked Max.

"We met at a dreary drinks party," said Anika. "It was so boring I went for a walk in the garden and that was where I met Thomas, looking for birds naturally, and he offered me some sloe gin from his hipflask. We have been very close friends ever since."

Max and Elodie said nothing.

"Very close," repeated Anika, veering left off the motorway towards Drummare.

Elodie tried to imagine Gramps and Anika as a couple. She couldn't have been more than forty-two or three.

"Sometimes people take a second glance at us," said Anika. "They think perhaps I am his daughter. Can you imagine? But I look at your grandfather and I don't see an old man. I see a wonderful man, full of life. Who cares what the age difference is?"

"People sometimes mistake me for a twenty-one-year-old," said Morag, preening herself.

"Anika, did you know Odette?" asked Elodie, ignoring Morag's attempts to join the conversation.

"No, she'd been dead a couple of years before I met Thomas."
Elodie disliked the casual way she said it.

"Anyone like a piece of gum?" said Anika, swerving as she passed the packet to Elodie.

"Actually, Anika," said Elodie, "any chance we can pull in? I'm longing for a ciggy."

"Are you crazy? No chance, and your grandfather is certainly not expecting a baby, so the sooner you land that bombshell on him, the better for all of us."

Chapter twenty-three

Bellamore

The pillars of the main entrance to Bellamore were submerged beneath sprawling hawthorn hedges and the gravel clearly hadn't been replenished for years, as a light hue of grass ran up the centre of the avenue. Anika drove much too fast, powering through the potholes.

"Why are the gates open?" said Elodie, holding onto the handle above the car window and feeling slightly uplifted by the daffodils coming up in the woods, as they had always done.

"Why wouldn't they be open?" said Anika.

"Odette always kept them closed."

"She's not here though, is she?" said Anika, turning to look at Elodie. "I hope you had a bath before you came."

"What's that about a bath?" said Morag, as Fleur began to wail.

"There hasn't been any water since last week," said Anika.

"You *are* joking?" said Elodie, running her fingers through her hair.

"Baby must have her evening bath!" said Morag.

Anika ignored her.

A sturdy three-storey Georgian house came into view, which Elodie instantly noted looked naked without its summer coat of thick Virginia creeper.

Pulling up in front of the house, Elodie opened the door and Bonnie and Clyde went flying over her lap and began circling around the legs of a big old Labrador whose long tail was acting as a rudder.

"Is that Bluebell?" said Elodie, stepping onto the gravel and kneeling down to the dog. "Oh my god, you were just a puppy when we last saw you. Look at you, you've got so –"

"Old and doddery like me?" came a familiar voice and, looking up, Elodie saw her grandfather standing at the front door, with two sets of spectacles hanging around his neck and thinning grey hair swept back from his forehead. He was wearing a purple jumper, a bright-green shirt and green cords.

Walking towards him, Elodie completely surprised herself by bursting into tears.

"My, my, Elodie, you've turned into a woman," he said, holding her. "There we are now, how did that happen?"

Standing behind her, Max reached out his hand to Thomas.

"And as for you, Max, where has my young grandson gone? You've shot up. I think you must be nearly as tall as I used to be."

Max was about to respond when Anika barged past, pushing her bosom into Thomas's chest and giving him a smacker of a kiss.

"Hello, sweetheart," she said huskily.

"Hello, darling," he said, patting her bottom. "You're so good to have collected the children – apart from the NCT being out of date, I couldn't possibly have fitted two of them into my sports car."

"I think you will find there are more than two, Thomas," said Anika.

Elodie watched anxiously as his head rotated back towards the jeep to see Morag approaching, with Fleur who was wearing a sheepskin coat, hat and soft leather booties.

"That doesn't look like a computer whatsit," said Thomas.

He always had a curious habit of making jokes without a follow-up smile but, in this case, it looked like he was definitely serious.

"Is that real? When you said you were bringing a baby, I thought it was some new thing on a computer. A FaceTube or what have you."

"No, she's definitely a baby, Gramps, not an app," said Max, taking his daughter from Morag. "Would you like to hold your great-granddaughter?"

"Her face is determined," he said, taking the baby into his arms. Fleur kicked out her feet and fists, then bleated a series of yells. "That's a cry for hunger, I'd say."

"She had a bottle an hour ago, my lord," said Morag, curtseying.

"And you are?"

"Morag, my lord," she said formally, brushing down the pleats on her skirt. "Lord Broadbent has placed me in charge of this child."

"Sheepskin? Won't she overheat in the afternoon sun?" said Thomas, not remotely interested in who was employing her.

"We must keep Baby warm, my lord," said Morag.

"Why are you calling me 'my lord'?"

"I'm so sorry," said Morag, getting flustered. "Would you prefer for me to address you as 'sir'? Or 'Lord Archdale' perhaps?"

"Why on earth would you do that?" said Thomas. "You can call me Thomas – or Mr Archdale, if you insist on formality."

Morag's face dropped. "But you are a lord, are you not ... my lordship?"

"I'm sorry to disappoint, but there is no title to be found here," said Thomas.

"I see," said Morag. "My aunt worked for a Lord Archdale years back, on the Isle of Rousey, and so I presumed you must be related."

"No connection, as far as I am aware."

Morag looked put out. "Then would you be so kind as to direct me to the facilities, *Mr* Archdale?"

"The WC in the stable yard has water fortunately, so it's the best option if you're in a hurry?" He pointed to a large archway. "Blue door on the right, you can't miss it – and watch out for the cobblestones, they can be slippery at this time of year."

Morag inhaled so deeply that her nostrils looked like they might stick permanently together before proceeding towards the yard, while Thomas whistled between his teeth.

"She's been hired by a family friend of Fleur's mother," said Max, as soon as Morag was out of earshot, "and, as neither Elodie nor I have a notion about babies, we had no choice but to bring her."

"No matter," said Thomas, gently patting Fleur's head and smiling at her. "I'm delighted to meet the next generation, although I honestly wasn't expecting a baby –"

"Her name is Fleur," said Elodie, as the baby reached both her arms out.

Thomas looked from Max to Elodie and back again.

"As I say, to see you both here ... well, let's just say I'm very happy about it. *Tempus fugit*. I take it your mother has no idea you're here?"

"None," said Max and Elodie in unison.

"Then let's cross that bridge later, shall we?"

Chapter twenty-four

As Morag followed Thomas along a corridor towards the kitchen, she observed an array of hats, piled high on a huge wooden trunk. Holding the door open, Thomas ushered her in and Bonnie and Clyde promptly began to slalom around her ankles, while old Bluebell, with her thick coat and long ears, looked on from the comfort of her beanbag by the Aga, her tail beating happily.

"The floor is flagstone," said Thomas. "Makes one less inclined to drop things."

"Flagstone is cold, in my experience," said Morag, folding her arms.

"Quiet down, you blasted dogs," said Thomas, lifting the terriers up and plonking them both next to Bluebell.

"What is that smell?" said Morag, leaning against the Aga, her nose wrinkling.

"You mean the orange peel??" said Thomas. "After I've squeezed out the breakfast orange juice, I put the pieces of peel into the bottom left of the Aga and they turn into homemade firelighters."

"It's a sickly smell," said Morag.

"How about a cup of tea?" said Thomas, ignoring Morag's negativity and taking a teapot from the dresser.

"Chinese or Indian?" said Morag, eyeing the cracked lid on the teapot suspiciously.

"Sorry?" said Thomas.

"The tea," said Morag. "Will it be Chinese or Indian?"

"It's what we call builders' tea," said Thomas, putting the kettle on the Aga. "SuperValu does an excellent blend."

"Hot water with lemon will suffice," said Morag, flattening her hands on an Aga lid.

"What are you doing?"

"The ten-second test," said Morag.

"Testing what?"

"If you can hold your hands down comfortably on an Aga lid for longer than ten seconds, the temperature isn't high enough."

"I see," said Thomas. "And?"

"As my hands are still lying flat on the Aga, the temperature isn't high enough, Mr Archdale. However, it will suffice for baby's fruit purées."

"Well, that's a relief," said Thomas.

"And why are there underpants on the Aga?"

"Doesn't everyone dry their underpants on the Aga?" said Thomas. "Now, where is the baby?"

"I've just put her down," said Morag. "She's in her Moses basket on the top floor."

"Far be it for me to criticise you, Morag, but is it really correct to use the term 'put her down'? Shouldn't that terminology be saved for the vet?"

"The baby is reconnecting with her routine after the unexpected disruption of the flight and the dogs," said Morag, narrowing her eyes. "She'll sleep for the next two hours."

"It's terribly damp up there," said Thomas.

"I imagine it's *terribly damp* everywhere in this house, Mr Archdale," said Morag. "Now, please, can you direct me to a pan? I'll cook up some apple first, and then I'd like to run a hot bath."

"Yes and no," said Thomas. "I can certainly provide you with a pan. Indeed, Le Creuset galore. Regarding the bath, however, as I mentioned, we we are out of water just now and unfortunately Niall the plumber is away and won't be back until next Tuesday – though which *next Tuesday* is the question."

"But that's four days away?" said Morag.

"At least."

"Wait, Mr Archdale – are you saying there is currently no bathwater in this house?"

"No, I'm saying there is no water in the house, except in this very kitchen," said Thomas, filling up a large aluminium kettle from the tap in the Belfast sink. "The plumbing in this sink is joined to the stable yard's supply, you see, so it's a completely different system to the rest of the house – and we have a tidy water heater in here, which supplies ample amounts of hot water to the kitchen. Hence my facecloth and toothbrush being here next to the washing-up liquid."

"I'm speechless," said Morag.

"Between you and me, Morag, the timing of your visit isn't particularly great."

"I can assure you, Mr Archdale, that coming to Ireland was not on my agenda."

"*Bugger off*," came a high-pitched voice from the corner of the kitchen.

"Who said that?" said Morag, spinning her head around the room. "Who is it?"

"Ah, of course, you have yet to meet Augusta," said Thomas.

Picking up a bowl of monkey nuts, he advanced towards a cupboard upon which, sandwiched between a bread bin and an old telephone, an African Blue parrot perched inside a large cage.

"She's been the chatelaine of our kitchen for over twenty years now," he said, offering the parrot a nut. "Haven't you, Missy?"

Augusta nodded her head from side to side before accepting the nut with her claw.

"Don't put your finger in, whatever you do," said Thomas.

"What would happen if I did?" said Morag, smiling strangely.

"She'd bite it off, plain and simple. No mustard required. Isn't that right, Augusta?"

"*Mustard*," repeated Augusta, standing skilfully on one leg as she shelled the monkey nut.

"That cage takes up a lot of space," said Morag, backing away. "I can't imagine it's hygienic to have a bird like that in a kitchen. I was brought up to believe that the only animals in a kitchen should be those that are to be plucked and drawn, or skinned."

"Which reminds me," said Thomas, taking half a packet of Rich Tea out of the bread bin, "Mrs Murray, my daily, mentioned that two large boxes came this morning."

"Well, that's something at least," said Morag. "Those will be my supplies from Sainsbury's. They could deliver across the border, thank goodness."

The terriers leapt off Bluebell's beanbag yet again when Max arrived into the kitchen and the room was filled with the sound of their barking once more.

"Don't mind Bonnie and Clyde, they'll only bark for a moment and then they'll get used to you," said Thomas. "How about a cup of tea?"

"Thanks," said Max.

"Elodie mentioned you've moved on to great things," said Thomas. "Hollywood? Must have been lucrative for you?"

"Not sure about that," said Max, distracted by a dripping tap in the sink.

"Don't let the drip bother you," said Thomas, following his gaze. "It's been leaking for months. Just ignore it."

But Max went beneath the sink and perhaps twenty seconds after his upper body disappeared the dripping stopped.

"How in Heaven's name did you do that?"

"The valve just needed a little tightening," said Max.

"Fair enough," said Thomas. "And where's your sister?"

"On the phone and having a smoke, two of her favourite pastimes," said Max, looking through the window over the Belfast sink. "Who's that in the yard?"

"What?" said Thomas.

"In the yard, that woman?"

"Can I have a peeler for the apples, please?" said Morag, who held a wooden chopping board beneath one arm.

"Who is it, Gramps?" said Max again.

"That is your aunt," he said, handing Morag a peeler from the drawer.

"Tess? I had no idea she was back in Ireland," said Max. "We haven't heard about Aunt Tess in years. I thought she had settled in

Africa? I'm sure that's what Mum said at some point."

"It was Ibiza," said Thomas, placing a few mugs on the table. "She came back just after your grandmother died."

"So weird," said Max. "I don't think we've ever met Aunt Tess."

"Would you have a spurtle, Mr Archdale?" asked Morag, searching through a pot of wooden spoons.

"A spurtle?" said Thomas. "That's a word I haven't heard in a while."

"Do you have one?" said Morag.

"Never had one in this house. My late wife was French, you see. Porridge was far from her mind."

"I'll make do with this wooden spoon then," said Morag, tapping it against her hand like a schoolmistress with a ruler.

"She lives here in the house?" said Max, still looking out the window into the yard, watching his aunt rinsing her wellies with a hosepipe.

"Tess?" said Thomas. "No, she's living in the gate lodge. Prefers the privacy and as the place only has a handful of rooms it's easy to keep. Now what about that cup of tea?"

"Actually, no thanks, Gramps. I'm going to try calling Charlotte again."

"Fine, but before you go, Max, I was just saying to Morag that this kitchen is the only room in the house with water at the moment, so you can bath the baby in this sink."

"I'll not bathe a charge of mine in a sink, Mr Archdale."

"Rubbish, it's perfectly adequate," said Thomas, patting the sink. "The only pity is that we adults are too big to fit in ourselves.

Chapter twenty-five

Peering over the stable half-door, Tess's heart pounded as she watched Max circling the cobblestone yard, speaking into the phone and looking pensive. He was unmistakable – as tall as his father, and every inch as handsome.

Tess looked at her hands, so lined and worn – old before their time. Why did her heart seem to continually feel like a horse's lip being twisted while having its mane pulled?

Tess didn't want the children to see her, not now. She ran around to the front of the house, passing mossy-edged pots filled with strong stems and beautiful blue heads of agapanthus, which she had carefully planned to flower from spring to autumn. Her breath tightened like a dishcloth being wrung out for every last drop as she reached the steps to the front door and pushed it open with her shoulder. She kicked off her wellies. Her socks had slipped, making her heels red and sore. She pulled the socks back into position and threw her jacket across a basket filled with tennis rackets and croquet mallets. She needed to sit and think, just for a moment, and then she'd get away. Tess looked up at the gallery above the hall, where she and Julia used to play with their dolls.

"There you are," said a voice behind her as she tiptoed into the yellow drawing room.

"Dad?".

"I went out to look for you and found one of your gardening gloves on the gravel out there."

Tess, her freckled face pale against her chestnut hair which was piled up with a fringe covering her eyebrows, stood by the fireplace for a moment and then pulled a gardening book from a pile beneath the coffee table.

"I realise I should have warned you," said Thomas, picking up a log from a basket by the sofa and throwing it on the fire. "I barely had time to think, Tess, and I said yes so instinctively. I really had no choice. They're all over the place, Tess. Really, I don't think they have anywhere else to go."

Tess sat down on the sofa, while her father sat in the armchair opposite her.

"You promised they'd never come here," she said, "not while I was around."

"Actually, that was your sister's promise on the day Odette died. Julia swore the children would never return, but they have minds of their own now."

Tess tried to say something but all that came out were slow wheezing tears from the back of her throat, which she quickly silenced by clasping her hands over her mouth.

"I honestly think coming here must have been their only option," said Thomas, interlocking his fingers, "which shows their relationship with Julia must be in some kind of crisis."

Tess looked at the muddy patch on the knee of her dungarees. Maybe she'd call Freddie and stay at Farley Hall for the time being, but then Freddie would fuss and want to look after her. Tess didn't want that. She didn't want anyone to look after her.

"Why don't you sit down properly, Tess. The arm of the sofa is wobbly enough without you sitting on it, not that you weigh much these days."

"I'm going to the lodge," she said, standing up and pushing her hands into her back, "and I don't want anyone coming to my house, or to the walled garden."

"Tess, you look worn out," said Thomas. "The garden is just too much for you."

"It's the only place I can bloody well find peace," she snapped, "and even then I can still hear Anika's bellowing voice trailing across the lawn."

"Yes, but –"

"And by the time I've finished with the garden, it'll take care of itself. I'm taking out anything that needs to be managed. As for the wild meadow, all you'll need to do is mow a few paths and it will look perfectly presentable."

"As if I give a damn about presentable," said Thomas. "How about a drink?"

"You know I don't drink anymore," said Tess, pressing her red, swollen hands against her face.

"I suppose I'll keep asking though, just in case you change your mind."

Tess walked to the door. "And how do you expect to cope with guests in the house and no water?" she said.

"I have a plan to fix the water problem," said Thomas.

"Oh really? And what about that massive leak in the top floor? You have a solution for that as well? As for the wiring, how many times do I have to tell you how much of a fire hazard this place is?"

"My grandchildren have come to me because they need my help," said Thomas calmly.

"What sort of help?"

"Max is the father of a baby. A little girl, six months old, whom he has brought to Bellamore while the baby's mother is otherwise occupied in England."

"A baby girl," said Tess quietly.

"Yes, a very sweet little thing too. Smiley and rosy-cheeked, just as they should be. They call her Fleur."

Tess inhaled deeply. "So why is her mother not here?" she said, getting worked up again.

"The mother's name is Charlotte and all I know is that she has some sort of family business to attend to. Before you say anything, they're very organised and they have brought a nanny with them, though a rather dour one, I might add."

"Then this emphasises my point even more," said Tess. "The house is far too damp for a baby."

"We have ten bedrooms, Tess. I think we can find one bedroom that will be suitably dry for a baby, don't you?"

"Well, don't expect me to get involved."

"No one expects you to," said Thomas, "and if I can find a way to straighten out the quandary my grandchildren find themselves in, I will do so. Allow me that, will you, please?"

Chapter twenty-six

Elodie lay back on a four-poster bed with her arms stretched out, the air so cold she could blow rings with her breath. Even having slept for fifteen hours straight, her shoulders still felt tense. Her iPhone mercifully had good reception in her bedroom and Sam had sent supportive messages, urging her to make peace with her mother as soon as possible and return to London. Easier said than done. Most uplifting was an email from Luke, wondering why she hadn't called and that he had hoped he hadn't blown it by trying to kiss her.

Being with Luke already seemed like a lifetime ago, since when she had acquired a niece, watched her brother fall to pieces and had flown several hundred miles to stay with a grandfather she had not seen since she was a teenager. Wearing a thick polo neck over her pyjamas, Elodie watched the tassels swinging like pendulums across the lining of the canopy above her, just as she had done when she was little, except now she could touch the quilted rose in the centre of the fabric with her toes. This was the bedroom Elodie had always slept in during her visits to Bellamore and she could almost catch the faint scent of her grandmother's perfume.

Jumping off the bed and onto creaking floorboards, she opened the shutters to behold the morning. A blue tit clinging onto the window ledge fluttered its wings in surprise and flew off to a branch on the laburnum. Seeing the mist rise over the drumlins, each hill rolling into the next like a patchwork quilt of green and brown, Elodie realised how much she had missed the view. Feeling her tummy rumble, she a flashback to Odette's breakfast tray, which Gramps had religiously brought to her bedroom every morning. A silver pot of coffee, another silver pot containing hot water, a silver milk jug, a linen napkin, a tiny butter dish, and a china plate with a single croissant, a constant supply of which were kept in the freezer, delivered monthly by a French bakery. A taste of Paris, Odette called it. Elodie wondered if Gramps did the same for Anika and quickly wiped the image from her mind.

In the adjoining bathroom, she thought longingly of a hot bath in the deep copper tub but turning the hot tap produced nothing more than a breathy hiss followed by a glug; as Gramps had warned, there wasn't a drop. Elodie noticed the ceiling was stained brown, and one of the glass panes in the sash window had cracked, letting in water and rotting the woodwork. It was all so different to when Odette was alive, the days of staff scurrying around with polish and fresh linen, when hot water flowed freely and towels were fluffy. The days when Odette would sit in a winged armchair like a throne, with a Tom Collins in one hand and a long crème cigar in the other.

Elodie scraped back her hair into a ponytail and, braving the cold, quickly tore off her pyjama bottoms, pulled on a pair of black skinny jeans and then a thick jumper over her pyjama top and polo neck – it was too freezing to do a complete change. With her clutch bag in hand, she walked to the landing and could hear Fleur crying from the top floor. As awful as Morag was, thank god for her as it would otherwise have been Elodie trying to comfort her niece. The stairwell landing, once lined with first editions on mahogany shelves, now had stacks of unwanted books as if awaiting a jumble sale.

Descending the staircase, Elodie could see outlines on the walls where several paintings had once hung, and in the hall a fan light above the front door poured light onto a sideboard which lay empty except for a stack of unopened letters and VHS tapes. It was as if a burglary had taken place.

Pulling back heavy velvet curtains from across the front door, she unlocked a large bolt and opening the door found the air outside to be curiously warmer than inside. She had forgotten the quirks of a country house, where windows frost up inside and out, and doors are kept closed, in the hope of keeping the heat in, or the cold out. Remembering Odette's yell if she left the front door open, Elodie pulled the door behind her and walked towards the yard, with her suede boots crunching into the gravel.

She stood beneath the bell tower and listened to her grandfather whistling in the middle of the yard. He wore a red cravat tucked inside an open-necked shirt, making him look like a cross between David Attenborough and Michael Caine.

"Morning, Gramps," said Elodie, as he pursed his lips and continued to whistle. "I forgot about this ritual."

Within moments of her moving next to him, a flock of squawking, feathery hens came flying around the corner and raced to a bucket of feed.

Jumping out of the way, Elodie landed in a thick carpet of mud.

"Gave you a fright, did they?" said Thomas, emptying the remains of the bucket between the hens. "Sorry about that."

"I'm more sorry about my suede boots," said Elodie. "I only bought them last week."

"Wellies, Elodie, you know that."

"I didn't exactly have time to pack them, did I?" she said, taking a box of cigarettes from her bag and offering one to him.

"No, thanks," he said. "Gave up since I last saw you. Too damned expensive."

Elodie nodded her head in agreement and lit up.

"I like the look of that hen over there," he said, pointing to a fat, red bird, "but I just can't bring myself to wring her neck."

"You are kidding? You'd actually eat one of your own hens?"

"Poulet au pot – nothing more delicious, though sometimes I like a good curry."

"No chance you'll catch Max, or me, joining you for homegrown chicken, and I can't imagine Morag would go for it either," said Elodie, checking her phone in case Luke had sent another email.

"I'd say that nanny won't touch anything unless it's been

stamped by HRH," said Thomas, walking towards the feed house. "Which leads me to ask, and without wanting to make you feel in any way unwelcome –"

"Yes?"

"Just how long are you lot thinking of staying?"

Luke had asked her the same question in his email, prompting her to think of the way he looked at her and to wonder why she hadn't kissed him back.

"Would you mind if we discuss this later, Gramps?"

"Fine," he said, kicking the base of the door with his welly boot and pushing it open, "though if you can give me a little inkling on the timeframe of your stay, it would be helpful."

He dropped the hen-feed bucket on top of a bag of grain.

"I thought you said we could discuss it another time?" said Elodie. "You know, my feet are still like ice-blocks, I'm surprised my hot-water bottle didn't freeze overnight."

"Try wearing a woolly hat in bed. Works a charm."

"No wonder Fleur was crying this morning – she probably has frostbite."

"Must you be so dramatic, Elodie? Let's get back to discussing the length of your visit, shall we?"

"Why do you need to know?" said Elodie, wondering if she'd have to come clean about being completely broke and potentially homeless if her mother really did give her the boot.

"A number of reasons," he said, pushing his glasses back onto the bridge of his nose, "including the fact that your Aunt Tess is rather under pressure with a garden project and doesn't like to be distracted."

"It's not as if we're going to have all-night raves," said Elodie defensively. "Besides, Tess lives at the bottom of the avenue."

"True, but she's just rather sensitive," said Thomas, reaching into his pocket, and producing a packet of Fox's Glacier Mints. "Like one?"

"No, thanks," said Elodie, holding up her cigarette.

"These mints replaced my morning puff."

"Clever," she said. "I might think about doing the same one day."

"My main concern, Elodie, relates to the fuse board. I'm not overly confident that it has the capacity for immersions being on for babies and so forth."

"I thought the immersion wasn't working?" said Elodie.

"But if it were, is what I mean. The same applies to the heating, which as you have pointed out, isn't working either."

"Yes," she said, making no effort to sound interested.

"It's a matter of oil, Elodie. Do you follow?" said Thomas, brushing hen food from his sleeve.

"Oil? Are you expecting some?" Elodie watched the hens frantically pecking up the pellets between the cobblestones and took a picture with her phone. "

"Well, I'm not sure – Elodie, you see, I haven't actually …"

"It's Sam," she said, waving her iPhone at him. "Sorry, Gramps, I'm going to take this call if you don't mind. It's my friend, and more recently, my boss, calling from London."

Chapter twenty-seven

Standing on the bank above the sunken garden, Thomas brushed his fingers along the snowdrops and studied the house. The wisteria, trailing, thin and leafless as it clung to the coarse rubble-rendered wall, framed the sash windows, many of which were in need of replacing – only a small number could be opened safely without the risk of a frame shattering to the ground. Also in view were several gaps in the roof where slates had blown off during winter storms, an open invitation for the wet to seep in and create further damp throughout the house.

"What are we to do?" he said to Bluebell, who flashed her white teeth, having chased a rabbit through the shrubbery. "How about starting with breakfast?"

Walking to the back garden, Thomas's heart was lightened by the sight of little birds filling their feathery bellies as they fed on peanuts from hanging feeders. Taking off his boots by the kitchen door, he could see Morag standing over a pan on the Aga and a regimental line of baby bottles and folds of muslin on the table.

"In good form today, are we, Morag?"

"Ample," she said.

"Any chance of a sausage?"

"No chance, Mr Archdale. I cook for Baby and I clean for Baby, exclusively," she said, tapping a spatula on the edge of the pan. "This morning I'm making purée for her."

"Fair enough," said Thomas, pulling out a chair and emptying his pockets onto the table before sitting down. "It was magnificence itself out there this morning," he said, flattening out scrunched-up pieces of paper with handwritten observations of the dawn chorus. "The blackbird led the chorus, followed by the thrush and then several chaffinches. The Albert Hall couldn't have put on a finer production."

"I could hear no birdsong from my room, Mr Archdale."

"I'm sure if you opened the shutters you would."

"I'm trying to keep the cold out, Mr Archdale. There's a howling gale coming through those windows."

"The old glass may be thin, Morag, but I think you'll find that it keeps any nasty bugs out."

"Speaking of mould, Mr Archdale, why are there pots of yogurt in the hot press?"

"That's my natural yogurt," said Thomas. "It's the perfect temperature for the bacteria to grow."

"That would never be allowed in a well-run household – most unhygienic."

"Nonsense," said Thomas as Bluebell leapt up from her beanbag with the arrival of a very flushed, moonfaced man through the door. "The bacteria is desperately healthy and that's why I'm fit as a snipe, isn't that right, Harry?"

"Wish I could say the same," said Harry Rose, a longstanding neighbour from Farley Hall, slapping a brace of ducks down on the table to Morag's horror. "Damned hangover after last night."

"A late one, was it?" said Thomas.

"The Rangers," said Harry, lifting the Aga kettle from the hotplate to the hob. "Still wild – age doesn't seem to make a blind bit of difference. Speeches didn't happen until after midnight, by which time half the chaps had passed out. However," he said, turning to Morag, "as Evelyn Waugh said, *'punctuality is a virtue of the bored'*."

"Is that right?" said Morag, unamused.

"Harry Rose," he said, offering his hand to her.

"Morag is nanny to my great-granddaughter, would you believe?" said Thomas, seeing that a handshake was not forthcoming from Morag. "Nanny training camp's best."

"Hello, Nanny Morag," said Harry, patting her arm instead. "I must say you don't look much like my old nanny. She had grey hair and wore a lot of lace, though not the kind I'm fond of, if you follow?"

"Tell me, Morag," said Thomas, "must you wear that brown uniform all the time?"

"It prevents a nanny from being mistaken for a housemaid," said Morag, staring at Harry until he moved away from the Aga.

"Rather old-fashioned, isn't it?" said Harry.

"On the contrary," she said. "Our turnout reflects our high standards, which are continuously reached in order to keep Baby happy."

"Speaking of high standards, you should meet our woofer," said Harry. "Pablo from Buenos Aires, who has taught Freddie how to make the most supreme mayonnaise, not that she'll let me eat it since my blasted heart attack last year."

"Funny you should say – I had thought about bringing in a team of woofers but I wasn't sure if I could afford to feed them. I hear they eat an awful lot," said Thomas.

"It's a rather double-edged sword for us," said Harry, "as we've ended up with a chef rather than handyman. He'll whip up a soufflé, but he has no idea about mending a fence, a fuse or painting a wall." He peered over Morag's shoulder as she poured the apple purée into small Tupperware pots. "What do you do in the evenings, Morag? Box sets, I suppose? That's what all the young seem to do these days." He went back to his tea-making, piling several tea bags into a teapot.

"Easy on the tea, Harry," said Thomas. "Can't we just use one bag?"

"How about we add a drop of whiskey into the pot, Thomas?" said Harry.

"No chance," said Thomas. "Besides, aren't you supposed to be off whiskey?"

"I don't usually make tea," said Harry, looking to Morag.

"Perhaps you might step in?"

"No, indeed," said Morag.

"Scottish, are you?" said Harry.

"Aberdeen," she said.

"Like a drop of whiskey, do you?" said Harry.

"Never touch it," said Morag, tightening the apron string around her waist.

"Very wise," said Harry. "Yesterday morning I used the breathalyser, which I keep in my glove compartment. I was all set to collect a trailer of compost for Freddie's border and the blasted thing told me I was over the limit."

"So what did you do?" said Morag.

"Well, I couldn't go anywhere, could I? And have to put up with Freddie telling me that I need to stop drinking by at least 11pm?"

"'*He who hoots with the owl at night, cannot soar with the eagle by day*'," said Morag.

"What else do you learn at the nanny training camp?" said Harry, getting bored. "Doesn't sound like much fun so far."

"Advanced driving skills," said Morag, her eyes brightening, "in case we need to drive away from chasing paparazzi and take corners at speed in the rain."

"Really?" said Thomas. "Is there really much call for racing away from photographers?"

"Not yet," said Morag, who looked like she was almost salivating at the thought of it, "but I'm hoping my next placement will be with an A-lister."

"Is that right?" said Harry, staring at Morag's bottom as she loaded several ramekins in the dishwasher.

"That's my goal," she said, "to travel the world with celebrity families."

"Can't say you've landed in the right spot here, I'm afraid, Morag," said Thomas.

"Mr Archdale, as you know, this role was meant to be based in Somerset," said Morag, turning to Harry, "where I lived at the residence of Lord and Lady Broadbent."

"Grow broad beans, do they? The Broadbents?" said Harry, trying to see if it was possible to make Morag laugh.

"Somerset is home to more celebrities per acre than anywhere outside London," said Morag, taking off her apron. "And speaking of nanny training camp, we also learned Taekwondo."

"Tae-*whatdo*?" said Thomas.

"In case I need to protect my young charges. You know, I can do several high kicks while pushing a pram," said Morag proudly.

"A rare skill, surely?" said Harry.

"I came top in my class," said Morag proudly.

"Well, it all sounds more James Bond than Supernanny," said Harry.

"I like to think so," said Morag, picking up the pile of muslin. "Now, if you'll excuse me, Mr Archdale and Mr Rose, I must attend to Baby," and walking out the door, she sneered at Augusta the parrot who wolf-whistled as she passed by.

Chapter twenty-eight

Somerset

Opening one eye, while sitting cross-legged in a circle of seven other women, Charlotte Wentworth spotted a woman in a fur-lined Barbour, headscarf and tortoiseshell sunglasses peering uncertainly into the yurt. She realised it was Petra's mum, Christabel Broadbent.

"Now, girls, I want you to inwardly say hello to your womb and wait for a reply," said the spiritual practitioner, who led the Womb Wisdom Circle as the chiming chillout music played in the background.

"Sorry to disturb you, girls, but I need a word with Charlotte," said Christabel and everyone's eyes opened.

"Mum, do you have to?" moaned Petra, wearing what looked like a hessian sack tied onto her head. "We're just about to make a deep inward connection and Charlotte's just beginning to get the hang of it now that the baby isn't here."

"Charlotte is going to be in deep something else if I don't speak with her," said Christabel.

Standing up, Charlotte tried to look as apologetic as possible as she made a Sun Salutation. Hiking up her long green skirt, she stepped across the thick seagrass carpet to face the formidable Christabel who directed her to follow her out of the large yurt.

127

Once outside, Christabel removed her sunglasses and fixed her eyes on Charlotte.

"Now, Charlotte, you know how open-minded I am about you all. And, for that matter, you know how long it took me to get Petra's father to agree to setting up this commune."

"Yes, Christabel, for which I am eternally grateful. Truly I am. As the sun rises, so does my heart."

"Charlotte, with respect, please spare me the hippy rhetoric. We've got rather more important fish than a rising sun on our plate."

Standing next to a fire-pit, Christabel pulled up the collar of her Barbour.

"I've had your mother on the phone."

"Oh."

"*Oh* is right, Charlotte," said Christabel, tut-tutting as she looked at a barbeque parked next to a large, silver campervan. "I thought you lot were meant to be vegetarian? How did Nigel's barbeque get down here? He'll go spare. You know how my husband likes his outdoor dining, even when it's freezing outside."

"I think Petra ordered a delivery from Goslings," said Charlotte.

"What? Goslings is far and away the most expensive health-food shop in Somerset, and no doubt it's the only place that deals with utterly organic beef."

"Yes," said Charlotte, smiling, "and it was very tender. Felix and Clementine made the most delicious horseradish to go with it."

"I am not overly interested in your attempts to recreate *MasterChef* in a *Bear Grylls* setting," said Christabel, as a silky Labrador flew down the steps of the silver streamlined motorhome, followed by a man sporting a beard and a man bun.

"Fancy a brownie, Christabel?" enquired Otto. "Raw chocolate, avocado, flourless and guilt-free."

"You do know my weak spot, don't you, Otto?" said Christabel.

"Every time, Christabel, and while I think of it I've a smashing new oven you're welcome to try out?"

"I'll stick with my Aga, but thank you. I take it that shiny camper van of yours was paid for by your trust fund too?"

"No need to be unmellow, beautiful lady. I like to think of that shining beauty as a gift from the lunar eclipse. My parents are cool with it. They are, as it happens, so in tune with my chosen direction that they're presently enjoying some time on a retreat of their own in California. I'm inclined to think the experience will really make them grow."

"Extraordinary. So, they clearly don't mind that your expensive education has been put to such little use?"

Otto suddenly knelt down on a Moroccan rug, crossed his legs and began to hum.

"What's this?" said Christabel, looking to Charlotte.

"I think it's his safe place," said Charlotte. "When Otto feels challenged, he meditates on the spot."

"Yes, well, I think these silk-lined commune days may be numbered. The hippies of my youth would turn in their graves to see the way you lot pamper yourselves."

As Christabel's voice rose, so too did Otto's humming.

"It's all yoga poses at sunset these days, isn't it?" said Christabel, setting off along a gravel path that led away from the edge of the woods towards the main house, with Charlotte trailing behind her.

"It might give the impression of a sustainable lifestyle but, when you return to the real world, I think you'll find this neo-hippy baloney really isn't what it's cracked up to be. Petra claims to be a vegan and yet she can't stop herself tucking into all sorts of delicatessen indulgences, including meat. Not only do they have luxury Portaloos, but they have even, I gather, hired Mrs Williams and her daughter to clean them."

"How does Mum know I'm here?" said Charlotte.

"You were spotted out shopping last weekend by a grandson of our church warden's sister, and our church warden, needless to say, is a friend of your papa's."

"We thought we'd try out some light-box therapy in the new spa that's just opened up," said Charlotte, sweeping up her blonde curls and twisting the locks into a topknot with a faux-fur hair-tie.

"You'll need a lot more than special light when you explain to your parents that you are not with your baby in Ireland. Why did you tell them you were going there, when instead you came back here?"

"I desperately needed time to myself, Christabel, truly I did."

"But surely the nanny gave you time to yourself when you were here? The whole point of keeping Morag on for another month was to teach you how to look after Fleur, not to come back here and connect with your womb."

"I just seem to keep doing the wrong thing, don't I?" said Charlotte, bursting into tears. "I miss Fleur so much, my little baby, and Max too. I miss them both, I can't tell you how much I miss them."

"Alright then, Charlotte, you miss them and so *go to them*," said Christabel. "Fleur is at a crucial age. She needs your love, Charlotte. No nanny can provide the love that you can give to your daughter. Then in due course you can get back on your feet and make the most of your gardening skills. You really have worked wonders on my Azaleas since you've been here."

"Really?"

"Really. Now, I suggest you prepare to say farewell to Petra and depart over the next day or two. Much as we've enjoyed having you, Charlotte, I want to focus on my garden, not on the comings and goings of my daughter's entourage."

"You have been truly wonderful," said Charlotte, who was now beginning to feel emotional at the thought of having to leave the security blanket Petra's family had provided.

"Whether I remain wonderful or not rather depends on how I fare when your mother waves that whisk of hers in my direction. Can you pay for your own ferry to Ireland?"

"I've got my post-office savings," said Charlotte. "Dad always instilled the rainy-day fund into me."

"Unlike Petra," said Christabel, standing next to one of the stone lions flanking the steps to the house. "However, I can't see her lasting much longer at the commune either. I think you'll find that your friend will reclaim her flat in Bristol – and her well-paid estate agency job – before you can say lamb curry."

"Thank you, Christabel."

"And do try to avoid the grass verge when leaving this time, will you, Charlotte? I honestly can't see how you ever managed to pass a driving test."

Chapter twenty-nine

Bellamore

"*Gramps?*" shouted Elodie from the back kitchen. "*Is there another fridge? This one is almost empty except for jars of chutney and half a roast pheasant.*"

"*What's that?*" said Thomas, taking a lamb bone out of parchment paper and giving it to Bluebell.

"*Would you have any mozzarella?*" said Elodie, with her head stuck in the fridge. "*And what about prosciutto? I'd love to put some on toast.*"

"You'll find butter in the dish by the bread bin," said Thomas.

"*But where is the other fridge?*"

"What other fridge, Elodie? And please don't shout. Come in here and speak to me rather than yelling, would you?"

"Sorry," said Elodie, coming into the kitchen. "Where is the other fridge?"

"There is only is one fridge," he said, rubbing Bluebell's ears as she chewed on the bone. "The butcher in Drummare sent a little treat over for Bluebell. Good to be free of those blasted terriers for the day, isn't it, girl?"

Elodie watched the dog chewing and felt put out. "Gramps, what about meat for us? The fridge out there is practically empty, except for milk and some funny-looking houmous."

131

"Beetroot houmous – beets grown by Tess and very good for Vitamin C."

"But about all the normal things you'd find in a fridge? Cheese or chutney. There isn't even any yogurt."

"Now yogurt we do have, except it's in the hot press."

"What?" said Elodie.

"We try to grow as much produce as we can in the Tess's polytunnel, and I make bread. Also, you'll find jars of pickled courgette and cucumber in the pantry – most delicious, and elderflower cordiale in the cellar."

"And meat?" persisted Elodie, sitting up on the Aga hotplate.

"Harry Rose, a neighbour, dropped over a brace of duck earlier. He's in terrific form, really has got his mojo back since the heart attack. I told him he can graze Penthouse in one of our fields, but he seems to love having him stabled at home."

"Penthouse?"

"His hunter. A huge animal, very beautiful and always hungry."

"Speaking of which, would you have any crisps?" said Elodie, trying again.

"You'll find potatoes in the back kitchen," he said. "Come to think of it, could you peel a dozen spuds for supper tonight?"

Elodie looked at her nails. "Sorry, Gramps, my hands are very sensitive to any sort of dirt. We always have pre-peeled potatoes at home. Why don't we eat bulgur wheat instead?"

"You are not in London now, Elodie. No wonder you and your brother are so thin," said Thomas, walking into the back kitchen and returning with a bowl of muddy potatoes.

"Now roll up the sleeves of your jumper and you can make a start on these."

"And what exactly am I supposed to do?" she said.

"Wash the mud off them in the sink – though use cold water. I want to save the hot water for Fleur's bath."

The afternoon sun streamed through the yew walk as Elodie strolled along a path, smoking a cigarette. She and Max used to run up and down the yew walk as children, Elodie dressed in Valerie Goad smock dresses and Max in corduroy shorts and Peter-Pancollared shirts. Odette had created model grandchildren and how disappointed she would be now, thought Elodie. She was like the single line of poetry she could remember from school, '*I wandered lonely as a cloud*', except unlike a cloud she had no freedom. She thought of Luke and what he had said in his recent email, about where he wanted to take her in London and how ambitious he was feeling for the future. She had added his number to her mobile and decided to bite the bullet and phone him.

"Luke?" she said.

"Elodie? How are you?" he said, his enthusiasm belting down the phone. "It's so good to hear from you. You got my emails?"

"Yes," she said, "and I'll reply, once I get a chance to."

"As you hadn't called and I didn't have your number, I figured I'd take a punt and bombard you with emails."

"I liked them," she said, feeling better on hearing his voice.

"And how are you?"

"So, so," she said, checked her bag to count how many cigarettes she had to keep her going for the next couple of days.

"Lying low?"

"You could say that," she responded, realising he didn't even know where she was.

"Cool. I've just had lunch with my father and, before you ask, I didn't mention your name."

"Ha! He wouldn't remember my name anyway, though maybe he will recall the girl who sent his smart client to the slums for a business meeting."

"He's got a sense of humour, really he has, but no, right now he's determined that I'm going to work for him and I've got exactly fifteen weeks left of my personal sabbatical, and then crunch time." His voice sounded so confident and straightforward. "I had a coffee at Sam's Kitchen this morning."

"So I heard – Sam called me this morning and said she'd seen you."

"As lovely as Sam is, the coffee didn't taste quite as good as when you made it."

"I doubt that."

"Seriously though, I want to see you – can I take you out for dinner tonight?"

Elodie saw the walled garden up ahead of her. "You know, I'd really love that," she said, lighting a cigarette, "especially as I'm bloody well hungry."

"Don't they have takeaway in Notting Hill? Or have you been detoxing?"

"Not exactly," she said. "The thing is, Luke, I'm actually in Ireland."

Chapter thirty

Standing on an upturned bucket, Tess hoisted up a branch of the fig tree with a pitchfork but it kept slipping when she got close to pegging it onto the hook. The tree had been espaliered against the garden wall, but the majority of it had come down during the winter storms. Her lack of energy was frustrating and, as she pushed the fork up once more, she knew her strength wasn't what it used to be.

Hearing a voice calling, Tess looked toward the archway of apple trees framing the entrance. "Damn it!" she said, then her foot slipped and the bucket flipped over.

"Aunt Tess?" said Elodie, sauntering through the archway, waving with cigarette in hand. "I thought I'd come and say hello."

Tess stood for a moment, then taking off her gardening gloves she put them into her pocket.

"I guess you know who I am?" said Elodie, looking like she was waiting for some kind of air kiss. "Julia's daughter –"

"I know who you are," said Tess. Picking up the pitchfork and stepping back onto the bucket, she tried again to lift the fig-branch upwards. "I left instructions at the house that I wasn't to be disturbed."

"Yes, I know," said Elodie, stubbing out her cigarette on the ground, "but I figured, as we are here, it would be crazy not to at least *meet* you."

Tess continued to fuss over the branch, pulling it one way, pushing it the other. As it collapsed for the third time, she stood down from the bucket and rested the fork against the rotting wooden bench.

"I take you're going to pick up that cigarette butt?" said Tess.

"Yes," said Elodie. Taking a leaf from the tree and wrapping it around the butt, she put it into her pocket.

Tess could see the extravagant mouth and the delicate jawline of Douglas in Elodie's face.

"Aunt Tess –"

"Please. Don't call me aunt."

"Okay, *Tess* then. Whatever you like."

Tess looked at the overgrown laurels sloping against the dilapidated glasshouse, the shrubs so unkempt, and the profusion of roses, brown and spindly in need of pruning. She felt cornered by Elodie and wanted to get away.

"This fig tree can wait for another day," she said and, picking up the pitchfork, she walked across the garden towards the shed.

"You look quite like Mum," said Elodie.

"Do I?" said Tess, trying to hold her patience.

"Just smaller," said Elodie, "and prettier."

Tess was determined not to engage.

"When did you return to Bellamore?" said Elodie, following her like a shadow. "Max and I had no idea you'd be here."

The paint on the shed door was peeling off and the handle had completely rusted over. Tess opened it and put the pitchfork inside.

"Elodie, if you'll excuse me, I've got things to do," she said, not making eye contact.

"Just one thing, Tess. I need to ask …"

Tess could feel her face stiffen.

"Can you tell me the reason Max and I were banned from coming here?"

"What?" said Tess, focusing on a mossy rock and wishing she could sink into its crevice. "I don't know."

"You know that Mum literally never mentions you?"

136

"Elodie," said Tess, closing her eyes, "I am actually at a loss as to how to respond – it's like being laid into by a lawyer."

"I'm sorry," said Elodie, "I didn't mean to –"

"To what? To ask me insolent questions? And how ironic that you should be standing next to an apple tree."

"Sorry?" said Elodie, reaching out for a branch.

"Because the apple never falls far from the tree, does it?"

Elodie paused for a moment and then seemed to grasp what Tess meant.

"You mean my mother? I'm not like her. How can you say that? You don't even know me." She took a cigarette and her lighter from her bag. The lighter didn't work the first time, but after a couple of sparks the flame held and she inhaled deeply. "I should have listened to Gramps and stayed out of the garden."

She walked away.

The guilt Tess lived with had always resulted in silence. Friends, boyfriends, she couldn't hold on to anyone. Closing the shed door, she could hear a buzzard shrieking in the distance, searching for food to feed its young. She sometimes wished that she could be a buzzard, and if it wasn't possible in this life, then maybe in the next one.

Chapter thirty-one

Elodie sat on the pink-velvet armchair in her bathroom, reading another email from Luke. He was very open about his feelings and really seemed to wanted to dive into her heart with both feet. He said that he couldn't stop thinking about her and how he could imagine her painting in a studio, and how he'd love to live in the countryside one day, live in a big house with a yard and he could convert the outbuildings into an art studio and gallery for her. It was amazing to read and yet unbelievably confident, which made her feel slightly terrified and excited in equal measures. He seemed generous and kind, and gentle, and the touch of his lips ... she could remember the touch, his breath, his scent.

Then her mind returned to Tess, and she decided not to let herself get upset about what she had said, or just how incredibly unfriendly she was. Instead she let herself get cross and uptight, feeling hemmed in and panicky, knowing she had no means to leave Bellamore. Not that she entirely wanted to leave, because a huge part of her felt relief to be back, especially with Gramps. Resting her legs on the edge of the bath, she began scrolling through a Facebook group on her phone for 'out of work artists' with links to placements in schools and colleges, painting theatre sets and making signs for events. There must be some way she could earn money without having to resort to sitting at a desk and shuffling a mouse in front of a desktop all day. Besides, temping for Giles Hampton for a day had put her off office work for life.

"*El?*" said Max, calling from her bedroom door. "*You up here?*"

"*I'm here – in the bathroom.*"

"What's up?" he said as he came in the door. "I've been looking for you.

"Nothing," she said.

"It doesn't look like nothing. You look like you're in a proper grump. Haven't you heard from lover boy in London?"

"Luke is actually my friend and, yes, he's just sent another lovely email, really sweet actually."

Max sat on the edge of the bath as Elodie tightened her cardigan around her. "So what's the grumpy face for?"

"I went to find Tess in the walled garden earlier."

"I thought Gramps said she was off limits?"

"I know, but I wanted to at least meet her. She's our aunt, isn't she? Surely we have a right to meet her?"

"So, what's she like?" said Max. "I saw her in the yard the first day we arrived. She was like a mini-version of Mum, you know, same type but just smaller."

"That's what I said to her, but it didn't seem to go down very well."

"People don't like comparisons, do they?"

"She doesn't wear make-up for starters," said Elodie, "and she has chestnut hair. She's much prettier than Mum – she didn't like me saying that either."

"I guess as she's a gardener she's bound to be natural."

"Naturally rude. No, actually, she was quite mean."

"What did you say to get her back up?"

"Why do you presume that I said something?"

"Alright, keep your hair on."

"All I did was ask her why we were banned from coming here."

"I don't know, El. Mum obviously had some kind of breakdown when Odette died, and I guess she had a barney with the family. Gramps and Tess. There's only two of them – not exactly difficult to fall out with two members of a family."

"I don't know what it is about this year," said Elodie. "I keep going over things, over and over, wondering how different things would be if Dad were here."

"Let's just hang out with Thomas while we're here, and try to look forward. Honestly, El, we've got to find fish to fry if we're going to get out of this mess."

"I've been job-hunting," she said, getting to her feet and pushing her phone into her back pocket.

"Which is exactly what I need to do," said Max, getting onto his knees and looking into the cupboard beneath the sink. "One sec."

Lying down on his back, he began to twist something.

"I'm trying to find out which pipes are linked to the main water system," he said. "I can't seem to find any pattern at all."

"Max?" said Elodie. "Since we've been here, I've noticed your interest in the water system."

"Of course I'm interested. Because we all need a bath and Morag is on about it on the hour, every hour."

"But where did you learn it?"

"Learn what?"

"This DIY stuff."

"El," he said, getting up from the floor, "I haven't been exactly straight with you."

"What do you mean?"

"You know, in LA?"

"Yes, where you were working on film scores with Hollywood composers and flitting around with the glitterati?"

"Well, not exactly."

"What do you mean?"

"The guys I was supposed to be interning with turned out to be a complete cokehead."

"You're kidding? I thought he was a big cheese?"

"Yes, he was, having snorted his way into the movie business, but it seems by the time I got there he had managed to snort his way back out again."

"But he was an award-winning composer!"

"Yes, he was, about a decade ago. No, the guy's off his head but I have to say, he has the most incredible secretary who set up the internship."

"Yes, which you paid for."

"Exactly, paying for his habit."

"So what really happened?"

"In a nutshell? I landed in LA and he wanted to party. He saw me as his summer sidekick, and had no interest in introducing me to anyone other than his dealers."

"And what did you do?"

"It's sounds random, but a plumber came round to take a look at the pump of the pool, and I got talking to him and, well, he's like the plumber to the stars."

"What? A celebrity plumber?"

"He is a plumber to celebrities, yes."

"So you're telling me that a plumber took you under his wing? God, if Mum knew this!"

"Anyway, the plumber and I got talking and he did the usual, said that I sound like someone from *Downton Abbey*. Next thing I know he hands me a wrench and asks me if I wouldn't mind holding onto one end of some kind of water-heating system. Turns out this guy is earning big bucks, I mean serious cash for the most simple of jobs."

"So you're telling me while you were in Hollywood, you were actually using those long elegant fingers of yours to fix celebrity bathtubs, rather than tinkle the ivories?"

"Bingo."

"You are in the double-merde with Mum, my friend, when she finds out."

"Tell me about it. I did manage to stash away some savings – how about that? And you know what, El, it feels so good to make my own money – one thing is for sure, I am going to bring Fleur up to be completely independent. I think our allowances have held us back."

"But what about your music? You are so good, Max."

"I think it's my hands that are good. Sure, I can play piano but, I have to tell you, maybe fixing things is an easier way to make a living than shooting for a star that I'm just not going to catch."

"I wish you could fix me," said Elodie.

Chapter thirty-two

Portland Road, London

Lorenzo stood at Julia's front door wearing a pale-pink tunic and Liberty-print shirt. "Welcome!" he said, greeting Charlotte's parents warmly. "Julia was happy to receive your suggestion of lunch and decided her home would make for a good location, no?"

Lorenzo watched as Mary, pushing Gerald ahead of her as they climbed the steps, balanced her shiny patent handbag on her arm.

"You must be Mary," said Lorenzo, kissing her on either cheek. "So youthful, no?"

"And you must be Italian," said Mary, blushing like a young girl. "I'm such a fan of the maraschino cherry."

"I'm actually Puerto Rican," said Lorenzo, and, turning to Gerald, he reached out his hand. "And you must be Gerald. You are very welcome."

Closing the front door behind them, Lorenzo took their coats and laid them on a chair in the hall.

"Julia will be down in a moment," he said. "She had Shakti Yoga this morning, so she's just cooling off."

"That sounds very exotic," said Mary, standing in front of a nude sculpture and nudging Gerald, "rather like this piece of art."

"Does the Hirst offend you, Mary?" said Lorenzo.

"Well, I couldn't quite say," she said. "He goes to a lot of trouble with the detail, doesn't he?"

"We watched a documentary about modern sculpture a few months ago, didn't we, Mary?" said Gerald, clutching a wine bottle wrapped in yellow tissue paper. "Fascinating to find out the inspiration behind these sorts of pieces."

"You are right," said Lorenzo. "These pieces aren't always what they seem, are they? That's what I say to my clients."

"Clients?" said Mary, as Lorenzo led the way to the kitchen.

"I'm a fashion consultant," said Lorenzo. "My clients come to me in search of a new look, and once they relax," he raised his arms as if he were conducting an orchestra, "they realise the true desires in their souls."

"I should take notes from you for my sermon on Sunday," said Gerald.

"I'm afraid I don't attend any church," said Lorenzo, "but I have respect for all choices."

"Pleased to hear it," said Gerald.

Lorenzo ushered Gerald and Mary along the corridor and into the kitchen.

"Perhaps we could start with a mint julep mocktail?" said Lorenzo, bringing a tray of glasses, filled with mint, to the table.

"A mocktail?" said Gerald.

"An alcohol-free cocktail?" said Lorenzo. "I prefer it that way, though of course I can add booze if you'd prefer?"

"Oh no, carry on," said Gerald. "In fact it sounds like the kind of drink I could serve at one of our church socials."

"This kitchen brings to mind an article I recently read about knocking down the wall between the kitchen and dining room," said Mary. "Open plan is very on trend, isn't that right, Gerald?"

"If you say so," said Gerald, who had swapped the bottle he was carrying for a copy of *Tatler* and was flicking through the pages as Julia strode into the room.

"Gerald and Mary, I presume," said Julia, stretching out her hand to greet them. "We were intrigued to receive your call."

Gerald quickly put down the magazine and, lifting up the bottle, he held it out to Julia.

"How kind," said Julia, taking the bottle and tearing off the paper, "but really, I wouldn't have bothered. I'm afraid we'd never drink this wine."

"Really?" said Mary, "I seem to remember from Charlotte that you liked red wine?"

"I do like red wine," said Julia.

"This bottle comes from the vestry," said Gerald, "and is proving to be rather popular with my regulars on a Sunday. In fact, since I brought in this label, I think numbers for Communion have risen."

"Is that right? You are kind," Julia said unconvincingly. "Lorenzo, Grey Goose with a twist, please. Mary, will you join me?"

"I was actually making a round of mint julep mocktails, Julia," said Lorenzo, trying to set the tone for a sober lunch.

"I wouldn't say no to a dry sherry," said Mary, "as we're in London."

"Splendid," said Julia. "There we are, Lorenzo, nobody wants your mocktails after all."

"I'd be partial to one of your mocktails," said Gerald enthusiastically.

"I do like the finish on your kitchen units," said Mary, "they look very –"

"Expensive," said Julia, who Lorenzo guessed may have poured herself a strong drink while getting changed.

"Shall we go through?" said Mary.

"Through?" said Julia. "Through to where exactly?"

"What a good idea!" said Lorenzo, who felt like a continual dousing blanket over Julia's flames. "Follow me."

Arriving into the lobster-red drawing room, Mary made a beeline for the striped sofa and rearranged the bow of her floral blouse once seated, while Julia sat by the bay window on an upright chair.

"I gather from your letter that you are keen to discuss your daughter with us," said Julia, "though why, quite frankly, I'm not sure. It's not as if we have met Charlotte that often."

"I do like to write letters, don't I, Gerald?" said Mary. " Royal Mail has always been a favourite of mine when it comes to communication."

"Indeed," said Julia. "As I was saying, Max has been in LA for the best part of a year and I gather the distance has enabled the children to embrace their different routes?"

"Different routes?" said Gerald.

"Yes," said Julia, flashing a white smile, "as Max and Charlotte are no longer an item."

"Oh lord, Gerald," said Mary, reaching out for his hand, "they don't know!"

"*They* don't know what exactly?" said Julia.

"They are more than an item," said Mary, taking a handkerchief out of her patent handbag.

"I'm sorry?" said Julia, looking at Lorenzo and leaning in Mary's direction. "Is there something in the sherry which has given you that peculiar look on your face?"

"They are in sin," said Mary, very quietly.

"In sin?" said Julia. "Speak up, would you? What are you talking about?"

"Fornication," said Mary in a whisper.

"Lorenzo, what is this woman saying?"

"Sex. That is what you are saying, isn't it, Mary?" said Lorenzo, thinking that Mary could do with chopping at least an inch off her hair.

"That's right," nodded Mary.

"Well," said Gerald, "there's a bit more to it than that."

"A baby," said Mary, pressing the handkerchief to her nose. "Out of wedlock. Our daughter Charlotte has produced a baby and Max is the father."

Julia stared at Mary.

"Of course we've had our challenges with Charlotte, she's always been one to go her own way – in fact she's been quite untruthful," said Mary, who began in sob into her handkerchief.

"She was meant to be in Ireland, you see," said Gerald. "Such a beautiful country."

"I'm sorry," said Julia, who looked quite stunned. "What has Ireland got to do with anything?"

"The baby," said Gerald. "The baby and Max, they're in Ireland, and our Charlotte had said she was going to join them –"

145

"But instead she only went back to Lord and Lady Broadbent's estate where their eldest has set up a hippy commune."

Julia rose from the armchair, pausing in a position somewhere between half-standing, half-sitting, trying to register what the Wentworths were implying.

"Where is Charlotte now?" she asked quietly.

"She's just left for Ireland," said Mary. "To join Max and the baby at their grandfather's place. And I gather your Elodie is there too, according to Lady Broadbent."

"*Whhhhatt?*" yelled Julia, and walking over to window, she drained her drink and passed the glass to Lorenzo. "Pour, Lorenzo, pour the damned vodka."

Julia looked at Gerald and Mary huddled together on the sofa. "I'll have you know that my children are in Cornwall staying with old school friends."

"I'm afraid you're quite mistaken," said Gerald.

Chapter thirty-three

"Shall I find the napkins?" said Mary, as they sat down for lunch.

"I was taught not to rely on napkins," said Julia. "Why should a napkin be necessary if one is a tidy eater?"

"Quite," said Mary, carefully forking up a mouthful of bulgur-wheat salad and salmon.

Julia took a small mouthful of fish and pushed her plate to one side then drank the remainder of wine in her glass.

"Now that we've let the dust settle, as you so wisely suggested, Gerald," said Lorenzo, "may I ask if –"

"I'll handle this, Lorenzo," said Julia, cutting in. "You have come to inform us that Max has fathered a child?"

"Yes," said Gerald, rubbing his eyebrows, "that about sums it up, and if it's of any consolation to you during your hour of need, Julia, we also have yet to meet the baby."

Julia couldn't decide what she was more upset about. The fact that Max had defied her wishes by returning to Bellamore, or that Max had fathered a child related to Gerald and Mary.

"And who is to say that Max is actually the father of this baby?" said Julia, slamming her hand on the table.

"Our Charlotte doesn't sleep around, if that's what you're getting at," said Mary.

"That is exactly what I'm getting at," said Julia.

"If I may interject?" said Gerald.

"Please do," said Lorenzo, "and ladies, let's keep this civilised, shall we?"

"We have actually seen pictures of the baby, and there is no doubt of her likeness to your son Max."

"Well, until I see the DNA I demand the subject be changed immediately. I don't want to discuss this any further."

Lorenzo observed as Julia found refuge in her wineglass over lunch. It seemed that Square One kept returning no matter what he did for her.

"So, Gerald, how is life in the church?" he said, trying to salvage the situation with his fluent small talk.

"Funny you should ask," said Gerald. "I've got rather a problem at the moment."

"Oh?" said Lorenzo, looking down to admire his own slender ankles as he crossed his legs.

"Funeral crashers. An epidemic really. Friends of friends of friends, seem to be coming, even though no one knows the deceased. Families of the bereaved most likely wouldn't mind so much except that these days a proper spread is laid on for guests. One man even asked for a doggie bag last week."

"Extraordinary! These funerals must be entertaining, no?" said Lorenzo.

"Some of the sermons are frightfully good," said Gerald, "but I think we are going to have to start insisting on formal invitations to be issued for funerals."

"They'll be turning funerals into a royal wedding next," said Mary, "and of course I'm all on for feeding and watering Gerald's flock, but this really is taking the digestive."

"Mary Berry," said Julia.

"Sorry?" said Gerald.

"You are a dead ringer for Mary Berry," said Julia, holding out her empty wineglass to Lorenzo. "Down to the shade of your lipstick, you are a dead ringer for Mary Berry."

"You are too kind!" said Mary, looking delighted.

"Our daily, Nosy Carol, the children call her, watched the *Bake Off* in the early days, but now Nosy Carol's gone towards *The Genealogy Roadshow*."

"That's lovely, Julia," said Lorenzo, hoping that she would keep things polite.

"Carol's got the most enormous nose, so she wants to find out which side of the family she should blame," said Julia, making a strained attempt to laugh, but not managing it.

Lorenzo beamed a smile at Gerald and Mary, who looked baffled by Julia's train of thought.

"Of course, my mother had a very simple solution when it came to working out where one came from," said Julia.

"Fascinating," said Mary. "Do tell?"

"Those who are blue have no need for the loo?"

"Julia," said Lorenzo. "I really don't think – "

"What do you mean?" said Gerald, who looked genuinely interested.

"Well," said Julia, taking a huge sip of wine, "those of blue blood don't seem to have urgency when it comes to having a pee."

"How fascinating," said Gerald.

"Quite," said Mary, who Lorenzo observed looked like she might soon need the little girls' room.

"Thank you, Julia, for that interesting insight," said Lorenzo, "but you know we have no such sayings in Puerto Rico. The salsa, bomba and of course cha-cha – it's in our blood and I think that is surely the finest blood of all, no colours or class restrictions necessary."

"I might well add that to my sermon on Sunday," said Gerald.

After lunch they retired to the drawing room for coffee.

Julia was still clutching her wineglass and Mary stood up just as she tapped the rim of it and gave Lorenzo a wink, suggesting a refill.

"Would you mind if I pop to the ladies'?" said Mary, looking embarrassed.

"The little girls' room?" said Lorenzo.

"She means the loo," blurted Julia.

149

"Only to blow my nose – a tissue would do, but perhaps I could touch up my lipstick while I'm there," said Mary, as if to reassure them all that she did not need to pee.

"Take your time," said Julia. "Can't be helped, can it?"

Mary hurried off.

Some minutes passed as Julia began to nod off, slumped on the sofa.

Glancing at her, Lorenzo said, "I like your watch, Gerald."

"Thank you," said Gerald, putting his wrist out in front of him. "I do like to accessorise where possible."

"And is Mary alright in the bathroom? She has been quite a while."

"I suspect Mary is knitting a row or two on the loo."

"Knitting?"

"Oh yes, she always carries her needles with her in her day bag. She finds it's a huge release should tension ever mount."

"Yes, I see," said Lorenzo, watching Gerald's eyes closely. "You know, Gerald, you could really consider manscaping your brows."

"Do you really think so," said Gerald, leaning in.

"And what of these clothes you are wearing?" said Lorenzo.

"I must admit to feeling rather tired in these old slacks," said Gerald, "and as for this check shirt!"

"A little dated perhaps?"

"You know, Lorenzo, sometimes I come across magazines which fall out of the Sunday newspapers in the parishioners' community hall."

"Some of them are very fine to spot the latest trends," said Lorenzo.

"Yes, exactly," said Gerald, "and when I see some of the fashion catwalks, well, I find myself wondering why my clothes must be formulaic."

"Quite," said Lorenzo.

"The church has long supported intricate designs – just think of the great cathedrals of Europe."

"And the Renaissance painters, Michelangelo's Sistine Chapel," added Lorenzo.

"I see Cristian le Croix and Stella McCartney's designs as just as important," said Gerald, who was thrilled to be giving dressing up a theological perspective. "I've always been interested in the theology of fashion and I've always wanted to dress in a way that reflects my personality."

"Why shouldn't a priest be interested in Prada?" said Lorenzo

"That's exactly what I've always wondered," said Gerald. "You've really hit on something, you truly have. I'm certainly in awe of Diana von Furstenberg, I think she's got a gift from God."

"Ah yes," said Lorenzo, rubbing his sideburns.

"You know, Lorenzo, between you, me and the four walls, I once wore Mary's Marks & Spencer wool dress. It was so stretchy beneath my robes and I did feel very good, I must say."

"I see," said Lorenzo. "Perhaps you would like to make an appointment to come to my studio on Bond Street and I can talk you through next season's collections?"

"You know, Lorenzo, I am blessed to have a wife to choose my clothes – however, to get beyond M&S is one of my dreams."

"I see. So Mary is aware of your interest?"

"No – I do keep it under the carpet – or, to be precise, under my robes. Though I sometimes wonder if she suspects."

"Gerald, my friend," said Lorenzo, topping up his espresso as Mary returned from the loo, "you are looking at the man who can make your dreams come true. Personal shopping and styling is my speciality. I can take years off you – ten, maybe even twelve years. You won't know yourself."

"Discussing fashion, are we, Gerald?"

"Yes," said Lorenzo, moving on to inspect Mary's nails, "and if I may suggest without offence, Mary, you must remember that you are never fully dressed without a good manicure."

"I put my flower beds before my nails, I'm afraid," said Mary, "and gardening is so unforgiving to long nails, not to mention terribly unhygienic."

"Everything in life has two sides, neither of which are perfect," said Gerald, quietly, as Julia began snoring.

Chapter thirty-four

Bellamore

"Who keeps leaving the blasted lights on?" said Thomas, walking into the dining room and stepping over a puddle on the floorboards. "And more dog pee – those wretched dogs!" Finding an old copy of the *Irish Times* in the study, he pulled out a couple of sheets of paper and returned to lay them on the floor. He looked up at the dining-room table, once surrounded by a dozen regency mahogany dining chairs, now replaced by white plastic garden chairs. He had come so close to selling the table, but with the memory of Odette sitting at the head, so elegant, commanding conversation, the epitome of the perfect hostess, he couldn't bear to let it go.

He let his eyes wander to where a sideboard once shone with silver, to a display cabinet once filled with antique trophies and, looking up towards the bleak pattern of damp on the cornicing, which was increasing by the day, he could only see gloom. The dehumidifier, chugging away in the corner, seemed to do little else except run up the electricity bill.

"Nothing's ever easy, is it?" he said, looking up at a portrait of his ancestor, who wasn't famous enough for the painting to be worth anything.

"Gramps?" said Elodie from the hallway.

"I'm in here, Elodie – talking to myself – first sign of madness, isn't it?"

"Perhaps eccentricity," she said, as her phone bleeped in her bag, "but I don't think madness."

Luke had sent a text message with a picture of a gorgeous landscape painting.

Thinking of you in an Irish field X

"What else do you carry in that little bag of yours, Elodie? It seems to stick to you like a limpet."

"Ciggies, my phone and a pencil."

"A pencil?"

"In case I feel like sketching, and if I can't find paper, there's always something to sketch on – a magazine, envelope or a paper napkin."

"Your grandmother used to carry a pencil in her hair," he said, pulling out a couple of chairs from the table.

Elodie had intended on having a ciggy but thought she could wait a few minutes.

"I wish I'd got to know her as an adult," she said. "I don't feel I really managed to ever get on a one-to-one level with her."

"I don't think anyone did. I feel I only scratched the surface in what I learned from her during our time together."

"And would you do it all again?"

"Not all of it," he said, pressing the palms of his hands onto the table. "However, if I hadn't met Odette, then I wouldn't be sitting opposite you now, and that would be a terrible shame."

Elodie smiled and felt a wave of something across her chest, maybe over her heart, and it was a good feeling. "Thanks, Gramps."

"For what? I'm not exactly plying you with luxuries, now am I?"

"For having us here," she said.

He took a handkerchief from his pocket and wiped his nose. "These chairs are uncomfortable, aren't they?" he said, getting up. "Damned plastic furniture. If you're wondering where the majority of things in here have gone to, Elodie, we have a dreadful man locally, thirsty for money. He rubs his hands when he sees me arriving with a portrait or curio."

"What about the painting that was over the fireplace? When I was a child, I always imagined he was the real *Black Beauty.*"

"I'm afraid your *Black Beauty* went straight to the south of France with a dealer, which paid for a new water pump, though now I think the water was just too hard for it – terribly hard water up here. Full of lime."

Elodie was about to ask as to the whereabouts of the pair of yellow-striped wing chairs, which she and Max used to pretend were their thrones, but decided it was all too depressing.

"Blast it," said Thomas, trying to open the lid of a wooden Jacobean trunk in the corner of the room. "The lid of this trunk has a habit of getting stuck." Stepping back, he swung his leg forward and gave the base a good kick with his boot. "There we are," he said, opening the lid and letting it rest against the dado rail. "Dip your nose into that, Elodie – very old paper, can you smell it?"

"Musty?" said Elodie, getting onto her knees and leaning into the trunk.

"Now, have a rummage in there and try to find your grandmother's sketch pad."

Beneath yellowing newspaper and discoloured linen tablecloths, Elodie pulled out a burgundy leather-bound book.

"That's the one," said Thomas.

Sitting cross-legged on the floor, Elodie opened the book and found ink and pencil sketches, page after page, in a style startlingly similar to her own. There were sketches of Chateau Versailles, a woman pushing a bicycle along a lane, a row of tents at the foot of a mountain, market stalls, ice skating and two small children climbing a tree with Bellamore in the background.

"The children?" she said. "Meant to be Max and me?"

"Expect so. I found this book in Odette's chest of drawers shortly after she died. I hadn't seen it before and, in truth, I haven't looked through it too closely."

"It's extraordinary," said Elodie. "I had no idea that Odette sketched."

"She was very private, as you'll remember."

"And are there any other books?"

"There were – but she burnt them, one by one. As soon as a

book had been filled, it went into the fireplace, with only smouldering leather left in the ashes as evidence of her work."

Elodie continued to turn the pages, noticing how the sketches grew darker in theme. Bonfires and empty bottles, chairs lying on their sides, and a cot sailing down a river, like Moses in a basket.

She turned to him. "Gramps, why do you think she kept this book and didn't burn it like the others?"

"That, I am not sure of. But I've always kept it and, if you'd like, you can have it now."

Elodie got up from the floor and, looking out the tall sash window, she watched the trees as they swayed together like an audience during an anthem at a massive concert.

"And what about Tess – does she sketch?

"Not that I know of – though she may have done while she was away."

"How long was she actually away for?"

"For a long time, Elodie, too long. I gather from Max that you had a rather tricky meeting with her the other day?"

"You could say that. I think I asked too many questions."

"Try not to hold it against her if you can," he said. "She's had a time of it."

Elodie looked at a photograph of Odette, holding a croquet mallet in one hand and a long cigarette in the other. "After Odette died, how did you find Tess to let her know?"

"Your mother's godfather, Cecil Brooks, came to see me. There was no funeral, as you know, because she donated her body to medical science, but he still came. Good sort of person really."

"And he knew where Tess was?"

"Not at all – but he was ex-army, SAS in fact, and of course I was rather down about everything, wondering what to do with this old place. Cecil set about finding your aunt."

"How did he do it?"

"He still had the contacts, despite having had to take permanent leave from the forces, and who could have blamed him for having a breakdown after what he saw."

"What did he see?" Elodie felt like a war correspondent.

"Never mind – the point is he tracked down Tess for me and,

following an exchange of letters, she agreed to come home to Bellamore and help me out."

"And what about Cecil Brooks?"

"It all caught up with him in the end, sadly. Threw himself off a bridge in Hungary."

Elodie looked at him. "Like my father," she said, "except he did it with a gun."

"I'm sorry I mentioned it, Elodie. Stupid of me, bringing up that sort of conversation."

"Don't be. I just find it baffling how, even though I am getting older, my understanding doesn't seem to be getting any better."

"People are complicated, Elodie. And why people do things? Well, I'm just not sure if it's worth spending time trying to work it out."

"I never heard Mum mention her godfather," said Elodie.

"No reason why she would. I don't believe she ever met him, apart from when she was a baby at her own christening of course, and I think he was only chosen because Odette liked the look of him, plus he had a title. Viscount, I think. Or the one before that, Duke maybe, can't quite remember."

Chapter thirty-five

Though Thomas knew Elodie's meeting with Tess had been less than smooth, at least they had laid eyes on each other and, as he looked out the window, seeing Max standing in one spot, pushing Fleur back and forth in her pram, he decided Max needed to do the same.

It seemed that Bellamore had become a refuge for the lost.

Taking up a couple of finely embroidered cushions from the sofa, he headed out to the garden. The herbaceous border was coming into bloom, despite having been largely ignored, but luckily there were so many plants they had a habit of overtaking the weeds.

Espying a wheelbarrow beneath the oak tree, he tipped out bark left over from the last collection of logs and dropped in the cushions.

"Hello, Max," he said, pushing the wheelbarrow towards him.

"Hi there, Gramps, how are you?"

"Still standing, as you see. Where's Nanny?"

"Morag has gone into the village and so I thought I'd push Fleur around in the pram."

"Fair enough, though it doesn't look like much fun in there, does it?" He peered in at Fleur, lying back with a hood covering the sky view. "Why keep the hood up, and what about this netting – afraid she'll swallow a fly?"

"Morag said to keep her completely covered," said Max.

"Yes, but is she having any fun, Max? And more to the point, are you enjoying each other's company? She can't even see you properly through all of this paraphernalia, let alone see the sky."

"She's a baby, Gramps. I'm not sure we'll be having many longwinded conversations just yet."

"Small steps though, Max." He patted the cushions on the wheelbarrow. "Come on – there's little point in preserving these cushions in the house, let's put them to good use."

"What?"

"Time for a change of steed for your daughter. Lift her up, Max, and lie her onto the cushions."

"You want me to put Fleur in the wheelbarrow?"

"Precisely. I want to take this baby for a walk down the avenue, so that she can take in her surroundings properly. No need for hoods and suspension – what this young lady needs is a taste of the good life."

"But she'll need to be strapped in," said Max, concerned.

"Nonsense – she can nestle nicely in this lovely soft valley between the cushions, and the sides are plenty high."

Max took the netting from around the hood of the pram and, shrugging his shoulders, he reluctantly unstrapped Fleur and lifted her out as if she were a cat, holding her somewhere in the middle.

"Support the head, Max. Didn't that nanny teach you anything?"

"I have zero experience, Gramps – how am I supposed to know?"

"You are now a father, Max, and it's time to take responsibility. Come on, that's it, rest her down on the cushions."

Fleur gurgled and, beaming a huge smile, she squeezed her chubby little hands together.

"Lovely little thing, isn't she?" said Thomas. "Now, as you can see, the cushions are holding her in position, she looks wonderfully comfortable and she has a view of the world around her. Isn't that right, little Fleur? Who likes being caged up in straps and netting?"

Adjusting the cushions to make sure Fleur really was comfortable and secure, Max began to gingerly push the wheelbarrow across the lawn.

"After all, it's not as if you're going to plough through huge potholes, is it?" said Thomas. "We can amble down the avenue and Fleur can look up to the sky and see all those birds in flight. You can be proud of your little daughter, Max, and I have reason to think that you will make a very splendid father."

"Thanks for saying that, Gramps. I just hope Charlotte will feel the same."

"You really want things to work out between you, don't you?"

"Yes, I do."

"You know, it hits you right in the eyes when it's really right." Thomas put out his hand to Fleur, who clutched his finger as they walked. "Is that how you felt with Charlotte?"

"From the moment we met."

"Then you have every chance of making it work."

"And if we don't?"

"Let's not dwell on that scenario, Max."

Avoiding potholes as he pushed along, Max smiled down at Fleur.

"Always better to get out into the fresh air and think things through," said Thomas.

"I'm not sure walking is going to solve my problems," said Max. "Almost a year ago, I was on my way to Los Angeles to work alongside a composer on film scores, all of which resulted in my learning how to deal with a blocked U-bend."

"You've lost me."

"Really, it doesn't matter. The main thing is that now I have a family to support and I have no clue as to how I can progress with my career."

Thomas stopped by a fence post to inspect an insect. "Dragonfly or keeled skimmer?"

"Haven't got a notion," said Max, resting down the wheelbarrow.

"We'll say dragonfly," and looking at Max, Thomas took hold of his hands. "You see these?"

"What? My hands?"

"These are your trump card, Max. Your grandmother always said it. You played so beautifully, even as a twelve-year-old. I can remember the pieces you played for Odette, and the moment she'd leave the room you'd break into freehand jazz, no music sheets required."

"I think I'd make a better plumber," said Max.

"Really?"

"It's a safer bet, isn't it? Plumbers will always be in demand."

"But is it your dream, Max?"

"It's my reality."

"Well, if you insist, then I may have a project for you tomorrow involving a bath and, in the meantime, let's push on to the gate lodge."

Max glanced at him, thinking of Tess.

"You see that Giant Redwood over there?" said Thomas. "It was planted to commemorate the Battle of Waterloo. And you see that wall? Used to have a deep border in front of it to supply cut flowers to the house – and look at it now."

"Tough to keep these places going, isn't it?"

"Not always. When my great-uncle bought Bellamore, he had made a fortune and extended both the house and the gardens."

"He was ambitious, I guess."

"Yes, and like some fortunes he lost it all, and now Tess has a dream about wanting to continue the horticultural work here but it's becoming increasingly difficult for her to get a handle on it by herself. I've tried to tell her that she's on a hiding to nowhere, but of course she doesn't listen. She never has."

"She's like Mum then," said Max.

"In what sense?"

"Mum doesn't like being told what to do. I'm sure that's why she was pushed out from the gallery she's been a patron of. She won't accept that the directors run the show and that no matter how much cash she throws in their direction, it won't buy her an opinion."

"Julia has been unsettled for as long as I can remember."

"What is it with our family?"

"I think the suppression and formality of Odette must have been suffocating – those girls couldn't move an inch without being corrected."

"But it didn't stop Tess?"

"No, but nothing ever stopped Tess. She has always paddled her own canoe, no matter what the consequences."

"Are you sure this is a good idea?" said Max, seeing the redbrick lodge up ahead. "Tess wasn't exactly over the moon to see Elodie."

"I think it's necessary," said Gramps, "and she'll come round – like a chaffinch to a new feeder, they first need to be sure there are no threatening birds lurking overhead."

The lodge was so pretty, with its entrance at the top of a short flight of steps and a portico flanked by windows set within a shallow archway.

"I suggest you lift Fleur out of the wheelbarrow and carry her from here," said Gramps, "and I'll go ahead and have a quick word with Tess first."

Max could hear raised voices coming from the lodge but decided to venture inside all the same.

"Like to meet your great-aunt, little one?" he said, kissing Fleur on the forehead. "We'll give it shot, shall we? But let's not expect too much."

Standing at the front door, Max could see Thomas standing in the kitchen at the end of the corridor. Tess's back was turned to him.

"There you are," said Thomas, turning to Max. "Come and join us."

Tess turned around, holding a basket filled with seed packets, as a little bird shot past and darted out the window.

"She's been in here all morning, poor thing, even though I've had the window wide open," said Tess. "That's the thing about little birds – when caught inside, they are at the mercy of those strong enough to release them."

"I'm Max," he said, stepping forward, uncertain whether to put out his hand or kiss his aunt, and so he did neither.

"Sorry, Max, there I am banging on about birds. Sorry if it's freezing in here, it's just that the window has been open, as I said." Tess put the basket onto the kitchen table.

"And this is Fleur, my daughter," said Max.

"Fleur – that is a beautiful name."

She reached out her finger and Fleur grabbed hold of it.

"She's strong," Tess said, smiling at Max.

"Yes," said Max. "I'm thinking that she has potential to be a drummer – you should see her in action with a spoon."

As the baby released her grasp of the finger, Tess stood back, looking mesmerised.

"How old is she?" she asked.

"Nearly seven months," said Max.

"She is lovely," said Tess, smiling at Fleur, and for a few moments nobody said a word.

"I was suggesting to Tess that she might join us for supper," said Thomas.

"And I was just explaining that I have plans this evening," said Tess.

"That's a shame," said Max.

"A plate of stew, Tess. Come on, the children won't be staying long – surely you can spare an hour? And you can even meet Sergeant Morag."

"Morag?"

"The nanny – she's a fierce one."

"If I stay for an hour, but no more?" said Tess.

"Good – especially as there's a particular bottle in the cellar that I'd like to try out this evening. Fond of wine, are you, Max?"

"I'm more of a beer drinker, Gramps, to be honest."

"But you're at least a quarter French! Come on, boy, a drop of cabernet, surely?"

"For you, Gramps, I'm sure I could manage a glass."

Tess had managed to spend the past two decades erasing her past, during which time she had gradually evolved from Wild Child to Plants Woman. Now forty-six, she had given up smoking and alcohol, leaving her days of hanging out with music-industry hippies on smart Euro yachts in Ibiza firmly behind. She could still remember the morning she decided to pack it all in, the scent of pine trees as she arrived back to her then boyfriend's beach house at dawn, having had a very bad trip on a cocktail of drugs and thinking how nice it would be to wake up in the mornings rather than collapsing into bed.

When Thomas, Max and Fleur had left the lodge, she sat at her desk in the sitting room and pulled a folder from the drawer. She only had three photographs, and they were worth more than any possessions she could ever have owned.

Since being at Bellamore, her rock-solid friend Freddie Rose had told Tess over and over that she had to forgive herself and that she had to let the past go. But letting the past go would mean leaving the affair behind – the perfume, the lunches, the dinners, hotel rooms, gallery alcoves, 'stolen kisses and near misses' as he had once said. Two years or twenty-four months, seven hundred and thirty days. It didn't matter what way she computed it, those two years had been the happiest of her life until the end, abrupt and final, everything taken from her hands in one swoop. She paid a heavy price, but no matter, the guilt was always there.

The sight of the veins on her wrists, risen and blue, shook Tess back to the present day. Maybe this evening she could make an effort with the children, especially as she had been so rude to Elodie. More mistakes, her life was full of them, but did she have time to start again? Her head said no, but her heart felt differently.

Chapter thirty-six

Portland Road, London

"Darling, I think I might actually die if I don't have a day off soon," said Lorenzo, pulling off his Chelsea boots. "Pass me your eye mask, will you, my love? I need to take five, just a few minutes of silence."

Lorenzo lay back on the armchair in Julia's bedroom and slipped the red silk mask over his eyes.

"I met Dominic on my way in," he said.

"I thought you were in silent mode," said Julia.

"What was he doing here?"

"That boy is heartbroken over Elodie and needed to talk about it, that's all."

"I think he's always had a thing for you, Julia," said Lorenzo, lifting up one side of the mask.

"Nonsense," she said.

Closing his eyes again, Lorenzo thought how he longed to tear Julia away from this roller coaster of a life she had created. Since the news of the children going to Ireland, and even more so the grandchild, she had said so very little. Last night he had filled the Jacuzzi with verbena-scented oil, he had chilled Bollinger in a bucket of ice and presented Julia with a plate of oysters, prepared by a chef from Bibendum, but her reaction was unenthusiastic to say the least. Even forty minutes of pure, orgasmic attention failed to bring much of a smile to her face.

"You've exercised today, my darling?" he said. "Or only your elbow?"

"What?"

"Your elbow, have you been exercising your elbow by lifting a glass to your lips all afternoon?"

"Maybe."

"And Dominic came to keep you company?"

"Why do you mention Dominic again? He simply needed a listening ear – we've always got on, you know that."

"Which is my concern, Julia. I'm wondering just how well you actually *get on*." He removed the mask and stood up. "He has a certain streak, that man, and I don't want him taking advantage of you."

"What kind of streak? Honestly, Lorenzo, anyone would have thought you were jealous."

"No, I'm simply looking out for you, my love," he said, unbuttoning his shirt and moving towards the bed. "Like to tell me more?"

"Not really," she said, taking a pillow from behind her head and throwing it to one side. "I think I need new linen, I can't bear this pattern anymore."

"I give you the best sex my fit Puerto Rican body can offer you," said Lorenzo. "I give you oysters and I rub every inch of you in your favourite cream. The royal Lorenzo treatment, darling, but I am getting no results. You want to talk about changing the bed linen, but material changes are not the answer, Julia, and you know it."

She turned her face away. "I need to sleep," she said, "and another thing, when you see Nosy Carol, can you make sure to tell her that the children have extended their stay in Cornwall if she asks? She'll want to know why they've been away so long and I can't bear for her to know where they are."

"Julia, my love, I'm sure your daily knows every detail. Isn't that how she earned her name in the first place?"

A faint smile crossed her face, but Lorenzo knew he needed to help Julia to escape from this frame of mind.

"Julia," he said, pushing back his cuticles, "how about I cancel my client list tomorrow and we spend some time together? No shopping, just relaxing."

"But shopping is how I relax," said Julia, turning to him.

"I think we need to change that, I really do," he said, sitting next to her and rubbing his hand around her waist between the sheets. "I realise that might sound a little odd coming from a personal shopper, but really, Julia, we need to take some time out from shopping."

"What are you thinking?" said Julia.

"I've got a range of ideas for you, Mrs Gold," said Lorenzo, sliding into bed next to her. "I would like to suggest Oxygen Freejumping – I hear it gets the blood pumping and endorphins flowing."

"Sounds similar to an afternoon in bed with you, Lorenzo," said Julia, picking up a little.

"Well, that's true," he said, pulling her towards him. "Or a sorensensistem facial at Triyoga? I can't quite pronounce it but it's a mix of Chinese acupressure and South American body-mapping methods – and, darling, you know that I know my way around your body very well." He began to undo the buttons of her silk pyjamas. "It's designed to relieve tension and lift where lifting is needed."

Lorenzo was now kissing his way around Julia's breasts, his fingers curling around her ribcage and gently down her back, feeling her taut muscles easing with every touch of his tongue.

"Julia," he said, his head disappearing beneath the sheets, "I want you to take it easy on yourself. Our bodies ... the tension," he said, taking a breath, "it is all reactionary to how we feel. The stress, the pain, it all reflects in these shells we are covered with."

As Julia's breath began to quicken, Lorenzo felt he might be making at least some progress in his efforts to soothe the inner distress that she was feeling.

Chapter thirty-seven

Bellamore

Tess arrived into the drawing room carrying a small basket. She was wearing a pale-pink skirt with a long grey cardigan and flat suede pumps. It looked like she was wearing a little make-up, her eyes and skin a little warmer.

"Aunt Tess," said Max, standing up.

She smiled shyly at Max, and took a package wrapped in parchment paper from the basket.

"This is for you, Max," she said.

Elodie continued to read her magazine as she sat on the sofa, wearing velvet slippers with a tiny crest on the front. Peering above her pages, she gave Tess a brief and frosty look.

"El?" said Max. "Aunt Tess is speaking to you."

"It's okay, Max," said Tess. "I've bought some fudge for you too, Elodie, by way of an apology for being so short with you yesterday, and unfriendly."

Like a hungry Labrador, Elodie's nose almost sniffed the air as she heard the word *fudge*. Taking the package from Tess, she untied the string and opened out the parchment.

"This looks good," she said. "I haven't had a proper sugar fix in ages. Gramps won't even stretch to hot chocolate around here." Like a thoroughbred filly, impossible to fatten up, Elodie crammed a piece of fudge into her mouth. "This is seriously good," she said, offering a piece to Tess who declined. "Max, go on, try some. It's delicious."

Max took a piece and then another.

Tess then took a small rag doll from the basket and passed it to Max.

"I wasn't sure, but I thought Fleur might like this little doll."

"It's sweet," said Max. "And old?"

"Very old, I'm afraid," said Tess.

"Was it yours as a baby?"

"No," said Tess. "I actually found it in a garden, when I was in Ibiza."

"A foundling, then?"

"Yes, when I couldn't see any children searching for her, I picked her up and kept her. I'm not sure why."

"This must have been the reason then," said Max. "Destiny knew you'd have a little great- niece in need of a little doll."

"If you think it isn't right for Fleur, I'll understand."

"It's perfect for Fleur," said Max. "I've been so caught up with everything I haven't even thought about toys for her. So far she's been given empty Tupperware containers and half-eaten tennis balls that Gramps rescued from Anika's dogs."

"I didn't even manage to make you a cup of tea yesterday," said Tess. "I was a little distracted, I think, but it was lovely to meet Fleur."

"No worries," said Max, with his hands in his pockets. "We landed on you unannounced. Mum finds that kind of thing really annoying too." Seeing Tess's expression when he mentioned his mother's name, he realised it had drawn an instant cloud on the conversation.

"How is the baby?" said Tess, sitting down on an armchair opposite the fireplace.

"Crying, a lot," said Elodie.

"Seems to be quite irritable," said Max. "Though when we walked down to you yesterday, she was like a little lamb. Mind you, she was in the wheelbarrow."

"Wheelbarrow?" said Tess.

"With cushions," said Max. "Didn't we mention? Gramps wanted to give Fleur a taste of proper country living, I think."

"Sounds like my father," said Tess. "Where is Fleur now?"

"Morag took her upstairs about half an hour ago," said Max. "She literally won't let me near her unless it's at an allotted time. It's as if a judge decided that the father should only have thirty minutes access per day."

"Does Charlotte know that she's such a control freak?" said Elodie.

"Good question? When she calls, I'll let you know."

"How is your eyesight, Mr Archdale?" said Morag, sitting at the kitchen table.

"Dreadful," said Thomas immediately, "and why the enquiry might I ask?"

"The loos, Mr Archdale. Without proper flushing facilities the loos are growing more filthy by the day. The occasional bucket of water doesn't suffice."

"Is that so?" said Thomas, glancing at Anika, who was mashing potato.

"Don't look at me," Anika said. "Mashing this potato is bad enough. That's for Old Murray Mints to deal with when she comes to clean."

"Darling, I do wish you wouldn't call her that," said Thomas, walking over and squeezing her elbow before taking a bottle of wine off the Aga hotplate. "Perfect temperature. How about a glass of red, Morag, and surely we can find a more interesting conversation than cleaning matters at Bellamore?"

"I wouldn't bet on it," said Max under his breath and smiling at Tess.

"Mr Archdale, the situation is intolerable," said Morag.

"Mrs Murray will be back on Monday," said Thomas, "and I'll ask her to give the bathrooms a good once-over then, how about that?"

"A once-over, Mr Archdale? I'd be thinking twice or three times if I were you."

"Well, thankfully, Morag, you are not me, and vice versa." He poured a splash of Chateau de Baume into his glass. "There we are," he said, swirling the wineglass and raising it towards Anika before taking a sip. "Now, Morag, as it happens, I have an announcement relating to the situation with the water."

"Let me guess – we're going to drive to a beach and skinny dip," said Elodie, feeling really well having received a deliciously long email from Luke.

"Do sit down," said Thomas to Bluebell who was pawing at his knee. "And how you stink. What have you been rolling in? Can you all smell her?"

"Mr Archdale, please!" said Morag, who was looking queasy.

"I'm terribly sorry, but whether she has rolled in a fox or something else, it's quite revolting. Which leads me on to my solution."

"Yes?" said Elodie, aching for a bath.

"I know how much we all enjoy a good dip," he said, "and I have lately realised that we've got a rather fine-looking bath in the paddock, which used to be a trough for the Thompsons' cattle back in the day – now the cattle are long gone, as is dear old Mr Thompson." Taking a pack of mints from his pockets, he held it out to Elodie. "Sorry, only one left, Elodie – can I tempt you?"

She shook her head. "What? You want to bring this 'bath' into the house?"

"No, no. We are going to bring the mountain to Mohammed, so to speak."

"Thomas, why do you insist on speaking in riddles?" said Anika.

"Gramps, surely it's water we need, not an extra bath?" said Max.

"Harry Rose has an old outdoor water heater at Farley Hall and he's very kindly offered it to us."

"What good is a water heater without water?" said Morag flatly.

"Ah," said Thomas, "and here lies the beauty of my thinking. As we have water in the yard, we are going to install the water heater in an outhouse and simply plumb a couple of pipes, hot and cold, naturally, to the bath."

170

"The bath? You mean the cattle trough out in the paddock?" said Elodie.

"Surely I do," said Thomas. "The so-called *cattle trough* is going to be returned to its bath status, and what's more we are going to relocate it to a spot that even Monty Don might envy."

"Monty Don?" said Elodie.

"A rugged, handsome dish on television," said Anika, her eyes brightening. "Keen on creating rooms for *everything* in the garden."

"Precisely," said Thomas. "Therefore we shall locate the bath in a discreet position so that we can be at one with Mother Nature."

"I can help with the plumbing, Gramps, if you like?" said Max.

"Thank you, Max, and Niall McNally has promised to appear with a mini-digger to lay the pipes."

"I don't understand," said Elodie.

"I think what my father is saying is that the household shall be bathing al fresco," said Tess.

"What an absurd idea," said Morag. "I assure you I will not be bathing outdoors for all to see."

"The Swiss do it all the time," said Anika, who appeared to find the idea perfectly acceptable. "In fact, I have a German friend who hoses herself down every morning outside with cold water. She has a great body."

"But what about creatures?" said Elodie.

"Don't worry, darling – I'm sure the frogs will leave you alone while you take your bath," said Anika. "Pour the wine, Thomas, would you?"

"None for me," said Tess.

Elodie noticed how Tess retreated further into herself when Anika was around.

"I left a bottle of elderflower in the drawing room – maybe I'll go and get it," said Tess.

"Or I can get it for you?" said Max.

"No, thanks, Max," said Tess, getting up from the table.

"Elodie and Max, a drop of wine?"

"Yes, please, Gramps," said Elodie, "and supper smells good whatever it is. I'm absolutely starving."

"Where there's salt and pepper on the table there is always hope," said Anika, putting a pot of potatoes on the table. "Thomas, can you dish up?" And pulling something out of her pocket, she threw it in the air as Bonnie and Clyde almost collided trying to catch it.

"Is that bacon, Anika?" said Thomas. "I really wish you wouldn't – you are ruining those dogs."

"You know I keep treats for them in my pocket," she said, sitting down at the table. "Besides, I have just cooked for you, so you are not in a position to criticise."

"True," said Thomas, blowing her a kiss while Max and Elodie squirmed at the sight of their grandfather flirting with someone who looked like she should be sitting on the lap of a man half his age.

"Giving my little dogs a snack before I eat settles them and stops them from begging," said Anika, refusing to be condescended to.

"But surely it must have the opposite affect?" said Thomas, watching the dogs scrambling over the ball of rinds and bacon. "Oh, blast it, not again, Clyde!"

Clyde had cocked his leg against the Aga.

"My word, that is too disgusting," said Morag, lifting her napkin to her lips. "I'm afraid my appetite has gone."

"It's only pee," said Anika, patting her lap, until Clyde leapt up for a back massage.

"That's it," said Morag, throwing her napkin down. "I'll be excusing myself from dinner this evening."

"Must you give this royal massage treatment to your dog at the table, Anika?" said Thomas, holding his wineglass, with a crack on one side, as if it were a chalice.

"Clyde is a nervous dog, you know that," said Anika.

"He's a scoundrel," said Thomas. "They're aptly named Bonnie and Clyde."

Morag was making for the door.

"Come back to the table, Morag – how about a drop of wine?" said Thomas. "It'll warm you up."

"No, thank you, Mr Archdale, I have excellent circulation. I've got a protein bar in my room, so that will do me for tonight." She stepped back from the door as Tess arrived flushed and breathless.

"There is a screaming baby up there," said Tess. "I could hear her from the hall."

"There's nothing to concern yourself about," said Morag.

"Max, your child is screaming her lungs out upstairs – I can't believe you are just sitting here," said Tess, almost in tears.

"I'm so sorry," said Max, standing up. "We can't hear anything from down here."

"I must say, Morag, Baby Fleur has been crying a considerable amount since she's arrived," said Thomas.

"Maybe she's missing her mother?" said Anika, refilling her wineglass.

"I actually think she's hungry," said Thomas.

"I don't agree," said Morag. "Her weight is entirely on target. It is more a case of Baby needing to learn to control her temper."

"Babies cry for a reason," said Tess. "Like a baby bird calling out for food from its nest, that must be what she's doing."

Elodie watched Max, who looked like a rabbit in headlights.

"Tess has a point, Max," said Thomas.

"With respect, Mr Gold, if you would like me to discuss Baby's routine with Ms Wentworth, I can do it tomorrow via telephone but, in the meantime, while I am in charge, I will implement my training in the interests of my client."

"How can a baby be a client, for goodness' sake?" said Tess.

"Quite easily," said Morag, clutching the door handle. "Along with Lord and Lady Broadbent who pay my wages and, as neither of them are present, I suggest this conversation is null and void."

"Nonsense," said Thomas. "Now, what about the baby monitor Freddie brought over the other day – why don't we use it?"

"I don't believe in baby monitors," said Morag defiantly. "All that electrical current whirring about isn't good for babies – it disrupts their sleep."

"Freddie asked us to test it out for her daughter, Anna, who's expecting a baby this summer," said Thomas, pointing to a box sitting near Augusta's cage. "I'm all on for a monitor as long as the damned thing doesn't use too much electricity. Morag, why don't you plug it in, and then we can all relax?"

"Fine," said Morag, taking the box and leaving the kitchen like a teenager in the middle of a row.

"Tess, you need to sit, and you need to eat," said Thomas, as Anika lifted a platter of guinea fowl with buttery carrots from the Aga hotplate onto the table. "Come on now, help yourselves, please."

"I'm really not hungry," said Tess, reluctantly sitting down, looking very pale.

"You look like you need a big meal," said Anika, joining them at the table.

"Do I? How kind of you to say."

"Steady, you two," said Thomas. "Anika, why don't you help yourself?"

"I will eat when I am ready. Don't treat me like a child."

Elodie looked at Tess, her face so stressed, and then at Max, sensing that he felt uncomfortable about how Fleur was being treated.

"Then, Elodie, please help yourself," said Thomas, as Morag arrived back into the kitchen and plugged in one end of the baby monitor next to Augusta.

"*Bugger off!*" screeched the bird.

"Back already, Morag? I thought you were dining on a protein bar this evening?" said Thomas.

"I decided it would be better for me to keep my strength up, and guinea fowl is a favourite of mine," she said.

"As long as the baby is settled, and the monitor is on," said Thomas, looking reassuringly at Tess.

"It is, aye," said Morag, helping herself to a large helping of guinea fowl and potatoes.

Sitting at the table, Elodie watched the monitor as the pips rose higher and higher.

"Max," said Elodie, "that monitor is going doolally."

Getting up from the table, Max picked up the monitor and, flicking a switch, released immediate shrieks coming from Fleur.

"Baby is overtired, that's all," said Morag, forking up the guinea fowl.

"Why not bring her to the drawing room?" said Tess, who had hardly touched her supper.

"I think that's a good idea," said Max, trying to assert some kind of parental authority but failing.

"I like to keep Baby in the bedroom environment," said Morag, through a mouthful of potato, "and we don't want her to think that she can disrupt social occasions, do we? That would be no way to raise a child."

"That can't be right, can it?" said Tess, looking around the table.

"I honestly don't know," said Max, wrinkling his forehead. "I really don't have any experience with babies." Then he turned to Morag and checked his watch. "Charlotte said that you had a routine all mapped out for Fleur, didn't she? I'm going to try calling her again. I tried earlier but her phone seems to be continually out of signal."

Tess grabbed the napkin from her lap and threw it on the table. "You can't ignore a screaming baby," she said, standing up.

"It may seem stern," said Morag, "but from the outset Baby must know who is boss."

"Listen to me, Morag," said Tess. "I don't care what smart training camp you came from, it simply isn't right. That little baby is up there all alone, terrified, wondering where her mother is. Can you imagine how she must be feeling?"

"Settle down, Tess, there's a good girl," said Thomas, putting his knife and fork together.

"A baby needs her parents," said Tess and, opening the door to the back garden, she walked out into the night.

"Gramps, is Tess okay?" said Elodie.

"Sigmund Freud said neurosis is no excuse for bad manners," said Anika.

"There's no need for that, Anika. Tess is tired, that's all," said Thomas.

"But there's no getting through to her," said Anika, pulling on a jumper that was much too tight for her bosom. "She does not take help or advice. Freddie Rose is about the only woman I know who can talk properly with her."

"I'll go up to Fleur," said Max, getting up from the table.

"No, leave it to me," said Morag, "I'll go, but it is against my wishes and I will be reporting your interference to Ms Wentworth."

"Baby is asleep and so I've come down to make a brew," said Morag, wearing pink slippers, which made her brown uniform look particularly unflattering.

"Excellent timing, Morag," said Thomas, having polished off another bottle of wine, with a small amount of help from Max and Elodie, as Anika had moved on to vodka. "I want you all up for the dawn chorus in the morning. There's no place better than four o'clock on a misty morning, standing in the woods, listening to a symphony of clicks, churrs and trills. It is an experience that will warm the belly."

"But that's practically the middle of the night," said Morag.

"On the contrary, Morag. It's when the birds are saying good morning to each other."

"Won't we freeze?" said Elodie, who had just received another text message from Luke, along with a selfie of him looking so handsome standing next to a bust of Oscar Wilde in Charing Cross.

"There are plenty of warm jackets in the tack room," said Thomas, "and scarves, and hats. Anika, darling, do you think you could do us all a favour and take on nanny duty for Morag? Say from four thirty onwards?"

"Thomas, you are kidding?"

"I promise I'll take you out for a slap-up dinner as a reward."

"What, you're going to fly me to my favourite restaurant in New York?"

"As you know, I can't stretch that far, my Dutch cream – however, I can take you to the pub for a most splendid Shepherd's Pie and bottle of red?"

Anika sidled her way towards Thomas, her blue eyes sultry, and slipping her arms around his shoulders, she smouldered into his cheek. "I find it impossible to resist your charm, don't I, Thomas?"

"So it seems," he said, winking at Max. "Lucky for me."

"For one night only, I will baby-sit," said Anika, "as long as Bonnie and Clyde can sleep with me."

"Of course, my darling," said Thomas.

"Not in the baby's room?" said Morag, looking alarmed.

"You can sleep in the room next door," said Gramps. "Make it up for her, Morag, will you? There's a good girl."

"I am no chambermaid, Mr Archdale," said Morag. "Haven't I made myself – *Aaaaaaahhh!*" Jumping onto a chair and then onto the table, she pointed to the floor. "*Aaaaaaahhhh!*"

"What on earth?" said Thomas, getting to his feet.

"*It's a rat, over there, it's a huge rat!*" screamed Morag, wrapping her arms around herself and twisting her legs together.

Thomas moved the platter of guinea fowl on the table away from Morag's slipper-clad feet.

"I see it," said Anika, remarkably calmly.

"*OMG!*" yelled Elodie. "*Max, do something.*"

They all watched as the brown rat, with a grotesquely long tail, tried to scramble up the corner of the wall behind a picnic basket.

"There it is indeed," said Thomas, folding his arms.

"Looks like poison," said Anika. "For a rat to be seen, it's almost always poison."

"*Throw one of your bloody dogs on it,*" roared Morag from the table.

The others looked at Bonnie, Clyde and Bluebell, all snuggled up on the beanbag, completely disinterested.

"It's a classic, isn't it, Anika?" said Thomas.

"It is," she said. "My little pair – butter wouldn't melt, would it?"

As Anika pulled opened the door to the back garden, Thomas took a sweeping brush from the cupboard, pulled back the basket with the head of the brush and released the rat from the corner. Galloping across the kitchen, at a pace worthy of an Attenborough slow-motion video, the rat exited through the door onto the garden.

"Oh my goodness," said Morag. "I don't think I've ever seen anything so disgusting in my whole life. I feel sick."

"No need to worry, it'll be dead in an hour," said Thomas, walking into the pantry. "Yes," he said loudly, "all the poison has been eaten."

Anika put out her hand to Morag and helped her down from the table.

"Makes me think of that UB40 track," said Max and he began to sing 'There's a Rat in Mi Kitchen'.

Meanwhile Elodie took a picture of the kitchen, so that she could send it to Luke to accompany her latest update of events.

"You mean to say, Mr Archdale, that you knew there was a rat in the kitchen?"

"That's right," he said. "I generally keep poison behind the pantry fridge. All part of country life. Now, how about a brandy to calm the nerves? Then I suggest we all get some sleep before our morning excursion."

Chapter thirty-eight

"Gramps, I don't think there are any batteries in this," said Max, shaking a yellow torch with both hands.

"Blasted thing," said Thomas. "What about yours, Elodie?"

"I can't find the button," she said, passing Max a blue plastic torch with a cracked handle.

"No, this one is dead as a dodo," said Max, letting Bluebell out of the kitchen to join them.

Morag, togged out in a full-length oilskin coat, boots and a woolly hat, was standing by the picnic table in the back garden, holding a tiny pocket torch.

"You'll have to lead the way," said Thomas, looking at Morag.

"Who, me?" said Morag.

"Yes, that light of yours is perfectly adequate."

"With respect, Mr Archdale, it is four o'clock in the wee small hours of the morning and unnatural for us all to be out here in the pitch black."

"Your eyes will acclimatise to the darkness. No need to worry. Now on you go, Morag." He shooed her on with Elodie and Max. "And, Elodie – *no smoking.*"

"Why did you think I was going to, Gramps? I hadn't even as much as lit a match."

"I'm getting to know you, you see? Call it pre-empting a situation. Smoking is absolutely forbidden when listening to the dawn chorus. Why should the little birds have to put up with your air contamination?"

"Alright, Gramps, I get the message," and, joining Morag in her grumpiness, Elodie stomped on towards the woods.

"Mind how you go, you two," he called after them. "The land is uneven underfoot."

"I've been trained for this kind of terrain," said Morag proudly.

"How?" said Elodie, wishing she were with anyone but Morag.

"During nanny training we had to run through woods carrying a fake baby – all while reporting an attempted abduction down the phone."

"Morag, seriously?" said Elodie.

"I never joke," said Morag.

"I think we figured that," said Max, catching up with them.

They trudged on and entered the woods. The birds were indeed tuning up.

"Over here, you lot." Thomas beckoned them over to stand beneath a giant oak tree. "What you are now hearing is the build-up to a sublime orchestra of birds singing their hearts out to stake out their territory and, at this time of the year, to attract a partner." Leaning on his stick, he closed his eyes. "You hear that? One chord after another," he said, almost imitating the voice of David Attenborough. "You see, there is no better alarm clock – these birds are always bang on time."

"I'm sure Augusta would prefer to be out with this lot rather than stuck in that cage," said Elodie.

"Hush, Elodie, be still and listen," said Thomas.

"Sounds like a series of shrieks to me," said Morag.

"Only to the untrained human ear, Morag."

"So, the male birds are out to woo the good-looking chicks," said Max, scratching Bluebell behind the ears.

"Yes, the birds you are hearing now are mostly males, perhaps with the occasional female joining it."

"Sounds very chauvinistic," said Elodie, thinking of Dominic, but then she thought of Luke and felt such a longing to see him.

"Actually, it's the females who call the shots," said Thomas. "The girls perch up high, working out which male bird has the best prospects. If the male hasn't got a good singing voice, then he doesn't stand a chance. The better and stronger the voice, the better and stronger the genes, do you follow?"

"It makes being a human seem very easy," said Max. "All we have to do is book a table in a restaurant."

"I can't believe how loud it is," said Elodie. "All those tiny voices."

"Terribly intelligent little things," said Thomas.

"And the pigeons, cooing away in the background, like bass guitar," said Max.

"God, it's freezing out here," said Morag.

"How about a nip of brandy?" said Thomas, pulling out a hip flask. "Go on, Morag, it'll warm up the toes."

"No, thank you," said Morag curtly.

"Don't mind if I do, Gramps, seeing as you aren't interested, Morag?" said Max. He took a hefty swig and gasped. "Wow, powerful stuff, Gramps." He handed the hip flask back. "Do you think Anika's okay with Fleur?"

"That woman managed to keep a houseful of Dutch reality stars in check – what was that dreadful show called?"

"*Big Brother*," said Elodie.

"That's the one. Anika also manages to ride like a demon with the hunt and last year oversaw the delivery of a foal when the vet was delayed."

"Well, it's hardly rocket science to sign a delivery docket, is it, Gramps?" said Elodie.

"Delivering a foal, Elodie. From the mare?" said her grandfather with lifted eyebrows.

"Ah, okay," said Elodie.

"I have no doubt Anika can handle a baby for a few hours," he said, passing the hip flask to Elodie. "And a pheasant between it all, did you hear it?"

"There we are," said Thomas, turning to Morag. "The chorus is dying down now and you're nearly home and dry. Wasn't so bad, was it?"

"I'm still in recovery from Ronald Rat," said Morag.

"Was that a joke, Morag?" he said, giving her a gentle nudge.

"Aye, maybe it was," she said, smiling a very pretty smile.

"Good to see," said Thomas, "good to see."

"Mr Archdale, if it's all the same to you," said Morag, "I'd like to get back to the house."

"Surely you can stay out a little bit longer, Morag?"

"I have standards to adhere to, and I will not be swayed," she said, any good humour retreating. "The house is this way, is it not?"

"Yes – follow your nose," said Thomas, watching her go. "I was almost tempted to send her in the wrong direction," he muttered. "What a killjoy that woman is."

"You're wicked, Gramps," said Max with a grin.

"See that fellow up there?" said Thomas, pointing to a greenfinch. A fine beauty, don't you think? Look, Elodie." He frowned. "Elodie, you aren't smoking, are you?"

"What? No, Gramps," she said, eyes wide and smiling as she held a ciggie behind her back.

"You are naughty," he said. "Put it out, would you? And put it out properly – you don't want to set fire to the woods." He watched while she did. "And then we have the yellowhammer," he continued, "see that fine yellow head and green body? When he's calling for his lady it sounds like he is saying 'a little bit of bread and *no chee-eese!*' Such fun, isn't it?"

"I'm beginning to see where Max inherited his musical talents from, Gramps," said Elodie.

"Ah, and there's the blackbird. My very favourite. He has a purity that is unrivalled. Listen to his call: *srreee, srreee.*"

Elodie glanced at Max, both of them smiling. She marvelled at the twist of fate that had led them here to this wood to listen to birdsong at dawn with their long-lost grandfather.

Chapter thirty-nine

Bonnie and Clyde raced down the basement stairs and, as Anika opened the door, they shot through to the kitchen and piled on top of Bluebell, who was lolling across her beanbag. Anika followed, wearing a full-length dressing gown, carrying Fleur in one arm and an empty baby bottle in her hand.

"What are you doing up?" said Tess. She was standing by the Aga in her wellies and didn't look up.

"I might ask you the same question?" said Anika.

"I always come in at six to collect Bluebell and I thought I'd have a cup of tea before starting work in the garden," said Tess, repositioning the kettle on the hob as if to make it come to the boil faster.

"After the fuss you made about the baby, I thought you'd at least say good morning to her?" Anika brought Fleur, who was clutching on to her little rag doll, towards the Aga but Tess moved away.

"I can tell you that neither the dogs nor I had a wink of sleep last night," said Anika. "Morag insisted I shouldn't give Fleur a bottle during the night, but of course I had to, as the poor baby was clearly famished."

Still no reaction from Tess, so Anika stamped her foot, strode across the kitchen and unloaded the baby into Tess's arms.

"What are you doing?" said Tess. "I can't hold the baby."

Anika felt completely fed up with Tess and her apparent fragility, having to tiptoe around her, listening to Thomas explaining that 'Tess needs her space, she'll come around, you'll see'. "You are at least related to the baby," she said, tightening the belt on her dressing gown. "I, on the other hand, am certainly not."

"I can't get involved," stuttered Tess, holding Fleur. "I've got the garden to look after."

"And I have better things to be doing. I didn't come to Ireland to get involved in someone else's family. Your father is presently in the yard with Elodie, who is hosing Morag down following her mishap."

"Her what?" said Tess, as Fleur slapped the rag doll against her face.

"Morag arrived back to the house from her dawn-chorus venture in the woods and got into bed – and as she settled beneath the covers she felt a wet patch seeping into her back from the mattress – and onto her head from the pillow, along with a stench of –"

"You don't mean to say that –"

Anika began to giggle. "Not only that, but her hand came across a rather unpleasant swirl of poop, right under the covers, can you believe it?"

"Bonnie and Clyde?" said Tess.

"My sweet little doggies, such discerning little creatures," said Anika, with a proud grin.

"Thomas and Elodie walked into the hall to find Morag running down the stairs in her starched white nightie with her hands in the air, pee in her hair, dog poop on her hands."

This was almost the longest conversation that Anika and Tess had ever had, and they were even laughing together.

"And that is why, if you look out the window you'll see Elodie with a bottle of Fairy Liquid, hosing Morag down."

Tess walked over to the sink and, sure enough, there was Elodie on the other side of the yard, trying to keep a straight face as Morag bent her head forward, scrubbing Fairy Liquid into her hair.

"I think that Thomas may at last begin to appreciate my dogs," said Anika, "now that the Morag has demanded transportation to Dublin Airport as soon as possible."

"She's leaving?" said Tess.

"Yes, I'm going to drive her and I'll take Elodie with me, as travelling alone for two hours with Morag is beyond the call. Can you take care of the baby until we get back?"

"What? No, of course not. I don't know the first thing about looking after a baby."

"You'll find the formula over there in the basket – naturally Morag has every possible item labelled, so making up the bottle will be easy."

"But I've never made up a bottle for a baby."

"It's no different than making a cocktail, I can assure you. Just follow the measurements."

"Okay," said Tess, her voice relaxing a little as Fleur took hold of her index finger.

"If you had seen the way Fleur drank from the bottle during the night, even managing to hold the bottle herself with both hands. She drank the milk with fury, which makes me think that the little one has been hungry all along."

"You seem to know a lot about babies," said Tess.

"My son is twenty-three now," said Anika. "I raised him by myself, while trying to make it in TV, and I can tell you, looking good on the screen, fending off execs who want to sleep with you and being a mother is no easy balancing act."

"I had no idea," said Tess. "And your son's father?"

"Dead. No need to be sorry, he was a snake. He made money, he lost money, and he made even more money, he lost even more again. It was like being married to a human casino."

"Was that why you came to Ireland?"

"I put my finger on the map of Europe and it landed on Ireland. That is the truth. My little Irish cottage is now my castle. It's easy to heat, charming to look at and I managed to hold on to most of my favourite paintings before the banks liquidised the rest. Life is so easy now, and I don't have to deal with leaking rooms or drafts, like your father does. I am very lucky."

"Sounds like it," said Tess.

"I've kept my looks, some money and my son calls occasionally, so things aren't so bad." Saying all of that out loud made Anika's stomach churn. 'My son calls *occasionally*.' She didn't have it all, not even slightly. She knew she had been a dreadful mother, and not much better as a wife, and on top of that she had slept her way into television.

"Anika?" said Tess.

"Yes?"

"Thank you for looking after Fleur."

"Well, it's over to you now."

"Maxy," said Anika, halfway up the stairs, "there you are. You've had an eventful morning?"

"You could say that," he said, stretching out his arms. "I'm longing for a snooze."

"You really shouldn't be seeing me in my dressing gown," said Anika, with a cheeky smile.

"No worries," said Max, "and thanks again for taking care of Fleur last night, and advance thanks for taking Morag to the airport."

"Thomas has promised me all kinds of things for my hard work," said Anika, "but you know, Max, maybe you and I could go out this evening and talk things over? A man of your age needs to have a little fun."

"I'll be looking after Fleur from now on," said Max, oblivious to Anika's advances.

"This dressing gown was your grandmother's, I take it?" she said.

"If it's silk, you can count on it being Odette's. She liked her luxury."

"It's rather revealing, though, isn't it?" she said, hating herself for trying to come on to Thomas's grandson, but she needed to do something to distract herself from thinking about her own son.

"Have you seen Morag in the yard? El is actually hosing her down, complete chalk and cheese compared to how Elodie's days usually are. If she were in London right now she'd be at the hairdresser's or trying on a pair of shoes that she doesn't need."

"Well, I guess we are all adapting, aren't we?" said Anika, losing steam. "Your baby is with Tess in the kitchen, so that at least is being taken care of."

"Right," said Max, putting his hands in his pockets, "I'd better get down to the kitchen then."

"Wait – Maxy?"

"Yes?"

"Do you like adapting to things, Maxy?"

"As in –"

"Things," she said, reaching out to touch his arm.

"You know, Anika, I think I'm going to check on the baby," said Max, at last registering that she was behaving rather oddly. "By the way, would you mind calling me Max? I'm really not keen on Maxy."

"Your grandfather says he wants me to be his *live in*," she blurted out. "He tells me that even Judi Dench has a *live in*."

"Sorry, Anika, gotta go – I'll see you later."

He hurried off downstairs.

"*Your grandfather is taking me for granted, you know?*" she called after him, but it was unlikely he even heard her.

Walking upstairs, she wondered what the hell she was doing in this house and with a man twice her age. Nothing was working out for her – it might be time to get back to the drawing board.

Chapter forty

"Hello, little one," said Tess, looking into Fleur's big, bright, staring eyes. "This isn't what I expected, how about you?"

The baby smell, powdery, milky, warm – Tess had never experienced it before, not properly, not like this. Propping Fleur on her lap, she smiled at her, taking in every inch of her soft face, her pinkish skin so smooth and perfect. Her little mouth, gurgling and making little 'ooh' sounds. Tess felt like she had arrived in heaven and felt a love so instantly for this baby that she could hardly grasp or explain it. Fleur was miniature perfection.

"Good morning," said Max. "Talk about early birds. How did you get landed with my little daughter?"

"I think Anika is pretty worn out and Morag has abandoned her post, I believe."

"I'm actually feeling pretty good considering I've been up since four," said Max. "I guess the thought of Morag leaving is such a relief I really don't care how little sleep I've had." He looked at Fleur. "I swear she's grown since yesterday. Hello, you." He knelt down in front of Tess and Fleur. "You must be the most relieved of all, little one, to see Morag leave."

Fleur grinned as if she understood.

"Would you like to take her?" said Tess.

"How about you hold onto Fleur and I make us a pot of tea – if that's okay with you?"

"Of course."

"She's really taken to the doll you gave her."

"Sweet," said Tess.

Tess smiled at Max as he picked up the overflowing compost bin.

"Better put this out here," he said, walking into the back kitchen. "Elodie can't bear compost."

He was so upbeat and gentle, and it was easy to imagine how he would have been as a little boy. She closed her eyes for a moment and thought of Max and Elodie as children, then Fleur tapped the doll on the side of her face. "Quite right, Fleur, this is no time for daydreaming."

"I'm going to have to work out how on earth I'm going to cope until Charlotte gets here," said Max, returning with a handful of eggs. "How about an omelette for breakfast?"

"Yes, please," Tess said.

"And tomatoes?"

"Except without the seeds."

"Couldn't agree more," said Max. "I can't bear the seeds either – so slimy."

"Has Charlotte told you when she'll get here?"

"No, she hasn't been in contact since she left her parents' house – where the news didn't exactly go down smoothly."

"Is she alone?"

"No, she went straight to her friend Petra's – it sounds like some kind of hippy commune set up on an estate in Somerset." He began to fill the kettle. "Charlotte kept saying that she needed time to herself, and I, maybe stupidly, told her to take as much time as she needed. I'm beginning to regret it. I have no experience of babies and I didn't appreciate how much Fleur needs her mother."

"And what do you need?" said Tess as she snuggled Fleur.

"It took me a while to figure that out but now I have. And I have you to thank for it."

"Why?"

"Last night, when you rightly pointed out that Fleur shouldn't have been left alone, my inner protective-father mechanism really kicked in. She's my priority now."

"Oh, it was nothing," said Tess, sitting Fleur down on a blanket on the floor. "Watch now."

Fleur's arms went out as she swayed forward and back.

"Look how full of concentration her face is," said Tess. "Learning to balance, isn't that what life is all about?"

"How come we never saw you, Tess? When we were growing up, I mean."

"Is the kettle boiled, Max?"

"Did you have some kind of falling-out with Odette?"

"What?" said Tess.

"You know, a barney."

"I don't know what you mean, Max, I'm sorry?"

"Mum goes mental when we talk about our summers at Bellamore."

"What does she say?" said Tess, bowing her head, hands on her knees as she watched Fleur.

"Nothing precise. She just basically has a complete hissy."

"Right," said Tess.

"She prefers for us to talk about Cornwall, or Le Plan de la Tour – you know, the so-called *family holidays* we had in our teens, though we were totally left to our own devices. Mum off meeting someone about material and then inevitably on to a drinks party. I won't put Fleur through that."

Tess felt great relief when a blonde in the shape of Freddie Rose arrived through the door, carrying a stack of egg cartons. She was dressed in burgundy cords and a cream round-neck jumper with gold bracelets jangling on her wrists and a gold necklace of a trout around her neck.

"Sorry I'm late," she said.

"You're not late, Freddie, you're early. It's eight o'clock in the morning."

"You must be Max," said Freddie. "Lovely to meet you."

"And you," he said, taking the egg cartons from her.

"You won't remember me, but I remember you as a child."

"You knew my grandmother?" said Max.

"A little," said Freddie. "She gave me some wonderful cuttings from the garden."

"And Freddie has a beautiful garden," said Tess.

"Well, I spent most of yesterday digging up dreadful bindweed, or convolvulus," she said. "Tess knows all the plant names in Latin, Max – unlike me, so badly educated. But I must say I slept like a dormouse last night, and as I was doing my yoga this morning I remembered your father asked me for a supply of egg cartons last week. I popped into the lodge, Tess, but you weren't there – obviously."

"I've been looking after this little one," said Tess shyly.

"Isn't she a darling?" said Freddie, bending down. "You two are getting acquainted then?"

"We are," said Tess.

"Such a carry-on with the nanny. I heard from Mrs Murray in the village."

"Already?" said Max. "How is that possible?"

"It's the village network. Your grandfather called the shop to look up the next flight to Edinburgh from Dublin. It's Mrs Murray's grandson, a proper whizz with technology."

"And?" said Tess.

"Mrs Murray comes to us on a Friday, and I met her on the avenue, so she filled me in."

"Who needs online news with your own private newswire, eh?" said Max. "Anyway, as you can see, Fleur is left with a pack of amateurs now – no disrespect intended, Tess."

"And none taken, Max," she said, beaming a smile that Freddie didn't think she had ever seen from her before.

"On the contrary," said Freddie, kneeling down next to the baby. "All Fleur needs is love. You don't have to be an expert parent, Max. No matter how many degrees you have, nothing prepares a human for this. You have to just learn as you go along, isn't that right, Tess?"

Chapter forty-one

Portland Road, London

With a trilby angled like Humphry Bogart, Lorenzo climbed the stairs carrying a tray with Julia's favourite food.

"Presenting lobster and crab crêpes for Mrs Gold," he said, imitating a movie trailer, "and not forgetting the Bacon Bling breakfast sandwich, which includes bacon from rare pig breeds, truffle, watercress, saffron and a single egg all cooked in truffle oil, and –" he tossed his hat onto the sofa, "the pièce de résistance? The dish has been sprinkled with real gold dust."

Julia lay on the bed and looked like she was trying to raise a smile.

"Oh no, darling, you are disappointed I didn't top it off with ten ounces of caviar?"

"It's all lovely, Lorenzo, really it is, but truly it's wasted on me."

Lorenzo put the tray down gently onto Julia's bedside table.

"Julia, we have discussed this," he said, with as much tenderness as he could conjure up. "First, we find a balance in our heart and then our mind, and the body will follow, yes?"

"I know I've said this over and over, Lorenzo, but I can't believe they've gone to Ireland. The thought of them being at Bellamore, I just can't explain it. And to think my father had the nerve to suggest me as a guarantor for that loan."

"Well, you quickly blew that one out of the water, didn't you?"

"Yes, and so he put the house against the loan, and lost the entire lot through unsafe investment. He has been so irresponsible, I just can't bear it."

"This is all history, Julia, and yet you bring it up over and over."

"How can I not think of Bellamore when my children are there?"

"Your father asked you because he was desperate," said Lorenzo.

"Yes, and he deserves to be and that is why I ignored his letter to bail him out when he lost his shares."

"You think Max and Elodie have received your messages?"

"Four voicemails each, that's eight in total. I would have thought so," said Julia dryly.

"And I suppose you left calm messages, suggestions you should talk over the situation? Or did you –"

"Lorenzo, you know perfectly well that I roared, swore and yelled down the phone to both my children."

"So, why do you expect them to return your calls?"

"Because I have a granddaughter, and I had to be bloody well told about it by that godawful woman and her muttering husband."

"No, Julia, that's too harsh. I like Gerald – but they are clearly a couple who need an injection of fresh energy."

"Unlike us?"

"There is nothing stale about us, Julia, and you know it."

"Do I?"

"Yes," he said, sliding his hands down her pants. "You're the sexiest woman I've ever known, and with all the women I've dressed, I know what I'm talking about."

"Oh, you're just saying that."

"No, my darling, I'm not, and I know exactly what always calms you, don't I? Now come on, let me give you one of my Giomatti specials."

Chapter forty-two

Bellamore

Max and Elodie sat on the club fender, either side of the fireplace in the drawing room. Elodie was still getting over the journey she had to endure with Morag and Anika, a double whammy of uptight women who wouldn't tolerate as much as a whiff of smoke. Meanwhile Max had spent much of the day with Fleur and Tess in the kitchen, before hiking several loads of wood in the wheelbarrow from an outhouse and into huge log baskets in the front hall. The roaring fire brought much-needed comfort to them both as they picked up phone messages from their mother.

"Maybe Lorenzo will talk her round," said Max, knowing that any form of optimism would be wasted on Elodie, but worth a try anyway.

"I doubt it," she said.

"We just need to keep things in perspective."

"Max," she said, sipping from her mug of tea, "our mother has told me that I am dead to her and that I'll find my belongings in bin liners by the front door. What kind of 'perspective' can we have on that?"

"Well, at least you don't have a baby to look after," he snapped back, and then felt sorry, for he had loved his day with Fleur and,

194

just as much, getting to know Aunt Tess.

"Look, El, this is a difficult time, no doubt about it – however, we have to keep it together if we are to stay on as guests here. If we get into a state there's no way Gramps is going to want us around, so we have to make the best of it."

Elodie looked in her yellow bag. Three cigarettes left to her name.

"Alright, Max," she said, thinking of Luke, which made her feel a little encouraged for the future. "I'll see if I can help Gramps some way while I'm here. Maybe I can do some painting or something – the walls are in a dreadful state upstairs."

Elodie looked at the silver-framed photographs around the room, depicting Odette as a mother and hostess of perfection. "Odette looks amazing in the photos, doesn't she?"

"Yes," said Thomas, standing at the door wearing a pink cravat, green chinos and a navy jacket. "The photo you're looking at was taken on the Blackwater."

"What about this photo of Odette with Mum and Tess under what looks like a magnolia?" said Elodie. "They look so happy – Mum couldn't have been more than eight or nine."

"They were good days, Elodie."

"Looking snazzy, aren't you, Gramps?" said Max.

"I'm taking Anika out to dinner," he said, "as a thank-you for her help with Morag."

"I really feel like I should foot the bill for dinner, having put you guys in this position," said Max.

"Nonsense – though wasn't it ironic that Morag took an outdoor bath after all," said Thomas, "albeit from a cold hose? And to think that she could have enjoyed a bath in the garden if she had stayed just a little longer. Lord, the atmosphere around that woman – she'd turn anyone to stone. I feel like we should have some kind of freedom party for Fleur."

"Max, why don't we order a takeaway?" said Elodie. "Would Anika be game to come here for supper instead, Gramps? And we can invite Tess, and Fleur can join us in the kitchen in her Moses basket."

"Is there a decent Indian takeaway, Gramps?" Max asked.

"Yes, there is – and if you're certain you'd like to, Max, that sounds wonderful."

"This is exactly where she should be," said Tess, as she, Max and Elodie watched over Fleur, sleeping soundly in the drawing room. "Not stashed away at the top of the house."

"Now that Cruella de Ville has left the building," said Elodie.

"Fleur really wolfed down the baby rice earlier, didn't she?" said Max.

"So sweet," said Tess.

"You lot really are smitten, aren't you?" said Thomas, nursing a whiskey on the sofa. "It's amazing what a baby brings to a house, isn't it?"

Tess began coughing and stepped away from the Moses basket.

"Tess, are you okay?" said Max.

"I'm fine," she said, wheezing a little, "I'm sorry, give me a moment," and she left the room.

"Gramps, is Tess okay?" said Elodie.

"She has a weak chest, plus she's had a long day, so she may need to take it easy this evening."

"Tess is pretty easy to get on with, isn't she?" said Max.

"Very different from my first meeting with her," said Elodie, "that's for sure."

Anika arrived into the drawing room, with Bonnie and Clyde at her heels, dressed in dark velvet trousers and a blouse covered in horseshoes.

"Anika," said Thomas, standing up to greet her, "you're steeped in good luck with all those horseshoes."

"I hope so," she said, kissing him on the lips.

"Darling, must you bring the dogs up here?" said Gramps.

"Gramps, they are the heroes of the hour, they must be here," said Max. "If it wasn't for their bad habits, we'd still have Nanny Morag to deal with. In fact, I believe they did it deliberately – you know, claiming their territory from her."

"Very likely," said Thomas, watching Bonnie and Clyde sidling up to Elodie's ankles. "And they seem to be especially fond of you, Elodie."

"No idea why, and don't even think about peeing on my shoe, Clyde," said Elodie, as both terriers looked up at her with innocent eyes.

"I'd suggest the reason they are lurking around you is because you all need a bath," said Anika. "The dogs like natural odours."

Elodie didn't appreciate Anika's comment and pushed the dogs away, though they came straight back to her like little boomerangs.

"So, where are we off to this evening, Thomas?" Anika asked.

"Actually, darling, Max has suggested eating in," he said.

"I see," said Anika. "Is this because you are allergic to spending money, Thomas?"

"It was my suggestion," said Max, cutting in, "as a way of thanking both of you for having us all here."

"In that case, it seems your grandfather is rather redeemed."

"Good to hear it," said Thomas, who seemed a little on edge. "Why don't you lot make yourself a drink? I'm just going to find out where Tess has got to."

"Weird," said Max, walking into the kitchen. "I can't find my bank card anywhere."

"Didn't you go to the village for baby rice?" said Tess.

"No, I've had it since then. I was sure I threw it down on the kitchen table, but obviously the combination of an early start and waving farewell to Morag was enough to tip my memory over the edge."

"I'm sure it will turn up," said Tess. "Houses like these have a knack of devouring things up, like reading glasses and phone chargers – oh, and books. I spent my childhood searching for half-read paperbacks."

"Not that it matters, as my bank account is completely empty," he said, "as I discovered in the village earlier."

"Oh dear."

"It's alright – I knew Mum would stop my allowance the second she twigged we were over here. But I've got a good stash from my earnings in LA to keep me going for the moment, though it's an old savings account so I don't have a card attached to it."

Tess was struggling to open the lid on the jar of Marmite.

"How about I open the jar for you?" said Max.

"Yes, please, the lid is a little stiff."

"You like Marmite then?"

"Yes, I'm firmly in the Love Marmite camp."

"Me too," he said. "Is the toast burning?"

Tess lifted the silver lid and took out the Aga toaster with bread inside. "I think it's just about perfect."

"You're quite right to have toast now – who knows when the Indian takeaway will arrive," said Max.

"You know, I think I might pass on the supper," said Tess, then seeing the expression on Max's face added, "but I'd love to help with Fleur tomorrow if that's okay with you?"

"More than," said Max, checking his phone. "Great, I've just got an email confirming our takeaway order – very decent of them to take a cheque considering they don't know me."

"Benefits of the countryside," said Tess, spreading butter on the toast, before putting on a smattering of Marmite. "Tonight, try praying to Saint Anthony. Freddie once lost her whopper of a diamond ring, she prayed to Saint Anthony and the next day she found her ring in the hen run."

Chapter forty-three

Emptying the last of the curry from a tin-foil container onto his plate before taking a large sip of wine, Thomas looked like he was in heaven.

"I haven't eaten like this in years," he said. "In fact, I don't think we've ever had a takeaway in this house."

"Who's for the last poppadom?" said Max.

"No, thanks, I'm well and truly stuffed," said Elodie, "but it was all delicious. Good call, Max."

"Anika will regret having bowed out of supper when I tell her how good it was," said Thomas. "However, when a lady says she needs her beauty sleep, who am I to argue when I am fortunate enough to be the one to lay eyes on her?"

Elodie thought of the palpable look of boredom on Anika's face over drinks before supper, but Gramps seemed oblivious.

"How's her ladyship doing over there?" he said.

Max got up and peeped into the Moses basket by the Aga.

"Sleeping like a baby," he said, smiling.

"Tess and Julia both slept in a basket just like that," said Thomas. "I'm sure it is still stowed away somewhere upstairs."

"Maybe you should open a museum, Gramps, charge a tenner," said Max, "and you could give them a glass of sloe gin on their way out – bound to get glowing reviews with that sort of liquor on board."

"If only life were so easy, Max – the only thing that belongs in a museum around here is me."

"Not sure about that, Gramps," said Elodie, grinning. "Some of the chutney in the pantry must be practically antique by now – maybe you could team up? One Man and His Chutney – could work in the Tate Modern if we got Tracey Emin on board."

"Though you'd have to stuff me first – and speaking of old things – Augusta," he turned to the parrot, "you've been very quiet lately?"

"Apart from swearing at Morag," said Elodie.

"Yes, apart from that."

Augusta stared at them with her piercing eyes.

"Maybe I'll take her out tomorrow for a little exercise," said Thomas.

"She wouldn't attack Fleur though, would she?" said Max.

"Certainly not, but good to see you being the protective father."

"Gramps, this seems like a good time to tell you that Mum knows we're here," said Elodie.

"Does she now?" he said.

"Not too happy about it either," said Max.

"And do you have a plan as to your next move?"

"Could we get Mum to come and visit Fleur here? No, I suppose not," said Max, seeing the expressions on their faces.

"Maybe we could write to her, Max, and explain how we all ended up at Bellamore," said Elodie.

"Your grandmother used to write letters," said Thomas. "Often illustrated with ink drawings of what was happening here, a basket filled with magnificent vegetables from the walled garden, fruit from the orchard or a meet on the lawn."

"It sounds like you did have fun with Odette in the early days," said Elodie.

"Certainly, and we threw some wonderful parties, no expense spared of course. Champagne and roast goose, always a highlight." He lifted his glass and tipped the remainder of the sloe gin in his glass from left to right.

Elodie wondered if it might be a good time to ask about his relationship with her mother, but his eyes were beginning to glaze over with the gin.

"Anika for some reason seems to like me," he said. "Who knows why?"

"I'd say it's your dress sense," said Max. "The powder-blue jacket and bright-yellow trousers you were wearing yesterday – very razzy."

"My old house master instilled the idea of dressing properly every day – 'you never know who you might bump into,' he'd say."

"On that note, I'm going to pop on my designer coat and go outside for my very last ciggy," said Elodie.

"Thank the lord for that," said Thomas.

"Only because this is the last of my supply," she said.

"As long as you pick up the butt. I can't abide litter."

"Neither can we – no need to worry, Gramps," said Max.

"*What's more, you can give the ruddy things up altogether,*" Thomas called after Elodie as she slipped out the door into the back garden. "Now then, Max, as it's just you and me, I'd like to propose a toast to Baby Fleur – may she grow to love and prosper."

"Thanks, Gramps," said Max, raising his small glass of sloe gin.

"Lovely stuff, isn't, Max? Which reminds me, at the other scale of potency I've got that little H20 project for you tomorrow."

"Elodie, so good to hear from you," said Luke.

"I'm outside having a ciggy, so I thought I'd call."

"Are you beneath the Irish stars?"

"I am – it's rather beautiful here."

"I bet it is," said Luke. "I've been thinking about you – a lot."

"Would you like to come over?" There, she'd said it.

"To Ireland?"

"Why not? I realise we haven't known each other for very long but –"

"Oh, I think we have a pretty good idea about each other, don't you? I'd love to see you, you know I would."

"It sounds busy where you are."

"New York."

"New York?"

"Seeing my mom. You know, family gathering, that sort of thing ... so, I can fly to Dublin?"

"Yes, and I'll ask someone to collect you."

"No, I'll pick up a car. I'll relish the adventure of driving in the wild Irish countryside. Is the house on Google maps?"

"I wouldn't say so, but type in Drummare, and when you pass through the village, drive along a narrow road and look for gates with a pair of donkeys in a field just inside, who usually rest their heads over the top of the fence."

Chapter forty-four

Portland Road, London

Amy Mahon's voice sang 'One Is the Loneliest Number' as Julia stood in her dressing room, which was styled on Carrie Bradshaw's *Sex in the City* clothes sanctuary. Dressed in a cream, ankle-length nightdress, Julia closed her eyes and pulled on the ends of her fingers as taught by her therapist to release tension, but it wasn't working. She could feel her shoulders mounting, becoming stiffer and more painful with every thought of her children. All she wanted to do was drink but, more than that, she wanted to stop. In fact, she wanted it all to stop: her bad decisions, her bad mothering, her bad everything.

Slowly, she circled the edge of the room, tapping her fingers on the hook of each clothes hanger and then, with a slow count to three, she released her raging bull and began pulling clothes onto the floor. Evening dresses, tailored suits, wool trousers, knee-length skirts, cashmere sweaters, whatever came to hand – and then she pulled open drawers, hurling nightdresses, scarves, lace camisoles … on and on.

By the time Julia had finished the purge, she could feel sweat seeping slowly into her hairline.

Stripping off her nightdress, she stepped into a three-way mirror.

"The lights in here aren't bright enough," she said, hearing footsteps in the bedroom.

"Julia, come out of there, I beg of you," said Lorenzo, on the other side of the double doors. "This reaction makes no sense."

A few moments later, Julia opened one of the dressing-room doors and looked at Lorenzo.

"I will be the judge of what makes sense," she said calmly. "Now, get out of my house and leave me to it."

"I wish you would listen, Julia," he said. "We have been here before and you know you will feel better once we talk it through. Things are always better when we talk it through."

"Not this time," she said, with her hand firmly on the door.

"How about we try some exercise, or we can go out for ice cream? Whatever it takes, Julia, please let me help you."

"No," she said, closing herself into the dressing room, but a minute later she opened the door again.

"*Lorenzo?*" she called. "*Lorenzo, come back.*"

"Julia, I'm here," he said, rushing back to the door. "Thank God – I knew you'd see sense."

"Get me a knife, will you?"

Lorenzo's expression darkened. "What kind of knife?"

"A sharp knife." She closed the door.

Looking around her dressing room, she considered adding the contents of her dressing table to the pile – but no, she was wise when it came to jewels.

"Julia?" said Lorenzo from outside the door. "I have a small knife, but first you need to tell me what you are going to do with it."

"No." Opening the door slightly, she slipped out her hand.

Lorenzo passed her the knife by the handle.

"I give you this knife because I trust you, Julia," he said, his voice slightly shaking, "and I know you won't do anything stupid."

"Close the front door on your way out, will you?" Shutting and locking the door, she retreated to her cavern of designer labels.

"You know where I am if you need me, Julia," she heard him say, his voice full of concern, but at this moment she didn't care how he felt.

Barefoot and naked, she sat on the floor and piece by piece, blouse or trouser, whatever came to hand first, she tore her way through thousands upon thousands of pounds worth of haute-couture collections. She didn't like what the clothes represented, how they had been bought, or more accurately with what they had been bought.

In complete silence, Julia lay on top of a thick, luscious mattress of ragged material and curled up like a cat. She wished she could cry, but not a single tear came. She couldn't ever remember crying and it had made life hard. This must be why people think I'm a cold-hearted woman, she thought to herself.

Chapter forty-five

Bellamore

Sitting on a stone bench in the garden, Elodie was wearing an old jumper that she found in a wardrobe on the top floor, leggings covered in Bonnie and Clyde's dog hair and a pair of luminous yellow socks that Mrs Murray had bought for her in the village hardware shop.

"Those terriers," said Elodie, hearing Bonnie and Clyde's yapping, which echoed against the house, "they must drive Gramps mad, don't you think, Fleur?" Bouncing her little niece on her lap, she wondered why the terriers seemed to like her so much. The moment they arrived with Anika, the dogs raced around the house in search of Elodie. Even if she was still asleep, they'd leap up on the bed and lick her face. She had never been a dog person, especially not little dogs, but she felt a little flattered that they liked her all the same.

Lifting a twig from the ground, Elodie passed it to Fleur who began waving it over her head. Elodie looked at Fleur's tiny golden locks, and then ran a hand through her own hair, which she'd half washed in the kitchen sink about a week ago until Gramps arrived in with a dead rabbit and so she abandoned her Vidal Sassoon moment. However, she was relishing the thought of a hot bath at Farley Hall later, thanks to a kind invitation from Freddie, after

Elodie explained that Luke was due to arrive tomorrow evening.

Leaning back, she looked up to see a pair of jackdaws moving at a pace as a buzzard swooped overhead. It was an incredible sight against the huge, blue sky.

"I think I hear your daddy coming," she said, hearing footsteps on the gravel. She gently pressed Fleur's little nose and they both giggled. "Would you like to see your daddy? Shall we see who it is?" Holding Fleur, she slowly got up from the bench and, turning towards the house, she waved at Max. "Say hi to Daddy." Holding up Fleur's hand, still clutching the stick, she waved it.

"How are you, girls?"

Gathering Fleur into his arms, Max sat on the bench.

"Da-da?" he said to Fleur. "Can you say Da-da? Maybe too soon for linguistics?"

"I think she prefers to chew on that twig," said Elodie, sitting next to him.

"We've been discussing the bird life, haven't we, Fleur?" said Elodie, resting her head upon Max's shoulder. "Sorry about my greasy head on your shoulder, by the way."

"Sis, never did I think I'd see the day when you'd not only be wearing zero make-up but wearing a pair of neon-yellow socks."

Elodie laughed. "I merely said in passing to Mrs Murray that my feet were cold at night, despite the hot-water bottle – which by the way leaked last night."

"Nice," said Max.

"And Mrs Murray came back with these beauties."

"Should you ever take up hill walking, there'll be no need for you to buy a high-vis jacket with those socks."

Elodie closed her eyes. "Anyway, it actually feels quite liberating – you know, not feeling like I've got to look like something out of *Tatler* all the time?"

"It was Odette's legacy that made you like that," said Max.

"What? Making me completely paranoid about how I look and feeling that I can't leave the house without make-up and a blow-dry? You got off lightly, Max."

As she felt Max's shoulder move, Elodie lifted her head and saw he was staring towards the house. She looked, and her heart yo-

yoed – first of all in a really good way, which lasted for a split second until she realised just how hideous she must look.

"Holy fucking hell," she whispered, "and to quote Augusta, *bugger, bugger, bugger.*"

"Who's this?" said Max.

Elodie watched as Luke walked towards them, wearing sunglasses, a blue shirt and a beaming smile.

Elodie took a hair-tie from her wrist and frantically pulled her hair into a ponytail.

"I cannot believe it," she said between gritted teeth.

"You're gorgeous," said Max, giving her a kiss on the forehead and slipping an arm around her shoulders. "Don't worry – just remember what we've been talking about, how you feel so at ease not having to dress up all the time."

But Luke's smile slowly turned into a strange expression as he drew closer.

"Elodie," he said, awkwardly, raising his hand. "Hello. Surprise?"

"Aren't you going to introduce us, Elodie?" said Max, with his arm around his sister.

"Sorry, yes, Luke, I'd like you to meet Max."

But Luke didn't say a word.

"Max, my brother?" said Elodie.

Then Luke's smile returned. "Your brother, ah, I see," he said, visibly relaxing. "Good to meet you, Max." He held out his hand.

"Alright, mate," said Max as they shook hands.

"And this is?" said Luke, smiling at Fleur, who held out her stick to him as if she wanted him to take it.

"This is Fleur," said Max, "my daughter."

"Hello, Fleur, I haven't seen such a tiny human for a long time."

Elodie desperately tried to think of something to say.

"I didn't hear a car arrive, only the dogs barking," she said.

"Google maps brought me in through the back entrance, but I think the jeep I picked up at the hire place was happy to have a little muddy adventure."

"Is this your first time in Ireland?" said Max.

"Yes, green fields and friendly faces," said Luke. "True to its word."

"How about a coffee?" said Max.

"Great," said Luke, just as Elodie said, "No."

"I mean, wouldn't you like to get settled into your hotel instead?" she said. At least then she'd have a chance to wash her hair if she could get over to Farley Hall, tidy her room and try to work out something they could eat for the next few days that wouldn't involve last night's stewed rabbit.

"He's hardly going to stay in a hotel," said Max. "There are at least ten bedrooms here – if you don't mind dry rot, leaking ceilings and damp, that is, Luke?"

"Not at all."

"Then welcome to Bellamore."

"Who's that?" said Luke, as a scooter drove down the avenue.

"Mrs Murray," said Max. "She helps Gramps in the house. She's got an OAP sign tied on to the tail-light with bailer twine – quite a character."

"Look, guys, would you mind if I leave you to it for a couple of hours?" said Elodie.

"No problem," said Luke. "I'm just taking in the views – the countryside here is incredible."

"Actually, El, would you mind taking Fleur with you? Tess is going to take her for the afternoon so she should be in the kitchen."

"Sure," said Elodie, taking Fleur into her arms so naturally now and so pleased to have an accessory to distract from her jumper.

"And Luke, mate, if you don't mind, can you help me with a bath in the garden?"

"As in a bathtub?"

"Welcome to Bellamore," said Max.

Each taking a side of the bath, Max and Luke heaved it across the paddock, under barbed wire and across a muddy lane until they reached the edge of the garden at Bellamore.

"I didn't realise a bathtub would slide nicely on grass," said Luke.

"Not surprising with all the algae and slime on this beauty," said Max. "Right – we're nearly there – we just need to push it about two hundred metres in that direction."

Along the length of the garden was a densely planted and shady border, which Thomas had chosen as the location for the bath.

"So it's going to be an Irish hot tub?" said Luke, as they slid the bath across the lawn.

"Exactly," said Max, "and thank god you're here – otherwise this would be me, myself and I pushing this beauty along – so the timing of your arrival is rather brilliant, even if you did catch my sister by surprise."

They pushed on, passing rhododendrons, acers and magnolias, supported by irises and a scattering of peonies.

"It's so good to see her again," said Luke. "You know, when I arrived in London, I had planned to be a complete loner and get my head around my future. I really had no idea I was going to meet such a girl. Honestly, she snapped up my heart in a second."

"How did you manage to get onto such a good footing with her?"

"Is that surprising?" said Luke as they came to a halt at the appointed location.

"Well, she's usually so guarded, very few friends – only close to Sam really."

"I fixed a coffee machine she was struggling with at Sam's place," said Luke. "I guess that did the trick."

"Ah, yes, it would. Right – let's lift this into place by the hydrangea." They heaved it into position.

"And you know about her ex-boyfriend Dominic?"

"We've met, actually," said Luke, raising his eyebrows, "very briefly."

"Big Bad Dom, bloody headcase. I can't tell you how happy I was to hear she had finally ditched him. He is seriously full of himself."

"Why was she with him?"

"Classic low self-esteem maybe? But I don't mean to blow any ideas you have about El – I absolutely adore her, and Fleur and I wouldn't be at Bellamore if it wasn't for her."

Wiping away moss from around the bath taps, Max got onto his knees to check out the potential for pipe work.

"Not sure where we're going to pipe the waste outlet to," he said. "Those plants won't want a heap of soapy water soaking into their roots."

"How do you know about plumbing?"

"Long story. Still, we won't need to worry about an overflow pipe, as we have no floorboards to worry about, do we?"

"Max, would you mind if I ask more about Elodie – you know, the lack of self-esteem?"

"I blame our ancestors," said Max. "Elodie has had to put up with our grandmother Odette and our mother, a formidable combination if ever there was one."

"I gathered," said Luke.

"Odette was all about manners, and Mum obsessed with image, so as a result El was always the kind of girl people would have a crush on, the whole way through school. I think she was unhappy and lost for much of the time. I know she sometimes seemed aloof and kind of haughty, but I think it was just a front to hide her misery."

"And how about you and your mom – are you close?"

"Not exactly – I just tend to nod accordingly and then ignore her. Anyway, I'm striking out for freedom, or at least about to."

"My old man wants me to get into the family business."

"You don't sound keen?"

"That's partly why I came to London, to take time out before I sign up to endless board meetings."

"What if you don't go for joining the firm?"

"I get to live my dream and set up my own business."

"So what's stopping you?"

"Maybe I'm lazy, and maybe a little scared of leaving a guaranteed life of comfort." Luke couldn't believe how honest he was being – it felt like he and Max had just swallowed truth pills. "So how long are you guys here for?"

"No idea. I'm trying to hold on to my cash from my year in LA, but Gramps is really strapped so I'm not sure how long this whole Ireland excursion is going to last."

"What about Elodie – what do you think she'll do in the future?"

"Well, not architecture, that's for sure. She ducked out halfway through her first year – as soon as Odette, our grandmother, died. She pretty much forced Elodie into that course, said she had to get a degree no matter what."

"Didn't your mom have a say in things?"

"Not while Odette was alive – no, she called all the shots, even from her deathbed."

"Sounds like a Dickens' tale."

"For quite a while after Odette died, I think El and I could both feel her shadow lurking, but I think we've shaken off that feeling now. But there's no doubt that the combination of Odette and our mother put the brakes on Elodie's ambitions."

"Isn't your mother supportive to Elodie?"

"El wants to be an artist and she should be an artist, she's bloody good. But the thing is, all Mum seems to want for her is to be a professional wife. It's been almost seven years since El left her degree course, and she has literally achieved zero in that time."

Chapter forty-six

"This place is turning into one of those *social hubs* I keep reading about," said Thomas, as a beautiful girl with misty eyes and flushed cheeks arrived into the hall, with a soft-toy fox in one arm and a bottle of scent and one of whiskey in the other.

"I'm so sorry to come barging in," she said.

He looked at the girl whose eyes were brimming with tears. "Darling Fleur has been blessed with your eyes," he said. "You are Charlotte, I presume?"

"Yes," she said, nodding her head and sobbing without wiping her eyes, "and I'm so ashamed. The way I abandoned Max and my baby – how can any of you even begin to forgive me?"

It had been some time since he had seen such unabashed outpouring of emotion.

"You have nothing to apologise for, not to me at least, for your little daughter has brought this house back to life."

"Do you mean it?" she said, blinking through the tears.

"Yes, I do, and if I know my grandson the way I think I know him, Max will feel the same."

"I do hope so," she said, taking a deep breath. She awkwardly put the two bottles down on the sideboard. "The whiskey is for you, Mr Archdale – and the scent is for your kind friend, who I gather collected Max and Fleur from the airport."

"Anika will be pleased, though not as happy as I will be when I charge my favourite tumbler this evening."

"I'm all over the place, really," Charlotte said, "and I got completely lost on the motorway, went miles in the wrong direction."

"Didn't you call Max?"

"I wanted to be a surprise."

"Well, there's no shortage of those around here. Now, Baby Fleur is with her Great-aunt Tess in the kitchen, but let's step outside for just a moment – there's something I want to point out to you."

As they walked down the front steps, Mrs Murray arrived up the avenue on her scooter.

"Hello, Mrs Murray," said Thomas.

"More mouths to feed, I see, Mr Archdale," she said, pulling off her helmet to reveal her grey hair in a purple hairnet.

"Yes, indeed, Mrs Murray," he said, taking Charlotte's arm and steering her away. "Mrs Murray and I have a rather old-fashioned relationship, as Max and Elodie have both pointed out to me."

"No first-name terms then?" said Charlotte.

"Lord, no. Mrs Murray would have a heart attack if I asked her to call me Thomas."

"It's such a relief to be here, Thomas, if I may call you Thomas?"

"Please," he said, pausing beneath an oak tree. "And just as well you didn't arrive yesterday, as we had Niall McNally here with a digger, while my genius grandson and an American fellow laid pipes and connected water to a bath. He's a talented young fellow, Max."

He looked at Charlotte, her eyes so pretty and brimming with tears.

"I'm sorry," she said, gently running her fingertips beneath her eyelids as if trying to stop any mascara from smudging. "I've missed Max so much, and my little Fleur."

"Of course you have."

"You must have plenty of bathrooms here," she said, looking up at the house.

"Plenty. However, and this is what I want to point out to you –

if you want to actually find a bath that fills with water and even better, hot water, behind the hydrangeas at the end of the garden is the place to find peace. Do you see the pink blooms towards the end of the garden?"

"I do," said Charlotte.

"There lies the most charming bath imaginable and, Charlotte, there's no need for you to feel any awkwardness here. I won't pretend that meeting Fleur wasn't rather a shock – however, Fleur has made me realise that there may be something in the future after all and I've stopped thinking about dying, and more about living."

"That certainly sounds like a good thing," said Charlotte.

"Though not sure I could say the same about your choice of nanny."

"Oh," said Charlotte.

"Oh, indeed. I'm afraid Morag has returned to Scotland following a certain unpleasant experience and, let's say, a fit of flighty temper. But no matter."

"Thomas, I have to tell you, I've been in a real state worrying that Fleur might not recognise me. And I feel so guilty for having left her with Morag and Max –"

"My dear, it all worked out for the best – and, as for Fleur recognising you, I believe that mother and child instinctively have a sense about each other. Now, let me lead you towards the kitchen – there you will find your daughter and her Great-aunt Tess."

Charlotte pushed open the kitchen door and found her little daughter snuggled into the arms of a very pretty woman sitting in an armchair by the window.

"Hello," whispered Charlotte, peering around the door.

The woman seemed to panic and, standing up, she held Fleur closely.

"I'm so sorry, you must be Aunt Tess? I'm Charlotte, Fleur's mother."

"Oh god, Charlotte, I'm the one who's sorry," said Tess, flush-faced as she passed Fleur into her mother's arms.

"Hello, my little angel," said Charlotte, trying to hold her tears, "Mummy's come back, and I'll never leave you again, never ever, never ever, my little darling."

"Max will be overjoyed," said Tess.

"Fleur looked so happy and comfortable with you," said Charlotte. "I can't thank you enough for taking such good care of her."

"No, I've done so little," said Tess, who had picked up a dishcloth and begun mindlessly wiping the kitchen table. "Nothing at all, and she's a lovely baby, a very lovely baby."

"I had no idea Max had an aunt in Ireland."

"No," said Tess, dropping the cloth in the sink. "Now that you're here, Charlotte, I really do need to get going, I'm so behind with everything." She gave Fleur a kiss on her forehead.

"Bless you, little darling."

"And Max?"

"I think he might be in the yard, helping the plumber to fit the water heater," said Tess. "But don't worry, he'll be in soon, so put on the kettle and make yourself at home."

"Are you sure you won't stay? Join me for a cup of tea?"

"I really do need to get on," said Tess, "but thank you, Charlotte," and she pulled on her boots and walked into the back garden.

Mrs Murray stood at the top of the ladder in the roomy old hot press, wearing a blue housecoat with a tiny gold cross hanging around her neck. Her tongue was squeezed out between her lips with concentration.

"Mrs Murray," said Thomas, "I didn't want to disturb you in the middle of such a vital operation, but should you really be at the top of a ladder at your age?"

"Sure, aren't we the same age?" she said, taking out the old light bulb and throwing it down onto the shelf of pillowcases. She then carefully pushed in the new light bulb and retreated down the wooden steps.

"Surely there's a year or two in it?"

"No, same year," she said, "and if it's a case of you or me going up them steps to change the blub, I'd be the more nimble of the both of us, and you know it."

"I don't suppose you spotted any jars of yogurt in there?"

"I did not," she said, patting her permed grey hair. "There be nothing but towels and linen in there, and moths."

"Moths?"

"Aye."

"Well, let's not dwell on life's irritations – a battle with moths is at the bottom on my list at the moment."

"Another thing, Mr Archdale –"

"Yes, Mrs Murray?" Now feeling older by the second, he wondered how he got tied into such formalities with his cleaner.

"Your business is your business, Mr Archdale, but I cannot abide that bedspread."

"The leopard print? Anika surprised me with it at the weekend."

"Moths, that synthetic material is a beacon for them moths," said Mrs Murray.

"Surely not already?"

"Those beggars will be all over that bedspread, mark my words. I'd be putting it into the bin, so I would."

"But Anika brought it over to liven up my bedroom."

"What do you mean, 'liven it up'?"

"Let's not go into the details, Mrs Murray," said Thomas, as Anika arrived onto the landing with a magazine rolled under her arm. "Ah, Anika, how about a siesta, darling?"

"No," said Anika, completely ignoring Mrs Murray, who proceeded to restack several piles of pillowcases and hand towels. "I've just been reading an article about my old director on *Big Brother*, so I'm going to go home and give him a call. For some reason, I feel so restless." She ran a hand through her hair.

"How about a walk then?"

"Not that kind of restless," snapped Anika. "I don't need a walk."

"You know that Anika used to present a big television show in Holland?" he said, turning to Mrs Murray. "A house full of people, living together, sharing bathrooms and all sorts of things."

"Sure doesn't it sound like this very house?" said Mrs Murray. "You could set up a programme here, so you could."

Anika glared at Mrs Murray.

"And we're out of bleach, so we are," said Mrs Murray, "for

when you're next in the village."

"Alright, Mrs Murray," said Thomas. "Are you alright, Anika darling? You truly look irritated."

"Can I leave Bonnie and Clyde here for the night?" she asked.

"Won't you stay for supper, darling? The children's other halves have arrived and I'm hoping Tess will join us. We'll have an impromptu celebration."

"Tonight, I choose vodka, in my house, alone."

"You might want to take that bedspread with you?" said Mrs Murray. "Only a matter of time before the mildew sets in. Like honey to bees, that synthetic material, so it is."

"Which reminds me, Mrs Murray, there's a matter of a bathtub outside and I was hoping you might run a cloth over it?" said Thomas. "Well, it may require a scrub."

Chapter forty-seven

If Elodie had been told she would bathe surrounded by hydrangeas in an overgrown Irish garden, she would never have believed it. It was late afternoon when she had walked out the front door wearing an old dressing gown of Odette's and cowboy boots. It was a case of needs must. Thankfully Max had taken Luke for a long walk to the village to sample an afternoon pint and, once satisfied that there wasn't a person in sight, Elodie walked through the garden.

It took both Elodie's hands to turn on the hot tap but, once she had, piping hot water gushed out, crystal clear. Having added cold water to the bath and double-checked that there was no one else around, she dropped her dressing gown to the ground and climbed in. She had even found a bottle of rose oil in her bathroom and, once she had washed her hair, she poured in the oil and luxuriated in the hot water.

That evening, wearing a grey polo neck and jeans, with dark pencil lining her eyes, Elodie felt like the best version of herself that she'd ever been.

"He seems like a nice chap, Elodie," said Thomas, standing over a pan of fried potatoes on the Aga. "He and Max were very excited to have got the bath going, and the water heater works like a

219

charm, doesn't it?"

"Are they back yet?" said Elodie, irritated that she hadn't seen Luke since before lunch.

"Boys will be boys, and it's good for Max to let his hair down for a change, though he'll jump out of his skin when he discovers that Charlotte is here."

"I met Charlotte upstairs a while ago – she seems to have made herself very much at home already."

"I'll leave it to you to sort out bedrooms with your American friend. Whatever arrangement you prefer."

"What else is for supper?" said Elodie, changing the subject.

"Leeks, home grown of course, beetroot and rabbit."

"Rabbit? Really, Gramps?"

"Really, Elodie, and let's open the last of the rosé this evening, shall we? Celebrate the arrival of Charlotte, and of your apparent *friend*."

"We are friends," said Elodie, smiling at her grandfather. "Will Tess and Anika join us too?"

"Anika seems rather low this evening, so she's going to go home and mull things over. Think she may be rather overwhelmed by our houseful."

"Sorry, Gramps," said Elodie.

"For what?"

"Messing up your routine?"

"Not at all. Besides, if it wasn't for you I most likely wouldn't have bothered getting that bath set up out there – which I've christened Maud, by the way."

"What's that about the bath, Gramps?" said Max, beaming a smile as he arrived into the kitchen carrying Fleur in one arm, and with his other arm around Charlotte.

"Home from the pub and reunited with mother and child. A fine afternoon for you, Max."

"Most certainly, Gramps, best surprise in the world," said Max. "Oh, and Elodie, we actually only had a pint. Luke's just making a phone call by the front door, he'll be down in a sec."

"I was saying as you arrived in, Max," said Thomas, "I've christened our al fresco bathtub 'Maud'. You know, the old love song – 'Come into the Garden, Maud'? No? I suppose you wouldn't."

"I like it," said Charlotte. "They would have lapped up the al fresco bath at the commune."

"As pure as spring water is, Charlotte, I'm not sure you'd necessarily like to lap up that bath water."

"I think Charlotte meant lap up the *idea* of the bath," said Elodie.

"Yes, it was one of my better ideas. Another one I've had is to ask Maurice Allen for a vat of his homemade cider, which is a much more economic option to wine."

"Not sure Anika would be too keen, Gramps," said Max.

"I thought she only drinks vodka?" said Elodie.

"Yes, but I'm thinking of the young," he said. "You lot."

"You must be longing for a night to yourself though, Gramps," said Max. "We can clear out for an evening if you like? Or we could have a carpet picnic in the master bedroom."

"Apart from the leaking roof in that particular bedroom, Max, I honestly would prefer to have your company. I'm not a big fan of dining alone as it happens."

"At the commune, there was no such thing as eating alone," said Charlotte, snuggling Fleur by the Aga. "When I left, the first thing I did was pull into a motorway diner to order a toasted cheese sandwich, which I then ate by myself. It was heaven."

Just then Anika arrived with dancing eyes, Luke in tow.

"Darling, I thought you weren't staying for supper," said Thomas, waving the spatula in her direction.

"I had a change of mind," she said, looking at Luke's behind as he walked over to Elodie. "How boring of me to stay at home when there is a cosy party here."

"Excellent," said Thomas. "Now all we need is Tess."

"Luke, how about a drink?" said Anika.

"Ah, there you are, Tess," said Thomas as she arrived in from the back garden. "Right on cue."

Anika looked put out.

"I've brought some chutney," Tess said shyly. Taking off her wellies and slipping on flat shoes, she made a beeline for Fleur. "I hope I haven't held you all up?"

"Not at all," said Elodie. "Tess, I'd like you to meet Luke."

Tess turned around and took Luke's proffered hand. "Lovely to meet you," she said. "Elodie tells me you're from California?"

"That's right," said Luke.

"Are the California girls as hot as the song suggests?" said Anika.

"Ah yes, the Beach Boys," said Thomas. "I've always been fond of them, excellent group."

"Actually, Thomas, I was referring to Katy Perry and Snoop Dog," said Anika, turning back to Luke. "I interviewed Katy and Snoop in New York for a *Big Brother* special."

"Snoopy, yes. Isn't *Peanuts* wonderful?" said Thomas. "Timeless really."

"Gramps," said Max, stepping in to rescue him, "I think the song Anika is talking about is more recent than the Beach Boys. Snoop Dog is an American rapper."

"So, Luke, do you go to many events in California? Are you on the social circuit?" said Anika, taking off her blazer and readjusting her thick gold necklace.

"Not really," said Luke. "My parents have a ranch there – otherwise I was brought up in New York."

"Where the city never sleeps," said Anika.

"So good they named it twice," said Thomas. "I got that one right, didn't I?"

"Yes, Dad," said Tess. "Shall I help with the gravy?"

"I had no idea rabbit could be so tender," said Luke. "I ate it in Ohio, years ago on a school camping trip, and it tasted more like shoe leather, but this really is good."

"Delighted to hear it," said Thomas. "It's the Drummare land, just damp enough to keep the limbs moist. Any more gravy at that end of the table?"

And the lights went out, completely.

"Oh," said Thomas. "Well, that's a fine thing."

"Max, can you put the light on your phone on?" said Charlotte, as they stood up to bring Fleur, who was asleep in her basket, closer to the table.

"Here you go," said Luke, passing his phone with its torch to Charlotte.

"Is she okay?" said Tess.

"She's fine, thanks, Tess," said Max.

"When did you drop the aunt part?" said Elodie.

"Max and I agreed that Tess is much easier," said Tess, "didn't we, Max?"

"We've got some candles by the sink, Max, if you can get them, please?" said Thomas.

Max fetched a pair of candlesticks with only the stumps of candles in them.

"These won't last long," he said.

"There are more in that cupboard," said Tess, pointing.

He retrieved a box of candles. "Anyone got a match?"

"I know a lady with a light," said Luke, rubbing his hand along Elodie's thigh.

"Here we go," said Elodie, taking a lighter from her pocket and lighting the candle stumps.

"Though you've stopped smoking, haven't you, Elodie?" said Thomas.

"Only because I haven't been to a shop," she said.

"Well, whatever works. Now, how about some whiskey to warm us all up? Max, will you do the honours?"

"I'd better go and check the fuse box first," said Max. "I suppose there's a trip switch? Though God knows in a house this old – has the electric system ever been updated?"

"Oh, never mind that," said Thomas. "I'll check it later. Let's get more candles lit – much better ambience and how about we open the lovely bottle of whiskey that Charlotte so kindly brought to us. I left it in the dining room on the table."

"Can you keep an eye on Fleur for a sec, Tess?" said Max. "Charlotte, come with me – I need someone to hold my hand – I'm scared of the dark."

Charlotte giggled and took his hand.

"Do be careful on the stairs, Max, won't you?" said Thomas.

"Aye, aye, Captain – I've got my trusty phone-light and a beautiful maiden to protect me," said Max, as he and Charlotte left the room.

"Tess, you've hardly touched supper?" said Elodie.

"I had an enormous lunch with Freddie," said Tess, smiling.

"That Freddie, she's got such appetite for life, hasn't she?" said Thomas.

"Did Max find his card?" said Tess, abruptly.

"What's that?" said Thomas.

"It has completely vanished," said Elodie, "and Max suspects that Morag might have taken it." She turned to Luke. "Fleur's ex-nanny. But luckily his current account was bone dry, so it really doesn't matter."

"Elodie, watch the candle, would you?" said Thomas. "Just so that it doesn't melt onto the table."

"It's fine, Gramps, don't worry," said Elodie.

"Where is Max with my whiskey?" he said, getting up from the table. "Excuse me for a moment, would you?"

"Everything alright?" said Tess, looking at her father.

"Yes, yes," he said.

"Got the whiskey, Gramps," said Max, arriving back into the kitchen with Charlotte, "and not a ghost to be seen up there."

"Don't say that, Max," said Charlotte. "You know what an utter wimp I am."

"Straight into the tumbler, please, Max," said Thomas, staring at the glass.

"And look what I found?" said Max, holding his bank card between his fingers. "It was sitting on the table out there – I must have left it there after all."

"Dad, wouldn't you like a proper glass?" said Tess.

"No, thank you, this will be fine."

Once the whiskey hit the glass, Thomas took a large drink and sat down again.

"Now tell us, Luke," he said, "how exactly did you meet my granddaughter?"

"Luke was helping me in Sam's Kitchen," said Elodie.

"Earning a few shekels? Not easy out there, is it, Luke? And what is it that you do?"

"I'm in between jobs," said Luke, smiling at Max.

"Reminds me of my days in the city . . ."

And as Thomas proceeded to tell tales of the days before he met

Odette, Luke ran his foot up Elodie's leg.

"Gramps, sorry to interrupt," Elodie said after a while, "but would you mind if Luke and I excuse ourselves?"

"Wouldn't you like one for the road?"

"No, thanks, Gramps," said Luke.

"Here's your phone, Luke," said Charlotte. "Looks like it may need a charge."

"Well, you'd better take a candle with you," said Thomas, "and I trust you'll guide Elodie safely upstairs, Luke?"

"Happy to," he said, looking at Elodie.

"And, Elodie, you know where the torches are in the tack room following our excursion to the dawn chorus?"

"Sure do, except they don't actually work," she said, picking up another candle by the sink and lighting it. "Goodnight." Slipping her hand into Luke's, she led him from the kitchen and they made their way upstairs.

"All the way to the top," said Elodie, "and I actually have a confession."

"Oh yes?" said Luke, kissing her neck.

"I'm afraid of the dark."

"Well, that's perfect," he said, "because that makes two of us, and I really think it would be better, in the name of health and safety, if we sleep together tonight, don't you think?"

"I do," she said.

The candle flickered as they walked into Elodie's bedroom.

She put the candlestick on the chest of drawers and then turned to him.

"You and I, by candlelight," she said.

"You and I," he said, as his hands ventured beneath her jumper.

When they kissed it felt like a perfect fit, and all the longing, the waiting felt like it had been worth it.

They climbed onto the huge bed and Luke smoothed back the hair from her forehead and kissed her tenderly.

"So, this is what it feels like," said Luke.

"My body?" giggled Elodie.

"Yes, that too, but what I mean is, this is what the real thing feels like. Because this feels like the real thing, don't you think?"

"Yes," whispered Elodie.

"I almost wish that time could hurry up," said Luke, wrapping himself around her.

Tess felt so cross she didn't know where to look, but she had to compose herself until Max and Charlotte, and darling Fleur, had gone to bed.

"I'll take a proper look at the fuse board in the morning, Gramps, if that sounds good to you?" said Max.

"Right you are, Max. Goodnight to you all, and to you, little one," he said, shaking Fleur's little hand.

Then he and Tess were left alone at the kitchen table, by candlelight.

"You're quiet," he said to Tess.

"Yes," she said.

"Might I ask why?" he said.

Tess shook out the napkin on her lap and began folding it with absolute precision.

"If you had used a ruler you couldn't have got that napkin to fold more evenly," he said.

"Stop it," she said, "just stop it."

"What's got into you, Tess? You were in fine form earlier on."

"You know perfectly well why I'm livid with you," said Tess, trying to keep her voice down.

"You're not going to rake up old coals, are you? I thought we've all been making such progress."

"Yes, and we were, until you bloody well had to go and ruin things."

"Tess?"

"It was you, wasn't it?" she said.

"I don't know what you mean?"

"The fuse hasn't gone at all, has it?"

"Well, of course it has, or if it hasn't I'm sure there's a simple explanation."

"You tried to use Max's bank card to pay the electricity bill, didn't you? And the card was declined because my sister has cancelled Max's allowance."

"Tess, you're quite –"

"Incredibly ironic, don't you think?" she said, getting up from the table and pulling on her cardigan. "How you could betray Max's trust like that? The children are just beginning to settle, and you had to go and do this."

"Tess, if you would just let me speak," he said calmly.

"Alright," said Tess.

"I admit I did take Max's bank card but –"

"I knew it," said Tess, "and you're such a fool – don't you know that if the transaction had gone through it would have appeared on Max's bank statements?"

"I wasn't thinking straight, Tess. It seemed providential that the card was there to hand, and I seized the moment."

"And now you want to blame fate or 'the universe' for what was just plain thieving?"

"Well, it wasn't really – the children and the baby need the electricity after all –"

"So now you're going to tell me that, because the children are staying here, it's only fair they should foot the electricity bill?"

"Not exactly, but yes, of course it is more expensive having them here. Elodie, God bless her, just has no idea about economising. Lights on all over the house, Dimplex heaters plugged in, phone chargers, it all adds up."

"But your little plan didn't work," said Tess, "and that's why we are sitting here in front of a single candle that is about to burn out."

Chapter forty-eight

Tess wanted to forget last night's conversation with her father. It was humiliating beyond words and the worst part of it was she felt such pity for him – he just didn't have the backbone to find solutions that wouldn't have bad consequences. To save both him and Max from embarrassment, having sipped the first half of her mug of hot water and lemon, she called the electricity board and settled the bill. After all, she reasoned with herself, it wasn't as if she paid her father rent for living in the gate lodge, nor, mind you, did he pay her wages for looking after the gardens. Tess had hardly touched the money Odette had given her when she was sent away from Bellamore – in fact, when travelling Tess had worked the most menial of jobs to avoid touching what her mother had given her so begrudgingly.

Puccini was playing on Lyric FM as Tess began to realise how Charlotte's arrival could only be a signal that the children would soon leave Bellamore. Taking the radio with her, she tried to distract herself by going into the potting shed, but all she could see were timeworn tools, chipped terracotta pots and grey cobwebs sweeping across the beams like streams of ancient crochet. She knew she had let herself feel a false sense of security, bonding with Fleur, getting to know the children and spending more time at up at the house than she had ever intended. Maria Callas sang *"Si, mi chiamano Mimi"* and Tess could feel her heart pounding against her chest, tears welling in her eyes as she felt an overwhelming urge to lie down on the ground and sob her heart out.

Catching her breath, she heard a banging sound coming from the front door.

"Tess?"

She could see Max walking around the house to the back entrance to the kitchen.

"Are you there, Tess?"

Pressing her face into the crook of her elbow and pausing for a few moments, Tess turned off the radio and stepped out of the shed.

"Max, hello," she said, smiling. "Please excuse my sniffing, it's very dusty in there."

"Not at all," he said. "I'm sorry to barge in on you, Tess. I know how you like your space. But I was knocking on the front door for a while."

"It was the radio, I turned it up much too loud, terrible habit."

"I'm the same, the louder the better as far I'm concerned."

Tess had another wave of sadness, she just couldn't help herself. "I'm sorry, Max," she said. "I'm so hay-feverish today, it's making my eyes run – excuse me for a moment, will you?"

Running into the house, Tess stood in front of her bedroom mirror and sobbed silently into her clenched fists.

"Oh god, oh god, oh god, I can't do it!" she said but, catching sight of her reflection, she stopped and began practising the deep breathing that Freddie had taught her.

"I've put on the kettle, hope that's okay?" said Max, as Tess reappeared in the potting shed.

"Of course," she said. "You'll find tea bags in the box and out-of-date biscuits in the cupboard."

"Ha, you and my mum are like complete opposites."

"Are we?" said Tess, without looking up, trying to concentrate on evenly dispersing seeds in the pots.

"Come on, you must know it. Mum's groceries come straight from Harrods Food Hall, and when she's on a health kick, every meal comes directly from Pure Package."

"Very smart," said Tess, not unkindly.

"Yes, though you know what? It's incredibly refreshing being over here, even though things up at the house are tight."

"You noticed?"

"Well, yeah," said Max, finding a couple of unwashed mugs in the sink and rinsing them under the tap. "I mean, if I so much as flick on a light-switch a look of horror crosses Gramps' face."

"Ah, it's the old tight Protestant coming out in him, nothing too serious," said Tess.

"And the roof?"

"Yes, the elephant in the corner – now that is a problem. Pass me the basket in the corner, would you?"

Tess began transferring potatoes, which had gone to seed, from a large hessian sack into an old basket. "These beauties are going to turn into new potatoes this summer."

"Have you always been so organised?" said Max, dropping a couple of tea bags into the teapot, before filling it to the brim from the kettle.

"No," said Tess, "quite the opposite."

"In what way?"

"Oh Max, where do I begin? In fact, no, you'd drown in your mug of tea by the time I bored you with the details."

"Go on," he said.

"Let's just say it took me longer than most to grow up, simple as that." Tess looked at him, so young and fresh, his eyes earnest and gentle. "But you have a real chance now to make a good life with Charlotte and Fleur."

"And it scares the hell out of me," he said, passing Tess a cup of tea. "Milk?"

"Oh, lemon for me please. I'm afraid I don't have as much as a drop of milk in the fridge."

"No worries at all, lemon is fine." He handed her half a cut lemon from a saucer on the table. "Okay, how about I sample some of your out-of-date biscuits, then carry those potatoes up to the vegetable garden for you?"

"It's a deal," she said.

Chapter forty-nine

Kensington Yoga, London

With red hair tied back in a purple ribbon, Nadine, the mistress of the yoga studio, stood in the doorway with arms stretched out like a starfish.

"You're American?" said Julia.

"I'm from Quebec," she said, leading Julia into a room with lights beaming from the ceiling against the parquet floor like tiny space-station satellites. "Now let's get straight to it."

Julia stepped onto a yoga mat opposite a huge wall mirror. There was no escaping one's reflection here, that was for sure.

"This morning, we shall substitute rage for the traditional feeling of serenity."

"Okay," said Julia, scowling at her reflection.

"I can see that you have too much going on in your head, so the usual yoga can't give you the outlet you need. Do you follow?"

"I think so," said Julia.

Squaring up to the mirror, Nadine let out a large, wheezy, rasping growl. Then wiping a hint of sweat from her upper lip she turned to Julia.

"This is what we're talking about, Julia. I want you to let it out from your heart – I want you to yell out the pain, the discontent and goddamn unfair things that have happened to you. This is your

231

sanctuary of scream and no-one is here to judge you, nobody is here to listen. I might as well be invisible."

Julia felt deeply uncomfortable but Lorenzo had assured her that this therapy would be worth trying.

"One more thing," said Nadine. "Rather than finishing each class with the traditional 'Namaste', I would encourage you to shout out a swear word. The majority go for the F-word, I have to tell you. However, it is totally up to you. Shout out whatever you feel like."

The Killers' 'Mr Brightside' began to play from the sound system. It started out softly, then the volume increased as Julia followed Nadine, moving fluidly from the Downward Dog into a Salutation, then to a Tree then to a Plank. Julia was just about keeping up, the volume still increasing. It was angry, it was strong. Julia felt every beat, every line. Next came Oasis with 'Wonderwall'. Every beat, every word meant something to Julia as she pressed her body against the mat.

"Are you doing okay, Julia?" Nadine said, red hair streaking across her chest as she lifted her head from the Sideways Snake.

"Yes, I think I am. I can feel my heart beating and that has to be a good thing."

"Definitely," said Nadine, catching her breath. "Okay, now Julia, let's keep this introductory session short, okay? I'm gonna step out of the studio now, and I want you to finish this class alone. And by finish, I mean I want you to shout out whatever word expresses how you feel."

Julia pulled one of her faces.

"Do you think you can handle it by yourself? I can stay if it would help?"

"No, thank you."

Once the door closed, Julia stood on the mat in a star-jump position, her reflection staring back at her beneath the lights. When she took a deep breath, she could see her nostrils flaring, just like her mother's used to. Staring at herself, she was determined not to feel anything, not to feel a single tear – no tremble of her lip, no more feeling sorry for herself.

And then she focused. Digging right into her heart she prepared to scream out the biggest, most excruciatingly rude word she could muster. And then it came out. *"Damn you,"* whispered Julia. *"Damn, damn, damn you!"* she roared, with all her might. And then it shot out. It really shot out, loud, furious, shrieking: *"Fuck it, every bloody part of it!'*

The release hadn't lasted long, and so today, thrusting his Mercedes convertible into sixth gear, Lorenzo drove up the motorway, Julia beside him with a bottle of Champagne between her legs. Lorenzo had always guessed it was her husband who lay at the root of her anxiety, and now she admitted to feeling like a complete failure having lost her children to Ireland and couldn't bear the thought of them getting caught in a life sentence like she had.

Swigging from the neck of the bottle, and encouraged by Lorenzo, Julia yelled from the top of her voice as they blasted along, *"Screw you, Douglas, screw fucking you!"*

Chapter fifty

Bellamore

The needle of the record player danced upon a Myles Davis vinyl before the turntable caught pace and bellowed out moody jazz in the library. The crackle from the speakers felt soothing to Elodie while she sketched her grandfather sinking into his armchair by the window.

"How many days have you been off the smokes now?" he asked.

"Nine, and it would have been utter hell if it wasn't for Luke. We've been having the most gorgeous walks and yesterday we had a picnic in the rain. I never dreamed I'd feel so happy getting utterly soaked."

"There's nothing so comfortable as the company of an old friend."

"But we're not old friends, Gramps, we only met recently."

"That may be, but it looks like you are, and what's more, if you are going to be more than friends, it looks like you're on a good footing."

"You think so?"

"I do, and I'm not sure what sort of job prospects he has, but I'd say that American of yours is rather a catch. Now look at that," he hunched in towards the window, "that little warbler has just managed to scam its mate out of a free lunch, pinched the bug right out of its mouth."

"Impressive eyesight, Gramps," said Elodie, putting down her sketchpad and curling up on the sofa. "It's cosy in here, isn't it? Books and paintings, best combination."

"I've always collected art, even before I met your grandmother, when I couldn't afford it. Sadly most of the good ones have been sold, except for that one by the door." He pointed to a small frame picturing a dark shadow of a woman's face. "It's of no monetary worth of course, but to me it's priceless."

"Is the shadow Odette?"

He looked at Elodie. "You are intuitive, aren't you?"

"Did you know Odette was the one when you met her? Was it instant?"

"You see, Elodie, it seems that life is all about timing. I think if Odette and I had met in Paris when she was at the height of her days as a deb, she wouldn't have looked at me once, let alone twice. Your grandmother's life hadn't worked out the way she might have intended. When we met in New York she hadn't been there long." He leant forward. "She was the most elegant of women on Fifth Avenue, and to see her ice-skating in Central Park you could never have known the turmoil she must have been feeling inside." He sighed.

"Go on," said Elodie.

"Her brother, your great-uncle, died in a car accident, and quite simply her parents blamed her."

"Was she driving?"

"Not at all. Odette never drove, never ever. Not in France, not in Ireland. Her brother had borrowed their father's sports car to take Odette to a party in Paris, and on his way back to the family house in Neuilly-sur-Seine – a magnificent place –" Looking towards the window, he pointed to a finch landing on a branch nearby. "It was black ice, at least that was the deduction of the Police Nationale – however, Odette thought he was most likely speeding. The crash happened at the end of a long stretch, just out of Paris, where a sports car could really come to life." He pressed his foot forward as if he were accelerating. "Odette's brother would have died instantly – those tiny cars were built for speed but not for crashing."

"That is horrendous," said Elodie, thinking back to her mother's drunken driving around London when she was a child. "And what was his name?"

"Maximillian."

"Max – he was named after him?"

"That's right."

"I had no idea," said Elodie.

"Why would you? It wasn't something your grandmother ever spoke about. Her parents blamed Odette for the accident – displaced, of course, but blame her they did – if she hadn't asked her brother to drive her to the party – you know, all the things you could understand running through a person's head when they are grieving."

He picked up a pair of binoculars and began adjusting the dial.

"As a result, the house, the family fortune that would have gone to Maximillian, passed directly to Odette, and I think that was why she struggled so much in her life. Every penny she spent made her feel guilty. It's the sort of thing no one could possibly understand unless they knew the background to the story."

As the needle on the record player began to hop at the end of the track, Elodie stood up and turned it off at the plug.

"All this time, and we never knew."

"You know, your grandmother never wore the engagement ring I gave to her, even though it was stuffed with diamonds."

"Why?" said Elodie, watching him as he squeezed his ring finger between his thumbs.

"She thought it weak to have something on her finger that she hadn't paid for herself. Even now I can hear the signet ring on her left-hand *tap-tap-tapping* away on her writing table when she became irritated by something."

Elodie wished she could leap inside her grandfather's mind to find out what she wanted to know without having to ask questions.

"There is so much we don't know, Elodie. Life is full of secrets, and the more I think about it, the more I realise that one of the reasons Odette was so fiercely independent was because she never wanted rely on anyone, not even her husband, having experienced the trauma of being shunned by her own parents."

"They disowned her?"

"Much worse than that, they literally stopped loving her."

"Like my father stopped loving us?" said Elodie.

"That's rather an out-of-the-blue question, isn't it? I suppose it's all my reminiscing that's egging on your mind, is it?"

"Did you like him? I mean, as your son-in-law, did you think he was a good choice for Mum?"

He put the binoculars down on the side table and, crossing his legs, he leant back into the armchair. "It was a long time ago," he said, looking awkward, rubbing his hands together, squinting his eyes. "Your father had a strong character, and well, Elodie, we just didn't spend that much time together, you follow?"

"But he was married to your daughter?"

"They lived in London, and he was terribly busy with his job."

"Resulting in him blowing his head off."

He picked up his binoculars again and looked at the window. Elodie wondered if he was going to say anything.

"It was tragic," he said, one long minute later. "I wasn't sure that you knew."

"I found out years ago – not that Mum told me – it was a friend from school whose parents knew."

"Not easy for you to find out like that."

"I knew there was something," said Elodie. "I even researched his death in online news archives, but it said nothing more than a 'tragic death,' no details."

"Quite the detective." But he wasn't making a joke, his face was deadly serious. "Your father was a risk-taker, Elodie, and he took a risk that resulted in a line of investors looking for his head."

"I know that."

"And it makes you angry?"

"No," said Elodie, who was feeling relief of some kind to have such a blunt conversation about this matter. "I feel sorry that he didn't give himself the chance to get to know me, or Max."

"I am also very sorry for that."

"He was the same age as the woman in the changing room," she said.

"What's that?"

"There was a woman in a changing room I was in – my age, she died from a drug overdose."

"Dreadful. She was a friend?"

"No, I didn't know her at all, but she made me realise how fragile life is and I think it forced me to open my eyes to what's really going on, you know?"

"Such as?"

"Well, for example, I get the feeling that you think I'm oblivious to your situation –"

"Situation?"

"It really seems like you are struggling moneywise."

He smiled. "So you've noticed then? Though it took you a while."

"Maybe," she said, feeling the tough old leather on the sofa.

"Families like ours, we're an old-fashioned lot, and I fear we are dying rather a slow painful death. Families, once rich and dysfunctional, are now poor and dysfunctional. The irony of it is that this place had been empty, a complete ruin, plundered and on the verge of collapse when we took it over. Your grandmother instantly fell in love with the house and devoted her life to restoring it, dressed it with antiques, paintings, handstitched upholstery, that sort of thing."

"And so, Gramps ..." said Elodie, leaning in.

"Yes? One last question then we must have lunch."

"Where did Odette's money go? She had millions, didn't she?"

"Your grandmother's money went to the place she felt it was deserved."

"What do you mean?"

"Your grandmother did what she thought was right," he said, "and it was her money after all."

"But what was that? What she thought was right?"

"I can't say, Elodie. It's confidential."

Elodie stared at him, wanting to press further, but realising she had no right to.

"It doesn't seem fair that you and Tess are living here, worrying about bills, while Mum is totally minted. Dad must have had the most enormous insurance policy."

"We make our bed and then we lie in it, isn't that right? Now, I think a pre-lunch glass of wine is in order, don't you?"

Chapter fifty-one

Despite the damp, the draughts, the lack of hot water and even the seemingly endless amounts of pheasant and rabbit that came out of the freezer for supper, Elodie felt happy at Bellamore. She had fallen for Luke in a big way, Tess was spending more and more time with Fleur, while Max and Charlotte worked their green-finger magic in the walled garden, planting vegetables and tending to the fruit trees. Mrs Murray baked bread, giving out about Thomas's habit of sweeping crumbs from the breadboard directly onto the floor and about frequent visits from Anika dressed in her inappropriate outfits for the countryside. It was a bubble of eccentric security and Elodie felt that she didn't ever want to leave.

Her mind began racing towards ideas as to how she could persuade her mother to pledge funds to lift Gramps out of the financial hole he had sunk into. Couldn't she play the family-values card? Urging her mother to dig deep for the sake of her roots?

Walking to a huge copper beech on the bank, Elodie nudged her back against the trunk, slid down until she was sitting comfortably and tried to visualise a scenario in which her mother would write a cheque.

"Elodie," said Luke, walking up from the stable yard, "I've been looking for you," and climbing up the bank towards her, he bent down and kissed her lips. "You okay? It looks serious – whatever you're thinking about?"

Elodie was feeling frustrated but also a little excited. She was devising her plan.

"I've just been speaking with Gramps."

"Cool," said Luke, "and I've been cleaning out the hens' laying boxes with Max – those birds are incredibly messy."

"Wouldn't it be lovely if one of them would lay a golden egg?" She got to her feet, feeling her heart rush. "So, Luke, I've been thinking."

"Go on, gorgeous," he said, leaning against the tree.

"First I need to work out how to get my mother to reinstate my allowance."

"Okay," said Luke.

"Then, I need to work out how I can persuade Mum to inject some serious cash into this place."

"Into your grandfather's house?"

"Bellamore is where my mother grew up – in fact she most likely played right here, where we are standing beneath this tree. To give up some of her cash, well, it's more of a duty, isn't it? What's more, all of her money came from my father. I'm not sure how – he had a huge insurance policy or something ... or maybe he robbed a bank."

"You think so?"

"I'm joking," she said, feeling like a live wire and wanting to get a huge canvas and write her ideas down in big black lettering.

"I wonder how comfortable your grandfather would be to have his daughter bail him out?"

"It isn't *bailing* him out, Luke," snapped Elodie, "Mum could solve the structural problems at Bellamore with a swipe of a pen, and then she could simply put a sort of monthly payment scheme in place, like giving Gramps a sort of pension?"

"But is that a realistic expectation? That she would agree, just because you suggest it?" said Luke, who just wasn't playing ball. "And, as for your request for your allowance, why do you need to rely on your mom? You can earn your own money."

"What?" Elodie took two steps back from Luke.

"Elodie," he said, moving towards her, "you are really talented

– your drawing is incredible and I'm sure if we can get you into the right gallery –"

"What do you mean *we*?"

"I'm saying I can help to get your art into the right hands. A guy I went to college with has a gallery in New York, and is about to open in Boston, and I can think of others who'd be open to viewing your stuff."

"Luke, I think you're missing the point," said Elodie, disliking the way he so arrogantly felt that he could fix her career. "This isn't about me, it's about Bellamore. Just look at that roof." She pointed to missing tiles and guttering hanging down with a myriad of weeds attached to it. "The walls are literally crumbling before our eyes and that's before we even think about the wiring, which is a disaster waiting to happen."

"But, Elodie, this is your grandfather's house – surely it's up to him."

"Luke?"

"I think you are using the house as a distraction from dealing with your own problems."

"Excuse me?" Elodie couldn't believe what she was hearing. "Problems? And what problems are these exactly? You've only known me for five minutes and now you are assessing my problems?"

The expression on Luke's face didn't waver as he spoke. "Well, from what I do know of you, Elodie, I think you're afraid to move on with your career because you're afraid of rejection, and now you've found a distraction with this place you want to preserve the house so you can stay here and hide away from taking responsibility for yourself."

Elodie felt like she was going to blow.

"You can't rely on an allowance, Elodie. That's the kind of thing a fourteen-year-old would say."

"And this is coming from the boy who was born with a silver spoon in his mouth?"

"Elodie, I'm trying to help."

"What, by insulting me?" Elodie began to search through her coat pockets. "I need to smoke."

"Elodie, don't, you've been doing so well."

"Oh, so you're actually keeping tabs on my smoking? You know what, Luke, I'm not sure I like having you around anymore."

"Elodie, all I'm saying is that I can see what's holding you back."

"Oh my god, Luke, this is like being on *Oprah Winfrey*. You know what? You go back to your family business, you have nothing to worry about."

"Is that right?" said Luke, looking incredulously at Elodie. "You seem to have this weird idea that I am from this perfect land of manicured lawns."

"Your father bought your flat, didn't he? There's even a Lichtenstein hanging in it."

"Oh, and that's impressive, is it?"

"No, yes, I don't know –"

"You know what, Elodie, I think you might just be the epitome of the poor little rich girl."

Elodie said nothing and, turning to the tree, she pressed her forehead against the bark.

"Tell me what to do, Elodie? I want to help you. What is it that you want me to say?"

"I want you to leave," said Elodie, without turning around, her eyes fixed on a tiny spider crawling out of a crevice in the bark.

"That's what you want?"

Elodie tried to think of something wise to say, to explain to Luke that she wasn't a lost cause, that she wasn't spoilt. That she missed her father even though she never really knew him. That the dead woman in the changing room had made her afraid of dying, and that she couldn't stop thinking about it. But hardest of all was that she knew she was her own worst enemy.

Elodie turned to watch Luke walking away and felt almost satisfied at proving to herself that she was right: it hadn't taken much to drive him away. She could hear Luke's voice, over and over, saying "*poor little rich girl*". Maybe he was right, she had nothing and she had everything – perhaps like Odette, she was trapped in a tangled web of money and love pulled apart by history. Can you blame history? Not as long as you are alive, she thought, and taking an elastic band from her pocket, which her mother would have balked at, Elodie tied her hair into a ponytail and walked towards the house. She had a suggestion to make.

Chapter fifty-two

Freddie arrived into the hall armed with courgettes and a bottle of whiskey.

"Hello?"

Pushing open the door into the study, she found Thomas sitting at his desk with a large brown file spilling out paper in front of him.

"You're laden, Freddie," he said, with half-moon spectacles propped on his forehead.

"Thomas, I hope you don't mind my dropping over, but I was keen to get this lot over to you before the weekend. I gather from Tess that her courgette crop failed?"

"Yes, not sure what happened, usually Tess is so on top of the polytunnel." He spotted the bottle. "Whiskey? Very good of you, and apologies for my study, it's a complete tip in here."

Standing up, he took off his glasses, kissed Freddie on both cheeks and relieved her of both courgettes and whiskey. "You look younger every time I see you," he said.

"You are very kind and, as I say to Harry, if you would join my yoga class I'd have you touching your toes in no time."

"Once I can still pull a cork from a bottle, that'll do me," said Thomas.

Freddie looked around the study, admiring the walls lined in original leather and curios collected from distant lands. She walked up to her favourite painting of a camel striding across the dessert.

"You're so lucky to have inherited all this wonderful stuff," she sighed.

"Yes, and if it wasn't for a hungry lion, I might be somewhere else entirely."

Thomas's great-uncle's brother came a cropper lion-hunting in Somaliland in 1896, and so the line of the house shifted and it came to him from his uncle.

Freddie thought of Tess and wondered how different her life would have been if it hadn't been for that same lion.

"You'll have to leave me this painting in your will," she said.

"Certainly. I'll call my solicitor immediately. After lunch. So how about a lunchtime tipple? I was going to suggest a lovely bottle of rosé, which I came across in the cellar last night – however, I do have a bottle of prosecco from Lidl, if that's of interest?"

"I'm keen to go to the lodge to see Tess," said Freddie.

"But she's here. Seems to have taken over from the dreadful nanny."

"She's still helping with Fleur?"

"Most definitely, while Max and Charlotte are romancing in the walled garden, and Elodie and Luke seem to be in seventh heaven, completely distracted by love. What it is to be young."

"In that case, I'll to pop into the kitchen to see Tess and the baby."

"And, you know, the baby monitor you brought over has been tried, tested and commended."

"Wonderful news – Anna will be pleased. Can't believe I'm going to be a grandmother."

"A sumptuous grandmother at that," said Thomas. "Now, let's make our way to the kitchen, shall we?"

"Just look at the swirl on that banister," said Freddie as they headed down the basement staircase towards the kitchen.

"Finest example of stucco in the country, so the Georgian Society says," said Thomas. "Just don't look up, whatever you do. With all the damp, the paper is coming away, revealing even further cracks in the ceiling."

"It is a very pretty ceiling though, isn't it?" said Freddie.

"Yes, and though I'm good at identifying problems, I'm less good at fixing them."

Anika arrived into the kitchen as Thomas popped a cork.

"Anika, darling, there you are. Freddie has dropped over courgettes and even whiskey," said Thomas.

Freddie smiled at Anika, who pouted her lips and seemed to breathe in and increase the size of her bosom and bum all at once.

"I'm starving," said Anika, plunging her hand into a Tupperware container, retrieving a couple of pieces of shortbread. "I was out with one of my riding friends last night and the portions sizes were outrageously small."

"You should have been with us," said Thomas. "The rabbit was delicious."

"I love rabbit," said Freddie, "though I much prefer to see them in the field than on my plate."

"At the restaurant, I challenged the maitre d' as to why they have removed the habit of stacking on the plate – you know, when beef was stacked on potatoes, stacked on courgette and a ladle of Hollandaise on top?"

"Awkward to eat though, always hard to know how to approach such a dish," said Thomas.

"Take a knife and knock it down," said Anika.

"So why bother with stacking?" Freddie asked, eyebrow raised.

Bluebell leapt off her beanbag as Elodie walked into the kitchen.

"Elodie," said Thomas, "there you are. I'm not sure if you've met Freddie as yet? Wife of wonderful Harry who brought over the brace of duck the other day."

"Hello," said Freddie, instinctively putting her arms around Elodie and giving her a healing hug. "You're tense, aren't you? Sorry, darling, to be so forward, I know we've only just met, but with my yoga culture I'm terribly sensitive to chakras."

Elodie's face was flushed and Freddie could see she was upset.

"Elodie, have you been crying?" said Thomas, pouring prosecco into champagne coupes.

"It's nothing, really," said Elodie, wiping her eyes.

"Is Max still in the garden?" said Freddie. "I'd love to meet him."

"You'll be more interested to meet Elodie's American," said Anika. "Very handsome."

Elodie ignored Anika and turned to her grandfather. "I've come up with an idea," she said.

"How about a drink first? And where has Luke gone off to? He popped his head into my study, but I was on the phone."

"No prosecco for me, Gramps," said Elodie, ignoring the mention of Luke.

"Who is Luke?" whispered Freddie to Anika.

"The American – a friend of Elodie's," said Anika.

"Friend my backside," said Thomas. "You see, my hearing isn't so bad, is it?"

"Hello," said Tess, arriving in from the back garden with Fleur in her arms.

"Sweet Fleur," said Freddie, rushing over and hugging them both. "Tess, I tried to call you earlier."

"I've been with this little one all morning."

"Can I hold her?"

"Sorry – maybe not at this moment," said Tess protectively. "She's sleepy – I'll just settle her down in the Moses basket for a little snooze first."

"Max and Charlotte are so lucky to have you here, aren't they?" said Freddie. "But you're looking pale."

Tess looked at Thomas, and Freddie wondered just how much he knew.

"Nonsense on both counts," said Tess as she put Fleur in her basket, "but Charlotte seems happy to spend time in the garden. She and Max are working wonders out there."

"The nanny sounded dreadful," said Freddie, then seeing the look of frustration on Elodie's face, she stopped talking. "Sorry, Elodie, you were saying?"

"Gramps, can I run my idea by you?"

"Yes, we'll be quiet, won't we, sweetheart?" whispered Tess, stroking Fleur's hair as she fell asleep.

Elodie stood next to Freddie, both of them leaning against the Aga.

"Okay, I know it might sound a little out of the blue," Elodie said, "but I've really been thinking about the state of this house."

"Haven't we all?" said Thomas. "Every morning I am amazed that a chunk of cornicing hasn't landed on my head and sent me to the grave."

"And so," Elodie persisted, "I wonder if we can hold some kind of fundraising event to fix the roof, for starters, and then once we get into our stride, we can hold more events and slowly renovate the house."

"What sort of fundraising event?" said Thomas, grimacing. "A cake sale? Because it'll take more than a few Victoria sponges to set this place right."

"I understand what you're trying to say, Elodie," said Anika. "You're thinking of a big party, with expensive tickets and celebrity entertainers."

"Something like that, I guess?"

"I think I should probably leave you all to it," said Freddie, seeing that Thomas was beginning to look irritated.

"Please stay," said Tess, sitting down at the table. "It's good to have you here – another voice of opinion."

"Elodie, do I need to spell it out?" said Thomas. "The roof is in tatters, and I suspect that every window needs replacing. This place is a noose around my neck, it's a bottomless pit, how many clichés do I need to pull out of my hat to explain that it is a pointless exercise to even try." He opened the lid of a jar of chutney and began spooning off the mould on top. "Everyone looks for the magic bullet to fix things, and I'm sorry to say this, Elodie, but in the case of Bellamore, there simply isn't one."

Chapter fifty-three

Tess, Thomas and Elodie were drinking tea in the kitchen when Charlotte arrived.

"Thank you so much, Tess," said Charlotte, pulling off her wellies as she came into the room. "You're brilliant to have looked after Fleur for the entire morning."

Taking her daughter from her basket, she lifted her high into the air. Fleur shrieked happily.

"It's my pleasure," said Tess. "She's an absolute joy to have around and … now then, don't you look well, Charlotte? So rosy-cheeked and beautiful and …"

"Ecstatic?" said Max, peering around the door with the widest smile imaginable.

"What's all this smiling about?" asked Thomas.

"Charlotte, would you like to do the honours?" said Max.

"We're getting married," said Charlotte, hugging Fleur and twirling in a circle before kissing Max.

"Oh, how fabulous," said Tess, throwing her arms around Charlotte, Max and Fleur. "I'm so happy for you both."

"That's great," said Elodie, trying to sound enthusiastic. Her heart was still pounding from her argument with Luke.

Thomas hadn't said a word. He just sat down in an armchair.

"Gramps, are you okay?" said Max.

Looking up, he shook his head and sank deeper into the chair.

"I'm simply relieved," he said, slowly rustling up a smile. "Profoundly relieved. You two are rock-solid at last and so too is the future of your child."

"I'm truly sorry again," said Charlotte, her eyes filling with tears. "Sorry to all of you. For putting Max through all that doubt. I should never have left him and Fleur."

"And I'm sorry you had to go through so much alone," said Max.

"This is starting to sound like a *Jeremy Kyle Show*," muttered Elodie, and then she covered her mouth when Max looked at her sharply. "I didn't mean it," she said.

"El, what's going on?" said Max. "I thought you'd be pleased for us?"

Elodie said nothing.

"It's good news surely, Elodie?" said Thomas.

Tess walked over to Elodie and put her arm around her. "Of course Elodie's thrilled, aren't you? She's just got other things on her mind, isn't that right?"

Elodie nodded, instantly comforted by Tess's gentle nature.

"What about a ring?" said Thomas.

"I don't need one," said Charlotte. "Fleur is the finest engagement present I could have wished for. We're thinking we could have a Humanist wedding in the garden. Something small, lots of wild flowers, that sort of thing."

"Love, my dear," said Thomas. "That's what it's all about. Once you have love, you can take on the world."

Elodie looked at her brother, restored to his happy and confident self, smiling into the eyes of his beautiful bride-to-be. They were a perfect match.

"Congratulations, Max," she said, hugging him. "Really, I'm so pleased for you, and you too, Charlotte."

"Celebrations are called for," said Thomas. "A slap-up family dinner, here, tonight. Elodie, let Luke know. Tess, you on?"

"Can I let you know later? I'd love to, but I do need to check a few things. It's been terribly busy and I'm so behind on everything."

"No pressure whatsoever," said Max, "but we'd be delighted if you could join us."

"Max has built two raised beds for your tomatoes in the tunnel, Tess," said Charlotte. "You're going to have a bumper crop this year."

Elodie noticed tears welling in Tess's eyes. God, it was so emotional in that kitchen, she really needed to get out, especially as she could guess how upset everyone would be when they realised Luke was gone from their lives. Her life seemed to be heading in the exact opposite of Max's yet again.

"Gramps, can I borrow the MG?"

"What? Are you sure, Elodie? I mean, can you actually drive?"

"Of course she can," said Max. "She's twenty-seven."

"Age offers no security when it comes to driving, Max. It's taken me seven and a half decades to reach that conclusion."

Chapter fifty-four

As she waited for the engine of the yellow MG to warm up, Elodie tried to wipe away the cobwebs from the inside of the tiny windscreen. She then released the clips on either side of the roof, knelt on the passenger seat and rolled back the soft top. She sat back down. The view seemed somehow more surreal as she looked out over the steering wheel – the redbrick yard walls crumbling onto the cobblestones, Mrs Murray's scooter leaning against the pump house and a large white hen, which must have escaped from the hen house. She wondered how much longer she would stay.

Putting on her sunglasses, she inched the car out of the yard as fantail doves circled around the wisteria-swathed pillars. Down by the avenue gates, the donkeys leant over the post and rails, their huge ears anticipating company, but Elodie drove past them without stopping. She pulled out onto the narrow road and drove towards the village, the exhaust rattling, the wind in her hair. To hell with Luke, and to hell with her promise to quit smoking; she desperately hoped that her loose change would add up to at least a box of ciggies. Tonight she'd sit down with a big glass of wine and smoke as much as she damned well liked. She would put her Bellamore plan down on paper. The longer it would take to fulfil that plan, the longer she could stay. Maybe it would take forever, chipping away at the decay.

Rounding the corner, Elodie saw a solitary magpie fly across the road and she automatically saluted to ward off bad luck. Putting the car into fourth gear she pelted onwards, trying to work out how to persuade her mother to cough up funds to save the house. She would open all the shutters in the house and turn on every light and lamp that worked. Bellamore would shine like a jewel. She'd take a marvellous photograph and email it to her mother, to remind her what a heavenly place it was, to inspire her to come and save the house. That was the answer. A surge of energy shot through her as she thought of how excited Gramps would be about the prospect of the house being renovated.

She began to slow down as a tractor up ahead, pulling a huge round bale covered in black plastic behind it, turned into the entrance of a field. Then a loose grey horse came cantering around a bend just ahead, its neck frothing with sweat. Elodie slammed her foot against the brake pedal. The car moved sideways, its tyres grinding on the dry tarmac. The horse was surely going to jump over the car. Elodie threw her body into the passenger seat and ducked her head. The world turned into slow motion as she saw the hooves rearing above her, the whites of the horse's eyes … and then silence as the MG slid to a halt alongside the hedge. Elodie looked down at her legs, which seems so thin and small, almost as if she was having an out-of-the-body experience. She thought of Maximillian, Odette's brother, her great-uncle, crashing to his death in the sports car. Looking up she saw the horse, his body trembling, nostrils snorting as he pawed the ground. Elodie unbuckled her seatbelt and, opening the door, she slowly got of the car.

"Hello," she said, crying with fear and also relief to be alive. "I'm so sorry, I've given you a real fright, haven't I?" Her heart was beating fiercely as she reached out to touch the horse's sweating body, but as she patted his neck she began to feel calm. "It's okay," she said, "I'm not going to hurt you." It had been years since she'd been around a horse and yet it felt like second nature for her to stand by his head, rubbing her hands along his mane and pressing her forehead against his cheek.

As both Elodie and the horse got their trembling under control, she realised she needed to get into practical mode.

"What we need is a head-collar, don't we?"

Taking off her long-sleeved grey top, Elodie felt like she was starring in a DIY YouTube clip: How to Create a Homemade Head-collar from a Piece of Clothing. First, she stretched out one of the arms of the top and looped the material around the horse's nose to make a noseband. She then carefully ran the other arm of the top behind his ears and brought it down to join the noseband on the other side.

"That's not too bad for a city girl, now is it?"

Luke was furious with himself for speaking so freely to Elodie. Behind her know-all attitude, she was such a fragile soul. If his father hadn't called, he might have driven all the way to Dublin Airport. He had his bags. All he had to do was to erase Elodie and her dysfunctional family from his brain. And then his father blew it. He tried to lay down the law, to force Luke to take up his role as vice president.

Luke whammed on the brakes, realising Elodie wasn't the only one who was running from responsibility. Why had he come to Ireland? To find Elodie, of course, but was that not also a convenient distraction from what he really wanted to do? The easiest route would be to accede to his father's wishes, a smooth ride and, in due course, a smooth inheritance. But his dream was music, had always been music, to have his own label, to scout for talent, to bring new voices forward. What was he waiting for?

Luke swung the car back around towards Bellamore.

As he rounded a bend just outside the village, he inhaled sharply at the sight of a dark-haired woman who appeared to be dancing with a horse in the centre of the road.

Elodie was wearing only jeans and a lace bra, as she tried to lead the horse up the road. She heard his car and swung her head around.

"*Luke!*" she called, as the restless-looking horse threw his head,

Luke leapt from the car, ran forward and took hold of the makeshift head-collar. "Easy, boy," he said, running his hand down the horse's neck. "I got you, okay, I got you."

As the horse calmed, Luke reached his other arm out towards Elodie, and pulled her to his chest.

"What on earth happened?"

"He came pounding around the bend and we very nearly collided. It was terrifying."

"Christ," he said, "but you managed to avoid each other – how did you do it?"

"I don't know, I put on my brakes and this amazing horse put on his."

"And you made this head-collar from your top? You must be freezing," said Luke, taking off his jumper and putting it around her shoulders. "So, it turns out you're a bit of a Bear Grylls?" he said, tightening his grip around her. "God, that was a near miss, Elodie."

Within half an hour, the immediate crisis was resolved, and the horse had been reunited with his very grateful owner.

"Elodie, I'm sorry about earlier – I went too far," Luke said, squeezing her hand, as they walked down the grassy lane back to the car.

"No," she said, "you did me a favour."

She halted and looked at him and then he held her face with both hands and they kissed.

"You," he whispered.

"Me," she said.

"Magic happens when you least expect it. That's what I've always been told. Now I believe it."

Chapter fifty-five

The next day, Luke, arrived into the greenhouse by the kitchen. "Elodie, there you are."

"Oh God, Luke," said Elodie, picking green beans and putting them into a basket, "I can't believe I'm out here in Odette's slippers. She would go crazy if she were here now."

"It's so sweet," he said, smiling at her. "Listen, there's something I want to tell you."

"Great – actually, wait, can you hold this basket?"

Luke took the basket and Elodie landed ten more long green beans into it.

"I've been thinking . . . well, I've been thinking a lot lately," he said.

"Oh yes?" said Elodie. "Oh god, here's a slug. Seriously, Luke, I can't handle slugs. Any chance?"

"Of rescue? Always," he said, winking, and gently picking up the leaf with the slug on it, he stepped outside.

"All done?" she said when he came back.

"Released to the wilds of Bellamore," he said.

"So, what do want to tell me?" said Elodie, wiping her forehead and leaving a sweep of earth across it. "Nothing heavy? Because I am so zen out here."

"Elodie, there's something I need to tell you. I really need to tell you, so that we can –"

"Look, another slug, Luke – yuck, it's in the basket."

"*Lunch,*" yelled Anika. "*Luke, Elodie, come on, you two.*"

"Hold on, with you in a sec. Luke's on slug duty."

"Feed the slugs to the hens," said Anika.

Luke raised his eyebrows at Elodie. "Really?"

"She's joking."

"No, I'm not," said Anika, appearing at the door. "Now come on, your grandfather has made omelettes and they'll go cold if you don't get a move on."

Luke transported the second slug outside.

"What did you want to tell me?" Elodie asked when he returned.

Luke shook his head. "It can wait," he said. "Sounds like we'd better get to the table."

"Before we go, I've got something for you," said Elodie.

"Sounds intriguing."

Elodie took a small drawing from her back pocket. "It's a drawing of a chaffinch perched on top of Big Ben."

"It's incredible, Elodie, and the streets are carpeted with wild garlic and bluebells. My god, it's amazing, thank you," and he kissed her so much that they both looked at each other, knowing that what they had really was something very, very good.

After lunch, in the back kitchen, Tess laid newspaper across the wooden draining board and one by one, took flowers which she had collected during the afternoon from the basket.

Elodie put her nose into a jug filled with flocks and Italian parsley with its tiny, lacy white flowers. "The scent from these flowers is amazing," she said.

"Pretty, aren't they?" said Tess, looking at Elodie, her nose crinkling as she smiled. "I usually deal with the long stems first," she said as Elodie passed a pink peony to her, "and if you cut each stem diagonally across the bottom, they have a better chance of drinking more water."

"Mum has flowers delivered to our house every week," said Elodie, twisting a piece of wild grass around her ring finger, wondering what sort of engagement ring she would like, "but your arrangements are so much prettier and more natural."

"This keeps the water in the vase clean and also allows the flowers to spread out nicely without getting their leaves caught up in each other," said Tess, pinching her fingers halfway down the stem and stripping off the leaves.

"Like this?" said Elodie, pulling the leaves off, one by one.

"Yes, you can do it that way, though if you actually pinch your fingers on the stem?"

"Like this?" said Elodie.

"Nearly." Tess held Elodie's hand, guiding her fingers to gently squeeze the stem, removing the lower leaves.

"Our hands are so similar," said Elodie, "even our cuticles."

"I suppose they are," said Tess, "though my hands are so scratched and worn from gardening. I have tried to make myself wear gloves, but I miss the feeling of the earth too much."

Elodie noticed how the sharpness in Tess's voice had gone and the scowl in her eyes had completely vanished, so different to when Elodie had first met her.

Getting to know Tess felt almost like eating an artichoke, removing the layers of leaves, one by one, before reaching the heart.

"There, you see," said Tess, as Elodie ran her fingers down the stem of a foxglove, "you're getting the hang of it now. They are pretty, aren't they?"

"I'd like to live in a house one day with a big round table in the hall and a huge arrangement of wild flowers in the centre," said Elodie.

"In England?" said Tess.

"I guess so? You know, this is the first time in my life that I've actually started to imagine what my future could look like?"

"Is it because of Luke?"

Elodie smiled and added a long stem of montbretia to the vase. "Maybe," she said.

"I think he's lovely," said Tess, "and very much in love with you."

"You really think so?"

"I do."

In the late afternoon, Luke went for a jog around the fields, wet and uneven, but the air was so bracing he felt that he could have run on, even though his runners were wet. Bonnie and Clyde had joined him, and an Irish band called the Coronas, which he had downloaded on Spotify, sang "Give Me a Minute" into his earpiece as he ran around the field. Luke had checked that the water heater was on before he left and, running back towards the garden, he could see the bathtub up ahead, surrounded by pink and blue hydrangea blooms.

Lying back in the bath, he felt so lucky to be at Bellamore. He had forgotten how it felt to be so deeply intoxicated by love. Knowing that he and Elodie were developing such a precious relationship was incredible and, though things were moving faster than he had imagined, it all felt so natural. He knew the timing wasn't exactly perfect, but he had never been one to wait – he was impulsive, a quick thinker and what was very clear in his mind was that he wanted Elodie in his life.

"Hey, you two," he said as Bonnie and Clyde came out from beneath the weeping willow, and Bonnie propped her paws on the edge of tub and attempted to lap up the water.

Hopping out of the bath to be on time for supper, Luke managed to land on a small, green and very prickly thistle.

"Is someone trying to tell me something?" he said out loud.

Luke heard music coming from the drawing room and, looking around the door, he found Max sitting at the piano, pencilling notes onto a sheet, with a MacBook propped on top of several books on a chair.

"You're recording something?" said Luke.

"Just messing around with some ideas. Hans Zimmer says that all you need is a microphone and an iPad, and that the creative process takes place in your head."

"You know him?"

"Hans Zimmer? I wish," said Max, tilting backwards on his chair. "The man is a complete genius. I've have been watching one of his Master classes on line and he says all you need is a story and then you start creating the world around it, and music is the world."

"Cool," said Luke, pulling up a chair.

"So, I've been practising my own story and thought I'd try writing a score to my life so far."

"Can I hear some?"

"If you really want to," said Max, stretching out his fingers. "It's kind of haphazard, but I'll give it a go."

Max began playing with the lightest touch on the piano, his slender fingers tiptoeing across the keys, often closing his eyes as he played. The chords began gently. "This is from when I was young . . . and then here's the dip, when my father died, not that I remember, but it happened." Max continued with the melody. "Next comes our summers at Bellamore . . . and this is Odette with her formality," he played some bass notes. "Now this is fun," he said, increasing the beat, "this is running around with Elodie as teenager . . . and now Odette dies, no more Ireland," the beat became slow and lethargic. "Next comes Charlotte," and the harmony of notes sang romance, "a highlight obviously," he said, "and then I lose Charlotte . . . I go to LA, and return to find Fleur . . . you hear this terrified rhythm?" His fingers pinged on the high notes. Then he stopped. "This is where I caught my breath," he said and, slowly returning his fingers to the keys, he began playing the sweetest, most gentle melody. "This is me getting to know Fleur – and Tess, that's been a big part of being here too. Discovering new family, an extraordinary thing."

"The score is enchanting," said Luke.

"And that's how it feels," said Max. "It feels enchanting, all of it."

"What I don't get is your idea of becoming a plumber?"

Max stood up from the piano and walked to the window. "One part of me is saying, don't do it, get a real job – that's what people tell musicians, isn't it? But the other part of me feels that the seconds of my life are ticking away and if I don't do it now, I never will. I feel like I'm going backwards and forwards."

"Are you still in touch with your Hollywood plumber?"

"He's a real character – Bob Paloma."

"What does Charlotte think?"

"She's so supportive, says we'll find a way and that I should follow my dream."

"And?"

"It's the practicalities. I've got some savings, may keep us going for a year tops, but what then?"

"What then? Look, Max, I'd follow my instinct, that's my advice. You say that composing is about creating words to a story? Well, this is your story – don't let your words be limited by a budget."

"That's what you would do?"

"Why else would I be here?" said Luke. "My instinct is often my best friend and when I met your sister, I knew, literally from that moment, that she was the one."

Lighting the candles on the kitchen table, Elodie felt good striking a match for a candle rather than a cigarette – maybe she really did have staying power after all – and, seeing Tess's arrangements of honeysuckle in the centre of the table, she felt truly happy.

"Are you up for a little twirl down memory lane, El?" said Max, connecting a speaker to his iPhone.

"*Give me a kiss to build a dream on*," sang Max, in time to Louis Armstrong, and taking Charlotte's hand, they began to dance and twirl around the kitchen table.

"I'm just in time, by the looks of it," said Luke, carrying a paper bag of cheese he had brought from the farmers' market. "Our first dance?" he said to Elodie.

Then the golden time happened, with Max and Charlotte, Luke and Elodie, dancing around the kitchen table, carefree for that moment, aware of nothing but their partners.

Thomas pushed open the door, holding a pair of tumblers. "I only came down to get some ice for Anika," he said, his eyes sparkling as he watched his grandchildren dancing.

"Like to join us, Gramps?" said Elodie.

"My bunions wouldn't take kindly to such moves, I'm afraid, Elodie, but don't let me stop you. I'm rustling up a voddy ton for Anika upstairs, though I'm sure she'd prefer to be down here with you lot rather than upstairs with me."

"Don't be hard on yourself, Gramps," said Max. "Anika

obviously likes distinguished company."

"That's very flattering of you, Max, but I'm not sure I'm quite up to keeping her entertained – still let's enjoy it while it lasts, don't you think?"

"Actually, Gramps, speaking of entertaining," said Charlotte, "could I ask you a massive favour and invite my parents to stay next weekend? I think it could be the perfect opportunity to introduce them to Fleur?"

"Everyone else seems to be descending on us here, so I don't see why not," he responded.

Over supper, they devoured a huge dish of Shepherd's Pie made by Mrs Murray, who had been concerned that they weren't eating 'half enough', and as Luke pulled another cork, Max brought his guitar to the table and sang a ballad about the Cornish miners. Even Bonnie and Clyde settled quietly on the beanbag next to Bluebell, listening to Max's dulcet tones.

"Max, you have serious talent – that's gorgeous," said Luke. "You really wrote that?"

"He did," said Charlotte, kissing Max. "He is brilliant, isn't he?"

"Ravishing," said Anika.

"I wish Tess had joined us for sups," said Elodie. "She would have loved to hear you sing."

"She was tired this evening," said Thomas, "and seemed determined to go back to the lodge."

"So, who's next to sing?" said Max.

"I might be persuaded," said Luke, "if that's alright with you, Gramps?"

"You're calling me Gramps too now, are you?"

"I never knew either of my grandfathers," said Luke. "I hope you don't mind."

"My dear boy, as you have such excellent taste in people," winking at Elodie, "it is my honour for you to call me that. Now, Luke, what are you going to sing for us?"

"You sound like Louis Walsh on *The X Factor*, Gramps," said Elodie.

Luke sat back in his chair, surprising them all with a short rendition of 'Raglan Road' in the most brilliant Irish accent. This was followed by rousing applause.

"Luke," said Elodie, "that was amazing."

"Not just a pretty face," said Anika.

"Next time, sing along to my guitar," said Max.

"Next time, I'd like to see you in my recording studio," said Luke.

"What?" said Max, just as Fleur began to cry.

And although Max didn't seem to catch what Luke had meant, it was at that moment that Luke realised that he truly did want to start his own music label. Things were becoming increasingly clear.

"You two seem to have struck gold after all," said Thomas, taking Max and Elodie's hands as he got up from the table. "I always wondered about the irony behind your mother's married name, but it's making sense to me now. Because you and your brother have hearts of gold, you really do."

"Gramps, how much have you had to drink?" said Anika.

"This is not the drink talking," he said, filling Elodie's glass and then his own. "I mean it. Because of what you children have brought to Bellamore during these past months, I honestly feel alive again."

"And what about me, Thomas?" said Anika, raising her glass of vodka. "Do I no longer serve a purpose?"

"Of course you do, my Dutch pussy," he said, as his grandchildren cringed.

Chapter fifty-six

The view from the coach-house roof was crisscrossed with old fences on pasture sheltered by magnificent stands of oak and beech, especially along the avenue. As Max held a stretch of felt across a row of broken slates, he wondered if he could combine being a handyman by day with writing music at night, until he *made it*, if such a thing was possible.

"Can you pull the felt a little tighter?" said Luke, from the other side of the chimney. "This is the closest I've ever been to doing a Spider-Man impression – how about you?"

"I was always a Batman fan, myself," said Max, straddled across a ridge tile, "and thank god this roof isn't too high. I've got a blinder of a hangover this morning."

"Your grandfather really knows how to push the sloe gin, doesn't he?" said Luke.

"Old dogs and old tricks," said Max.

It felt good to have Luke at Bellamore. His perspective on things was fresh, he didn't appear to have any baggage, and best of all he made Elodie happy.

Bluebell and the terriers came flying around the corner of the house to greet a very shiny Mercedes.

"Who's this then?" said Max, taking off his sunglasses.

"No idea," said Luke, until a tall man dressed in a tweed suit got out of the car and taking large strides made his way towards the yard.

"No – *effing* – *way*," said Max.

"What?"

"Luke, where's Elodie?" said Max, crawling across the roof towards the ladder.

"With Charlotte, I think, giving Fleur a bath. What's up?"

"Bloody Dominic," said Max. "That's what's up."

"Max Gold on a roof, fancy that," said Dominic, his blonde hair freshly combed back. "And a grotty-looking roof at that."

Max noticed that, by the expression on Luke's face, he recognised Dominic.

"I didn't think the world was really that small," said Luke.

"Mr America, isn't it?" said Dominic, wiping either side of his nostril. "You have one of those faces that seems to engrave on the brain for some reason, or maybe it's that rather annoying accent of yours."

"To hell with you," said Luke.

"No need to be so unfriendly," said Dominic. "We don't exactly know each other very well, do we?"

Luke climbed down the ladder, following Max, and the three men stood in a triangle on the cobbled yard, all equal in height.

"This is rather like that Irish joke," said Dominic. "An Irishman, that's you, Max, an Englishman, me of course, and an American – I had no idea you were out for hire as a bricky, Mr Hampton. Your surname is Hampton, isn't? As in Giles Hampton Advertising."

"What's it to you?" said Luke.

"I knew I recognised you when you tried to fob me off at the café. We've done business with your father – quite ruthless, isn't he? Though he's clearly a family man, he even has your picture in his office and told me that you were taking a personal sabbatical in Europe. I gather you're taking over the New York office?"

Luke shook his head and smiled the kind of smile that means quite the opposite.

"Funny how rich boys manage to stay out of the limelight, isn't it?" said Dominic. "I was doing a little research on your family, on behalf of Peregrine Properties of course, we like to be familiar with our clients, and I couldn't find a thing about you online, not even on social media. How did you manage that?"

"Cut it out, Dominic, and tell me what the hell you're doing here?" said Max.

"It's business, I'm afraid, as much as I'd like it to be pleasure, particularly as I gather Elodie is here."

Max put his hand on Luke's shoulder as he was clenching his fists.

"Easy, boy," said Dominic. "She's got under your skin, hasn't she? But don't worry, it won't last. You'll soon find out what a basket case she is." Looking down at his shoes, he grimaced as Bonnie dropped a dead rat in front of him.

"Gramps will be pleased," said Max. "We'd wondered where the poisoned rat had got to – he came to visit us in the kitchen the other evening."

"Revolting," said Dominic. "Give this to your grandfather, will you?" He handed an envelope to Max. "I'll be staying locally in some dump of a hotel for two nights, so that I can discuss procedures."

"You've become your uncle's delivery poodle then?" said Max, seeing a Peregrine Properties stamp on the envelope.

"Watch your mouth," said Dominic. "You lot are in no position to take the piss."

"Bugger off then, Dominic," said Max, as a series of barks came from the garden.

"More dogs?" said Dominic, looking nervous.

"Didn't you know about the Archdale Rottweilers? Especially vicious to men with bleached-blonde hair," said Luke, as Dominic began to retreat towards his car.

"Those grins on your faces won't last for long," he said."

"By the way, Dominic?" said Max. "You've forgotten to wipe away the remainder of white power on your left nostril."

Dominic stormed towards his car, looking over his shoulder in case the threat of Rottweilers was for real, and starting the engine he drove off at speed down the avenue.

"He's a piece of work," said Luke.

"Yes, and his uncle, Bruce Finchley, owns Peregrine. Bloody asshole, I bet, like his nephew."

"To do with the house?" said Luke.

"I fear so," said Max, folding up the envelope and putting it in his back pocket. "First though, I'm going to bury this rat in the compost heap and then I'm going straight to Gramps."

"Shame we can't bury the letter," said Luke.

"That would only put off the inevitable, mate," said Max. "The question is, how are we going to break the news to Elodie that Big Bad Dom is in town."

Thomas sat at the kitchen table and poured the last finger of whiskey from the bottle into what coffee remained in his cup.

"Do we know who the buyer is?" said Max, trying to work out why Gramps wasn't taking the news harder.

"Someone in the UK most probably, perhaps a Russian, particularly as they are prepared to transfer funds immediately," he said.

Elodie burst into the kitchen, followed by Luke.

"He had no right to come here," she said, flushed and shaking. "I can't bear the thought of him being here."

"Come, sit down, El, let Gramps explain," said Max, pulling a chair out from the table. "There's more to this than we realise."

"I don't understand," said Elodie, her voice breaking. "Why would Dominic and his uncle's company be involved, how did they know, where did the offer come from? You can't just lay down the law and buy a place, it has to be for sale first. Gramps, how has this happened? You can't sell Bellamore."

"Elodie," he said, shaking his head, "the banks have been chasing me for years."

Luke sat down next to Charlotte, who bounced Fleur over her shoulder to keep her occupied, while Max and Elodie sat on either side of their grandfather.

"But it doesn't make sense. Odette had all that money and she gave it away, you said. How could she? Did she *want* the house to crumble away?"

"And me?" said Thomas.

"But what did she *do* with all that money?"

"Elodie, where Odette's money went at this stage is irrelevant."

"But –"

"No, Elodie, that was Odette's business, and that's that. When your grandmother died, I put the house on the market, and when no buyers came forward I had no option but to take out a loan against the house."

"But why didn't you ask Mum?" Elodie looked at Max, imploring him to join her in trying to get to the bottom of what had happened. "Don't you think, Max? Surely Mum would have given you whatever you needed?" She looked around the room, at Luke, Max and Charlotte. Where is Tess? She should be here, we all need to be here."

"Elodie, you need listen, darling," said Thomas. He bowed his head and spoke so quietly it was difficult to make out what he was saying. "When I received the loan from the bank, an investment opportunity arose and I took a chance."

"What happened, Gramps?" said Max, taking Fleur from Charlotte.

"The investment collapsed within six months – all the money was gone."

"*What?*" said Elodie. "Didn't you have any insurance behind it or even some kind of security? Even for a percentage of it to come back?"

"No, Elodie, I didn't, which is why I'm feeling a certain degree of relief to know that an offer has been made on the house."

"Relief? How can you feel relief to be told that you are being booted out of your ancestral home?" said Elodie, her voice rising.

"But, Gramps, you love this place," said Max.

"I realise it's difficult for you all to understand, but my relief is huge because it would take thousands to put in a new heating system, whatever about the wiring – a new well would have to be sunk, along with a new pump or even worse go on the godawful mains – and that's before the house and yard are reroofed."

"You've been stringing us all along," said Elodie. "Max and Luke fixing things, Charlotte working in the garden? What is Tess going to say? She'll be heartbroken. The garden is her sanctuary."

Elodie, with her head in her hands, sat at the kitchen with Luke's arm around her shoulders. "How long have you known the bank were going to enforce a sale, Gramps?" said Max.

"Years. And on the month, every month, they send a polite letter to remind me of the fact that the moment an offer is made, it must be accepted."

"Is it a good offer?" said Max.

"Enough to pay back the bank, yes."

"No wonder you weren't keen on my fundraising idea," said Elodie. "All this time, the house has been on the market. I can't believe it."

"Max and Elodie, if I could leave Bellamore to you I would in a heartbeat, you need to know that."

"We do, Gramps, of course we do," said Max, dropping a kiss on Fleur's head.

"But you've been here for a lifetime. They can't expect you to simply pack a case and go?" said Elodie.

"Why not? Anything of value has been sold. Clothes and photographs are all that I'll be taking with me, and you pair are welcome to anything you'd like, of course."

"That's not what I mean," said Elodie. "I'm talking about practicalities."

"Such as?"

Elodie looked exasperated, "As in where you're going to live, and what about Tess? Does the sale include the lodge?"

"It does."

They all shook their heads.

"My god, this is impossible," Elodie said.

Luke knew that she was also facing the realisation that she would have to return to London and face her own reality.

"And from the sale," said Elodie, "will there be enough left over for you to live on?"

"I'll get by." He stared into his now empty coffee mug. "But there's no need to worry about me, or Tess."

"But where will you go?" said Elodie.

"We've got time."

"How much time?" said Max.

"Enough time."

Chapter fifty-seven

Elodie was curled up on the study sofa, with her knees pulled into her chest, listening to an old Beatles record.

"Sweetheart," said Luke, sitting down and putting his arm around her, "I've been looking for you."

Her eyes had narrowed, reminding Luke of how uptight she had been when they first met in Sam's Kitchen.

"Tough day," she said.

Luke held her close, as Paul McCartney's 'Blackbird' played softly from the record player.

"You don't have to see Dominic, ever," said Luke. "I'll make sure he never comes even close."

"How can you say that?" said Elodie, looking at him. "Dominic was here this morning. He delivered a letter sealing the future of Bellamore."

"In the future, I mean," said Luke. "Dominic has made his delivery, it's up to his uncle's company what happens next."

"That isn't Dominic's style. He knows exactly what he's doing. He's here to rub salt into the wound. This is his payback and it's all my fault."

"I don't think this has anything to do with you, Elodie," said Luke. "It's a coincidence, for sure, that Peregrine happens to be the buyer, or at least is representing the buyer, but it's nothing more than that. Dominic will go back to London and you'll never have to see him." He held Elodie's hands and kissed them. "I'll look after you, Elodie."

The music continued to play, filling in the silence until Elodie spoke.

"My mother used to listen to this piece when we were children," she said. "It almost feels as if the past has never existed, you know? As if Odette was never here. I can't explain it, I just can't believe that Gramps is in this position. He's about to be homeless."

"Is it worth letting your mom know?"

"I thought you said I shouldn't go running to her?"

"I think the fact that your grandfather is losing his home warrants a call, and by the sound of it the bank will take most of the cash from the sale."

"He'll live with Anika," said Elodie. "He'll be fine."

"And Tess?"

Elodie shrugged herself out of Luke's arms. "Luke, stop trying to fix things."

"Elodie, I think if we talk things through it will be helpful."

"You are not my therapist," she said.

"And if I were, what would you tell me?" he said. "Come on, Elodie, what would you say? What do you *need* to say?"

Elodie sat on the armchair by the window and looked towards the door.

"At this moment, I'd tell her that I'm fighting with this weird memory."

"Go on," said Luke.

"I was about six years old, and I walked into my parents' bedroom. It was at night, I had woken up from a bad dream or something."

"And your parents were in the room?"

"My father was," she said, "but he was with another woman, who was meant to be our baby-sitter."

"Not what a little girl would expect to find."

"She had long brown hair and was lying on the bed, laughing, while he pulled down her jeans. God, it's a strange memory to have,

270

isn't it? Sometimes I think I must have made the memory up, and maybe I wish I had."

"And what happened?" said Luke, his voice so patient.

"I remember the woman was wearing tanned tights under her jeans, and my father paused for just a moment, before saying 'Mummy's gone out'."

"And where had she gone?"

"I found my mother sitting next to Max's cot bed – he couldn't have been more than one at the time. Really little. She was trying to get him to settle and I can remember her face, just exhausted."

"Why did he say she had gone out?"

"I don't know. I suppose he thought she had?"

"And did she know where your father was?" said Luke.

"I have no idea, and that is a classic example of what my memory pattern is like. I feel so messed up. My father had affairs right under her nose, almost literally."

Luke crossed the room and gathered Elodie into his arms.

"You aren't messed up," he said, "and none of it is your fault. You were only a tiny child and even now, what's happening now, none of this is your fault, you have to believe that."

"He died soon after that," she said, "my father, maybe six months later."

"I'm so sorry," he said.

"I guess we've discussed a lot, haven't we, since we've been together?"

"And we are together, aren't we?" said Luke.

"Yes," said Elodie, "we are."

"I told you my father had the same mistress for at least ten years, didn't I?"

"And now? He has the same mistress?"

"No, I don't think so," said Luke. "There's someone new, or at least she's been on the scene for the past couple of years. My mother has learnt to look the other way."

"As my mother did, perhaps?" said Elodie.

"It's her choice to ignore it, makes her life easier that way."

"But don't you say anything?"

"No," he said, "it's just the way they are, I guess."

"Do you know who the mistress is?"

"No clue and it's none of my business. I think of it as their own arrangement." Luke slid his hand beneath Elodie's hair and around the back of her neck. "You know Mrs Murray has just left the house to go to Mass? I met her downstairs earlier, in fact I had a cup of tea with her. Man, I can't believe how Irish I sound."

"Is this a premeditated seduction?" said Elodie, as Luke scooped her up into her arms.

"I like to think so. How about we see if we can improve this day, which needs so much improving. I want to take care of you, Elodie," he whispered and, he held her hand all the way up the stairs to the bedroom where their clothes were rapidly unbuttoned, unzipped, unbuckled and undone, before they tumbled into bed.

Chapter fifty-eight

Anika arrived at Bellamore feeling agitated. Last night she had spoken with an old friend from her TV days and felt pure jealousy when she heard about new shows in development. She tried to make her life in Ireland sound exciting but she couldn't muster enthusiasm when describing her James Herriotesque adventures with her horses and dogs.

The telephone message from Thomas had done nothing to improve her humour, asking her to come over and cut his toenails. This was not romance, nor was it Sugar Daddy behaviour, not that he was ever a Sugar Daddy but he had always treated her so sweetly and the sex had been very pleasurable until in recent months it had taken a nosedive.

"The garden is teeming with lovage, Anika. It's a fabulous herb and can take on anything from rheumatism to indigestion, certainly worth trying."

"Neither rheumatism nor indigestion are my problems, Thomas – and you look dreadful."

"It's most likely the shock of knowing that I won't have to worry about this place in the future."

"You really mean that?" said Anika.

"I do. Now what is it that's bothering you?"

"Your voicemail this morning, it really upset me."

"I'm hardly over the moon about the news either, Anika darling, and I don't want you to feel that you have to take me in. I'm sure I can think of an alternative, and we have four weeks to get organised."

"It isn't about the house, though I'm sorry for it, of course I am." Anika looked at him seriously. "On the voicemail, you asked me to come over and trim your nails."

"Yes, and?"

"Your toenails."

"My back has been playing up, you see?" he said, turning around and pulling up his jumper. "I've got an awful rash."

"No," said Anika, standing up, "I don't need to see it, Thomas."

"Darling, I know how you like your men to be well shod, which is why I wanted you to cut my nails."

"I am not a blacksmith, Thomas. I am meant to be your lover."

"And, darling, you are, though I haven't been as attentive as I'd like recently."

"I think I'll fix a drink in the drawing room."

"Darling, I'm afraid the drinks cabinet is dry."

"Then I'll go home and have a drink there."

"But don't leave like that, Anika."

"Like what exactly? There is enough mud in the yard to cover your doormats, and I refuse to be another one."

Thomas looked genuinely surprised, despite Anika having fetched and carried, cooked on numerous nights and put up with moody Tess.

"Besides, I think you have greater problems than your toenails."

"I'm sorry you feel like that."

"So am I," she said, and she really meant it and felt guilty as hell for almost calling him 'old man'. How was she going to get out of this?

"Here comes Anika in another country classic," said Max, as he and Charlotte walked in the garden with Fleur.

"She definitely likes tight clothes, doesn't she?" said Charlotte.

"And she doesn't look too happy," said Max, waving at Anika who completely ignored them.

She got into her jeep and her tyres spat out gravel as she sped off down the avenue.

"*Max?*" called Thomas from the yard. "*Can you come here?*"

"*Coming!*"

Max and Charlotte crossed the lawn and found him by the hen run.

"I've had an idea," he said.

"About the move?" said Max.

"No, not about the move – we all know that is inevitable and I've never been one to worry about the future. No, my idea is that I'd like to throw a little party to celebrate your engagement."

"Really, Gramps, I think we've got more to think about, don't you?" said Max. "We've got to work out where you and Tess are going to move to? And there are tea chests and all kinds of boxes on the top floor that you'll need to decide about."

"Old clothes. They can all go to the recycling plant. I'll be packing one suitcase and that's that."

"And Tess?"

"Max, let Tess come to her own conclusions. She's going to need time for the news to sink in and, quite frankly, at this moment I want to focus on something that doesn't involve packing."

"And another thing, Gramps, we can't afford a party," said Max.

"Let's not worry about the details. Anyway, I feel that Anika is rather fed up with me and so I want to show her that I can still party – you know, give the girl a twirl and an excuse to dress up."

"But Anika always dresses up," said Max.

"Yes, she does, doesn't she," he said. "We'll keep it small and ask some local friends to bring a bottle and a salad, how about that? Nothing like a little impromptu gathering."

"Very modern of you," said Charlotte, "and I think it's a brilliant idea, and my parents arrive tomorrow so even better."

"There we are then, tomorrow night – and now I'm going back to bed as I have been up since 4am listening out for the warbler."

"Any sign?" said Charlotte.

"Not yet, but she'll come back, I'm sure of it."

When they first met, Thomas had a huge appetite for sex and was amazingly fit for his age, showering Anika with frisky love as he lacked the funds to buy her presents. But since the children had arrived, he had become completely distracted, so much so that they had barely slept together for over a month.

"Typical," said Anika, as the light for coolant lit up on the dashboard of her jeep. Putting on the indicator, she pulled into a small petrol station on the outskirts of Drummare.

In the shop, a teenager, wearing a hoody, sat on a stool behind the counter, laughing as he texted on his phone.

"Coolant," said Anika, looking down upon him.

"Coolant?" said the teenager, reluctantly putting his phone into his pocket and standing up.

"Yes, please," said Anika, "do you have any?"

"I dunno," he said, shrugging his shoulders, and sitting back down on the stool he took out his phone and began texting again.

Anika was about to swear at him and then decided no – she would be the elegant lady and keep her dignity intact. Scouring a shelf filled with dangling air-freshener and oil containers, she found the coolant.

"Buy yourself a lollipop with the change, little boy," she said, throwing a twenty-euro note on the counter.

At least the afternoon sun was out, which meant Anika could feel like a Hollywood actress as she opened the bonnet with her shades on. She often imagined herself as an actress when she had to carry out annoying tasks.

"*Where does the fucking coolant go?*" she yelled at the bonnet. "*Godverdomme! Where do you go, you bloody blue liquid?*"

A man joined her at the bonnet.

"To the left," he said, "next to the oil lid, you see?"

"Right. Now I see."

"I take it you're not a local then?" he said, adjusting his tie.

"It depends," said Anika, dipping her sunglasses down to appraise his sallow skin and beautiful nose. "I'm a town and country kind of girl."

"So I see," he said. "How about I pour this coolant into your bonnet and then we discuss that funny accent of yours over an early evening drink?"

"I'm very fussy," said Anika, pressing her fingers against the silver buckle of her belt.

"That makes two of us," he said. "Why don't you stay warm in the jeep while I deal with your engine?"

Getting into the car, Anika spritzed her hair with a cloud of perfume.

Chapter fifty-nine

Charlotte held Fleur in her arms and stood next to Max as her parents arrived into the hall. Catching sight of his daughter, Gerald took off his hat and looked as if he might have been reciting a prayer.

"Hello, Mum, and Dad, hello," said Charlotte.

"Please, Gerald, take my handbag," said Mary and, readjusting her floral silk scarf, she stepped towards Fleur.

She stood silently, staring.

"Mary?" said Gerald, tilting his head. "Aren't you going to say anything, Mary love?"

"She's got my mother's eyes," whispered Mary, with a tear running down her cheek, "the very same blue," and, opening her arms, she hugged Charlotte, Max and Fleur all at once.

"I'm your Nana Mary," she said to Fleur, "and it's lovely to meet you, precious."

Max felt such utter relief to see Charlotte's parents smiling at him, and when Fleur slapped her hand against Nana Mary's cheek, everyone burst into laughter, feeling all the tension release.

"I can be a silly old goat sometimes," said Mary, dabbing her eyes with a lace-trimmed handkerchief. "I shouldn't have said those things to you, our Charlotte, and I hope you can forgive me."

"Of course I do, Mum," said Charlotte, as Luke appeared at the front door with two large suitcases. "I'm so glad you've come, and you too, Dad,"

"Room service," said Luke, smiling and handsome in the doorway.

"You did send the most handsome driver to collect us," said Mary, "and American too, very exotic."

"Golly, I thought you were just coming over for the weekend?" said Charlotte, looking at the luggage.

"You did say you were having a party," said Gerald, passing Mary her handbag, "and we wanted to bring some wardrobe options. As Lorenzo says, 'one must be prepared for every occasion'."

"You've met Lorenzo?" said Max.

"Oh yes," said Gerald, "several times by now."

Luke found Tess in the dining room, piling forks into a basket.

"That was kind of you to collect Charlotte's parents," she said.

"The relief on Max's face was something else," said Luke. "Getting thumbs up from the in-laws makes life easier, I guess?"

"I wouldn't know," said Tess. "I haven't ever had any in-laws to deal with."

"You haven't come close to marrying?" said Luke.

"No, and I'm much too set in my ways now."

"You never know," said Luke. "You could meet someone when you least expect it."

"Like you and Elodie?"

"Exactly like me and Elodie," he said, straightening a line of wineglasses on a tray.

"Charlotte's mother would get on well with my mom, actually. Same kind of woman, I think – she seems like a homemaker."

"And is that the kind of woman you like?" Then she corrected herself: "I'm sorry, I don't mean to pry."

"No, it's okay, and no, not necessarily. I love free spirits, you know?"

"Yes. Does your mother have a career?"

"She's big into charities and on the board of all kinds of things from environment to children's hospitals, and she has a strong work ethic. So when I was a kid, if I wanted something I'd have to earn it."

"Sound training," said Tess.

"I got my first job when I was eight."

"That's young."

"By the time I was nineteen I opened a stock portfolio."

"No help from your parents?"

"Totally independent, and I guess that it's given me a great freedom."

"I imagine it must."

"I'd love Elodie to have that freedom," said Luke, "and I don't just mean financial, but to start doing what she loves. She is such a talented artist, and I really think with the right backing she can go far."

"I'm afraid we don't have a huge amount of self-belief in our family, Luke."

"I hope I can change that for Elodie," he said.

"So do I. She's going to need support after this, Luke. Bellamore really will go under the hammer this time, and these past few months will have to be swept away from Max and Elodie's memories if they are to get on with their lives."

Chapter sixty

The breeze brought a perfume of Philadelphus with it, making Elodie feel nostalgic as she kicked off her wellies by the front door of the gate lodge. Pulling up her socks, she picked up the paper bag of eggs, pushed open the door and walked along the short corridor to find Tess there, snoozing in an armchair.

"Tess? I'm so sorry – did I wake you?"

"No," she said, getting to her feet and pushing her fingers through her hair. "It was so busy at the house this morning, I thought I'd have a quick sit down before I make some mayonnaise for the chicken."

"This room is so cosy," said Elodie, noticing how the whites of Tess's eyes were almost pale yellow in colour. "How will you bear leaving it?"

"Quite easily," said Tess. "Mainly because I don't have an option – and sometimes in life you just have to take the cards you are dealt."

"Do you really think so?" said Elodie.

Tess smiled at Elodie, "I do," she said.

"Charlotte's mother seems very keen on catering – lucky for us, within an hour of arriving she was making cheese straws in the kitchen – oh, and I brought you some eggs. All intact, I think – I managed not to smash them as I walked down the avenue."

"Very sweet of you, Elodie."

"Are you really okay? You look tired."

"I'm fine," said Tess. "I didn't sleep very well last night, that's all. Let's put the kettle on."

In the kitchen, Tess took a box of tea bags from a cupboard above a white gas cooker.

"I had a good chat with your boyfriend earlier," she said, leaning one hand on the table and looking at Elodie with eyes full of warmth.

"I guess he is my boyfriend now, isn't he?"

"Seems that way," said Tess, dropping a couple of tea bags into a red pot, "and there's actually something I'd like to give you for tonight. I was going to bring it up to the house but, now that you're here, you might as well take a look."

"Sounds intriguing," said Elodie, following her aunt to a bedroom to see a full-length cream dress hanging on the side of a wardrobe.

"I bought this in New York in the seventies."

"It's incredible – the cut is amazing and look at the stitching," said Elodie, running her fingers along the material. "Such tiny petals of pink and green."

"I'd love you to have it, but only if you think it's something you might wear? Please don't feel you have to take it."

Elodie whisked off her top and, taking the dress from the hanger, she slipped it on over her jeans.

"It fits perfectly," she said and stepped in front of a long mirror. "Even the length is perfect. I can wear it with my little pink flats."

"I used to wear it with outrageously high heels," said Tess, standing next to her.

"Apart from height, our figures are so similar, aren't they?" said Elodie, studying their reflections.

"Yes," said Tess, "you're right."

A white damask tablecloth covered the dining-room table as Bonnie and Clyde pointed their little noses upwards, sniffing the aroma of Mary's Parma ham pillows filled with salmon paté and cream cheese. Crusty bread, huge wheels of Cashel Blue and Gubeen cheese awaited hungry mouths.

Rumours were rife about the fate of Bellamore. Those without knowledge of Thomas' penury suspected the grandchildren had instigated the sale, ousting Thomas for an early inheritance. Others suggested the American actress, Sofia Tamper – once linked to Harry Rose's son-in-law, George Wyndham – was buying the place, having lost out on her chance to own a Scottish estate a couple of years ago. Then there was an idea that Thomas's feisty girlfriend was pulling him away from Bellamore to her roots in Amsterdam.

"We're devastated by your news," said Harry, arriving with a bottle in each hand. "I couldn't believe it when Freddie told me."

"Nothing we can do about it now," said Thomas who was dressed in a turquoise-velvet suit and white shirt, "and I thought gathering the locals would at least give me one last memory of the place, seeing my friends here."

"It's too bad," said Harry.

Thomas swirled the bottom of his glass and knocked back the remainder of the sloe gin.

"Who's the buyer?"

"No idea," he said. "They're represented by an English property company, could be a Russian."

"At least the arctic temperatures of this place wouldn't be too much of a shock for them if that was the case. I remember being in St. Petersburg years ago – bloody freezing."

"That silly woman from the bird society has just asked me if she can take the stove from my study before the sale," said Thomas.

"More vulture than tit, I'd say, Thomas," said Harry Rose.

"Yes, well, no point in worrying about it now. I must say you're looking well, Harry."

"That'll be the whiskey," said Harry.

"You've given it up?"

"Lord no," said Harry, "I'm back on it."

"Well, whatever works."

"Try not to be down, old boy," said Harry. "Surely it will be a relief to live in a place where the plug, sockets, rooms and roof are intact?"

"I think it will, though where this new abode will be remains to be seen."

"Your Dutch crumpet will surely take you in, won't she?"

"Not so sure. I'm thinking of picking up a camper van on Ebay."

"You are joking, Thomas?" said Harry.

"I'm not actually joking, Harry. I'm clean out of jokes. Clean out."

"Dad," said Charlotte, walking into the hall, "have you been waiting here long?"

"No, we've just arrived and your mother's run straight to the ladies' to powder her nose – she wasn't happy with the lighting in our hotel room."

She felt stunned, but only for a moment and not because her father was wearing a full-length dress, along with a pearl necklace and earrings, but because her mother knew.

"Mum's really okay with –"

"Surprisingly so," said Gerald, "and you look beautiful, our Charlotte. Letting your hair out of its plait like that, it really looks good."

"Thanks, Dad, but tell me about Mum. When did you explain?"

"You know, she's been absolutely marvellous and, just like you, she knew all along, or so she says anyway."

"I thought I was the only one who knew. Remember when I was little and we used to play dress-up? I'd put that awful blue eyeshadow on you?"

"I do, Charlotte, that I do. But no, she knew all along – and I may have stretched one or two of her frocks when trying them on at home. It was following our trip to London, to have lunch with Max's mother."

"I can only imagine how that went," said Charlotte.

"There was a big silver lining as it turned out, as I met Lorenzo, who made me feel proud of who I am, who I really am inside."

"Dad, that's just so good."

"And a day or two later, I told your mother. Before I knew it, we were with Lorenzo in his London studio, trying on all kinds of dresses and accessories."

"I am amazed."

"You know, Charlotte, with your mother, beneath all that self-raising flour and cocoa powder, not to mention the doilies, there really is a rather understanding woman."

"Is that a Prada?" said Charlotte, peeking at the label of his dress.

"Yes," said Gerald, looking bashful. "Lorenzo suggested I wear long tonight."

"So, the Vicar Wears Prada?" said Charlotte, hugging her father, feeling the softness of his satin dress with cuff sleeves and a sash around the waist.

"Of course, if word were to get out, I'd have no chance of becoming a bishop. I'm afraid the distance between traditionalists and progressives is wider than ever."

"I can't really see a traditionalist wearing Louboutin leopard-print heels at the pulpit," said Charlotte.

"Still, I don't have to officially declare myself to the church, and over lunch with Thomas I was rather tickled to be offered a delicious cheese with the rather extraordinary name of The Stinking Bishop."

"Cheers, Dad," said Charlotte, raising her glass as a man with a freshly oiled bald head, dressed in black tie, tails and very shiny shoes paused by her side.

"May I refresh your glass, madam?" he said.

"This party is turning into *Downton Abbey*," said Gerald, elbowing Charlotte.

"Lionel is my name," said the man. "Your butler for this evening."

"How smart?" said Gerald.

"May I refresh your glass, sir?" said Lionel.

"I do hope you aren't alarmed by my dress," said Gerald, checking that his clip-on pearl earrings were in place.

"Sure, it's nothing I haven't seen before," said Lionel. "When I was a butler down there in Kells, didn't the rose in the dining-room ceiling collapse onto the table as I was dishing out the soup."

"No," said Charlotte, enthralled, "and what did you do?"

"Weren't the guests well-oiled after two hours of drinking so they split their sides, they did," said Lionel, lifting his hand to his mouth, imitating a glass of wine, "and that was before a woman's boob fell out of her dress she was laughing so much, so didn't I have to use the soup ladle to scoop it back in?"

"You didn't?" said Charlotte.

"Did so," said Lionel, with a cackle, "and by the time it came for the cheese course, the very same woman was pouring Champagne into her shoe and feeding it to her husband."

"My," said Gerald.

"Ah, sure they were grand days," said Lionel.

"Freddie sent you, did she?" said Thomas to Lionel, arriving into the hall, with a well-primed glass.

"She did, Mr Archdale, along with several cases of wine."

"She is good," said Thomas. "Now, Lionel, I'd appreciate it if you can keep an eye on those blasted terriers, who keep trying to pull the tablecloth to get to the Parma ham."

Chapter sixty-one

Men dressed in tweed sports jackets and women in striped dresses and pleated skirts were clutching their drinks as they pointed their noses towards each other, exchanging gossip about the Bellamore sale, when Max arrived into the drawing room with Gerald by his side, followed by Mary.

"Isn't this room a lovely colour?" said Gerald, trying to rise above the aghast looks from the old cronies by the mantelpiece.

"I love it," said Elodie, putting out her hands and kissing Gerald on either cheek. "And your dress is fabulous, I wish I had one as beautiful."

"I say!" said Gerald, who turned to Mary with a large smile.

"Come and meet Charles," said Elodie. "He's an old friend of my grandmother's."

"And to meet a friend of Odette's granddaughter is an honour," said Charles, leaning on his wooden cane, and bowing his head to both Gerald and Mary. "I can still remember taking tea in this room while you and Max played checkers on the low table over there."

"I forgot about the checkers," said Elodie, as Luke joined them.

"I do like a game of checkers as well," said Mary, looking increasingly comfortable.

"It's a game rather like marriage," said Charles, greeting Luke with a handshake. "I've been married three times, and I've loved every one of them."

"Aren't you lucky?" said Mary, sipping a glass of sherry.

"Blessed," said Gerald.

"My second wife was the trickiest – such energy, she had such an appetite for everything," he said, putting his arm around Elodie. "She loved to eat, to drink, and to make love, and I'm sure she was the reason I married a third time."

Elodie couldn't take her eyes off Luke as the old man reminisced.

"You have added another couple of years to my life," Charles said to Elodie. "Now, go on, you two, leave us oldies to it and make the most of your time."

"That's right," said Gerald. "You won't get this time back, so make the most of it."

"Elodie," whispered Luke, as they moved to an alcove, "I have to tell you something."

"Yes?" she said. "I can't believe this is Gramps' last party here, Luke. I can hardly bear to think about it."

"I know," he said, "it must be cutting you all up, and I just want you to know that I feel so lucky to be here, with you, and that you look incredible in that dress. Every inch of you is incredible."

"Is that what you wanted to tell me?"

"Yes," and sweeping a strand of hair out of her eyes, he added, "and to tell you that I love you."

"You do?"

"I do," he said, and he kissed her. "It's you, Elodie Gold."

Feeling a hand on her elbow, Elodie turned to find Lionel standing next to her.

"A top-up, ma'am?"

"Yes, please," said Elodie and, as Lionel hiccupped and swayed slightly, he poured white wine down the front of Elodie's dress. "Oh no," she said, leaping back. "That went right down my front."

"Are you okay?" said Luke.

"I'm terribly sorry, madam," said Lionel, patting Elodie's cleavage with a white napkin in an effort to dry her.

But Elodie didn't mind at all, her mind was already intoxicated by Luke, telling her that he loved her. She remembered when Dominic had said the same words, except he was spread-eagled on the floor, drunk.

"Don't worry," said Elodie, stepping back to avoid further efforts by Lionel to dry her.

"I'm going to run to my room for a moment, won't be a sec."

Turning on the light in her bedroom, Elodie found Bonnie and Clyde snuggled up between her pillows.

"You two," she said, rubbing both their tummies, "what are you doing up here? Has Bluebell pushed you off her beanbag? Can't say I blame her."

Finding some wipes, she mopped her sticky cleavage and examined Tess's cream dress to make sure there was no damage – it seemed okay.

She could feel a breeze coming from the thin window glass and, closing the shutters, she thought of how Luke had made her feel last night. She had never felt like this before and now he'd said he loved her, he really loved her. Looking in the mirror, she decided not to reapply her eyeliner. She ran her fingers across her collarbone and remembered the fragility she had felt in the past. Dominic's torment about how she was never quite perfect enough, and her mother constantly telling her to smarten up, to look better, to be better. But Luke didn't seem to want anything of her except to be herself. Being at Bellamore, she was beginning to think positively about her future and tomorrow she'd begin a new series of drawings.

Adjusting the straps of her dress, Elodie heard the sound of a phone ringing and, put out by the noise, Bonnie and Clyde leapt off the bed from where it came. Following the sound, Elodie found Luke's mobile under the duvet and, as the call went to voicemail, a text message flashed up.

Luke, call me. I need to speak with you. You promised!

Elodie's heart began to thump, and then the phone rang again, the name *Star* appearing next to an American 001 number. Elodie pressed accept and put the phone to her ear.

"Luke?" said a woman in an American accent.

"No, he isn't here," said Elodie quietly.

"Who is this?"

"It's Elodie."

"Are you the maid?"

"What? No, who is this?"

"This – *this* is Star Hampton."

"Oh, are you a cousin of Luke's?" said Elodie, relaxing a little.

"Cousin? I am not his cousin goddammit, I am Luke's wife, and if you aren't the maid then who the hell are *you*?"

Elodie could feel her hands beginning to shake.

"Hello? I said who is this?"

"Nobody," said Elodie. "I'm nobody."

"Tell him to call me, will you? I need to speak with him urgently."

Lowering the phone from her ear, Elodie felt the blood drain from her face. She sat on the bed, and couldn't feel anything, not a thing. She felt completely numb. There was a photograph of her on the screensaver of his phone.

Squeezing it in her hand, she went to the chest of drawers where she had kept an emergency rolled-up cigarette. Putting it into her mouth, tears ran down her cheek, damping the thin white paper around the tobacco.

Then taking it from her mouth, she scrunched it up in her hand.

"*No*," she said out loud and, turning off the light, she walked along the corridor and slowly made her way downstairs.

Chapter sixty-two

Elodie stood on the staircase, watching Luke gather logs from the basket in the hall and, as if he could sense her standing there, he turned his head and looked at her. Elodie could see the panic in his eyes as the wood tumbled from his arms.

"Elodie?"

She hurled the phone at him, missing his shoulder, and it hit the brass door handle behind him.

"*Don't you even say my name,*" she hissed, as Luke picked up the phone and frantically swiped on the messages.

"Star," she said, "your wife? And you had the nerve to arrive here as Mr Bloody Perfect?"

"It's not what you think, just let me explain, Elodie, give me a minute to –"

"All this time," she said, "all this time –" She was so shocked she didn't actually have the energy to scream at him.

"I didn't want to bring the past into it, Elodie, it was too complicated. I split from Star a couple of years ago, and when she finally gave in to the divorce I came to Europe."

"*I don't want to know,*" screamed Elodie, "*Just shut up and get out of my way.*"

Luke stood in front of her and reached for her hand. "I know

I'm impulsive, Elodie, but I've never been so sure about anything in my life. I want you, Elodie, it's *you*."

"No," she said, "get off me. I can't believe I let myself trust you – what was I thinking?"

"I know it sounds bad, Elodie, but I swear to you, it isn't what you think – it was a college thing that spilled over, we should never have married –"

"Spilled over? Relationships don't *spill* over, Luke," she said, wondering where she would run to.

"You remember when I flew to New York a few weeks ago?" he said.

"To see your mother? Or let me guess, to sleep with your wife?"

"To sign divorce papers," said Luke, "but Star backed out."

"Stop lying."

"Her lawyers advised her to hold out for a bigger pay-off – we didn't sign a prenup."

"A prenup? Luke, I don't want to hear about your fucking business."

"Elodie, what we have –"

"We? Luke, there is no *we*."

"I know how much you've been messed around, Elodie."

"You are a joke, Luke, I can't believe I fell for it," she said, and taking the stairs to the basement two steps at a time, she almost went over on her ankle.

"I'm telling you, Elodie," said Luke, running after her, "that's why I moved to London, to work out what I wanted. Elodie, I swear to you –"

"Don't bother," she said and, pausing for a moment outside the kitchen, she slapped his face so hard it made her hand ache, then she slammed the door in his face.

In the kitchen she found Lionel having a one-sided conversation with Augusta.

"I'm looking for Tess," said Elodie, breathless and wiping her mouth with her hand.

"She's just gone down to the lodge," said Lionel. "Doesn't this parrot ever say anything?"

Ignoring him, Elodie pulled on a pair of boots by the door to the back garden and, with just enough battery in her iPhone to use the phone light as a torch, she picked up a bottle of red wine from the Aga and walked outside.

"*Bugger,*" said Augusta, as Elodie left the kitchen.

Luke stood outside the kitchen not knowing what to do, then steeling himself he pushed open the door.

"Would you like a drink, sir," said Lionel, pressing his forehead against Augusta's cage, who whistled and bobbed her head at him. "I've been teaching this parrot some etiquette. I'd suggest that her manners need a little work."

"*Bugger off,*" said the parrot.

"Nothing to drink," said Luke, seeing the door to the back garden open. "Elodie went that way?"

"Yes, and without a coat," said Lionel, hiccupping again.

Luke called Elodie's phone as he walked back upstairs to the hall to find Max, but it rang out. Arriving into the drawing room he found Freddie and Harry balancing a very drunk Thomas on each arm.

"Can I help?" said Luke.

"It's been an emotional evening for him," said Freddie. "If you can make sure the guests are okay. Charlotte has gone upstairs to give Fleur a bottle with Mrs Murray and Max is about to play piano."

"Of course, leave it to me," said Luke, who had never felt such a fake.

Elodie's dress was soaked through, and her hair had tumbled down from the gorgeous style Charlotte had piled up for her earlier. Stopping intermittently to take mouthfuls of wine from the neck of the bottle, she could see the blurry lights of the gate lodge through her tears. Throwing the bottle into the hedge, she began running to the lodge and, rounding the corner to the entrance, she tripped on a wedge of granite and fell hard onto the ground.

Getting to her knees, she picked up her mobile, its screen cracked, and could feel a warm ooze of blood coming from her forehead.

"*Why won't you let me be? Why won't you let me be?*"

She wasn't sure who she was shouting at – maybe Odette, or her father – but Elodie felt a weight on her shoulders that was almost unbearable, as if her time at Bellamore had been one big tease. It had been a taste of real happiness, being with Luke, living at Bellamore, feeling like she was part of something solid, something real. But now it was over – the house, Luke, it was all over.

Elodie made it to the front door and hammered the brass door knocker against the wood.

It opened.

"Elodie, my god, what has happened to you?" said Tess.

"I tripped," said Elodie and, stepping inside, she noticed that Tess was wrapped in a coat. "Are you on your way out, Tess?"

"No," she said, "I've had my coat on since I got home and even though I turned the heating on it's still freezing, isn't it? Why you didn't you drive down, Elodie – it's a dreadful night out there."

Elodie notice how tanned Tess looked as she stood by the fire, holding onto the edge of the mantelpiece – she looked almost a little yellow.

"I don't know where to begin," said Elodie quietly.

"Why are you so upset, darling?"

"It's Luke," said Elodie, bursting into tears.

"Take your time. What will I make you? I'm not sure another drink is what you need. How about a cup of tea?"

"I don't want anything," said Elodie. "Luke is married."

"*What?*"

"He has a wife," said Elodie, between gasps, "an American woman and she called his phone, she bloody well called his phone and I spoke with her. I actually can't believe it."

"Are you sure?"

"Her name's Star," said Elodie, rubbing her eyes and feeling her mascara smudging into her face. "He has a *wife*, I can't believe it."

"And have you asked Luke about it?"

"He says the marriage is over," said Elodie, pacing up and down the room, almost hysterical, "but of course he's going to say that because he's a bloody liar. All along, he's been lying. Helping everyone, behaving like he's some kind of Romeo, stringing me along."

She joined Tess by the fireplace.

"He said he loved me – Tess, how could he have done this to me?"

"No, Elodie," said Tess, shaking her head, with both hands now holding on to the mantelpiece. "There must be an explanation?"

"He says he came to London to get away from her, but after this, after everything, why should I believe him?"

"I think he's genuine, Elodie, I really do."

Elodie noticed a photograph lying on the desk. It was of Tess holding a tiny baby.

"Tess?" said Elodie, picking up the photograph.

"Please put that down, Elodie. I meant to put it …"

Elodie noticed how Tess's voice had changed. She was speaking more slowly and her voice was weaker.

"Tess?" said Elodie. "Are you finding it hard to breathe?"

"Elodie, put down the photograph, please," said Tess, gravitating to the floor, "put it away," and putting one hand out in front of her, she tumbled to the rug and lost consciousness.

"Tess?" said Elodie, putting her cheek to Tess's mouth to check if she was breathing. "Oh god."

Elodie reached for her phone on the coffee table and dialled 999. Speaking steadily, she managed to give the address of the gate lodge at Bellamore and then she tried to call Max, but his phone was turned off. Then she called the landline of the main house but no answer.

She had no choice but to call Luke.

"Elodie? Thank God. I need to –"

"*Tess has collapsed,*" she screamed.

"Elodie, where are you?"

"I'm at the lodge. I've called the ambulance but it could be forty minutes before it arrives, I don't know what to do. Luke, tell me what to do, I don't know what to do?"

Luke ran to the front hall and passed a woman trying to hold a glass of wine and a canapé in one hand and squinting as she texted on her phone with the other. Rain pelted against the granite steps by the front door. He ran to his jeep and managed to squeeze through the atrociously parked cars. Halfway down the avenue, he found that a huge beech tree had collapsed across the drive, its branches stretching out as if in a Californian Pilates class. He couldn't get around the branches as there was fencing on either side of the drive. Grabbing his phone and the medical kit from the glove compartment, he thought of his uncle, who worked in the emergency rooms in Palm Springs. He was big into first-aid kits, just in case the equipment could by the grace of god make a change to a patient's outcome in the hands of a civilian.

He clambered over the fence, then climbed back onto the avenue beyond the fallen tree. Running to the lodge as fast as he could move, stretching out into huge paces, he darted over potholes, gusts of wind pushing him, as his heart reeled, not from exercise but from Elodie.

The front door was unlocked. Inside, he found her red-eyed and shaking.

Getting onto his knees, he put his cheek over Tess's mouth.

"She's breathing, but it's very light," he said.

"It happened so quickly," said Elodie.

"Can you pass me the rug on the chair, please," said Luke, moving Tess into recovery position and putting the rug over her as lights flared up the window.

"It's the ambulance," she said.

Luke got up and opened the front door to a team of paramedics.

"We know the way," said a woman in a luminous coat, with two men behind her carrying a stretcher, "though it's been a while since we've seen Ms Archdale."

Luke followed the paramedics into the sitting room.

"You've treated Tess before?" said Luke. "Do you hear that, Elodie? Did you have any idea?"

She shook her head.

One of the paramedics knelt down next to Tess, gently slipping an oxygen mask over her nose and mouth.

"You've been here before?" said Elodie.

The woman looked at Elodie for the slightest moment but said nothing. Pulling up the sleeve of Tess's blouse, she tore the top off a small plastic pouch and slipped a drip into a needle entry.

"And why is there a needle entry already in Tess's arm?" said Elodie.

"Bad night out there," said one of the men, and counting to three they lifted Tess onto the stretcher.

"Hello there, Tess, can you hear me?" said the woman. "You'll be grand now, won't you?" Tess began moving her head from side to side.

Elodie stood next to the stretcher and took Tess's hand.

"Tess, it's me," said Elodie.

"Elodie?"

"Yes, I'm here."

"Step back now," said the man. "We'll take her into hospital, set her right."

"Can I travel with you?" said Elodie.

"Of course you can," said the woman who had kind eyes.

"I'm coming with you," said Luke.

"No," Elodie said, firing him a look that made him back off immediately. "I want you to leave."

"Elodie, what's going on?" said Max, soaking wet and breathless, as he ran up to the ambulance. "I'm so sorry, I've only just found all these missed calls on my phone."

"Max, let's go with Tess," said Elodie.

"Mate, can you go up to the house and make sure everything's okay?" said Max to Luke. "And can you explain to Charlotte where I am?"

"I'm on it," said Luke.

Chapter sixty-three

Luke had been up all night, having explained what he knew to Freddie and Charlotte, before waving off guests and then tidying up with Charlotte's mother at the helm. Mary had quickly kicked the drunk butler to touch. She was like a whirlwind with a J-cloth, washing glasses, cling-film-wrapping canapés and putting manners on Bonnie and Clyde who were salivating for the Parma ham fancies she had kept for special guests but which had sadly been forgotten about.

Luke couldn't bear to be inside himself – he wanted to tear off his skin and run for shelter. Gathering his things, he took one last look at the view from Elodie's bedroom window. It was nearly light outside, the misty outline of the drumlins reflecting in the sunrise. There was nothing he could do now, except hope that Tess would pull through in hospital and that Elodie's family could help her through what he had done. It had been the greatest of misunderstandings. Luke could never resist taking risks, but this time he had taken it too far, and his carefree attitude wasn't going to save him this time.

He walked to his jeep by the collapsed tree on the avenue and, reversing up the hill, he drove out through the stable yard and back to his own reality.

Thomas walked into the kitchen, dressed in his turquoise suit from the night before.

"How are you?" said Charlotte, leaning against the Aga.

"Delicate," he said. "I'm afraid I can't even remember going to bed."

"Freddie and Harry walked you to your room."

"I have a vague recollection," he said, reaching down to rub Bluebell's ears and then thinking better of it as he felt nauseous.

He sat down at the table.

"Was that Luke's jeep I just saw driving through the yard?" he asked.

"I'm not sure," said Charlotte. "Max did send a message to say that there was some kind of misunderstanding with Elodie but, with everything happening with Tess, he didn't go into any detail."

Thomas took his glasses from around his neck and put them on the table.

"Freddie called earlier," said Charlotte, turning over Fleur's little cardigan as it dried on the Aga hotplate.

"I've just been speaking with her. She's going to collect Elodie and Max in a couple of hours from the hospital, and Tess will come here by ambulance after lunch."

"I hope you won't mind me saying, but you don't seem surprised?" said Charlotte.

"Tess has always been a mistress of disguise. She's the definitive of private."

Charlotte put a couple of pieces of brown bread onto the Aga toaster.

"How about I make you some breakfast?"

"A small breakfast, please, Charlotte, though if Mrs Murray were here she'd force a greasy cooked breakfast inside me as a 'cure' – thankfully I gave her today off."

"She was so good with Fleur last night, but she didn't mention anything about the sale of the house. Does she know about it?"

"Everyone knows about the sale, talk of the town."

"At least Tess is coming home, that is good news," said Charlotte, trying to be positive.

"The consultant has already had it out with Tess that she'll have to stay with us for the time being, so at least that's one battle I won't have to face."

"I'll make up a bed, shall I?"

"That would be very kind."

"Do you have any idea how long Tess will need to recover?" said Charlotte.

"Is that toast burning? Actually, Charlotte, maybe a poached egg?" He couldn't face those sort of questions, not this morning. Looking through the open door onto the back garden, he thought of something he had once read by Elizabeth Bowen, *Fate is not an eagle ... it creeps in like a rat.* Never had the quote been so true.

"I hardly saw Anika last night," said Charlotte.

"I have a feeling that the novelty of going out with an old dog has worn off."

"I'm sorry."

"Don't be," he said. "Everything in life has a cycle, and I feel that my cycle is drawing to a close."

Elodie sat in the hospital waiting room opposite an unbelievably depressing painting of empty chairs lined up in a garden. Still wearing her evening dress, she was wrapped in a scratchy hospital blanket, which Max had managed to persuade one of the nurses to lend to them. Handsome in his suit, Max had had several nurses offering him cups of tea and jammy dodgers through the night.

"That was Luke on the phone again," said Max, holding a plastic cup of tea. "You'll need to find your phone. I can only imagine the voicemails he's left you."

"I told you, I don't want to talk about Luke," said Elodie, flicking through an out-of-date magazine.

"He didn't want to put you off, El, by telling you about his broken marriage. He says if he had known things were going to become serious between you so quickly, he would have told you from the start."

"Don't you dare take his side, Max."

"I am on your side, Elodie, I am always on your side. But I think Luke is a good guy."

"He's a liar."

"Look, I agree he screwed up by not telling you, but El, I think he's a genuine guy."

"Why do you have to see the best in everyone?"

"I just think he was trying to protect you."

"By hiding the fact that he has a fucking wife, Max?"

Max put his arm around his sister. "I'm sorry," he said. "I just hope to god that Tess is going to be okay."

"She will be," said Elodie. "The paramedics didn't seem flustered about it at all, did they? It seemed so routine. So weird, that."

"We're so lucky that we've got to know her, and if it hadn't been for you we'd never have come back."

"If it hadn't been for Fleur, you mean?"

"It was your idea, El, and even though Bellamore is coming to an end –"

"Don't, Max, I don't want to think about leaving."

"Hello, you two," said Freddie, wearing a long fuchsia pink scarf around her neck. "Elodie, what happened to your forehead – that looks so sore?"

"It's nothing," she said, "I stumbled on my way to the lodge last night, that's all."

"The nurse put some cream on it," said Max, hugging Freddie, "said it was better to let the air at it than cover it with a bandage."

"Anyway, the nurses were much more interested in giving Max VIP treatment."

"I can imagine," said Freddie, who always put her best foot forward, bright and upbeat, even when her best friend was in hospital.

"You look tired, Freddie," said Max.

"Do I?" said Freddie, beaming that gorgeous smile of hers. "Now, I'm your pumpkin to drive you home, and the better news is that Tess is being released after lunch."

"How did you hear?"

"Tess called my mobile about an hour ago."

"One of the nurses could at least have told us," said Elodie, stretching out her arms. "Those chairs are incredibly uncomfortable."

"You two have been marvellous," said Freddie, "and Elodie, darling, I've brought you a cardigan. That blanket doesn't look up to much."

"The caffeine has made us so wired, I don't think our bodies can differentiate between temperatures at this stage," said Max.

"Come on," said Freddie, linking her arms through Max and Elodie's. "Let's get you two back to Bellamore."

On the drive to Bellamore, they travelled mostly in silence, expect for Freddie's frequent words of positivity, pointing out how lucky Tess was that Elodie arrived when she did and how good that the ambulance got Tess to hospital so quickly. But Elodie thought about the photograph on Tess's desk, when she was banging on and on about Luke before Tess collapsed. She tried to stop thinking of Luke, the way he held her as she slept, his breath on her neck and then she thought of Star, imagining that she must have been very beautiful, maybe a Yale or Harvard graduate, an Upper East Side Star.

"I'll jump out here, Freddie, if that's okay?" said Elodie, as they approached the gates of Bellamore. "I left my mobile in the lodge last night." As much as she didn't want to hear from Luke, in a way she wanted to see a string of missed calls, to have the satisfaction of knowing that he was desperate to speak with her.

"I'm not sure if the front door is locked, Elodie, but you'll find a key in a tin over the potting-shed door, just in case."

Walking towards the gate lodge, Elodie looked up at the sky full of house martins, swooping and weaving, while a buzzard shrieked over the distant woods.

Finding the front door open, the first thing she noticed when she walked into the sitting room was the torn end of a syringe packet on the floor. She found her iPhone on the mantelpiece, out of battery, dead. Searching for a charger, she looked on the desk and found a black wire, except it was for a different make of phone. There was an orchid on Tess's desk that looked in need of water though she remembered from her mother that there was some particular way of watering them, so she wasn't going to try. Funny how Tess kept orchids, just like her mother did.

Elodie picked up the photograph of Tess, wearing a long-sleeved nightdress, sitting in what looked like a hospital bed, holding a baby.

Elodie looked away and then looked again. She knew that baby. She got a strange feeling in her heart or her chest, she couldn't decide, and she could feel her face scrunching up, her eyes now filling with tears. She realised, at that moment, why she had never understood Julia, why she had never felt at home with her and why they were like opponents in a fencing competition. She was not her mother.

But if she was Tess's daughter, then who was her father? Elodie held on to the photograph and, grabbing her iPhone, she ran out of the lodge, her body shaking, feeling like someone was tricking her. Luke had lied to her, so why not her family? What if Max had known all along, and Gramps? Maybe Freddie too.

She winced when she pressed her fingers against the graze on her forehead and wondered if she was on the wrong track. But then why did she feel such a connection with Tess? Even when she had first tried on the long dress in Tess's room, the fit was almost perfect, and the similarity of their hands when they were flower-arranging was striking.

The puzzle was fitting more and more by the second in Elodie's mind. But what now?

Chapter sixty-four

"Hello, Anika," said Freddie, quietly arriving into the kitchen from the back garden with an armful of hydrangea.

"Hello," said Anika, who felt like a rat deserting a sinking ship. She'd needed to tell Thomas that there was no way he could move in with her and that she was bowing out of the entire relationship.

Anika followed Freddie into the back kitchen.

Freddie took a large crystal vase from a cupboard and filled it with water. She began to arrange the hydrangea in the vase.

"Freddie, what is really going on with Tess?"

"What do you mean?" said Freddie, adding the flowers at speed.

"I'm not sure that Thomas is aware of how ill Tess is – in fact, I don't think any of us are."

Freddie took a handkerchief out of her back pocket and wiped her nose.

"Anika, I feel it is up to Tess to let us know when the time is right."

"But surely –"

"No, Anika, I can understand your concern for Thomas, but Tess is my friend and it is not my place to discuss her private life."

"But surely if we had more information, we could get better medical advice?"

"I don't believe that there is better medical advice, not for Tess, not in this case," said Freddie, blowing her nose. "Tess will come home this afternoon. Charlotte is making up the bed in Odette's room with her mother, while the baby is with Gerald."

"In Odette's room? But nobody has slept in there for years? Not since I've been coming here."

"We'll move in an electric heater," said Freddie, "and the nights are getting so much warmer, don't you think? Anika, I can understand it seems strange, given her estrangement with her mother, but I believe this will be healing for Tess." She was trying to be diplomatic, keeping Thomas's girlfriend on side. "Is that alright, Anika, does that help with your concerns?"

"If I had known Tess was unwell, I would have been more –"

"She's a very private person, Anika, you must have realised? Now if you'll excuse me, I'm going to help Gerald with the baby, I'm in training, you see?"

"For?" said Anika.

"For being a granny. My daughter Anna is due in four weeks and I'll be flying over to Rousey, their house in Scotland, just before the birth. I couldn't be more excited."

Anika could tell that Freddie was putting on a brave face.

"It's in my nature to be positive, Anika. Today I am here for my best friend, and I am also looking to the future with my daughter and grandchild."

"Can you let Thomas know that I've gone back to my house to run a couple of errands?"

"I will," said Freddie. "And Anika?"

"Yes?"

"Things have a way of working themselves out."

In the kitchen, Freddie found Elodie, leaning against the Aga, her eyes red, her face so thin.

"Elodie?" said Freddie, giving her a hug. "Naturally you're upset about Tess, but she'll be home this afternoon. As for Luke, Max mentioned you'd had a row. I'm sure you can work it out."

Elodie stared at the floor and shook her head. "We've got to stop the sale," she said, "we've got to stop it."

"Elodie, your grandfather doesn't have a choice and we are all devastated for him, of course we are, but it's in the hands of the banks now and the estate agent."

"You don't understand," said Elodie. "We need to stay here. I belong here, with Tess, I belong here."

Freddie put her arms around Elodie again, "How about a cup of camomile?"

"I don't want tea," said Elodie through gritted teeth, "I need everyone to see sense."

Elodie left the kitchen and climbed the stairs to her bedroom in silence. She would stay at Bellamore, Gramps would live with Anika, and Elodie would live with her mother, her real mother. For the first time in her life, she would be properly loved by someone who understood her, who felt a mother's natural love. She could feel the dots joining and relief in realising that her disjointed life wasn't her fault after all.

Most probably due to sleep deprivation, she had half expected that Luke to be waiting in her bedroom, but there was no one there. The room was empty and felt like a murder scene, where she had taken the call from Star, her name still burning into her skull. Elodie felt like her whole life had crescendoed to this point and no matter how much she knew she needed sleep, she had to fix this.

Looking almost ghostly, wearing a long camel coat over a pair of jeans and a blouse, her hair frizzy from being in the rain the night before, Elodie walked into the hotel.

"I'm Mrs Finchly," she said to the receptionist. "I've come to surprise my husband."

"Well, isn't that just lovely," said the girl. "Nothing like a bit of old-fashioned romance, is there?" and, reaching for the room key, she handed it to Elodie. "I don't think Mr Finchly is in at the moment."

"That's okay," said Elodie. "I'll wait."

"Would you like me to send up a nice bottle of something?" the receptionist said. "Maybe a bottle of sparkling wine?"

"No, thank you," said Elodie, and then she thought again. "Actually, yes, a bottle of Champagne, please, and you can put it on my husband's bill."

"Right you are, Mrs Finchley."

The room was painted salmon pink, with a large oval mirror mounted above a pine table with several fliers neatly fanned out. Dominic had left his striped dressing gown on the bed, along with an iPad and a copy of *The Economist*. Elodie dropped her coat to the floor and turned on the taps in the bathroom. Then she answered the door and took a tray with the ice bucket, a bottle of Champagne and two glasses from the porter. Putting it on the dressing table, she undressed and thought of the weekends she had spent with Dominic, when he had lavished her with expensive dinners and hotel rooms, to counteract his cruel commentary.

As steam came from the bathroom, she sat on the bed, held the bottle between her legs and popped the cork. Taking a sip from the neck of the bottle, foam spilled out of her mouth, the bubbles were so strong, but by the third sip she could feel the rush of alcohol. She stood in front of the mirror, holding the bottle above her head, telling herself how lucky she was.

She was going to have it all. Her real mother and Bellamore.

As she stepped into the bath, the water was so hot it stung her body but the pain felt almost good. At least she was feeling something. Putting the Champagne between the taps and lying back in the water, with muffled sounds in her ears, she watched her breasts rising above the surface. She would do whatever it took to get what she wanted. Luke was a spineless liar – she wasn't going to make the same mistake twice. Managing to get out of the bath, though she was lightheaded by now, she pulled a small white towel from the silver radiator and, taking the Champagne bottle with her, she pulled the curtains and got into bed. The sheets felt coarse against her skin, and the thin, foam duvet so light. Elodie lay back and could only see Luke's eyes, pleading with her to believe him, just as she remembered her father's eyes, so desperate.

"Elodie?" said Dominic, sitting on the edge of the bed, running his fingers across her forehead. "This is an unexpected pleasure, isn't it? I came back to pack my case and what do I find but a goodbye present waiting for me."

She had fallen asleep and for a moment had no idea where she was.

"I was hoping to catch a glimpse of you when I went to Bellamore the other day, but I was there so briefly and your brother wasn't exactly welcoming, not to mention that American of yours."

He stared at her, trying to work out what was going on.

"Been in the wars, have you? That's a proper shiner on your head, and I'm surprised they have Champagne in this place," he said, picking up the bottle, now three quarters empty. "Did you drink this all by yourself, you naughty minx? Or have you brought a friend with you, Elodie? Could you be branching out into a little experimentation?" He rubbed his warm hand on her shoulder and down her arm. "I've missed you, Elodie, though you have got thin, haven't you?"

Elodie pulled the sheets across her chest, like a strapless dress.

"Dominic," she said, shaking out her hair and kicking her plan into motion, "I've changed my mind."

"Go on," he said.

Leaning forward, she tried to kiss his mouth, but he moved away.

"Elodie, what are you up to?"

"This is what you want, isn't it? And I'll give you what you want."

"Is that so?"

"In exchange, I want you to stop the sale."

"Darling Elodie," he said, looking at her, "you make it sound like we are on a Wall Street trading floor." He got up from the bed, pulled a roll-neck jumper from his case and slipped it over her head. "It's cashmere," he said. "Your skin won't object to being next to it."

"I'll sleep with you, Dominic, that's what I've come to do," she said. "If you'll get your uncle to stop the sale, I'll do anything."

"Hey," he said, pulling her gently towards his chest, "what are we going to do with you?"

Elodie got up to her knees, the jumper skimming her slender thighs.

"Don't play games with me, Dominic – I said I'll do anything."

"I'm afraid it's too late, gorgeous, much too late. The sale has gone through."

308

"It can't have gone through so quickly," she said. "I'm not stupid, I know how long paperwork takes, legalities and everything."

She tried to pull off the jumper again until Dominic stopped her. The expression on his face was unlike anything Elodie had seen before, and the tone of his voice almost tender.

"Elodie," he said, pressing her gently back onto the pillow, "you've had so much Champagne and I imagine you haven't eaten for hours. You need to sleep, come on."

"You can stop the sale, please stop the sale. There'll be nothing left otherwise, I have nowhere else, I don't want to be anywhere else."

In the silence, he looked at the girl he had once loved, at least in the beginning, during the chase, and looking at her he couldn't believe how much she had changed. The aloof, haughty Sloane had crumbled into a waif, lost and desperate.

Hearing a pair of heels walking along the wooden-floored corridor, Dominic got to his feet and opened the door. He was met by a heavy waft of perfume.

"Mr Finchley, good evening."

"You're late."

"I had arrangements to make," she said, "and a lady must not be rushed."

"Anika –"

"A word of warning, Dominic Finchly. I'll come with you, in fact I've been shivering with excitement all day – but I –" she said, pushing him towards the wall, "*will*" walking further, "*not*" and pressing her crotch against him "be pushed around, got it?"

"I think so," he said with a large grin.

"What time is our flight?"

"We've got an hour before we need to leave for Dublin."

"Well, then," she said, opening his belt buckle, "let's keep ourselves occupied, shall we?"

"Slight problem, darling," he said. "I'm afraid Sleeping Beauty has passed out on the bed."

Elodie woke up to find a cheque on the bedside table along with a note from Dominic.

"I've been a shit and I'm sorry. Take this and start again – no strings, I promise, D."

She looked at the almost empty bottle of Champagne and pieced together what had happened. Still wearing Dominic's jumper, she got out of bed and pulled on her jeans and boots. Before putting on her coat, she folded the cheque and put it into her pocket, next to the Polaroid photograph.

"How did the surprise go, then Mrs Finchly?" said the receptionist.

"Stupendous," said Elodie.

Elodie was feeling an almost delirious realisation. It didn't matter about Bellamore – with Dominic's money she and Tess could start again. They could move to a city, rent an apartment and Elodie could sell paintings to support them both.

"Elodie, dear?" came a voice from across the hallway. "We're so sorry about your Aunt Tess, aren't we, Gerald?"

"That we are, Mary, that we are. Your Aunt Tess is in our thoughts, Elodie, and I'll say a prayer for her in church on Sunday."

"Thank you," said Elodie, managing to smile at Charlotte's parents.

"We're leaving for the airport in a couple of hours," said Gerald. "We'll be thinking of you all."

"Gerald," said Elodie, "if you don't mind me asking, was it hard making a change in your life? Facing up to how you really want to be?"

"No, Elodie, in fact it couldn't feel more natural," said Gerald. "Lorenzo gave me the courage to be true to myself, as did Max and Charlotte in the way they steered through their obstacles. I think that's all we can ask of ourselves."

"Gerald, do mind your hem," said Mary. "What would Lorenzo say if you tore your new frock?"

Chapter sixty-five

"I'm like *The Princess and the Pea*," said Tess, lying in the large double bed, with brass pillars at each corner, in Odette's bedroom. "I can't seem to get comfortable in this bed."

"The hospital called to say that the nurse is coming back this afternoon to 'assess your needs'," Max said, putting on an Irish accent, trying to lighten Tess's mood, "now that you are home. Also, I've been thinking, Tess," he said, taking a stem of sweet pea from the vase on the bedside table and handing it to her, "if you and Mum can put your differences aside, you could come and live with us in London. Mum's guest rooms are like the Four Seasons, and you'd have Nosy Carol at your beck and call – in fact Gramps could come too."

"You are sweet, Max, truly you are, but I can't see how your mother and I could live under the same roof."

"Will you think about it at least?" he said, holding her hand. "At least think about it?"

"I don't think so," said Tess, and looking up she saw Elodie standing at the door, her hair falling around her shoulders, looking almost too heavy for her fragile face. Her eyes were still smudged with old make-up and her forehead marked with the blue bruise.

"Elodie, darling," said Tess, "I'm so sorry about Luke, but I'm sure he meant –"

"I need to talk to you, Tess," said Elodie, rushing into the room, jittery and excited.

"El, have you been sleeping all this time?" said Max.

"I haven't been here," said Elodie, nervously smoothing her hair down the back of her head.

"Then where have you been?" said Max.

"Elodie, you look like you need to sleep, sweetheart, and Max and I are having a chat. Why don't you get some sleep and come back later?"

"Tess, I understand what's been going on," said Elodie.

"Elodie –" said Tess.

"I found the photograph where you left it," said Elodie, tears building in her eyes. Taking the Polaroid from her pocket, she pressed it into Tess's hand. "I wasn't snooping, I swear – I was looking for your phone charger."

"Can you pass me a glass of water, please, Max?" said Tess, her voice stiffening.

Max topped up a glass of water from a jug on the bedside table and passed it to Tess.

"Elodie, why not have a rest and come back later?" he said, seeing that Tess was becoming distressed. "The nurse is due to call by soon."

"I had always felt different," said Elodie, "and now it all makes sense, don't you see? It's so wonderful."

"Elodie," said Tess, "please – we can talk later –"

"I feel you understand me, Tess, and now I know why."

"Wait, Elodie, *wait!*" Tess held up a hand. "There's something I have to tell you. Both of you."

"It's me, isn't it?" said Elodie, her voice getting louder.

"Elodie, please," said Tess, shaking her head.

"What's going on?" said Max, looking from his sister to his aunt.

"I know it's true. For some reason, you gave me away to Julia, but it's okay now, because I'm here with you."

"What are you saying?" Max asked. "Gave you away? Did you say 'gave me away'?"

"Sweetheart," said Tess, taking Elodie's hand and pulling her to sit on the bed, "just wait a moment."

"I know it's true," said Elodie. "I'm your daughter, aren't I?" Her eyes were blinking through heavy tears. "Please tell me the truth, Tess, please tell me."

"Elodie, I'm so sorry," said Tess.

"All the falling-outs – you and Julia, and Gramps and Julia – you gave me to her because you were too young to look after me, isn't that right? Please tell me."

"Elodie, what in God's name are you saying?" asked Max. "Where did you get that idea?"

"Elodie, my darling Elodie," said Tess, "I'm so sorry. I'm afraid you've misunderstood."

"No, I haven't," said Elodie. "Don't lie to me again. I've had a lifetime of it and I can't bear any more."

Tess shook her head and turned to Max. "I wanted to tell you before now, I swear I did, but I didn't know how to."

"Look at the photograph of the baby, Max," said Elodie, picking the photo up from the bed and thrusting it at him. "It's me."

"I realise this is difficult," said Tess, looking at Elodie and then at Max. "Your father and I, we were very young."

Max couldn't speak. He felt completely choked as he stared at the photo.

"It's you, Max," said Tess. "I am your mother."

"*What? No*," said Elodie, pressing her fists against her head.

"Yes," said Tess.

"No," she sobbed, "I don't want to be Julia's child, I don't want to be like her."

"It wasn't Julia's fault. I didn't want to give you away, Max, you must believe me. It was Odette."

Tess saw huge eyes staring back at her. Max and Elodie, both completely stunned.

"Is this why Mum has been a royal bitch to you all these years, Max? Constantly on your back. Is this why, Tess?" Elodie shouted. "Because she *had* to take in your son?"

"Elodie, for Christ's sake, stop it," said Max. "Tess, is this for real?"

"Our family is like a kind of fucked-up Greek tragedy," said Elodie.

"Please don't," said Tess.

"Why didn't you tell us before now? Not a word from you," said Elodie.

"I didn't know how to, or if I should," said Tess, looking at Max. "I'm so sorry."

"My brother is now my cousin," said Elodie. "No wonder you're so much better than I am, Max, so kind and lovely. But me, no, not me, I'm Julia's daughter."

"Elodie," said Max, "I don't know what to say."

"How about saying that I'm your fucked-up cousin?" said Elodie. "That just about sums things up." And she fled the room.

Chapter sixty-six

"Hello, Dad," said Julia, standing by the drawing-room door.

Thomas looked up and felt no surprise to see her, the tangled web slowly unravelling.

"You've got old," she said.

"You've come to visit your children, have you? And the baby too?"

"The baby, yes – you've had quite the household. All flock to Thomas, the saviour, when in fact it was you who caused the godawful mess in the first place."

Standing up, he hovered over the coffee table and lifted the bottle of wine, which felt like a lead weight as he filled his glass close to the top.

"Sit down, Julia, and have a drink with me, then you can relish the moment before you finally get to shut Bellamore down." He immediately regretted his words.

She crossed the room, tall and elegant, and sat on an armchair opposite her father.

"I'll sit down," she said, "but nothing to drink."

There she was, sitting so perfectly, legs crossed at the ankle, just like Odette had done. Except unlike Odette, his eldest daughter had a fragility beneath her shell, and immense sadness. All she had wanted, and he remembered this so clearly, was a tidy family, and a tidy husband. It was little wonder she had turned into a warrior who would take what was owed to her. He knew the debt of his actions was so great that it could never be repaid.

"It is you, isn't it?" he said, sitting down with his glass in hand. "You've bought this place."

"Ten out of ten," she said.

"Booting me out of my own home, the final punishment?"

"That had been my original intention, until –"

"Best served cold, isn't that what they say? I don't blame you," and he meant it. "My entire life has been a fiasco, and worst of all I let Odette take the lead."

"Like I said, it *had* been my intention, until Tess called."

"She called you?"

"Last night."

"It would have taken a lot for her to call you," he said.

"Yes." Julia sat forward and pressed her hands between her knees, almost childlike. "I'd like to sign the deeds of Bellamore over to Max and Elodie."

"What?" He was astounded but fought to conceal it. "Who says they'd want to live here?"

"I don't know," said Julia, "or they could sell it on, if they wanted to?"

"And what about me? You'd like me to rot in a stable? And I can't say I'd blame you."

"I want you to be part of it, if that's what you'd like?"

Putting down his glass, he burst into tears and covered his face with his hands.

"Dad," said Julia, "I'm so sorry it's taken me so long."

"How can you apologise? None of this is your fault, none of it."

"There were other women, you know, it wasn't only Tess. An affair to Douglas was like water off a duck's back, I don't think he felt as much as a trickle of shame running down his neck. But still there was the build-up of stress – by the time he actually got caught, what else was he going to do but blow his head off?"

"You've had to carry so much, Julia," he said.

"I only stayed with him for fear of being alone with two children, but he didn't honour that either, did he? He just couldn't handle any form of responsibility."

"Life as a cheat is tough," said Thomas. "I could swing for him if he were here now."

"Dad," she said, "I don't expect us to be close again, but we have to forgive each other, if we're to get through this."

"Thank you," he said. He got up and pressed his hand gently on her shoulder. That was as much of an embrace as either of them could manage.

"I'd like to see Tess," she said, standing up, "and the children – are they here?"

"I haven't seen Elodie – sleeping I presume following the late night at the hospital, and Charlotte has gone to the village with Fleur. Nappies, I think. Max may be with Tess."

"Then I'll sit in the garden," said Julia, "and wait until people are ready to see me."

Thomas climbed the staircase, carrying a jug filled with Philadelphus and stood outside Odette's bedroom for several moments before opening the door.

"It's been an age since I've been in here," he said, putting the flowers on the dressing table. "The light is so beautiful and look at those views. No wonder your mother chose this room."

"No wonder."

"I've seen you look better," he said, lifting a wooden chair and putting it next to the bed. Sitting down, he reached for Tess's hand.

"Are you hungry?"

"No, thank you," she said.

"Julia is sitting in the garden," he said, watching the light resting on Tess's cheekbones, delicate and so very like Odette's for that moment. "It would take a crisis for you to have called your sister," he said, "and to have a crisis, three things have to happen."

"Would you like me to count?"

"What is the point, Tess?"

"Point?"

"I know you want to tell the children and I am here to urge you not to."

"No need," she said.

"If you tell the children their relationship with Julia will be over."

"I said there is no need," said Tess, pushing herself up in the bed and resting on her side. "Max and Elodie both know."

"Oh." He paused. "I always thought I would take our secret to the grave."

"It's the right time," she said.

"Tess, my darling," he said, bowing his head, "if I were back there now, I would have gone against your mother."

"Dad, we don't need to go over it."

"You were only twenty-two – how could you have raised a child without your mother's support?" He closed his eyes.

"Max has me now, that's what is most important."

"For how long, though, Tess?" he said, squeezing her hand. "You have to acknowledge the reality of what's happening, as much as neither of us want to."

Tess looked at her hands, the earth still embedded in her palms, and the lines in the palm of her hands made her remember the day her mother laid down the law.

"Has someone died?" said Julia, standing in the drawing room at Bellamore, aged twenty-four.

She crossed the room.

"Tess, darling, what is it?" she said, putting arms around her sister, holding her shoulders.

"Julia," said Odette. "You sit next to your husband, over there."

"Alright," said Julia, kissing her sister on the head before walking across the room, smiling the kind of smile that only comes when the body is uncontrollably nervous.

Odette stood in front of the mantelpiece. She had been a judge with no need of any jury and stood holding her hands together, her petite waist beneath gathered tufts of tweed, haute couture for her country life.

"Julia, you asked if someone has died?" said Odette.

"And has someone died?" said Douglas.

"No one has died," said Odette in her French accent. "It is a birth."

Douglas and Julia looked at each other.

318

"Dad?" Julia looked to her father. "What is going on?"

"Listen to your mother," he said, gesturing to Odette, and he looked out the window, as he couldn't bear to make eye contact with his daughters.

"I have called you and Douglas from London, because I need to tell you –"

"Tell us what?" said Julia, taking Douglas's hand and holding it to her chest. "Why is Tess crying? Tess, why are you crying?" She dropped her husband's hand and crossed the room to her sister. "What is this all about, Tess? Tell me, you can tell me."

"Enough," said Odette, firmly. "Julia, leave her and sit down."

Julia went and sat next to her father on a tapestry stool, making her lower than anyone else in the room.

"Thérèse has had a child," Odette said as a spark jumped out of the fire, but nobody moved to stamp it out. They all watched as it burnt a tiny hole into the carpet.

Douglas, flushed, took out his handkerchief from the pocket of his cords and shook his head.

Julia didn't say a word; she didn't even flinch but just stared at her hands.

"You have disgraced the family," said Odette, glaring at Tess, while Thomas reached for his glass of whiskey.

"Mrs Murray?" called Odette. "Mrs Murray."

The door slowly opened and Mrs Murray appeared, holding a baby.

Douglas wiped his forehead again with his handkerchief.

"We are not going to make this more complicated than it needs to be," said Odette calmly. "Julia, you and Douglas will take the baby to London and rear it there."

Tess heaved herself off the sofa and onto the floor, covering her eyes as she whimpered.

Julia shook her head. "But why? Why can't it stay with Tess?"

"Don't be ridiculous," said Odette. "It cannot."

"But – but it's not our responsibility."

"It is," said Odette, pointing her bony finger at Douglas. "This baby has been fathered by your husband."

Julia felt she was going to be sick,

"I've thought this through, Julia. Your friends will assume you adopted. Besides, I'm about to make you so rich you can buy new friends. You will be the sole benefactor of my estate, Julia, and, until I die, you will receive a payment that will give you anything you want."

Tess could remember all of her family's expressions, especially the guilty sweat on Douglas's brow.

I'm going to get better, Tess thought to herself, and be a real mother to Max and grandmother to little Fleur.

Julia tried not to appear shocked by Tess's appearance, her eyes and skin now so jaundiced, her tummy bloated, her breath short.

"I had a bed bath in hospital yesterday morning – rather boring compared to Dad's bathtub in the garden," said Tess, breaking the silence with the kind of joke she might have made when they were children.

"I saw it earlier," said Julia, wondering where they could begin, having not seen each other for over twenty years. Nothing could have prepared her for this moment. She didn't know how to feel or how to react, a waterfall of heartache and sadness was pouring over her,

"What I've put you through," said Tess, lying back on several white pillows.

"We could have stopped Odette, you and I," said Julia. "We could have gone against her."

"It was a different era," said Tess. "She was the ruler and we were so young, so naive."

"Did Douglas instigate the affair?" said Julia.

"I was so naïve, Julia. It started out as a game and he knew all the tricks."

"Yes, he knew all the tricks."

"Why did you marry him?"

"He was charming and handsome, promising on paper, but by the time I discovered he was a born liar it was too late. And they got him in the end, those lies. Even if I had been prepared to bail him out, he would have had a custodial sentence."

"Instead he chose to take his life."

"Yes, he did," said Julia.

"Max told me about Lorenzo," said Tess. "I am glad you found someone so good."

"He's teaching me forgiveness, and I desperately want to forgive you," said Julia, lifting Tess's hand, so cold, to her face.

Tess could feel Julia's tears.

"I can't never forgive myself, Julia, so why should you forgive me?"

"Because we owe it to each other, and if we don't Odette will have won," said Julia. "I've come to fix things, Tess, to make things right."

"Elodie has taken it badly," said Tess.

"And Max?"

"He is as I imagine he always has been – gentle and understanding beyond belief," said Tess.

"That's because he's like you," said Julia, "and Elodie is reacting just as I would have done, head under the covers."

"Yes," said Tess, "but she'll come round, won't she?"

"In time," said Julia. "I've got a lot of making up to do. I've been so hard on her, and Max. I'm so ashamed. I don't know what I'll say to them when we meet."

"You are here, and we are together. I know it's an odd situation but there has never been anything stereotypical about our family, has there?"

"No," said Julia smiling, "and I notice Augusta's language hasn't improved either. When I walked into the kitchen earlier, she told me to 'bugger off'."

"Hah!" said Tess.

"So I think I will."

"Will what?"

"I'll go to Dublin, just for a few days, to give Max and Elodie a moment to come to terms with the news. You have my number."

"I do," said Tess.

"Thank you for calling me here, Tess," said Julia, kissing her sister's forehead.

Chapter sixty-seven

The ladies from the village quickly became part of Bellamore's routine. They arrived in pairs, right on time, thrice daily. With bright smiles, they breezed into Tess's bedroom, checking her medication, freshening her bed and, as each day passed and her illness deepened, ensuring she had as much comfort as possible. Nothing was too much trouble for them and Thomas couldn't get over how such a service was supplied by the health board. "These women are like harp-strumming angels from paradise," he said. Tess had never been so well looked after in her life.

The flowers by her bedside were replaced each day, filling the room with the aromas of the garden that she missed so much. Bonnie and Clyde had taken up residence on an armchair in the corner of the room by day. At night, they would go into Elodie's room and sleep at her feet. Max set up a CD player in Tess's room. Paul Simon, James Taylor, the Rolling Stones, Fleetwood Mac, conjuring up memories for Tess of her nomadic existence before her return to Bellamore. On request, Max hung her favourite painting on the wall opposite her bed, a landscape of Connemara.

The sound of raindrops bouncing off rose petals seeped through the window as Max folded a blanket and put it at the end of Tess's bed.

"You like to be organised, don't you?" said Tess.

"Preparation is key," he said, "and that made the arrival of Fleur all the more of a shock."

Tess laughed and then winced as a spasm of pain shot through her. She held the bedpost for a few moments as Max placed his hand on her arm.

"Why won't you put on the morphine patch?" he said. "The nurses are very keen that you get going with them. Nobody's going to give you a medal for not using them."

"No, Max. I want to keep my marbles intact. Morphine clouds the mind and I don't want a cloudy mind. I want absolute clarity because I don't want to miss a moment of being with you. Not a single moment."

Her eyes had filled with tears and Max fought to keep his voice steady. He felt such a strange yet immense love for this woman.

"When I first saw you in the yard, the day we arrived, I can't quite explain it, but I think I knew then," he said.

"Really?" said Tess. "But I was so unfriendly to you when we met. And to Elodie. In hindsight, I was appalling and I'm really rather embarrassed by my behaviour."

"Don't be," said Max. "How can any of us know how to react in a situation like this? There's no need for you to feel bad about it."

"Do you think Elodie will come to see me today?"

"I don't know," said Max. "That's the honest answer. And of course she won't even let me mention Julia."

"You're calling her Julia?" said Tess, moving onto her side.

"Yes, I've been practising. I've discussed it a lot with Charlotte and I've decided I'm going to call her Julia when we meet. I don't want to hurt her, but we do need to start on a new footing."

The next day Elodie arrived at Tess's room with a posy of sweet pea.

"Can I come in?" she asked.

"El," said Max, standing up. "I'm so glad you're here. Come, sit down."

Elodie sat in a chair beside Tess and held her aunt's hands, now so cold.

Tess gave one of those smiles that made it look like she didn't have a care in the world.

"Elodie, and Max, I want you both to know that your father and I, we were so young and dumb. Having Fleur at Bellamore has been like reliving the baby years that I missed. I never thought I'd have that experience. Elodie, you brought my son and grandchild home to me and I cannot thank you enough for that. Max, I have thought of you every single day of my life. I wanted to tell you before. Truly I did, but I didn't want to jeopardize our short time together by confusing things."

Max wiped a tear from her cheek with his palm but he could not speak.

"Know that I have always loved you, nephew or son, it matters not. And now you have given me a grandchild, a beauty beyond my wildest dreams. You children have bought me more love and joy since you came here then I have had in my whole life. Elodie, you will look after Max for me, won't you? Max ... my son Max."

"We will all look after each other," said Elodie, trying not to cry. "All of us together and then we can go on a big sunny holiday when you're better, can't we, Tess?"

Tess smiled but the pain was taking a hold.

"Please take the morphine, Tess," urged Max.

"Okay, I will," she said. Closing her eyes, she turned her face to the wall, her breath heavy and slow.

"Mum," Max whispered into her ear, and she smiled. "My mum."

As Tess drifted off to sleep. Max turned to Elodie. "El, you are still my sister. Nothing changes. Nothing."

Tess did not wake from her sleep. A second bed was moved into the room and Max, Elodie, Thomas and Freddie took it in turns to spend time with her. A nurse came at night to administer medication and delicate care, instinctively knowing what was needed. Three days had passed. The food cooked by Mrs Murray was hardly eaten by anyone. Gin and tonics were poured, and drunk.

"Pot of tea, El?" Max asked, failing to concentrate on a crossword.

"I'll go," she said. "How about I bring Fleur back with me? I'm sure Tess can tell we're all here."

"I hope so," said Max.

Kneeling next to the bed, he reached for her hand and pressed it gently onto his cheek.

"Mum," he said, "you know I'm here, don't you?"

There was complete silence, except for the dogs snoring in the armchair.

"I found you," he said, giving her hand a kiss, "and I hadn't even realised I'd been searching for you, Mum, and there you were."

Looking up, he watched as Tess opened her eyes very slightly for just a moment, and then, like a dove resting its head in its plumage, her head tilted towards her shoulder and her eyes closed for the very last time.

Still holding Tess's hand, Max sat still. He felt such peace and couldn't quite understand why, but he knew it didn't matter. He had found his mother and had the magnificent opportunity to tell her that he loved her and now, drifting towards the bedroom door, he could hear his little daughter's musical chatter.

Turning his head to the door as it opened, he looked at Elodie arriving into the room carrying a tea tray followed by Charlotte with Fleur in her arms.

He waited until she had put the tray down. "I'm sorry, El," he said and shook his head.

"Max?" she said, holding her hand over her mouth, trying to catch her breath, gasping and letting out a yelp of utter pain. "No, Max, she can't have gone, not yet. I wasn't even here. Why wasn't I here?"

Max stood up and tried to put his arms around his sister but she pulled back. "It's okay, El, really it is. She's at peace now, you have to believe that."

"Max? I can't bear it," she said.

"God bless you, Tess," whispered Charlotte, a tear falling down her cheek. "I'll do my very best to look after your boy."

Tess had left a letter of instruction with Freddie, requesting that her body should go to science and even though Thomas and in particular Freddie wanted to hold a service for her, Tess had stipulated that she wanted no more than a glass of whisky to be lifted after her death, so there were no sandwiches to be made or cakes to be filled for well-intended mourners.

Julia arrived into Tess's room carrying a bunch of white roses.

"Max, Elodie," she said, crossing the room.

Max turned to Julia and hugged her.

"Oh Max," said Julia, "I'm so very sorry, sorry for everything."

Stepping back, Max looked at Julia and, for a brief moment, closed his eyes as if to gather himself.

"I didn't expect you to speak to me ever again," she said, taking his hands and turning to look at Elodie. "You understand we had no choice, don't you? I want you both to know that. Elodie? Tess was so young, and your grandmother, she insisted. We had no choice, no choice at all."

But Elodie knelt on the floor, ignoring her mother's plea. She could only think of how Tess's voice had now gone forever and how wrong she had got everything, thinking that Tess was her mother, and all the lies her father must have told, to her mother, to the bank, to them all. Why did the truth hurt more than the lies? It didn't make sense.

"Elodie?" said Julia, holding out her arms to her daughter.

Standing up, Elodie kissed Tess's forehead one last time. "Goodbye, Tess."

Leaving the room, Elodie chose not to look at her mother, who felt like a stranger to her now.

Chapter sixty-eight

Elodie barely left her bedroom and what food arrived on a tray from Charlotte was mostly gobbled up by Elodie's fan club, Bonnie and Clyde. She hadn't said goodbye to her mother when she left, nor had she cried a single tear since Tess had died. There was so much for her to be upset about, she found it hard to know where to begin.

Another long letter had arrived from Luke to say how sorry he was about Tess and how deeply in love he was with Elodie, but she could barely read it, skimming over the words and then taking out her lighter, burning it page by page in the fireplace. She wished so much that she could have been part of Tess's secret, that she and Max could both have been Tess's children. She felt cheated.

"Can I come in, El?" said Max, knocking gently on the door.

Inside, Elodie was on the pink armchair in her bathroom.

"A team of plumbers had already started work on the house," he said. "You'll be able to have a bath in here soon," but no smile was raised. "Elodie," he sat on the edge of the bath, "so much has happened to us all. It's going to take time to work through it."

"That's life, though, isn't it, Max?"

"If you could start with Mum, Elodie, if you could talk to her? She desperately wants to talk."

"Don't call her that," said Elodie. "She isn't your mother. She lied to you, Max, she lied to all of us. They all did."

"If it hadn't been for Fleur, the chances are we might never have returned to Bellamore," said Max. "Fleur gave me the chance to spend time with my real mother, and I can't regret that, I can't regret any of it. It was Odette who did this – she made the decision for the whole family."

"How could she have done it?" said Elodie. "She bribed Mum to take you. How could Mum have accepted?"

"She didn't have a choice, El – surely you can see that?"

"And Gramps? He knew all along. How can you take this so easily, Max?"

"I am not taking it easily," said Max, "but Gramps must have had his reasons."

"I just don't understand how you can be so forgiving."

"Because I have to be. I don't want to be a bitter man. I'm Fleur's dad now and I want to be a proper father to her, birthdays and school plays, summer holidays and Easter egg hunts. All the times that our own father missed. You need to forgive too."

"I'm sorry Max, but I can't," said Elodie, "I can't forgive her."

Max left a piece of paper on her bed. "I'll leave this for you, in case it helps. I'll see you later, sis."

When Max left the room, Elodie reached over to her bed and picked up the piece of paper. It was a printout from the *New York Times* social page, reporting that the divorce had gone through between Luke and Star Hampton, also revealing that Star had a longstanding affair with Luke's father, Giles Hampton. Elodie thought back to when she was temping, sending the Boodles package to Mrs Hampton – the wrong Mrs Hampton – '*mon étoile*' – 'my star'. The package had been meant for Luke's wife all along. It felt like an octopus's tentacles connected them all.

"I thought you might like a cup of herbal tea," said Charlotte, her voice the epitome of calm and sympathy. "Grieving brings on a feeling of cold, for some reason. I think that's why people drink so much tea." Charlotte didn't crowd Elodie, she was clever like that, she seemed aware of space. "How are you feeling?" she said, standing by the window.

Lying across her bed, Elodie wondered how to reply. She didn't know how she was feeling – mostly sad and confused, or cross and confused – but Charlotte was so gentle, Elodie managed to rally her manners.

"I feel like I've practically ignored you since you've arrived, Charlotte, I'm so sorry."

"There's no need," she said. "It's been a complicated time."

"What about your parents – was their visit to Ireland a success?" said Elodie.

"They loved Gramps' little party, and they are completely obsessed with Fleur, as I hoped they would be."

"And how do you think Max is coping?"

"It's going to take time," said Charlotte. "Max is desperately sad but I think immensely grateful too."

"I just can't get my head straight," said Elodie. "The way Max went straight to Mum when Tess died. How can he forgive her like that? After all the lies, I just can't understand it."

"You know, Elodie, I honestly think that Fleur is the reason why Max is doing well. He's feels somehow grounded, like he has a proper understanding of where he's from, having been here with Tess."

"Whereas I feel like I'm being continually tested, or maybe punished," said Elodie. "Which is it?"

"I'm not particularly religious, despite my father being a vicar," said Charlotte.

"I liked his dress by the way," said Elodie, winking.

"Thank you," said Charlotte. "You see, nothing is as it seems, is it? But you know, Elodie, I do think there is something to be said for hope. Wanting something so much, you know, really wishing for something, and maybe there is a sense of power that can help things to work out." Charlotte looked so at home at Bellamore, her hands already pitted with earth from the garden, her hair tied in a scarf, and seemingly very content. "I understand it seems impossible to believe, right now, but you are going to feel better."

"It's just that on top of everything, I'm terrified that I'm in love with Luke."

"But, Elodie, isn't that's wonderful?"

"It isn't," she said, shaking her head. "He lied so badly, completely fooled me and now I'm in a heap, and what's worse, I'm afraid of returning to London. I have no purpose there, I'll just dwindle away." Elodie felt so worthless compared to Charlotte. "Since I've been at Bellamore, I feel in some way that I have been helpful, feeling like I'm actually needed. I'm just so selfish."

"You are not selfish," said Charlotte. "It was your idea to come here, Elodie. You united Max with his mother, and Fleur with her grandmother. Truly, the good you have done is more than you can possibly know."

A cool breeze came into the kitchen as Elodie sat on the armchair sketching Bluebell, who had passed out on her beanbag by the Aga. She thought how pleased Tess would be with the rain for her garden, and Gramps less so for the house martins, due to fly any day now. The little birds had crafted their nest in the eaves of the house, and for days Gramps had been sitting the back garden, surrounded by flocks and pink and blue geraniums, and white lilies in the border, looking like a water colour.

With her pencil and sketchpad in hand, Elodie walked out to the garden and towards her grandfather who wore a pink sun hat and binoculars around his neck, with a half-drunk mug of tea on the table in front of him. His reaction to Tess's death had been silence, but the pain in his eyes said it all.

"Gramps," said Elodie, "can I join you?"

"Elodie, yes, of course you can," he said, patting the stone bench. "I suppose I should be sitting on a cushion. I hear that sitting on stone isn't good for the kidneys, though what does it matter now?"

"I can get you a cushion?"

"Your company is all I'd like now, but thank you," he said softly, taking the binoculars from around his neck. "We're all miserable, aren't we, and who could blame us? I'm eighty-six and my youngest daughter has died before me." Taking off his hat and looking up, he squinted at the sun.

"Did you know it was going to happen so fast?"

"You know, Elodie, when I think about it, it wasn't fast. Tess had been living with her illness for years, at least five years before she returned home. I suppose we both treated her cancer like some sort of unwanted guest, and we simply tried to ignore it and carry on regardless. She knew the day would come, but somehow she waited, didn't she? Her body gave her time with Max, and I believe that when she delivered the truth to him, she felt at peace. Tess loved you very much too, I know she did."

Elodie nodded, but no tears came – she couldn't, she felt so cold still, right into her bones, so cold despite the late summer sun.

"You know, Elodie, I don't believe your father ever wanted Max to be parted from Tess, and neither did your mother," he said. "It was your grandmother and I'm afraid I was too weak to stop her. There is a cowardly side to my character, which I detest."

Elodie willed herself to listen, and to forgive.

"That day may be such a long time ago, but it feels like the other day, truly it does. Odette slamming down her hand on the table, I can remember every word of the exchange. The tears, the horror, from both Tess and Julia. She'd always sparred them against each other, but the Douglas situation took things to a different level. There's even a part of me that thinks Odette wished for your father to make a play for Tess. Odette used to get so bored in the country, and so bored to see our daughters getting on with me. Can you imagine being jealous of your own children?"

"I think I've been spoilt all my life," said Elodie.

"Yes, you and Max were both brought up in luxurious circumstances, but I believe you all, and I include your mother in this, were emotionally bereft. That is not your failing, Elodie."

Elodie turned to her grandfather. "Can I change, Gramps? Is there time for me to change?"

"My darling girl," he said, reaching out for her, "you already have."

"Have I?" She hid her face in her hands, loathing herself, thinking of all the time she had wasted achieving nothing.

Then he took her hand and she felt the sense of hope that Charlotte had talked about.

"I went to the walled garden earlier," he said. "The ginko has at last started to grow up the wall. That would please Tess if she could see it."

"And how about this?" said Elodie, holding up a drawing of Bluebell on her beanbag.

"A perfect likeness – those sorts of drawings would sell like hot cakes in Chelsea, all those dog owners?" He looked at his granddaughter and saw such potential in her. "I think it may be time for you to return to London, Elodie."

"Do you?"

"I really do," he said. "You need to see your mother, and she needs to see you, I am sure she does, and unless *The New York Times* has got its reporting wrong, it seems that what Luke was telling was you the truth. Seemed awfully nice, that American chap."

"You've got your place in Central Saint Martins," said Max, chopping up strawberries for Fleur, who was holding a seed catalogue in one hand and a twisty spoon in the other. "I'm really chuffed for you, and watch out, because you'll be our number one baby-sitter when we come to London for injections of urban sophistication."

"I'll be at the ready, won't I, my little darling?" said Elodie, kissing Fleur on the forehead. "I'm going to miss you all."

"'*Elodie Gold is going to make it as an artist*' – I want that to be your daily chant," said Charlotte.

"You think I can do it?" said Elodie.

"I know you can, sis," said Max, "and when we convert the outhouses into tearooms we'll hang your work there."

"Watch out for flying slate in the meantime, the builders are really going for it out there," said Elodie.

"We're really going to give this place our best shot," said Max.

"I can see that."

"And who knows, maybe we'll have enough children to fill all ten bedrooms," said Charlotte.

"Steady on," said Max.

Chapter sixty-nine

Portland Road, London

"There you are," said Lorenzo, and with both arms open wide, he hugged Elodie like she was a luxurious pillow.

"How is Mum?"

"She'll be so happy to see you. She's squeezing juice in the kitchen."

"For a screwdriver?" said Elodie.

"Not this time, Elodie. I think we've well and truly, what is it you English say, *nailed it* on the alcohol front."

Elodie looked at Lorenzo, his exuberance and warmth completely disarming her.

"I'm so sorry for your loss, Elodie, it's been a rough time for all of you," he said, his skin so perfectly moisturised, pale pink jacket so exquisitely pressed, his shoes with a perfectly rounded leather toe. "Do you feel ready to see your mother?"

"Yes, I think so," said Elodie.

"And shall I hold onto these little dogs for you? I must say they are very cute."

"Bonnie and Clyde," said Elodie, passing the leads to Lorenzo, "my new allies."

"How about I take these little guys for a walk while you catch up with your mother, Elodie?"

Walking into the hall, Elodie made her way along the corridor,

333

which had been repainted to a much brighter almost primrose colour. Reaching the kitchen, she saw her mother standing on the terrace.

"Mum?" said Elodie.

"Elodie," said Julia, "darling Elodie."

And as Julia held her, Elodie cried her heart out with relief to feel proper love for her mother.

"I have something to show you," said Julia, blowing her nose.

She led her daughter to Douglas's study. She had hung one of Elodie's paintings over the fireplace and had changed the room completely, with floral wallpaper and an art deco desk.

"My new office," said Julia. "I've gone into business with Lorenzo, a sort of fashion meets life-coaching business."

"Mum, this is so good," said Elodie, smiling and feeling so at ease in the house for the first time in her life.

"One more thing," said Julia. "Come with me."

Downstairs in Elodie's flat, Julia stood outside Max's bedroom.

"I read that every artist needs their own space, an engine room, or sometimes just a hiding place?" And she opened the door.

Elodie walked into a large, white studio.

"The architect seemed to think that the natural light in here is excellent," said Julia.

"I don't know what to say," said Elodie, taking in huge blank canvasses leaning against a wall, a table with tubes and chalks, brushes and pencils.

"And this doesn't mean that Max won't be back," said Julia, "but he has a family now, so he can take over the guest wing when he comes. We are a family together now, with Charlotte and Fleur."

"Thank you, Mum," said Elodie, "thank you."

Chapter seventy

Spending four days a week at St Martin's Central, Elodie was painting every day, either at college or in her studio at home. She looked at her hands, her nails multi-coloured from acrylics this morning. As for her heartache, it would take time, but she had a feeling she was going to get through it. Over drinks last night, Sam had gently tried to suggest that she might call Luke and told her that he had been coming to the café every day in the hope Elodie might be there. She was also very keen to show Elodie something in Sam's Kitchen.

Walking along Lombard Street with Bonnie and Clyde, Elodie looked at the afternoon light, thinking how lovely it would be to capture the skyline with pastels. A vintage car passed by with a white ribbon tied from the windscreen to the angel at the tip of the bonnet, tooting its horn as a man waved his top hat out the window, making her think of Gramps and his yellow MG.

On the corner of the street, Elodie took an envelope from her handbag. It carried a bank draft for £120,000 made out to Hillview Home, the right home for Dominic's money. As Elodie pushed the envelope through the mouth of the letterbox, Bonnie and Clyde began to bark and pulled on their leads to cross the road. On the footpath opposite her, she saw a figure standing there and looking straight at her. He didn't move as people shuffled to avoid him, and she could feel his eyes sinking into her, but when he put up his hand, mouthing her name, she pulled the dogs away and walked in the opposite direction. She couldn't do it, just couldn't face him, and instead of going to Sam's Kitchen she returned home.

Elodie went straight to her studio and began to paint on a huge canvas mounted on her easel, but all she could paint were his eyes, staring back at her. It was almost as if she hadn't seen him, maybe she had imagined it. She didn't want to need anyone, she could do this on her own and she knew peace would come, eventually.

"*Elodie?*" she heard Julia calling. "*Something's arrived for you.*"

"*Okay, Mum, you can leave it in the hall, I'll come up later.*"

"*Lorenzo will bring it down to you.*"

Elodie carried on painting and smiled to herself at how she and her mother had got into this rhythm of being friendly to each other.

"Elodie?" said Lorenzo's gentle voice. "I leave your delivery for you out here, okay?"

"Thanks, Lorenzo."

Putting down her brush, Elodie pulled on a jumper over her shirt and jeans and thought about maybe going to Sam at the café before she closed up this evening. She stepped out into the corridor.

And there he stood. He had cut his hair much shorter and looked almost like a businessman, dressed in a shirt and chinos. She noticed his face, so pale and drawn.

"Elodie," he said, so quietly she could hardly hear him. "When did you get back?"

"A few weeks ago," she said.

"I met your mom."

"Yes."

"And Lorenzo, nice guy."

"Yes."

"How is Max? And Charlotte and Fleur?"

"They're going to stay on at Bellamore," she said. "Keep Gramps company for a while and maybe try opening a guest house, or something. They're not sure yet."

"Sounds good," he said.

All was silent, except for a radiator pipe that kept clanking.

"I wanted to show you something." He held out a black folder.

She looked at him and took the folder, his scent reminding her of how much she missed him.

Opening the folder, she pulled out a piece of paper with a series of small circles and a drawing in the centre. It was the chaffinch she had drawn, perched on top of Big Ben with *Wild Bird Records* printed beneath it.

"Your record label?" she said. "This is your logo?"

"I wanted to ask you first, but –"

"Ask me what?" said Elodie quickly.

"If I can use your drawing. This is a mock-up for the logo."

"I thought you might have gone to work for your father, the way you're dressed."

"My father is selling up," said Luke, raising his eyebrows, "and is now in the Bahamas with my ex-wife. And just to round off the weirdness of that episode, it didn't come to me as a surprise – we hadn't been married long before it became obvious they had a thing for each other."

"You weren't upset?" said Elodie.

"I wasn't upset because I didn't love her, and I can say that honestly, because now I know what real love feels like."

Elodie looked down at her hands, in which she held so much hope, a career, a future.

"And I've taken a good look at myself," he said, "realising what a mess I've made of things and that I need to take responsibility for my actions."

Elodie sat down on the window seat and didn't make eye contact with him.

"I'll go – and I don't blame you for despising me," he said.

He walked up the stairs and her heart ached.

And then he was beside her again.

"Elodie?"

"Yes?"

"I'm so sorry about Tess, so very sorry. I liked her very much."

"Thank you," she said, "and you for your letter, or letters."

"You got them all?"

"Yes."

"Elodie?"

She looked at him and stood up, and like the strongest magnet imaginable they moved towards each other and they kissed.

"I'm so sorry for what I've put you through, so sorry, I can't tell you," said Luke, holding her so tightly. "I've died every day waiting for you."

Elodie woke up in her bed and, stretching her arms across the soft sheets, she looked at the bedside clock. She must have slept for hours. Squinting as the morning light streamed through the gap in the curtains, she could hear mellow jazz coming along the corridor. Slipping out of bed, warm and naked, she put on Luke's shirt, which he had taken off when they fell into bed the night before, pulled together by passion and a love that had grown despite the complications and sadness. Elodie felt safe and strong for the first time in her life, ambitious, ready for independence and at the same time to be with Luke on an even footing.

Walking towards the kitchen, her hair falling around her shoulders, she breathed in the aroma of coffee.

"Good morning, beautiful girl," he said, with a napkin over his shoulder and a spatula in his hand.

Bonnie and Clyde were lazing across the window seat, bathing in the sunlight and looking very content.

"I'm guessing my little dogs have been given some morning bacon, judging by their smiling faces?"

"Maybe just a little," said Luke, moving her towards her, "and as it happens, I was about to bring you breakfast in bed."

"Does the menu include a tall, handsome American?"

"I think that can be arranged," he said and, dropping the spatula to the floor, Luke kissed her all the way to bed, and Elodie Gold she knew she had found the man she could love, with no strings attached.

THE END